TRUST ME

ALSO BY JEFF ABBOTT

Do Unto Others
The Only Good Yankee
Promises of Home
Distant Blood
A Kiss Gone Bad
Black Jack Point
Cut and Run
Panic
Fear
Collision

TRUST ME

JEFF ABBOTT

DUTTON

DUTTON

Published by Penguin Group (USA) Inc.

375 Hudson Street, New York, New York 10014, U.S.A.

Penguin Group (Canada), 90 Eglinton Avenue East, Suite 700, Toronto, Ontario M4P 2Y3, Canada (a division of Pearson Penguin Canada Inc.); Penguin Books Ltd, 80 Strand, London WC2R 0RL, England; Penguin Ireland, 25 St Stephen's Green, Dublin 2, Ireland (a division of Penguin Books Ltd); Penguin Group (Australia), 250 Camberwell Road, Camberwell, Victoria 3124, Australia (a division of Pearson Australia Group Pty Ltd); Penguin Books India Pvt Ltd, 11 Community Centre, Panchsheel Park, New Delhi—110 017, India; Penguin Group (NZ), 67 Apollo Drive, Rosedale, North Shore 0632, New Zealand (a division of Pearson New Zealand Ltd); Penguin Books (South Africa) (Pty) Ltd, 24 Sturdee Avenue, Rosebank, Johannesburg 2196, South Africa

Penguin Books Ltd, Registered Offices: 80 Strand, London WC2R 0RL, England

Published by Dutton, a member of Penguin Group (USA) Inc.

First printing, July 2009

1   3   5   7   9   10   8   6   4   2

 REGISTERED TRADEMARK—MARCA REGISTRADA

LIBRARY OF CONGRESS CATALOGING-IN-PUBLICATION DATA

Abbott, Jeff.
Trust me / by Jeff Abbott.
p.   cm.
ISBN 978-0-525-95121-6
1. Online chat groups—Fiction. 2. Terrorists—Fiction. I. Title.
PS3601.B366T78   2009
813'.6—dc22   2009003611

Printed in the United States of America

Set in Adobe Garamond Pro

Designed by Leonard Telesca

PUBLISHER'S NOTE

For Travis Wilhite
because there is always hope

TRUST ME

"I wouldn't mind being a Pawn, if only I might join."

—Alice, in Lewis Carroll's *Through the Looking-Glass*

1

The old man had spent his entire life surrounded by unimaginable power and wealth—except for today. He was dressed as if for regional theater, playing the part of a retiree who'd failed to save for the long stretch of old age, wearing decrepit khakis and a threadbare jacket, mud sliming the heels of his boots, sitting on a park bench in the gray London afternoon, tossing stray crumbs to the pigeons. The crumbs were tiny, the size of diamonds.

The man in the gray suit, standing near him, pretending to talk on a cell phone, didn't look at the old man; instead he watched the people strolling in the park, his eye keen for an enemy. A young couple walking hand in hand; two teenage boys ambling, trying to look cool and tough and failing; a well-dressed mother pushing a stroller, laughing on a cell phone, tucking a blanket around a baby; a pair of old ladies, clutching purses close to their coats, one talking a monologue, the other listening and nodding. No danger here.

The man in the gray suit fought the urge to smile at the disguise the old man had chosen, but to laugh would be fatal. One had to indulge people with money. And one did not laugh at a billionaire, no matter how eccentric.

"I hardly recognized you, Your Majesty," the man in the gray suit said. He cast his gaze around the park again, the silent phone close to his ear.

"Look at them go to war," the old man said in soft Arabic as the pigeons battled over the bread, pecking at one another and the bare ground. "They dance for me. As if I have strings on their wings." He threw another scattering of food to the flock's left, laughed as they scurried to the crumbs.

The birds aren't the only ones, the man in the gray suit thought. But he waited for the old man to speak again. Like most bullies, the old man loved the sound of his own words.

"All is prepared?" the old man asked.

"Yes," he said. *Nearly so* would have been a more exact answer but the old man had never cared for details. Everything would be ready soon enough. Then he could start to change the world.

"Your people are ready for the money?"

"Yes. Your banker has been a great help. He's set up accounts, he's covered our trails so as to not raise suspicion." It was an effort to control his temper, to not say, *Yes, you old fool, now just give me what I want and get out of the way.* The man in the gray suit asked the question he'd come here to ask. "I need only to know the amount you're willing to invest."

"Fifty million dollars now." The prince dressed as a pauper tossed his last handful of stale bread to the pavement, watched the pigeons dart and peck for the scraps. A smile played across his face as the birds battled. "If your proposed attacks succeed over the next five years, then another fifty million for further work."

The man in the gray suit felt a heaviness seize his chest, felt the thud of blood in his ears. A hundred million dollars, to flow through his hands. But he showed no emotion. He kept the cell phone up to his ear. "September eleventh didn't even cost a million dollars to carry out."

"Yes, but it was not a long-term investment. I offer you much more. I give you many times the resources of September eleventh." The old man glanced up at the man in the suit and for a moment he smiled, an awful flexing of skin and teeth. "Give me many times the results, for years to come. Make them bleed for a lifetime."

"I will."

The old man paused, and for a moment there was only the whisper of the nearby traffic, of the wind creaking through the tree branches. "It is an investment. In the future of a better world." The pigeons pooled around the man's feet, hungry for more. He kicked them away from his foot with a disgusted snarl.

"You are generous."

The old man looked up. "If you fail me, you and anyone you care about will die."

The man in the gray suit said, "Threats and kicks work on a dog, sir. Not on me. You needn't worry." He didn't like being threatened. But he didn't let his feelings show.

"You have selected the right . . . people? I don't wish to trust fools or amateurs."

"Yes. We have a willing cadre and we are recruiting more. There will be a first wave of attacks. To distract, to confuse, to panic. Then those fighters who successfully carry out those initial operations will get the honor of participating in the second phase, which is actually a massive attack. We call it Hellfire. Heavy loss of life, devastating economic damage. I promise you will get your money's worth, sir."

The old man smiled again at the man in the gray suit. "Spend my money well." He rose from the bench, dusted the bread from his lap, and walked away through the rising cloud of the birds.

Fifty million, the man in the gray suit thought. It was everything he had hoped for. Enough to make the world pay. Enough to make him respected. He turned and walked away, folding the unused cell phone, dropping it into his pocket.

Fifty feet behind him, the woman with the stroller giggled into her phone. She leaned down and eased the blanket around the sleeping infant she was pushing in the baby carriage. She'd offered to take her friend's baby for a stroll—give the friend a much-needed break. The young mother had barely slept in the past few days and the offer had nearly made her cry in gratitude. "I know you're not in town long, Jane. Don't you have things to do?"

"Nothing important. Darling, please, take a break from nappies and crying. I'll take her for a long walk." And Jane had, giving the baby a dropper of allergy medication as soon as they were out of sight of the house so the darling would sleep the whole time.

The baby, nestled in its stroller, made for perfect camouflage for Jane's afternoon.

Jane checked the settings on the parabolic microphone and digital recorder that lay next to the dozing baby. Holding a modified cell phone, she heard the old billionaire's and the man in the gray suit's words as clearly as if they were standing a foot in front of her. They both spoke Arabic but that was not a concern to her. She understood every word.

The money would be on the move. It was time for her to put her plan into action. A tingle of anticipation and fear tickled her spine.

She turned on her real cell phone and dialed. She steered the stroller away at an angle from two approaching older women, walking arm in arm. Old ladies liked to look at babies. She didn't want them to notice her eavesdropping gear.

"Yes?"

"It's Jane," the woman said in English.

"And?"

"The money is headed to America. Fifty million. We start tonight. Rock and roll."

"Rock and roll."

Jane hung up. There was nothing more to be said.

Jane pushed the stroller out of the park, humming a jaunty tune to the sleeping baby. The sky was going gray but Jane thought it the loveliest day she'd ever seen.

Fifty million dollars, for years of 9/11s to come. Her throat went dry behind her smile.

She dropped off the microphone and its gear at her hotel room. She had a flight to catch tonight, a report to write for her bosses. It would not mention the fifty million, or the impending attacks, and she would have to edit the recording she'd made. The baby began to wake and cried. Jane sang to her softly, all the way home.

2

Luke Dantry was now the most dangerous man in the world. He had no idea of his status, of course; right now he wanted only a mind-clearing jog.

Luke ran. No one watching him could have guessed the danger he represented; they would see only a lanky twenty-four-year-old, curly dark brown hair a bit long over his ears, his strong build dressed in shorts and a T-shirt that read PSYCHOLOGISTS DO IT ON THE COUCH. He didn't much like the shirt, a gag gift from a former girlfriend, but it was the only clean one he had for today's run along Lady Bird Lake, in the heart of Austin's downtown. His blue eyes focused on his path through the crowd. He did not pause to linger on the faces of pretty girls, or the shine of the light on the water he ran alongside, or the shifting shadows cast by the oak branches, jostled by the wind. He dodged slower runners, faster bicyclists, leaping dogs tethered to leashes. He had to hurry, get back to work. The work possessed his thoughts, day and night.

The Austin air was cool, not too humid: It was mid-March, and the long steamy summer bake hadn't yet gripped the city. The breeze felt delicious on him, clearing his head of his worries, if for just a few moments.

Luke crossed the bridge into downtown, slowed his pace. He bent over, breathing hard. His medal slipped free from under the tacky T-shirt, the silver of the angel's sword cutting the sunlight. He was careful to tuck the medal back under his shirt; it lay cool against the sweat of his chest. He stood and walked the last three blocks to the high-rise condo his stepfather had bought him when he'd moved back to Austin for college. He waved at the doorman, who gave Luke a slightly disapproving look as he waited.

"How many miles?" the doorman asked.

"Only two."

"Only two, get your lazy butt in gear." The doorman was a more devoted runner than Luke.

"I was up late."

"Why you bother to live downtown if you never go to the clubs, go out and party?"

"How do you know I don't?" Luke gave the guard a half-smile.

"On night shift, I see who parties, who's been down in the Warehouse District, who's been on Sixth Street. You never stagger in late."

"I'm on the Internet most of the time right now."

"Well, get the hell off." The guard gave him a grin. "Life's too short."

The elevator arrived and Luke said, "I'll try to fix that partying deficit."

"Not tonight. Your stepfather is waiting for you. Got here a few minutes ago."

"Thanks." The doors closed and Luke punched the tenth-floor button. Henry was back again, all the way from Washington, and Luke hadn't finished the project. He took a deep breath.

The elevator door slid open and he walked down a short hallway to his condo. The door was barely open; Henry had forgotten to shut it. Typical. He opened the door and called out, "Hey, it's me." Luke closed the door behind him and he could hear the scratch of pen on paper, the sound he always associated with Henry.

Henry sat at the dining room table, in his slightly wrinkled suit, his luggage at his feet, writing on a yellow legal pad, a thick book open in front of him. Luke knew better than to interrupt Henry when he was thinking, and Henry's thoughts could be long, tortured affairs. Henry raised one hand slightly from the table as he wrote, begging for patience, and so Luke went and got a bottle of water from the refrigerator, drank deeply, listened to the scratch of Henry's writing, looked at the stunning view that faced the lake and the green stretch of Zilker Park beyond.

"Sorry, Luke," he said with an embarrassed smile. "I'm working on a dozen position papers at once, and all my ideas are sprouting like weeds."

"That's too many."

"I think a lot of change is in the wind. Did you have a good run?" Henry looked up from the paper. Fiftyish, lean, but with slightly mussed gray hair—standing in stray stalks from his fingers' constantly running through it as he spoke—and an equally rumpled suit. Henry never traveled well.

"I only sweat in front of the computer these days." He went over and Henry stood and gave him an awkward embrace.

"Well, go get showered and I'll take you out for a decent dinner. You've got nothing edible in that fridge." He leaned back, studied his stepson. "You're pale, thin, and you need a shave. I've been working you too hard."

"I wanted the research project to go well. But I worry I'm not delivering what you need."

Henry sat down, put his glasses back on his face. His nose was slightly crooked—he'd always kidded Luke that it had been broken in a bar fight, and Luke knew Henry had never set foot in a bar. "The data you've sent me has been extremely . . . compelling."

"I'm afraid it's nothing more than the crazy Internet ravings of vicious losers."

"But you never know when the crazy raving is the seed of something bigger. Something dangerous."

"Collecting crazy ravings isn't necessarily going to help identify and stop extremists before they turn violent."

"That's for me to decide."

Luke finished his water. "I would like to know who your client is. I want to know who wants to find potential extremists on the Internet."

Henry folded the paper he'd been writing on, tucked it in his pocket, and shut the book. The name of the book was *The Psychology of Extremists*. Henry's own masterpiece; he'd written it years ago in the aftermath of the McVeigh bombing, to little acclaim, until 9/11 changed everything and his theories about the mental makeup of terrorists bore fruit. After holding a series of professorships around the world—sort of a traveling scholar, much as Luke's own father had been—last year he had set up a small but success- ful think tank in Washington called the Shawcross Group. They studied and wrote about psychology and the role it played in governance, in terror- ism and extremism, in international crime, and in a host of other topics. His clients were the movers and shakers in Washington, London, Paris, and around the world: key government decision-makers and multinational companies who wanted to protect their operations from terrorist and extremist threats.

"I can't tell you. Not now. I'm sorry."

"I just think . . . we should give this information to the police. Or your client should."

"Have you found evidence of actual criminal activity?" Henry took off his wire-rim glasses.

"Um, no."

"But you've found the potential for criminal activity?"

"Come see the latest from the Night Road for yourself."

Luke sat down at his computer.

He had a list of more than a hundred Web sites, discussion groups, and online forums to survey, where he would try to draw in and talk with people who had extreme and even violent responses to the world's problems. A window opened to report on the responses to his many varied comments from before he'd gone on his run. He kept his user names and passwords in a text file on his Mac because he could not remember them all. He logged on to the first online discussion group, where topics ranged from immigration reform to privatization of Social Security. This one tended to be far-right wing and multiple retorts to his mild comments had sprouted up since yesterday. Luke scanned them; mostly, the contributors agreed with one another, but they fueled one another's anger. He signed on as MrEagle, his pen name, and posted a far more moderate view of the immigration issue. It would not take long for venomous arguments against his position to flow in for him to collect and measure. He would also post under other names, agreeing with those who attacked his initial postings, seeing if they were interested in violence as a solution.

Sometimes they ignored his prods; other times, they agreed that violence was the answer.

Luke jumped to another forum, found another pot to stir on a far-left discussion group. His middle-of-the-road comments, left last night on the issue of military contractors, had produced everything from abrasive disagreement to incoherent fury that practically blazed fire through the computer screen.

"The Night Road?" Henry asked. "Oh, yes. Your nickname for these people."

Luke had been using the nickname for a while, but typical of absentminded

Henry to forget. Henry had been traveling a lot in the past few days and apparently the jet lag weighed hard. "I used to call them the Angry Bitters but that sounded like a punk band. I dreamed one night that an angry mob of extremists of every stripe was chasing me down a long dark road. So I call them the Night Road."

"The Night Road. Right. Rather dark of you." Henry had an odd look on his face, as though a light had suddenly shut off behind his eyes. Then he smiled.

"So far this evening my masculinity, my patriotism, and my intelligence have all been called into serious question." Luke shrugged, let a smile play across his face. "Then the ones I pretend to agree with, I have to get them talking to see if they really are interested in violence."

"The troublemaker, as always." Henry flicked a smile. "So you're continuing to get a lot of responses."

"Fifty percent more than when I started back in November. I think it's the anonymity of the Net; people express themselves a lot more strongly. And these people, they're looking for others to reinforce their views. So the anger, the perceived injustice, ratchets up, higher and higher."

"How much data do you have so far?"

Luke glanced at a screen. The most interesting and extremist ravings on the Web sites and forums were scanned, copied, and uploaded into a database. "Close to ten thousand comments now, from roughly six thousand individuals, over the past four months."

"Wow."

"It's weird. I feel like a cop who pretends to be a thirteen-year-old girl luring the old perverts. But instead I'm trying to draw out the next Timothy McVeigh, or the next Madrid bomber, the next al-Qaeda wannabe here in America."

"You really think some of them are that dangerous?"

"Look at today's batch." He pulled up a comment from the day's database. "Not surprising a lot of them are antigovernment."

Let's start fresh. End their lifetime appointments; kill all the judges.

"Now, maybe this guy's just venting, maybe he's harmless. It's the first time he posted. I have to wait and see if he amps it up. If he does, then he's a possibility to follow."

Henry rubbed at his lip. "Prod him harder. See what else he says."

"Here's one from one of my more consistent correspondents," Luke said. "ChicagoChris. He's on a number of discussion boards for anarchists . . ."

"Organized anarchists. I love the concept," Henry said.

". . . and he loves to talk about ecoterrorism." Luke hit a button and a long series of comments made by ChicagoChris over the past few days rolled up the screen:

> Burn every McMansion to the ground, that's the start. A serious attack on a gated community would send a message. Don't kill people, warn them first, but level the houses. Sabotage the construction equipment. Get busy to save the earth.
>
> People who destroy the earth deserve whatever bad stuff happens to them.
>
> Killing our environment is akin to the greatest murder ever committed. I blame the oil and construction companies. I know those guys, what they're like when the attention isn't on them, and they're scum. Kill them, kill all of them, and there would be change. A change is in the wind, I know it. It's coming, fast. I want to be a part of the storm of change.

"He's a charmer," Henry said.

"And he believes every word he says. He e-mails me a lot, through the boards. I'm his new best online friend. And he's not just crazy, Henry, he's *focused*. That's what's scary."

"You said in last month's report you think he's one of the most likely to go violent."

"Yeah, he's promising." Luke made a face. "But crazy."

"I'm not interested in the crazy ones. I'm interested in the committed ones. There's a big difference."

"I can't really diagnose these people, I can only catalog their comments. I hope this is enough data for your research." Looking at all the hate made him tired. "For your client."

Henry heard the stubborn question in Luke's voice. "I told you, I have to keep my client confidential."

"Let me guess. It's the government. They want to watch these people, make sure they're only hot air and not actually acquiring weapons or putting bombs on buses or targeting politicians."

"I can't say. But I know my client will be extremely pleased with your work."

Luke said, "I'm surprised you don't trust me. You always have."

"And I always will. But the client set very specific parameters for me. If you worked for me full-time, were officially on the payroll, then maybe . . ." Henry gave a shrug, a half-smile.

"I'm not a think-tank kind of guy."

"Please. We're academics, just in nicer suits," Henry said. "Let me guess. You would like to get a paper out of this data yourself. Maybe the foundation of a doctoral dissertation."

Luke nodded. "Yes. I would. But I respect that you hired me to do the research. It's your data, not mine."

"Luke. I understand why you're driven to dissect the minds of those who think violence is a solution to every problem." The silence between them felt suddenly awkward. "But understanding why violence happens, that's the puzzle that can never be solved. And it won't bring your father back." Henry cleared his throat, looked at the picture of Luke and his father. His lips narrowed and he bowed his head slightly, as if under a weight.

Henry was a giver of speeches, and his phrases worked at podiums, not at dinner tables. He'd spent so much time with his books and found his family so late in life that Luke had gotten used to his stepfather's well-meant but flat-footed phrases. "I know. But I would hope this research would find the next asshole who wants to kill innocent people for a cause." Luke didn't look at Henry. He didn't look at the photo of his father, the one decoration on the fireplace mantel. A photo of Warren Dantry and Luke, age seven, holding a freshly caught bass, dripping from a Virginia lake. He could remember the smell of the clean fish, the scent of the pines, the warm sun against his skin, his father's quiet laughter. A happy memory of a rare time with his dad, long before evil in the form of a cold-blooded airplane mechanic named Ace Beere stole his father away from him. Evil that Luke felt compelled to understand.

Reading Ace Beere's rambling, incoherent suicide note—left at the airport hangar after he had killed Luke's father and several others—had fueled Luke's desire to understand the psychology of the violent mind. *I did it because God said I must, the only way to get my pride back, to strike back at my* *employer and I had to pick a flight to kill and since they were professors, they* *were useless to society, no one will miss them.* Rambling garbage, but inside the long letter there must have been the seed of an answer, a cogent reason why. Luke had never found it.

"Tell me this," Luke said. "Your client. Whoever it is, they want to find nascent terrorists before they move from ideology to violence. This isn't just a fancy profiling project."

"Luke. Identifying terrorists is far bigger than simply drawing out the disaffected on Internet forums."

"But we already know that plenty of extremists connect through the Internet. If we could narrow in on them, discourage them before they take those final steps, make the choice of violence unappealing or impossible . . ." Luke got up from the computer, went to the window. "Any of these people might be harmless or be a time bomb. Ten thousand comments, thousands of people, but I can't *prove* any of them will turn terrorist. Really, the next stage of the project should be to follow them, to see if there are ways to convince them that violence isn't an option."

"You've done a fantastic job, and my client will sift through all the data. You never know, maybe you did find the next McVeigh or the next person who'd mail anthrax to Congress or decide to take up the mantle of al-Qaeda. But you've spent so much time on it; I'm starting to think this is an unhealthy obsession."

"No. I want to finish the project. But . . ."

"But what?"

"The mail accounts I had to set up—the e-mails make clear that these people all think that I'm ready to join their battle. . . . I'm worried they might find me. Even though I post from different addresses, use a bunch of fake names. I could be traced if someone tried hard enough."

"But they're on the other side of the glass, in Wonderland." Henry tapped the computer monitor. "You don't exactly live in a dangerous world, Luke."

"I suppose not." Not anymore. He never spoke with Henry about the time after his father died, when he ran away and lived on the streets for two months. There was no point; that was a darkness in his life on which he'd long ago shut the door.

"I wonder if you might take me to the airport tomorrow. My flight's in the afternoon. I have meetings at the university all morning." As though his stepfather hadn't heard his concerns. Henry, he thought, had just moved on to his next idea.

"Sure." A response to one of Luke's fake comments popped up on the screen: *Your right, A race war is in-evitible in this country. What's got to be done is get all the un-desirables to leave this country. Killin em will encurage em to go faster. Maybe you and me can get together and talk about it. I could see if your serius or not.*

Henry read the message. "You bait your hooks well, Luke. Very well. I want you to listen to me." And Luke thought, with affection, *Here comes Henry trying to be a dad. Here comes the hand on the shoulder . . . yep. And now here comes the fumbling advice.* "Luke. You know I loathe sentiment. But—"

"I'm the only family you've got." Luke paused. "And this greeting-card moment is brought to you by the Shawcross Group."

"Now, Luke." But Henry offered a rare smile. "I promised your mom when I married her that I'd take care of you if anything happened to her. To me that was a solemn vow."

His mother. He took down the photos of her when he knew Henry was coming for a visit; the sight of them was too raw, too painful for Henry. The car crash had been only a year ago.

"Henry, don't treat me like a child. You don't have to watch out for me."

"Habits are hard to break." He cleared his throat, as though preparing to deliver another speech or presentation. He seemed to have trouble looking at Luke. "Aside from you, the think tank is my life. Come work for me. I would love to pass the think tank on to you one day." The final words came in a rush.

"Henry, wow. I don't know what to say." He felt touched. Honored. Henry was a bit of an oddball—all into his researches, his pondering about the political trends of the world, his books and papers—but he was the only family Luke had. A world without family was a lonely place, and Luke thought it had been an unbearably lonely place for Henry before Henry married Luke's mom. It had not always been an easy road for him and his stepfather but Luke never doubted that Henry, in his own way, loved him.

On the screen a comment appeared: *You're right, what we need in America is a nice dirty bomb set off in the beltway, clean up the whole act, make the Potomac a toilet for all the human waste in DC, start fresh.* Another loon chirping to be heard. A *nice* dirty bomb, as opposed to an awful dirty bomb. These people made his blood run cold.

"My God," Henry said, blinking at the comment. "This is the other reason I want you working with me. You get results. Say yes. Please, Luke. Please."

Begging was most un-Henry-like and Luke felt a swelling of gratitude. "I will sleep on it. After I wander a bit down the Night Road this evening."

"Fair enough. I need to make a couple of a phone calls and then we'll go out to dinner. Go get cleaned up." His stepfather patted his shoulder and went off to the condo's guest room.

Luke turned back to the computer, eight more bits of poison on his screen, and had to smile at the viciousness of the responses. He didn't want to admit it, but this taunting of people with such strong opinions was addictive. He wondered, despite all his worries about the people he angered, if he could give this work up so easily. Behind the mask of the Internet he was a badass, a troublemaker, a take-no-prisoners tough guy. Nothing like the mild academic who typed on the keyboard and thought hard about what precise words would evoke what terrifying responses.

Luke went to his bathroom and showered. Rubbing the shampoo into his hair, he wondered about the thousands of people he touched—angry, bitter, so convinced in their hate that they were blind to nuance or circumstance or even to a basic morality. The Web connected them all, electronic threads spanning the country, and he had the uneasy feeling that the people he called the Night Road could reach out and touch him, know him for the fraud that he was, in an instant.

Luke hated airports. He had last seen his father alive at Dulles ten years ago. Every time he stepped into the wide, cool expanse of a terminal he thought of his father; a dark-suited arm raised in good-bye, Luke's clothes still wrinkled from the force of his father's parting hug.

"Have a good trip, Dad," he'd said.

His father had stood close to him. He was a handsome man, with a trim beard, a full head of hair going gray early, and bold blue eyes. "I'll be back soon. Mind your mother."

"I will."

"You want me to bring you back some fish? In my pocket?" An old joke between them, from when Luke had caught a perch when he was five and promptly stuck it in his pocket and left it there for a few hours. They'd burned his shorts.

"No. Mom will get mad."

"Mom will be buying you new clothes," Mom had said, with a smile, touching his father's arm.

Then his father had rumpled Luke's hair, gently. "I'll miss you every moment."

"That's way too much missing," Luke said. He was fourteen and easily mortified in public by parental affection. He wanted to get back to the car, crack open his computer game, finish the level he was on. He let his impatience show with a sigh, an eye roll.

"When you have a kid, you'll understand what it is to miss someone each moment."

"You'll be relieved to know I just got a girl pregnant."

"Ha-ha," his father said, then looked at him with mock surprise.

"Kidding," Luke said. "Two girls."

"Funny man." His father kissed the top of his head. "Be a good boy. I got to go catch up with the others." A quick, firm kiss for his mother, and then his father had gone. Walking away, with his fellow professors, for a fishing trip in North Carolina. Gone forever. Luke did not even get to see him in the coffin. The Atlantic had hoarded his father's body in its gray clutches. He had walked on the beach closest to where the plane had gone down, wondering if he could hear his father's gentle baritone in the crash of the surf. It had been a crazy thought, but after the long darkness of his grief and the long weeks wandering the roads as a runaway, being close to where his father died had been a strange comfort.

His father had become a regrettable haze, defined by only a few sharp memories—swimming at home in suburban Virginia, walking on the Georgetown campus to his father's office, enjoying a Redskins game when Luke was five, hoisting Luke on his shoulders, a finger moving across the night tapestry, naming every star in the constellations. *That light,* Dad said in his quiet voice, *it's taken lifetimes to reach us. Starlight is long-term. Big picture. Always remember long-term and big picture, Luke.*

He needed his father's advice now. He knew he was facing a crossroads in his life.

Luke parked the BMW Henry had bought him as a graduation gift in the short-term parking lot. On the passenger side, Henry huffed out of the car. His appointments had run long and they were pressed for time. Luke pulled Henry's small bag from the trunk of his car.

"I put a copy of my latest report in your bag, and a copy of the current database," Luke said. "You can scare your fellow passengers by reading the report aloud. Fun for everyone."

"What did you call it?" Henry gave him a smile as they boarded the parking garage elevator.

"'A Drive Down the Night Road.'"

"It sounds like a bad heavy-rock album."

"Yes, but the subtitle's pure jazz: 'A Continuing Analysis of Extremists on the Internet.'"

Henry laughed. "Thanks for all your work on this, Luke. Seeing you was the best part of my trip; trying to convince my fellow academics about the threats we face was much less fun."

"Your peers won't listen to you?"

"I believe huge attacks are coming. But they're treating me like I'm saying the sky is falling." Henry couldn't keep the anger out of his voice. They walked toward the main terminal of the Austin airport; the spring breeze was cool but the sunshine was bright and hard against their eyes. "So. What about the job offer?"

"If I take it, then my job is now to officially . . . think. Mom would be amused."

"Your mother would have been incredibly proud of you." Silence then, for always about ten seconds, when they both spoke of Luke's mother. "Proud of us working together." They waited for a security officer to wave them across the walkway, stopping traffic with a gesture. Henry gave the officer a polite nod.

"I'm not sure this is going to put my psychology degree to real use. But playing tag with the crazies is slightly addictive."

"Danger is addictive," Henry said. Luke thought Henry's sense of danger was probably double-parking or placing a five-dollar bet at a casino. "But what your research is, Luke, is important." Henry stopped in front of the terminal. His sharp-planed face made a frown. "The hinges of history are at a critical turn right now, Luke. The world has grown far smaller than we ever dreamed it could be. It's easier than ever for people with certain . . . violent intentions to find each other. You could help us find ways to understand them, and fight them."

"Us. I wish you'd tell me who your client is."

"Take the job and you'll know." They'd stopped at the American Airlines check-in touch screens. Henry tapped in his info and the kiosk spat out his boarding pass. Luke followed him to the line of people waiting to thread through the security checkpoint.

"I don't want . . ." Luke stopped.

"What, son?" Henry didn't often call him son. Only when he was worried about Luke.

"I don't want a pity job offer, Henry. Just because you made a promise to Mom."

"Good, because pity doesn't play with me. You've done brilliant work for me, Luke, on researching the, um, Night Road, as you charmingly call it. But I would never offer you a career out of pity for you. I respect you and my company far too much."

Nice, Luke thought, how does that shoe taste? Your one family member offers you a job and you manage to insult him. "I didn't mean that. I know you're serious." Luke cleared his throat and his stomach gave a nervous lurch. "Yes. I'll take the job."

A surprising relief lit Henry's eyes. "You've made me happy. And proud. Us working together, it'll be, you know, cool."

Luke couldn't resist a smile. Henry's definition of *cool* was singular. Monographs on political economics, treatises on the history of terrorism, all qualified as Henry-cool. And maybe it would make their relationship easier . . . more adult. He wouldn't be seen as just a kid anymore. "You're right. It'll be cool."

Henry did a poor job of keeping the happiness from spreading across his face. "I'll call you tomorrow, and we'll get the paperwork started."

"Thanks, Henry."

"Go home and get some sleep. Stay clear of the Night Road for a while. Hang out in the sunshine."

"I'll miss shaking the tree and seeing the rotten fruit fall."

"You and me, we're going to change the world."

"Tall order."

"We can change the world. Trust me." And then Henry shook his hand, gave him an awkward hug. Luke hugged him back. Then Henry turned and joined the security line.

Luke walked back out into the glare of the afternoon and headed toward the parking garage.

We're going to change the world, Henry had said. At least he didn't lack for ambition.

Luke stopped at the edge of the parking garage, trying to remember where he'd parked his BMW.

"Luke, hey, how's it going?" A heavy arm went around his shoulder. A man's face—thirtyish, brown-haired, a crooked, nervous smile—was close to his. Too close. Luke started to pull back.

A metal object darted into the small of his back.

"Don't yell, Luke. Don't run. You have a very large gun against your spine. Can you stay calm for me?" The man had pulled Luke close so he could whisper in his ear. He was dressed in an expensive pinstripe suit, a conservative navy tie. His face was a little fleshy and soft; he did not look like a man who routinely carried a gun. Luke could smell his mint-drenched breath, his nervous sweat.

"Don't—"

The man pressed the gun harder into Luke's back. Luke hushed. He could not remember how to breathe. Not with a gun in his back, against his spine, up under his jacket. This couldn't be possible. It wasn't happening.

"You parked in row H. Let's go. Easy. Stay calm."

"Take the keys. Just take them." Luke found his voice. He held up the BMW keys with a tremble. Panic swept through him. That was what you were supposed to do; just let them have the car. The car could be replaced.

"No, you keep the keys, Luke. You're driving."

"What do you—"

"We've got places to go, people to see." He steered Luke toward row H. "It'll all be fine."

A family, young mom and dad, two daughters maybe six and four, approached them from a minivan. The younger girl was singing loudly off-key, dancing in the rows.

"I'll make you a deal," the man said quietly. "You yell, you run, and I'll shoot all four of them in the head. Be good and they live."

This cannot be happening to me. Luke made his mouth a tight, thin line. His skin prickled away from the gun's barrel. He tried not to look at the parents' faces while the girl mangled her tune with off-key gusto. He just kept walking.

Five feet away from the family now, and the man with the gun said, in a calm, businesslike voice: "So what I need for you to do when we get back to the office is to review all the accounts. . . ."

"Yes," Luke managed to say. "I understand." Every fiber in him wanted to run, to get away. But the family. Jesus. He couldn't risk their lives.

The older girl, moving away from her sister's annoying singing as it echoed in the concrete garage, met Luke's eyes.

She smiled, and they moved past, the mother chiding the younger, "Emma, okay, enough with the singing. Mommy's getting a three-pill headache."

"Well done," the man hissed into Luke's ear. "We're going to get into your car. Fight or yell and I'll shoot that nice dad dead." Luke heard a click in the man's throat as he swallowed.

"The car's yours, just take it, *please.* . . ."

"Do as you're told." He forced Luke to enter the BMW from the passenger side, awkwardly scooting across the gearshift, the gun firmly planted in his back. Luke settled into the seat and the man closed the passenger door.

"What the hell do you want? Please just let me go. . . ."

"Drive. Don't draw attention to us, or I'll kill you and then I'll kill whoever notices us." He pulled out a steel knife from a holster under his coat. The edge looked brutally sharp. Luke's throat turned to sand. "You see? It's worse than a gun. I can hurt you and keep you alive to hurt some more. Start the engine."

Luke, hands shaking, breath coming in hollow gulps, obeyed. He told himself to stay calm. He thought of those long weeks he'd spent on his own, fourteen years old, running away from his grief, hiding from the police, walking along the back roads, hitching rides, desperate to get from Washington, D.C., to Cape Hatteras. To the beginning of the long stretch of ocean where his father had been lost. He'd seen knives and guns then, once, and he'd gotten away. He could get away again. The key was to wait for the right moment.

"Head out. Say nothing to the attendant."

Luke backed out of the parking space, drove out of the garage, blinking at the sunlight. Two of the tollbooths were open; it was midafternoon, the rush of late-day flights not descending yet.

"Here's money for your parking," the man said. "My treat." He stuck a five-dollar bill under Luke's nose and the money trembled slightly.

He's scared, too, Luke realized and the thought did not comfort. A panicked man with a gun and a knife was more frightening than an icy calm kidnapper.

Luke closed his fist around the money, powered down the window.

"Your ticket, sir?" the attendant asked. He was a big kid, college age, dark hair cut in a burr, a wide friendly smile.

Luke dug into the pocket of his coat and felt the knife nestle into his ribs, where the attendant couldn't see it. He yanked the ticket from his pocket, handed it to the attendant with the crushed fiver.

The attendant returned his change in ones. "You all right, sir?"

Most people would never have noticed. Luke heard himself say, "Airsick. Rough flight." He sounded unsteady.

"Feel better." The wooden gate rose and he drove forward.

The bite of the knife went through his shirt and he nearly drove off the road. "Do you think I'm stupid, Luke? Do you? Were you *trying* to make him remember you?"

Luke winced at the sharp pain. The knife withdrew from denting his flesh and he now felt the barest trickle of blood ease along his ribs. "No, I didn't mean anything, I did what you asked. . . ."

"You just paid for short-term parking but you complain of a rough flight. Fliers don't park in short-term. You tried to stick in his memory. For when he talks to the police."

Luke flinched, then put his eyes back to the road. "I didn't know what to say. You cut me . . . are you crazy?"

"I'll make you a deal." This was apparently the guy's favorite phrase. "You cause trouble and I'll cut your stomach open and you can see what your guts look like. Do you understand?"

"Yes. I understand."

"Exit the airport. Head east on Highway Seventy-one."

"Look, seriously, I didn't know what to say. . . ."

"Don't pretend to be stupid. It will just piss me off."

Luke turned onto Highway 71, which threaded through the outskirts of Austin and eastward toward Houston. He eased into the traffic. The knife left his side but the gun returned to his ribs.

"Drive to Houston."

Three hours away, three hours sitting next to this lunatic. The suggestion unnerved him. What did this guy want? *He knew your name. He knew where you parked.* "Houston . . . why?"

"You'll find out when we get there. You pull over or try and wreck us, or get brave and fight me, you're dead. You obey me, you get out alive. Now, shut the hell up and drive."

"You're crazy, man. Please, just let me go!" *Crazy.* The word thudded past all his fear. A guy who looked ordinary, but had a single-minded mission of violence. Luke glanced at him again.

"I'm not crazy," the man said, and Luke saw that he wasn't. Not a glint of madness in his eyes. He was utterly and completely intent on what he was doing.

Are you one of them? Luke thought. *One of the people I drew out of the darkness?*

The Night Road, Luke realized, had found him.

3

Highway 71 curled past the towering lost pines of Bastrop County, crossed over the Colorado River as the waterway snaked south and east toward the Gulf of Mexico. The land was rolling as it slowly flattened into the coastal plain. Traffic was light.

I am being kidnapped. The realization cut through the shock in Luke's brain. No one would be missing him until tomorrow. Henry said he'd call tomorrow—an eternity, now. No one else would be expecting him or looking for him. Maybe the doorman at his condo, but if he didn't see Luke, he wouldn't think much of it. He wasn't on duty every day. *Maybe,* Luke thought hysterically, *the doorman'll think I've finally gone out to party.*

He drove in silence.

Luke ran the options through his mind, trying to calm his nerves. Stopping the car and simply running would get him a bullet in the back. He rejected the idea of crashing the car; if other drivers stopped to help, he'd be putting them in danger. Brawn couldn't beat a gun. He needed to figure out how he might reason with the guy. But everything he knew about the psychology of violence seemed to evaporate from his brain. He kept thinking about the knife and the gun.

"Don't quit your day job to play poker," the man said. He had not spoken since ordering Luke toward Houston. Forty minutes of gallows silence.

"What?"

"You're thinking it through. How soon you'll be missed. How long it will take for someone to realize you're not where you should be. Plan A is obeying me. You're trying to hatch plan B."

"I wasn't."

"You live alone in a tower condo in downtown. You're sort of friendly with your neighbors, but not so much that they'll notice you're not around tonight or tomorrow or even the day after. It's spring break; you don't have classes."

"You know a lot about me." *Maybe,* Luke thought, *because he's one of the people you went looking for.* He played out the times when the Night Road had responded to his postings via private messages to his online accounts, engaged him in long conversations about their obsessions and agendas. He'd been most careful not to reveal any real information about himself. But this man had still found him.

"What do you want from me?" Luke's voice was steadier.

"I just want you to come with me. Play nice and you don't get hurt."

Draw him out, Luke thought. *Draw him out the same way you would if he was on the other side of the computer monitor.* "If I understood what you were trying to accomplish . . ."

"You don't."

"Have we talked before? Maybe online?"

The man gave a soft laugh. "I'm not one of your research projects."

He definitely knew about the Night Road, then; at the least he knew what Luke was doing for Henry. "My stepfather will call me as soon as he lands."

"Give me your cell phone." The gun's barrel dug into his ribs.

Luke winced and fished his smartphone out of his jacket pocket. The man took it and tossed it to the car's floor. He crushed it under the heel of his heavy shoe. "Instant peace of mind."

Luke glanced at the radio. Above it was a button to a locator/monitoring service—one that would call him if the car was in an accident or that he could call if he needed directions or assistance. But he remembered, with a jolt, that he hadn't bothered to renew the service contract last summer. The monitoring service was useless.

"If you let me go," Luke said, "I won't tell the police. We'll pretend this didn't happen. I never saw you."

"It can't work that way." The man's voice went quiet and low, but not calm. "I'm sorry for you. But this is going to happen."

Going to happen. He thought of all the empty side roads that lay between Austin and Houston. The woods. Places a body could be dumped. He made himself stay calm.

"Doesn't have to," Luke said. "We'll say . . . you let me out here, by the time I walk to a town you're already halfway to Houston. I've already forgotten what you look like. . . ."

"No negotiation." The man wiped his lip with his finger.

"Trust me, I don't need to remember you, I won't. I am very practical that way."

"We're already past the point of no return."

"Wrong. You can always turn back." He didn't want this guy feeling more desperate than he already was. "You have a choice."

"You haven't gotten out much in life, have you?" The man choked on a nervous laugh.

Luke couldn't tell how to read this guy; one second he seemed like a hardened criminal, confident in his capacity for violence, the next he seemed nervous, fretful, as though he'd taken on the wrong job and he knew it. "Look. Mistakes were made. Things were said. It's all in the past. I'm the world's most forgiving dude. Also the most generous. Just let me go."

"We need us some bright and cheery tunes, and for you to shut the hell up." The man fiddled with the radio and spun past stations but found nothing he liked and switched it to silence. "I hate not having driving tunes. Or even the news. Except all the news is bad these days; it's the way we've made the world, nothing but bad, bad news."

Luke drove on in eerie silence. The man just stared out the window, lost in thought. But the gun stayed steady in Luke's side and he kept imagining the blood and torn intestines that would gush into his lap.

Luke saw a sign for Mirabeau, a good-sized town halfway between Houston and Austin. He remembered there was often a speed trap on the eastern edge of the town. He pressed gently but steadily on the accelerator. Rev the speed up past the limit, slow enough where the man wouldn't notice. For the first time in his life, Luke hoped he'd fall into a speed trap.

Talk to him; don't let him notice what you're doing.

But before he could say anything, the man's cell phone rang. He pulled it free of a pocket and read the display.

"You stay quiet," he said. He flicked the knife up along Luke's ribs and Luke winced and nodded.

"Yeah?" the man said into the phone.

Luke heard a woman's voice crackle through the cell, saying, "Eric, this is Jane. How goes the project? Gathered the nerve to grab our boy yet?" Her accent was British. Luke pushed the car to four miles an hour over the limit.

"It's—it's under control. But I really cannot talk right now."

"Hard for you, I'm sure, to do two things at once," the woman—Jane—said. She gave a sick, cruel laugh. "But hurry—time's running out."

The man thumbed the volume control on the phone, making Jane's words into a murmur.

Eric. His name is Eric. Luke kept eyes on the road. *Under control.* This Jane woman must know what Eric was planning and why. A barely felt tap, and he was six miles an hour faster than the limit.

Eric, huddled, listening on his cell, wasn't watching the speedometer or Luke, and Luke jolted the speed up higher. Eight over the limit. And then ten. He debated in his mind as to whether to push it higher, to risk it. No. He couldn't risk Eric noticing. He squeezed the steering wheel hard.

Eric listened to the phone and finally he said, "I'll call you when the rest is complete and you better keep your side of the bargain."

The rest is complete. Keep your side. What did Eric mean? And why would a British woman be involved in his kidnapping when his focus was on finding American extremists? He didn't look over as Eric switched off the phone without a good-bye to his caller.

Mirabeau spanned a few exits on the highway—the BMW shot past a McDonald's, a bakery/gas station selling kolache pastries, an exit for the downtown business district. No sign of a patrol car. *Please, please be up ahead,* Luke thought.

Eric seemed lost in thought and didn't notice. *Let's keep it that way,* Luke thought. *Let's make him just a little mad. Enough to keep him distracted.*

"Was that your girlfriend?"

"Shut the hell up."

"I bet she doesn't know you're carjacking innocent people at airports. She'd be so proud."

"This isn't a carjacking."

"I thought most kidnappers did their own driving. You're a cheap-ass kidnapper, making me do my own driving."

Eric stared at him. "Are you trying to be funny?"

"Yes. I want to lighten the mood." Luke risked a bad imitation of a smile. Where the hell was the cop who was, on every other trip Luke had made through this stretch of highway, so ready to give out a ticket? He wanted to pound his fist against the steering wheel in rage. But he had to keep Eric's mind engaged, his eyes off the dashboard.

"There's nothing funny about today." But Luke heard a jagged curl in Eric's words, nerves on end. "The hell I'm trapped in is not a joke!"

"Exactly what hell are you trapped in? You have the gun," Luke screamed back in his face. They shot under a bridge and on the opposite side, a Mirabeau police cruiser sat, waiting like a spider in the heart of its web.

Yes, Luke thought, *thank you, Jesus, and the patron saint of speeders.* He was saved.

Eric glanced in the rearview, saw the blues and reds flash to life. "Slow it down!" Eric yelled.

Luke obeyed but it was too late. The cruiser launched itself off the incline onto the highway.

"Oh, you rotten prick!" Eric screamed.

"I'm sorry. You made me nervous. I didn't watch . . . should I pull over?"

"If I have to kill this poor stupid cop it's your fault!" Eric hissed.

"Don't kill anyone. You don't really seem to want to do this!"

"I can't, I can't! You don't understand! You don't know what you're doing!" Eric steadied his voice. "Pull over and say nothing. Not a word."

"And he won't notice the gun in your hand."

"I'm going to put the gun out of sight."

Luke thought: *Good, because then I'm going to yell my head off.*

"Because if you say a word I don't like, if you do anything other than take the ticket and thank the officer, I'm going to shoot you both. You just put this cop's life in needless danger, because, yes, I will kill him, and if I have to kill him, you die too. I always have a plan B and this is it. Right now that cop is walking into a trap you set for him, you stupid heartless moron." An icy certainty colored Eric's tone now, unmistakable resolve.

"Heartless? You're the goddamned kidnapper!" Luke stopped the BMW, the police car stopping behind it.

Bile clouded into Luke's throat. In the rearview he saw the officer get out of the car and start to approach.

"Get out your insurance and registration. Now. I have the gun where I can reach it instantly. You warn him, you both die."

Luke gathered the papers. The rising courage he thought he'd feel if he could attract police attention was crushed. He powered down the window as the officer reached the door.

"I'm sorry, sir," Luke said.

The officer was middle-aged, tall, heavy-built. He wore the professional look that said he'd already heard every excuse a hundred times before. His name tag read Moncrief. "You didn't pull over very fast, sir."

"No, sir, I didn't." Luke handed the officer his license and registration.

"That's my fault, Officer," Eric said with a crooked, wan smile. He sounded like a disappointed big brother. "I was yelling at him about his speeding and he's already upset. We just got word of a death in the family, our grandma, and we were heading fast, too fast, I guess, to Houston."

"I'm sorry for your loss," the officer said, real sympathy in his voice. But still, he began to write the ticket.

Luke watched the pen move across the paper; the cop's hands busy and not near his gun. The chance had passed. Luke squeezed the steering wheel with frustration. If he called for help now Eric would shoot Officer Moncrief before he could react. He glanced at Eric and the barest smile of triumph flickered on Eric's face.

Officer Moncrief handed Luke his ticket and Luke signed. He wanted to write *HELP ME* on the signature line but he could feel Eric watching him. He paused halfway through his scrawl and he could hear Eric's very quiet intake of breath, readying the gun.

He wrote his last name, handed the pad back to the officer.

"Slow it down, gentlemen. If you're dealing with one tragedy, you don't want another."

"Words to live by, Officer, thank you," Eric said.

"Yes," Luke said. It was true. As soon as the officer turned away and started back to his cruiser, the gun moved to Luke's hip.

"Back on the road. Now. Speed limit."

Luke obeyed, his hands shaking on the wheel, raging at himself for his lost nerve.

"I'll make you a deal," Eric said, breaking the silence as they left Mirabeau behind them.

"You and your deals. Your deals only benefit you."

"Another stunt and I shoot off your big toe. I don't have to deliver you in perfect condition. We don't have much time."

Deliver, Luke thought. He was now a delivery. Who wanted him?

4

HOUSTON

The city spread out across the vast coastal plain, a seemingly endless quilt of shopping centers, office buildings, housing developments, all connected by a stitching of highways. Haze moped above the horizon. It was a city of drivers, a constant thrumming jolt of energy and movement. As the afternoon rush hour approached, I-10 traffic headed east into the city slowed in fits and starts.

The creeping pace of traffic gave Luke a fresh hope. He kept cussing himself, inside his brain, for his fear in not having tried to escape when the Mirabeau police officer was there to help him. But he believed it would have gotten them both killed. The desperation in Eric's eyes was a fierce, awful fire.

They'd hit their first real traffic now. If the car came to a full stop maybe he could bolt. Eric might not be eager to shoot him in front of dozens of other people. Or he could mouth a plea for help, if anyone would look at him. The drivers kept their eyes on the road. Strangers did not exchange glances in cars in Houston.

"The knife likes you to have your eyes forward," Eric said.

"The knife likes to not stab me when I'm driving because we'll crash. But God knows we want to keep the knife happy."

"Stay calm. Tonight you'll be safe." Eric sounded hollow. He had shushed Luke the few times in the past hour when Luke had tried to speak again. "Stay in the middle lane until we get to the downtown exits."

Traffic slowed again. And for the first time, Eric clutched Luke's shirt, grabbing the seat belt in his fist as well.

"You're considering making a run. I'm telling you I will kill you."

"You don't need the threats. I'm done fighting you." He was gripped by a panic that someone would see Eric threatening him and try to help him, making it worse. Luke glanced at the car on his left. He saw a woman driving a minivan, a bored teenage girl in the passenger seat, texting on a phone. To his right, an older man in a pickup truck drummed a beat on the steering wheel. None of them looked over, lost in the world of what was directly ahead of their windshields.

"Strange to be so alone, each of us, when surrounded by thousands of others. We don't even know who we can reach out to, who will understand us." Eric gave a ragged laugh. "That's why the world's going to hell."

"Then let's not take one further step into hell. Please. You're not a bad guy."

"You need to be afraid of me, Luke."

"I am. But . . . you don't want to hurt me. I can tell. You're not a criminal, you don't want to do this. Let me help you get out of whatever mess you're in." He had to convince Eric it wasn't too late to stop, to let him go.

"You are helping me. You just don't know it yet." Eric's jaw clenched.

"But . . ."

"It changes you, breaking the law," Eric said quietly. "I can't go back. I made my choice. And I want you to shut up now."

They had to work past a traffic jam caused by a chain reaction of fender benders, and by the time they reached the heart of the city night had begun its slide over the sky. Eric got more agitated, checking his watch every half-minute. Sweat was bright on his face. Downtown Houston rose in light-bejeweled towers. It had undergone a renaissance in recent years; old abandoned hotels and buildings reborn into new establishments, lodgings, and office space. Luke steered the BMW through the weaving pedestrians— office workers heading to the light rail and bus stops and parking garages, or to trendy new bars and restaurants. Luke had always thought Houston a place of unbounded energy and bustle, but right now he just wished someone would slow down long enough to notice he was in trouble.

"This is about to get dangerous," Eric said. He leaned forward, as though scanning the pedestrians for a face, for a threat.

"Like it wasn't already."

"Turn here."

They drove past Minute Maid Park, where the Astros played, then deep into a neighborhood that had not yet benefited from the economic renaissance of downtown. The buildings were older, the businesses humbler. Unrepaired potholes, a by-product of Houston humidity, pocked the pavement.

Luke reached a small parking lot and Eric said, "Pull in here."

Luke did, parking in a slot closest to the street at Eric's order. They had a view down the street. The sidewalks were less crowded; fewer pedestrians strolled to their evening's entertainment. Luke saw an old couple ambling slowly, carrying grocery bags; a young woman hurrying past, chattering on a cell phone and gesturing wildly; an older woman dressed too young, venturing into the twilight with her painted, pained smile. Down the street Luke could see a small bar, a homeless shelter operated by an Episcopal charity, a liquor store, a clothing resale shop, a neon-signed Tex-Mex eatery. The storefronts were weathered and worn.

"Now what?" Luke asked.

"We wait."

"For what?" Was someone coming here to meet them? To collect Luke? This might be his one remaining chance to escape. But no way he could get clear of the car without Eric shooting or knifing him. "What are you going to do?"

Eric glanced again at his watch, tugged nervously at his lip. "Everything will be okay. Trust me."

Twenty minutes passed; sundown completed its glory. The night threw its stars across the dark-purpled sky. Eric's gun rested back in its second home, Luke's ribs. Luke's legs ached from sitting so long. Hunger rumbled his stomach, but he kept fighting off a fear-induced nausea. He'd already decided if he puked he was aiming at Eric's rotten face. Puke and run for his life. A mark of real heroics. He thought he was starting to lose his grip.

He closed his eyes. He wondered if this sinking acceptance in his chest that the end was close was what his father had felt in the moments before he died, if Dad had realized the plane he was on was doomed.

Luke's hand found the medal under his shirt and clutched at it. He thought of the conversation he'd had with his father, his mom asleep in the sleeping bag, he and his dad sitting by the soft flicker of the campfire.

"I want you to have this, son, keep it close to you always," his father had said. "Always. It will shield you from danger."

"Dad. Seriously? You're not religious." His father had been raised Episcopalian but he wasn't a churchgoer, except maybe at Easter and Christmas, when Luke's mom insisted.

"No atheists in foxholes, Luke," Warren Dantry had said.

"We're camping, this isn't a foxhole," Luke said. He raised the medal to the firelight's glow: a faceless angel, muscular wings, holding a sword and shield.

"Saint Michael the archangel is an emblem of strength and determination, of order and reason overcoming chaos and violence. He's special in that he figures in Christian, Jewish, and Islamic traditions. He's a hero for the world, good overcoming enormous evil."

"Evil. Like Darth Vader?" He didn't remember the story of what Saint Michael had done, what evil he had defeated.

"Worse than Darth Vader," his father had said. "Saint Michael will keep you safe, Luke. If not now, then someday."

"Safe from what?"

"From whatever darkness comes into your life. You might be called to fight one day, Luke. Think of Michael. Think of strength and know you can win."

"Brains are better than strength, Dad."

His dad smiled at him. "Yes. But together, they're unbeatable."

"Thanks, Dad." Luke didn't like jewelry of any sort. He thought this a goofy gift and most unlike his dad and he put the medal in his pocket. His father had said nothing more, poking at the fire with a stick.

And a month later his father was dead, and Luke had worn the medal every day since.

"What are you doing?" Eric's voice rose.

Luke opened his eyes. "Nothing."

Eric jabbed the gun hard into Luke's side, pried his fingers from the medal, pulled it from Luke's shirt. A flat circular medal, with an angel armed with a fiery sword. The angel's wings were wide, strong, like an eagle's.

"What's this?" An edge came to Eric's voice.

"Saint Michael. The archangel. My dad gave it to me."

"You—you don't need to be praying. Everything's cool if you do what

I say." Eric let go of the medal as though it burned him; Luke tucked the silver back into his shirt.

Eric put his gaze back to the street. "Saint Michael. He's the one who casts Satan out of heaven, right, sends him plummeting to hell?"

"Yeah," Luke said. "Who sent you to this hell, Eric?" This might be his only chance to reason with him. They were waiting, for God knew what, and Eric was scared. He swallowed past the broken-glass ache in his throat. "The woman on the phone? Who is she?"

"Shut up."

"She's giving you orders."

"Shut up."

"She ordered you to kidnap me. Why?"

Eric kept his eyes locked on the street. "Hello," Eric said. Luke followed Eric's stare and saw a flicker of light as the homeless shelter's door closed. A tall older man approached their car, his weathered face lit by the juxtaposition of passing headlights and the pool of a streetlamp. He was dressed in the uniform of the homeless, a shabby coat, a bandanna secured over greasy hair.

They waited in silence as the man approached.

"Start the car." Eric's voice crackled energy, as though the exhaustion of the past several hours were forgotten. "Pull out into the street."

"Why?"

"Just do it."

Luke started the engine and pulled out onto the street. The homeless man was forty feet ahead of them, walking on the left.

"I have to be sure," Eric said to himself. "Stay close. But not too close."

Luke stopped the BMW at a light. The homeless man kept walking, stare fixed ahead on the buckling sidewalk.

The light flashed green.

"Go," Eric ordered.

Luke drove the car, closed the gap on the homeless man. They drove past him and the man glanced up.

"Drive another block, then go back," Eric ordered.

Luke U-turned at the next light and now the passenger-side window was closer to the homeless man. Eric studied his quarry.

"It's him," Eric said. "Okay. Be cool, be cool."

Luke wasn't sure if Eric was talking to him, or to himself.

The homeless man raised his head as he walked on in his broken shuffle. He wiped at his nose with the back of his hand. Another man waited at the street corner, leaning against the traffic light, turning to watch as both the first man and the BMW approached. The second man—dressed in a leather jacket with a colorful bald eagle stitched on the back, jeans, and heavy dark sunglasses unneeded at night—seemed to sense trouble rising; he turned and ran into the shadows of an alley at top speed, glancing once over his shoulder. Luke saw naked fear on his broad, scar-cheeked face.

"That guy in the eagle jacket was going to talk to the homeless man," Luke said. He was not sure why he said this thought aloud, but he had seen a smile of expectation rise and then fade in the second man's face. Luke had the sense they were interrupting something—a rendezvous or an appointment. The homeless man stopped as the leather-jacketed man rushed away from the scene.

They drew level with the homeless man and he paused as the BMW crawled to a stop, Eric lowering the window.

The homeless man took an awkward step forward into the pool of light.

Then he turned and began to hurry away. Walking with purpose, digging into his pocket.

"Follow him," Eric ordered with a hard jab of the gun into Luke's tender ribs.

The homeless man broke into a run. He cut across the street toward the parking lot of a bank. The building looked new, the foothold into the neighborhood for the revitalized edge of downtown.

"Catch up with him. I have to talk to him," Eric said.

The homeless man ran toward the narrow, empty drive-through lanes, toward the soft glow of the ATM.

"Cut him off, don't let him get away," Eric said.

Luke cut the BMW between the homeless man and the building. He glided into the ATM lane and slammed to a stop; the driver's side was close to the ATM, the passenger side fronting the running man. The homeless guy rocked on his heels, and then lurched to retreat the other way.

The gun left Luke's ribs.

"No!" he yelled, but Eric leaned out the window and fired. Three loud pops. The homeless man jerked, fell, collapsed in a huddle. The back of his head welled bone and blood.

Luke lunged at Eric's arm, at the gun; he stepped off the brake and the BMW lurched past the ATM. Eric socked his elbow back hard and Luke's head snapped into the driver's window. Pain lashed his nose, his face. The gun, warm from duty, pressed against the side of his throat.

Eric turned, held up his phone with the other hand, and snapped a photo of the dead man. He closed the phone and jabbed the gun harder against Luke's throat.

"Oh, God, you shot him," Luke whispered.

"Drive fast. Now."

Luke drove, his hands shivering, his whole body numb with shock. He steered back onto the road. The gun was warm against his skin. Holy Jesus. He had just witnessed a murder. Fear pounded an ache into his chest. He wasn't sure what he felt except that he did not want to die.

"Get us onto the highway." Eric's voice broke. "Go, go."

"Which—which one?" As if it mattered, Luke thought. Eric had just killed a man and Luke knew he was next.

"Just get us on a highway, get us out of here." Eric flipped open his phone. Worked the keypad with his thumb. Then he punched in another number, shaking. He emitted a hard, nervous laugh—an awful mockery of a laugh—and put the cell phone up to his ear.

"It's done. He's dead. I just e-mailed you the proof. So you tell me where she is."

Luke felt Eric's stare come onto his skin. He drove like a robot; he tried to focus on the driving. *Where she is.*

Eric closed the phone. "Get us to Highway Fifty-nine and head northeast."

"What, so I can drive you to kill someone else?"

"No. Now we go save a life." And the gun went back against Luke's ribs, like an old friend.

5

They were well past the city now, past the sprawl of lights and the scattering of outer suburbs and smaller towns, into the denseness of the piney woods. Luke kept a hard grip on the wheel. He badly needed to go to the bathroom and hunger clenched its fist around his stomach. The gas needle hovered toward the red zone of empty.

"We need to make a gas stop," he said.

"You'll pull over when I say."

Two minutes later they came upon a farm-to-market road, empty of traffic. Beyond its edges, heavy growths of loblolly pines stood like guardians.

"Drive a ways down the road," Eric ordered.

He's going to kill me now. Whatever strange reason I was useful to him is over and he's going to kill me. Terror rose in his throat.

"Stop."

Luke stopped.

Eric removed the keys from the ignition. "Get out of the car. Slowly."

The last movements his muscles would ever know. Luke obeyed. He'd been stuck behind the wheels, body locked in fear for hours. The night was silent, the stars mute witnesses.

"You need to pee?"

"Yes." Was this a final kindness? What did it matter?

"Go on the other side of the car." He stuck the gun between Luke's shoulder blades.

Luke relieved himself. When he was done, Eric steered him toward the trunk. He popped it open with the remote.

"I'm going to give you a break from driving. But if I hear one peep out of that trunk, you're dead. As much fun as we've had together, I'll just pretend you're the guy I killed and it's boom, you're done." The shakiness was gone from Eric's voice. He'd said earlier that breaking the law changed you, and now he had broken the greatest law of man. He had taken a life.

"I know." Shivering, Luke climbed into the trunk. The lid slammed down. Darkness. The engine revved. The tires hissed softly on the gravel, and the car backed and pulled into a U-turn.

Luke, alone, stretched his legs out as far as he could. *You may be called upon to fight,* Dad had said. The time was now. He had to think of something.

The car stopped and Luke opened his eyes in the dark.

He heard Eric's soft whisper near the trunk. "Filling the tank up. No noise from you or I'll kill the clerk inside."

Luke pressed a fist against the trunk lid.

"The funny thing is . . . shooting that man was much harder in my mind. I'd built it up as this terrible thing, but after the first squeeze of the trigger my mind turned off a little bit and it wasn't too bad." He sounded almost surprised.

I have to stop you, Luke thought. *I can't let you hurt another person.* The pump clicked as Eric settled it back into its slot.

Luke groped in the darkness. He needed a weapon. He felt a circular shape—a set of jumper cables. He groped past the cables and his fingers closed on a pile of plastic boxes. Old cassette tapes. Nothing beneath. He kept searching, turning over to face the front of the trunk. He felt the rim of the spare tire. There were tools to change it, but they lay under the tire, and he couldn't get to them with the trunk closed.

He reached out and touched the coil of the jumper cables again. Heavy plastic, like a thick braided rope, with the copper clamps on the end.

As the car started and pulled away from the station, Luke began to uncurl the coil.

6

Luke lost the sense of time. He kept the jumper cables close to him and he thought, long and hard, about what he would do when Eric—the murderer—opened the trunk lid.

Finally the car stopped.

Luke tensed. He pulled the cables close to him. He practiced what he was going to do, best as he could, given the tight quarters. It was insane to try but to not try was worse.

He heard a voice close to the trunk. "Luke? You awake?"

As if he could sleep. "I'm awake."

"I'm going to open the trunk now. You will get out and you will do exactly as you're told."

The trunk opened. The dark night had become gloomier, gray clouds obscuring the stars. In the distance thunder rumbled. He could see the shadow of Eric standing centered at the trunk's opening. The arm, cocked, holding the gun, aimed toward him.

Luke snared the cable over Eric's arm, one neat quick motion, and yanked down, pulling Eric toward the trunk. Then he kicked out hard, caught Eric in the chest.

"Dumbass!" Eric roared. Now Luke yanked Eric toward him, keeping him off balance, trying to scramble out of the trunk. The pistol, bound in the cables, was caught between the two of them.

Eric fired.

Heat. Burning. Luke heard the thump of bullets ripping into the trunk's body. He kicked out again, suddenly afraid of a bullet smashing into the now-full gas tank. The two men hit the ground, scrambling for the loose gun. Eric twisted his hands free of the cables. Luke tackled him, drove knees into Eric's back as he lunged toward the weapon. The gun lay close to his reach, lying now on the grass, lit only by moonlight peering through the clouds. Grass and dirt clogged Luke's teeth as Eric pushed him off.

Luke's fingers closed around the barrel and then the heavy rope of the jumper cables looped around his throat.

The cables tightened into the flesh of his neck like a noose. Eric's knee ground hard into his spine. Luke struggled to turn, to better the grip on the gun and aim the gun at Eric, but he couldn't move.

Eric began to strangle him. The pain—from the pressure, from the lack of air—burst in Luke's throat. "Let the gun go, Luke," Eric yelled in his ear. "Let it go."

If he let go he would die. If he didn't let go he would die. He couldn't turn the gun around to aim it at Eric; he didn't have the leverage or the grip on the trigger. He released the gun, spreading fingers, feeling the cool of the grass instead of the heat of the steel.

The noose didn't loosen, but Eric yanked him several yards away from the gun, dragging into the dirt and grass, then pounded him with a brutal kick to the back of the head.

Darkness, pain. Luke lay stunned, gasping, the ache in his head as bright as fire. Blood oozed on his ear, on his jaw. The gun barrel nestled against his hair.

"You're not going to screw me over!" Spittle hit the back of Luke's neck.

Luke, hardly able to speak past the pain in his throat, nodded, facedown in the grass.

Eric yanked him to his feet and shoved him toward a dirt road that cut through the grass. Loblolly pines rose in thin majesty around him and the air smelled of wet earth and gathering storm. In the distance, thunder sounded, clouds clearing their throats.

Luke and Eric moved down the road and suddenly a light flickered on, high and bright. Luke blinked at the harsh brightness. He could see a chained gate cutting across the road. A light above the gate glowed. No person stood on the other side of the gate; the light must be keyed to a sensor.

Eric shoved Luke against the gate. The links clattered as Luke stumbled against it.

"Turn around."

Luke did and Eric held up a cell phone.

"Smile."

Luke didn't.

"I want that bitch to see you're being delivered in good condition. Smile."

Delivered. Luke bit his lip, then smiled.

"Good." Eric fiddled with the smartphone. He clicked buttons, kept his gaze flickering between the keypad and Luke. Luke guessed the pine forest had been cleared of a width about forty feet for the scrabble of road. Eric could gun him down before he reached the woods.

Eric put the phone up to his face. "I just sent you a photo of Luke Dantry. Where is she?"

Eric listened, said, "You better not be lying." He clicked off the phone.

"You called the British woman," Luke said.

Eric didn't answer. He powered a bullet into the chain's lock. It shattered in the quiet, sent birds flocking up from the pines. Eric unwound the chains, creaked the gate open. He produced a small flashlight from his pocket and waved Luke forward with it.

Luke shambled along, gravel kicking under his shoes. The road looked like it had been built for quiet murder. The only noises were his footsteps, the hiss of the wind, and a low song of owls. The dark smelled dank and the circle of flashlight danced at his feet. A soft rain began to fall.

"Who'd you send my photo to?" he asked. First the dead man in Houston, now him. "Who am I being delivered to?" He risked a thrust. "Is it Jane?"

Eric stared at him, shook his head. "You are done talking, period. You don't say a word. I don't need you making things worse for me." Like Eric was the victim, more than Luke or the dead homeless guy.

The road split and Eric said, "Turn left. And hurry up. Hurry." He prodded Luke in the shoulder blades with the gun. Ahead he saw a soft glow of light.

Luke stumbled forward, Eric urging him into a loping run.

Suddenly the trees on each side opened up and a small cabin stood in the clearing of the pines. A thin light shone from a small window near the front door.

Eric stopped him as they reached the door. He kicked over a flowerpot filled with dead remnants of rosemary. In the puddle of the light Luke saw two keys. One large, like a house key. The other was smaller, similar to the kind to undo a luggage lock.

"Open the door," Eric ordered.

Luke slid the key into the lock, eased the door open.

They stepped into a dark, short entryway. The thin framing of light came from a closed door on his right. Eric put a hand on his shoulder—almost gently—and opened the door.

It was a small room and it smelled of cleaning fluid and sweat. A small lamp was in a corner and in its feeble circle of light Luke saw a woman. She lay on a metal bed. She was in her mid-twenties, dark haired. She wore jeans and a thin sweater. Her black hair was a tangle over her face and she smelled of having gone a couple of days without a good washing.

She stared at Luke in complete terror.

"Baby, it's me," Eric said, stepping from behind Luke.

The woman coughed a whisper that sounded like *Oh, God, Eric,* and she trembled. "Oh, my God, why, *get me out of here. . . .*"

"It's all okay. It's all okay," Eric said. Luke could see that shackles bound the woman to the bed—a set of chains braceleting her to the cot, at her wrists, another set of shackles at her feet.

Eric hurried toward her but stopped himself. He made sure to not turn his back on Luke and he backed away from the bed. He pressed the small key into Luke's hands. "Set her free."

"Eric, who is he? Where are the police?" the woman asked.

"Say nothing more. You're safe, that's all that matters." Eric stepped back, the gun not aimed at Luke but at the ready.

"Why the hell do you have a gun?" the woman demanded, an edge in her rising voice.

"Just hush, babe, you're safe now." Iron in Eric's voice, a huge relief. "Safe and sound."

Luke fumbled with the keys. He unlocked the chains cuffing her wrists and the links fell to the mattress. She slapped the constraints away as if they were radioactive. The links tinkled as they slid to the hardwood floor.

"Thank you," the woman said to Luke. "Thank you so much—"

"Don't thank him," Eric screamed. "Don't say a goddamned word to him!"

Luke unlocked the shackles on her legs. He met the woman's gaze; she was confused, glancing at him and then Eric. She kicked the chains away and wriggled past Luke off the bed. She fell against Eric's chest, drinking in the comfort of his touch. He kept the gun aimed at Luke.

"I want to go home," the woman sobbed into Eric's shoulder.

"So do I," said Luke.

Eric kissed the top of the woman's head, stroked her shoulder. He eased her toward the door and turned back to Luke. "Get on the bed."

Luke sat on the mattress's edge.

"I've moved heaven and earth to keep you safe," he said to the woman.

She nodded, looking confused, and he kissed her forehead.

"But I need you to do what I say. I need to keep the gun on him. So I need you to lock this guy to the bed."

Luke's throat froze and the woman mumbled, "What?"

"Lock him to the bed. He's taking your place."

"Eric—" the woman began. "You can't abandon a person here. No. Let's just go to the police, please, let's just go to the police."

At the same time Luke stood. "No."

"Sit down!" Eric shouted.

"You're not leaving me here."

"Aubrey, please," Eric said. "Do as I say."

"I don't understand—" the woman started to say, and Eric yelled, "Don't question me, not after I've put everything in my life on the line for you. Just do it, goddamn it!" Eric pushed her toward the bed and following her, put the gun to Luke's temple. "Stay still. Don't struggle." He swallowed. "He's a bad guy, baby. Don't feel bad for him."

"Don't listen to him, he kidnapped me—" Luke shouted. He stopped. If he told this woman Eric had committed murder, then Eric might kill him instead of leaving him here. He shut his mouth.

"He's one of the guys behind your kidnapping," Eric said. "I grabbed him, he's your ransom. So don't feel bad for him, babe."

The woman—Aubrey—stared hard at Luke and Luke shook his head. He grabbed at her smooth wrists. "He's lying. I'm not a bad guy. Please."

"Let her go!" Eric roared. He fired a bullet past Luke's head, into the wall.

Luke and Aubrey froze, doubled over in surprise. She trembled at the gunshot and Luke released her. She raised the cuffs to his wrists and clicked the shackles on him. "I'm sorry," she murmured. "I'm sorry."

Aubrey glanced at Eric. Then she attached the chains to his ankles.

"He's lying to you. I'm innocent . . ." Luke said.

"All I did," Eric said, "was deliver a ransom."

Aubrey stepped back, shaking, and the man embraced her again. "Go outside, wait for me. We're going home."

Aubrey stumbled out of the cabin.

Eric unfolded the phone. He pulled a small metal device from his pocket—Luke guessed it was a modulator, designed to mask his voice—and snapped it over the phone, and he punched in a number. He raised his finger to his lips in a hushing motion.

The phone was on speaker and Luke heard Henry say, "Hello?"

"Henry Shawcross. I have bad news. Your stepson, Luke Dantry, has been kidnapped."

"What? Who the hell is this?"

"Let's just say I'm passing the baton to you," Eric said. "Listen carefully. To get your stepson back, you must wire fifty million dollars to a series of offshore accounts."

"Henry doesn't have fifty million dollars. Are you insane?" Luke said softly. The idea was ridiculous. "You've made a serious mistake."

A long, agonizing beat of silence. "I wish to speak to Luke," Henry said.

"Tell him you're alive and well. Nothing else." Eric unhooked the device from the phone and put it close to Luke's face.

Luke said, "Henry?"

"Luke." Henry sounded stunned. "Is this a joke?"

"No. He grabbed me at the airport. He had a gun. He—"

Eric stood and replaced the modulator onto the phone. "He's alive and unhurt. Do what you're told or your stepson is dead."

Another long stretch of silence; Luke could hear the rasp of Henry's breathing. "I'm sorry. I will not pay."

Luke froze. He thought he had misheard. He said *will not.* Instead of *cannot.* "What?"

Henry's voice sounded thin, tinny, a ghost of his usual confident baritone. "I don't know what money you're talking about. Please don't hurt Luke. But I don't have this money you want."

Eric said, "Don't lie. You know you have the fifty million, you bastard."

"I do not."

"For God's sake, give him what he wants!" Luke yelled. He was thinking: *If you don't have the money, just tell them that you do. Stall them; make them think the money is coming; get the FBI on the job.* "Please, Henry. Tell him you'll cooperate." Maybe Henry was too stunned by the ransom demand to know what to say.

"Luke, I cannot. I cannot."

His stepfather—smart, determined, more than capable of thinking on his feet—was not willing to bluff. He was not willing to lie, to promise complete cooperation, and get off the phone and call the police. He was leaving Luke to the murderous mercies of a kidnapper. The realization hit him like a stone hammering into his chest.

Why wouldn't he lie, say anything to save Luke?

"You don't understand, you don't cooperate, he will die," Eric said.

"I can't help you," Henry said, unyielding.

"He's already killed one guy. He knows about the Night Road!" Luke yelled. "Give him what he wants!"

Silence, like a thread pulled to a breaking point. "I suspect this is a sort of very bad joke. Luke, why are you doing this?"

Eric retreated across from the room, holding the phone still, a look of disbelief on his face.

What does a kidnapper do when the family tells him to screw himself? Luke thought. "Henry! It's not a joke!"

"I am going to hang up now," Henry said.

The line went dead.

Eric and Luke stared at each other in the dim light of the cabin. After their yelling the room seemed to echo with the silence.

Luke was afraid to speak, instinct told him to be silent, that Eric was on the brink of either killing him or calling Henry back or calling back Jane, the British woman—the master pulling the strings—to report Henry's refusal.

Eric stared at him. Raised the gun.

Luke stared back in his eyes. It was his only defense. Eric had shot the homeless man in the back; he hadn't had to watch his victim face death.

"She'll hear," Luke said. "She'll hear and she'll know what you did. Know what you are."

The gun wavered.

"You can't talk about this," Eric said. "Your stepfather's in deep. That's all I can say. You're in deep as well."

"Deep in what?"

"The woman who took Aubrey, Jane, she'll call Henry again. I'm sure they'll work out an exchange for you." Eric's voice broke.

"I just want to go home. Please." Luke rattled the chains.

"I'll give you a bit of advice if you get free or Henry pays up. Find a place to hide if you can. Trust no one. That's your life now."

"You know Henry. You know about the Night Road. How?"

Eric leaned against the wall, as though the weariness of the past day had drained him of bone and blood.

"What the hell is my stepfather involved with? Why would he have fifty million dollars? Tell me."

Now Eric looked at him again. "I can't afford to feel sorry for you. Goodbye." He walked toward the door.

"Don't do this. Don't leave me here." Luke struggled against the chains. "For God's sake, no one knows I'm here in the middle of nowhere."

"You're right. And that ignorance buys me time." Eric turned and he left, slamming the door behind him.

A few minutes later Luke heard a car—his car—start, in the far distance, past the grove, past the gate. The BMW's engine gave what sounded like a joyful revving. Of course. Eric's and Aubrey's ordeal was over.

His sure as hell wasn't. He was alone, chained to a bed. In the middle of nowhere. With no way out. And no one to help him.

7

The bombs required a high level of trust. It started with several hundred pounds of high-grade Semtex explosive smuggled out of the Czech Republic and then sold to an operative in the FARC terrorist group in Colombia.

The explosives were then bartered for detailed intelligence on a new surge of antinarcotics operations supported in Colombia by the American government. This trade resulted in the eventual torture and murder of four undercover agents.

The Semtex was muled into America by the most trusted couriers of a Mexican drug lord in exchange for the name of a key government informant inside his own ring. The informant was tortured for three days. Her body, with her throat slit, was left on her mother's doorstep in a quiet Mexico City neighborhood.

Once the explosives were in the United States, the construction of the bomb was completed in a suburban garage outside of Houston, Texas, by an American woman who felt a deep and abiding hate for the government. Her nickname was Snow. It did not matter who was in power; Snow loathed all authority figures within the government with a fevered intensity. Snow had learned how to make Semtex-based bombs when she was a youngster, from her father, before he died. She refreshed her knowledge by perusing instructions found on the Internet and studying worn, tea-stained manuals left over from the Irish Republican Army's campaign in the 1980s that she had acquired on an online auction site.

Snow made many of them, in careful and rote fashion, one after another, for weeks, working in the quiet of her aunt's house. Her aunt had died a year ago and Snow'd kept the house as a workshop. Her boyfriend grew tired of her long absence; they fought on the second day, when she came home exhausted, her fingernails nicked from cutting wires, her nerves raw, and he left for a friend's house. She was glad he was gone. He wasn't committed to the cause; he was a pain in the ass. Fortunately he didn't know about the bombs. She went and bought her own supplies: cell phones, wire, blasting caps.

Then she made one special bomb, shaping the plastic to detonate in a certain way, with a calculated force to produce an exact result. Snow was so proud of it; she called this bomb Baby. She was drinking juice, waiting at her house for the man to pick Baby up, hoping that her boyfriend wouldn't show up, wanting her back. She was done with the boyfriend.

"It's lighter than I thought it would be," Mouser said when he picked up the bomb. He stood in Snow's suburban kitchen; she had, as ordered, placed the bomb inside a reinforced canvas carryall. He picked up the duffel bag, measured the weight. Heavy but manageable.

"I do good work," Snow said. Mouser thought the nickname fit her; her hair was dyed a stark white, cut short. Her gray eyes were like flecks of ice. Her body was muscled, not afraid of hard work. There was a thin crinkle of scar on her jaw and her neck; she'd been burned once. Maybe one of the bombs had backfired on her. She watched him with crossed arms. "Assuming your people provided the correct specifications."

"They did."

Snow raised an eyebrow. "If you're wrong about the tank thickness, we'll have a problem. Or rather, you will."

"It's been double-checked. Three-fourths of an inch thick, nonnormalized steel. More brittle. The cars are old." Mouser didn't much like his facts being called in question. "You put in too much explosive, we'll have more burn than drift."

"I guarantee my work." Snow sipped orange juice. "You don't look like how I pictured you."

She was not at all what Mouser had expected in a bomb maker. He knew a few and they were foreigners, often older guys (he suspected incompetent bomb makers died early), and frequently missing fingers. But she was supposed to be one of the best.

"How did you picture me?"

"Arab."

Mouser cracked a grin with no humor in it. "Sorry to disappoint."

"I'm not disappointed," Snow said. "If you were an Arab I wouldn't have let you have the bomb. I don't much like Arabs. They're worse than the government."

Mouser said, "Nothing's worse than the Beast."

"The what?" A light hit her eyes; she tilted her head to look at him.

"The Beast—that's what I call the government. I'm curious as to how you could have gotten the bomb away from me if you didn't like the look of me."

"Oh, I would have just detonated it once you were about three miles away," she said lightly.

"Ah." Mouser raised an eyebrow.

"Joking," she said.

Mouser was careful to keep his expression neutral. "I'm not much for jokes."

"No. You shouldn't be. This is important work. Take good care of my baby"—she put a proprietary hand on the duffel bag—"and she'll take good care of you."

It creeped him out a bit to hear her call a bomb a baby. "And the rest?"

"Ready when you are." She watched him with a bright interest. Maybe making bombs, living constantly on the edge of disaster, made her eager for physical sensations, for release. He had no interest in complicating his life with a woman. He had the mission he had appointed himself in life; to him, the mission was everything. The government had to be shown for the Beast incarnate that it was, the ravager of liberty, the ruination of hope, the devil that destroyed what had made America great. That was all that mattered.

"I'll call you when it's done," he said.

"I'll watch it on the news."

"And then the next stage."

She nodded, but she didn't seem to care so much about the money. She watched him with an intensity that made his stomach twist. Strange woman, he thought, but useful.

He got into his car and drove through the quiet streets. Spring break was this week. Freed from the mind-numbing indoctrination of government schools, lots of kids played on the lawns, riding bikes with those dorky helmets that the Beast insisted they wear for their protection, another emblem of its constant meddling. One girl waved at him and he raised his hand in a brief wave.

Honey, I'm going to set you free, he thought. *Bring you a different world where the Beast has broken legs and dulled claws.*

Mouser drove through Houston, the bomb sitting on the passenger seat, the duffel bag wrapped in a cloth cover. He listened to speeches he had written for himself on his cassette player and thought he needed to polish his metaphors a bit; he spoke too much of purpose, not enough of battle. He was firing the first, carefully considered shot in a long war and the realization thrilled him to the bone. More shots would come in the next couple of days.

The resting place for Snow's baby had been selected with great care: a quiet bend close to the rail switch station in Ripley, Texas, forty miles northeast of Houston. Ripley was a small town of two thousand people, a few farmers and ranchers, mostly blue-collar workers employed by the oil refineries and related service industries. Mouser had no specific quarrel with the people of Ripley; but he had no regard for them either. They'd chosen to live in a dangerous place. Ripley lay in a small depression along the railway, with a heavy growth of trees ringing the entire town. The people of Ripley could suffer the consequences of their poor planning, he thought. It had taken him weeks to find and select the right spot.

He wore a carefully chosen costume: jeans, a shirt with the logo of a railway freight line. No jacket because he wanted the railway's logo visible. He walked along the railroad with a cell phone in his hand, pressed to his ear, laughing as though someone on the other end had told a joke. The duffel bag was fashioned of camouflaged fabric, painted to match the gray puzzle of stones along the rails. He set the bag down close to the rail as he walked, in view of the train station, but no one saw him. He put a foot on the rail and waited until he felt the barest vibration of the approaching train. He walked across the grassy slide down to the road where his car was parked, closing the phone that he wasn't looking at, and glancing at his watch. Three minutes, he guessed.

Mouser got in the car. No one had seen him, no one had noticed him. A pickup truck drove past him, loud country music spilling from the windows. Two young men, laughing, on their way to an evening shift at the railway. Mouser liked the song they were playing; he started to hum it under his breath. He used to sing, back in church when he was a kid, and he was a fine tenor.

He drove away from Ripley, the farm-to-market road that led back to the highway. The pavement threaded alongside the rail track. A pickup truck, with a bunch of young Mexican workers in the bed, shot past him. Then another car, a minivan, a harried mother at the wheel. He could see she was yelling at the kids bouncing in the back.

You should take the time to tell them you love 'em, lady, Mouser thought, *instead of yelling at them.*

He heard the approaching train before he saw it; a long low whistle of approach. Ripley was a scheduled stop—a water treatment plant was nearby that served much of the northern stretches of suburban Houston.

He pulled his cell phone back out, dialed a number, poised his finger over the button. Snow had given him a choice on the bomb: timer or detonation through calling the phone. He'd picked calling.

The train wasn't impressively long, just a stretch of old, weathered railcars, each carrying ninety thousand tons of chlorine gas.

He pushed the car up to a hundred miles an hour, counted down another minute, and pressed SEND.

Ashley Barton drummed her fingers on the steering wheel. The kids were wearing on her last nerve but the morning was nearly done. Thank God. She'd had her two boys and her sister's girl and they'd zoomed like little rockets. She was exhausted. As it was she would get home from the shopping trip to Houston just in time to get a lunch of hot dogs and carrot sticks and an ice-cream sandwich in each kid. Park them in front of Cartoon Network while she caught up on laundry and had a glass of iced tea and a moment's delicious peace and quiet.

She aimed the air-conditioning vent toward her face; the day had grown warm and she felt sticky. She'd taken the kids to one of the big Houston malls to get clothes, where the kids begged her to buy toys for them. She knew she was an easy mark. She'd let them pick out a toy each, nothing too expensive, though. They were still paying for Christmas.

"Give it back!" her seven-year-old, Kevin, yelled behind her, and she heard the familiar sound of a boy-fist hitting a boy-shoulder.

"Kevin's hitting Brandon," her niece Megan announced in a tired voice. "Over those stupid trading cards." Megan's tone made it clear what she thought of trading cards.

"Kevin," she said, glancing back at him. "We don't hit."

"You don't, but I do," Kevin said. "He's gonna tear my card, Mom!"

"Brandon, give him his card back. Kevin, do not hit your brother. If I have to get on y'all again, no dessert." She drove past the Ripley rail yard; her own house was only two minutes away.

In the rearview mirror she saw Kevin had his face pressed to the window glass, watching the long freight train lumber into Ripley. Kevin and trains. He'd been fascinated with them from when he was a toddler. God, that was only a few years ago. They were getting so big so fast.

Suddenly a roar pounded her ears, the minivan bucked on the road, and at first Ashley thought she'd blown a tire. The sound of the derailment was deafening, steel hammering onto steel, metal tearing in a horrific screech she felt in her bones.

"Jesus!" she screamed. Then Kevin was hollering and she braked to see that the windows were broken, one of the back ones blown in, glass dusting the kids. The noise had been so loud she hadn't heard the shattering. All three of the children screamed. She stood on the brakes, wrenched around in the seat.

"The train derailed!" Kevin screamed. "Mom, I saw it, I saw it!" His forehead trickled blood from a cut, Megan kept shrieking, Brian covered his face with his hands, still clutching his brother's Japanese game card. Ashley only had eyes for the children and she did not see the men in the rail yard—some of them men she had gone to high school with, to church with—staggering, dropping as they hurried toward the accordion of derailed tanks, as though slapped down by an unseen fist.

"Mom! It hurts!" Kevin started to cough, started to rub at his eyes.

"What?"

"Throat . . . my throat," Kevin moaned and then Ashley felt it, too, a terrible burning in the back of her throat, her eyes. Her eyes, her throat, burned like matches had been jabbed into the skin. A heavy smell, like an ocean of bleach, swamped her. The children clawed at their eyes, their mouths.

Get out of here, Ashley thought. Something awful had been freed from the broken jumble of railcars. A haze blanketed the ground, coiling, the green-yellow of a snake's scales.

Oh, my God. Not my kids, no, she thought. She managed to shift gears, her eyes and nose and throat aflame. Nausea roiled her stomach. Her upper airway constricted like a fist closing. She jammed the accelerator to the floor. Blinking and gasping through the agony, Ashley saw the turn to her house, half a block away. Best sight in the world. Get home, call 911, wash the kids in the tub, everything would be okay, it would *have* to be okay.

She was dimly aware of people running on the streets, running from the rail yard. Collapsing as she roared past them.

Just get away, get away, get the kids inside, this can't happen to us.

Ashley Barton took the turn too soon and far too fast, fueled by her blind panic. She missed the street and plowed through the front of a small liquor store. She went through the windshield and she thought, *Not happening not happening,* and then the pain was gone, the screams were silent.

The explosion wasn't as loud as he'd thought it would be; but then the bomb had had to be calculated to precision. Big enough to rupture the chlorine tanks, but not so powerful that the extreme heat would either oxidize the chlorine, rendering most of the gas nontoxic, or burn up much of it. The shape of Snow's charge was designed to puncture the tanks. Derailment was a given.

He could imagine the chaos in his mind's eye: Everything within a thousand feet of the derailment site would be enveloped in a choking cloud of chlorine. The cloud could expand, if lucky, to a mile and a half in width and, with the boost from the wind, carry close to eighteen miles.

Twenty thousand people would be within the cloud's path.

The Beast would of course order evacuations, fight like the wounded giant that it was, but the death toll could easily be in the hundreds or even the thousands. He smiled.

He hoped, as a first shot, this would prove a great success.

He drove fast on the empty road, heading toward Houston. He had a gas mask but he didn't feel he needed it; Ripley was far enough behind and a wet finger out the window told him he was driving into the prevailing wind.

He drove south back to Houston, to Snow's house without calling, because he thought the Beast, with its thousands of eyes, would be tracking every cellular call made near Ripley as part of the town's postmortem. He listened to the radio, the music interrupted by a news bulletin, the increasingly frantic coverage, and the order for immediate evacuation.

When he got back to Snow's house, the yards were empty. He saw cars filled with families, heading out, even though the cloud was far away and the wind wasn't moving the poison this direction. People panicked so easily.

He got out of the car, breathed in the cool air, and walked inside the house.

Snow was sitting on her couch, watching CNN, eating pretzels and sipping a congratulatory beer.

He watched the coverage, the panic, the horror, thinking, *I did that. Good for me.*

She looked up at him. "I guess my baby delivered."

Mouser had a sudden hunger to touch her throat, feel the taste of her skin. But he barely knew her, so it would be wrong. The mission first, the mission always. He went and got a glass of water.

"Only one car punctured by the blast," she said, watching the TV coverage. A satellite image of the derailment was on the screen. "The cloud is going to be big. They're evacuating everyone within twenty miles."

He could see the dead by the rails, on the streets of Ripley. He counted a dozen bodies as the camera's eye moved along the main drag. He saw a wrecked minivan, halfway in a storefront close to the rail yard, a flipped pickup truck. The chattering experts said the chlorine cloud was not likely to move south toward Houston and heavy rain pushing in from the Gulf would help ground the gas. But the situation was already being labeled a chemical attack, not simply an accident, and the words *al-Qaeda* and *terrorists* were already on the commentators' tongues.

"Al-Qaeda. They always think of them first," Snow said.

My God, Mouser thought. That was simple. And cheap. What blows to the Beast could he inflict with real money, money to last him for years, now that he had proven his worth? He nearly laughed in joy.

The doorbell rang. Snow glanced up at Mouser. "You expecting anyone?"

"Maybe my ex. We broke up, he might come here begging."

Mouser pulled the gun, went to the window. "Answer the door. Move out of the way if you don't know 'em."

"If it's police . . ."

"I'm not being taken. You?"

She shook her head without hesitation.

Mouser positioned himself. Snow answered the door.

"I thought you were in Washington," Snow said.

On the porch, Henry Shawcross said, "We have a serious problem."

8

"Please tell us you're here to celebrate," Mouser said. He knew it wasn't the case, but he wasn't ready to let go of the euphoria he felt.

"No. My stepson has been kidnapped." Henry stood against the living room wall, arms crossed. Exhaustion marked his face.

Mouser sat on the edge of Snow's couch. "And I care why? That's not our problem."

"Wrong. Luke's kidnapping affects everything—the first wave, and the Hellfire attack." Henry told him about Luke, the demands of the kidnapper. "They want the fifty million for his safe return."

"Then no safe return. They can't have it," Mouser said. An absolute statement, no room for discussion.

"I am not going to let them kill my kid."

"I'm not going to let them have our money," Mouser said. "And he's Warren Dantry's kid, right?"

A long pause, a curled lip that told Mouser Henry was uncomfortable with Mouser's knowledge of his family. Mouser studied the professor in front of him. Henry always looked like he was running late for a lecture and he looked the same now, except in his gaze an intense anger steamed.

"Yes. He was Warren's son." Henry unfolded his arms. "I think of him as my son now."

"Answer me one question. Do you have our money, Henry?"

Henry stared at him, as though anticipating the sight of a gun or a knife. "No. I tried to access the accounts; the passwords have been changed."

All of Mouser's pride, all his excitement over the mission well done, the blow against the Beast, turned to ash.

"You can't access the money?" Snow asked, as though she didn't understand.

"Not for you. Not for anyone in the Night Road." Henry crossed his arms again. "I rushed back here as soon as I could, so we can figure out what to do. . . ."

"No. No." Mouser lurched forward, to seize Henry. Henry raised a gun from under his own jacket. Mouser stopped.

"Stop. We can't fight amongst ourselves. What's done is done. Listen to me. We're going to fix this. We have to move forward with the first wave. And Hellfire stays on schedule."

Mouser stopped himself. He wanted to strangle the life out of Henry Shawcross at that moment. Another betrayal, that's all this was, just like every other moment in his life where he'd approached greatness, only to see his glory snatched away. He forced calmness into his breath. He felt the pressure of a hand on his shoulder; he glanced behind him.

Snow said, "Was there any mention from the kidnapper about the first wave of attacks?"

"No."

"Or of Hellfire?" Her eyes were bright.

"No. So the kidnapper is interested in the fifty million—not in stopping the attacks themselves," Henry said.

"All right. They asked for a ransom of our money. What did you say?" Mouser sat back down on the couch.

Henry returned his gun to his jacket. "I wasn't willing to acknowledge that I had the money in case the conversation was being taped."

"So you refused to ransom your own kid. Your loyalty is an inspiration."

"I may have saved us all by doing so. Because I know who kidnapped Luke."

"Who?"

"The banker who was in charge of setting up the financial accounts around the country for the fifty million is missing. Eric Lindoe. He hasn't been at his job in the past three days."

"Who could have shut you out of the accounts?"

"Only Eric. Only he and I had access. Mine is under a false name, of course."

"You're not making sense, Henry. If Eric Lindoe took the money, he has no reason to kidnap your stepson," Snow said in an even tone. She kept her grip on Mouser's shoulder and he shrugged it off.

"I think there is a simple explanation. If Eric was just a common embezzler, then he could simply steal the money and try to hide from us. There would be no reason to involve Luke. If the government—the Beast, as you so charmingly say, Mouser—has discovered us and turned Eric against us, again, there would be no need to kidnap my son. The FBI would freeze the funds, arrest Eric, and arrest me, try to force your names and those of everyone in the Night Road from me. And they would care about stopping the attacks, and then stopping Hellfire—they wouldn't have the money as a focus. We face contradictory facts. Ergo, we must follow a third alternative: Eric wants everyone—us and our enemy—to think he doesn't have the money, and our enemy is not the government."

"Ergo, so who?" Mouser asked, mocking.

"Our enemy wants the fifty million for themselves. It might be someone in the Night Road, turning traitor against us, although no one in the group knows that Eric is our banker. Only I know him. So. I believe it's an outsider, who has discovered the existence of the fifty million and knows we can hardly report the theft of it to the police."

"But why would Eric ask for a ransom that you couldn't pay, if he knew you couldn't access the accounts?" Snow asked. A sharpness like a new-forged knife's shone in her words. "What's the point?"

"The point of the ransom may have been to get me to agree to pay the money, get me on tape acknowledging that I knew about the money. Blackmail me. Maybe our enemy grabbed Eric, but couldn't get the money from him because he'd changed the access codes to protect it. He lied that he had no access to the money, and so the enemy panicked and grabbed Luke—or had Eric grab Luke—thinking I could still deliver the funds. And Eric let the enemy think he didn't have the funds. But . . . this is all theory."

"You mean we can't even confirm if our money is still in the accounts?" Mouser said in a cold whisper.

"No. Not without knowing what the passwords are now. He took my name off and changed the access. I'm sure he's hidden the funds. With that much money, Eric can hide forever. He can buy serious protection."

"How could he . . . ?"

"He's an officer at the bank. He could manipulate the system to hide the money in a hundred places. I have one of our hackers trying to break into the bank's database, so we can see if and where the money was transferred, but he's had zero success."

Mouser began to pace, a cold fury moving his legs. "Without the money, Hellfire doesn't happen. Everything we've worked for doesn't happen. Every risk we've taken . . . wasted."

"I want to aim you at the problem. Under one condition," Henry said.

"What?"

"No harm comes to my stepson."

"He can't know about us, Henry. Not unless he joins us."

"I will deal with him. But you will not harm him. He could be very valuable to us."

After a moment, Mouser nodded.

"We need to find Eric, and we need to find Luke."

"How?"

"I've got a Night Road contact working on hacking the GPS system on Luke's car, see where it is, see where it's been. Then I want you to go find Luke and stash him somewhere so I can talk to him. Failing that—or if they've killed him—find his kidnappers. I will work on locating Eric."

Snow said, "You turned down their ransom demand. They'll have killed him."

"They won't give up on fifty million just because I said no the first time. They might conclude I was worried about being taped or trapped. They'll let me squirm, then send Luke's finger to me, or an ear"—Henry stopped a moment to steady his voice—"to prove the channels of negotiation are still open."

"All right."

"I am going to return to Washington. I'll let you know what the hacker finds on Luke's car. If you find his kidnapper, keep him alive for questioning. Do you understand me?"

"I'm taking an extra risk here," Mouser said.

"And you'll be rewarded with a greater share of money for your cause and glory."

"I need backup."

"I'll go with you," Snow said.

Mouser made a noise in his throat, lowered his voice. "No offense, but you're a tech-head, a bomb maker."

"I'm a soldier, same as you," Snow said. "I know how to fight and fight hard. And no one is going to derail Hellfire. No one. Not after all the work I've done. I risked my life, every day, for weeks to build the bombs."

"I would rather you stay here," Mouser said. "You've got more to do for Hellfire."

"Let me help you. We can make quick work of finding these people together."

Henry said, "I agree with Snow. I'll call you as soon as I know something."

"You sure got here quick," Mouser said. "Maybe you took the money, fed us this story, and you're walking off with it." He put his hand back on his gun.

"I wouldn't have built Night Road if I was going to betray it," Henry said. "I have to be back in Washington immediately. I can hitch a ride back on . . . a friend's plane." He shook Mouser's hand, Snow's hand. "We're off to a brilliant start today. We'll get the money back, we'll make Hellfire happen." He stood, leveled a look at them both. "Take care of Luke. No harm to him. I have your word."

Henry left.

"He must be scared to death. He could have told us this over the phone."

"Better to tell us face-to-face," Snow said. "Especially since he's asking you to save his kid."

Mouser considered. "You have a point. Disappointment is always easier in person."

"You want something to eat? I'm hungry. Gonna make me a sandwich," Snow said.

Mouser shook his head. She went into the kitchen. He sat on the edge of the couch and thought how he'd sunk from the joy of the bombing to the anger of the missing money. Rescue a snot-nosed grad student who had been taught in the Beast's tax-funded universities, where his mind had been poisoned to think the Beast's system was good and noble. Did Henry honestly think he'd let the kid live? If the kidnappers knew about the Night Road, then they were all at risk and Luke Dantry was just an unfortunate witness. A risk.

He walked back into the living room. Snow had opened him a beer, left it for him on the coffee table. She was watching the coverage from Ripley. "I might have put too much oomph in the baby. Ruptured two tanks for sure, they say now, but a lot of the chlorine must've burned off. It's given them time to evacuate more people."

"Ripley's served its purpose, drawn the Beast's stare right where we want it to be."

She glanced at him. "Poetic."

Mouser made a face at the idea of being poetic, and she laughed. Quietly. He ignored it. "I need to crash here."

"Guest room's down the hall." She put her eyes back to the television screen.

"You sure you can help me if we run into trouble?"

"I can be whatever life needs me to be," Snow said, watching the dying town on the television, not looking at him. "You're gonna kill his kid."

Mouser didn't answer, and that was answer enough.

Henry Shawcross did not take a commercial flight back to Washington, as he had the day before. Rather, he returned to Washington the same way he'd flown down this morning: He went to the airport and boarded a Travport freight cargo jet by flashing an ID and driver's license that confirmed him as a Travport consultant, entitled to fly at a moment's notice on any of the carrier's flights, domestic or international.

He sat in one of the few passenger seats, watched the plane fly over East Texas. He would be home in a few hours.

"What's wrong with you?" Luke had screamed. "Give them what they want." His stepson's pleas tore at his chest but he had to keep his heart of stone. *I will get you back,* he thought. *I will get you back and I will make you understand, Luke.*

He used the plane's Internet connection to watch the news coverage of the chlorine disaster in Ripley. The most visible attack so far in the first wave. The bomb had burned up more of the gas than it should have, but it had gotten the world's attention. Security was being raised at chemical plants and railway stations and airports, analysts pontificated on news stations as to whether it was an al-Qaeda attack or another jihadist group or a domestic terrorist or an accident. Every chemical facility in the country would be on heightened alert. Too many cities, too many water treatment plants, had massive stores of lethal chlorine, and Henry had long thought this a terrible weakness of American infrastructure. He had published a paper about such a threat a month ago; he checked his e-mail. Now his paper held an urgency it had not a month before. He'd been proven smart and in tune with terrorist thinking. He was being flooded with requests from new and old clients on how to deal with the threat, and what the next threat might be. He smiled, fleetingly, for the first time since Luke's ransom call.

It was all a delicious prelude to Hellfire.

Very different from the first time he'd written a paper about the possibility of a major terrorist attack, and been ignored and jeered. He had been right then; he was making sure he was right now.

Now he had struck, made his point, and all the government's resources would go to stop a repeat occurrence.

Which was perfect.

Henry arrived in D.C., picked up his car, drove for an extra hour to be sure he wasn't being followed, and went home.

He waited for another ransom call. He was prepared to talk this time; he knew what he would say that could shield him if the call was taped. He kept calling Eric Lindoe; no answer. He did not want to call the prince he'd met in the London park three days ago and explain that the fifty million was missing. It would be an immediate death sentence. Unless he ran. But if he ran, Luke was dead.

He got up, paced his floors. He listened to Bach, to Mahler, to settle his mind, to try to determine what he could do.

He tried to distract his mind by going back through Luke's Night Road database, reading the postings Luke had made while playacting at extremism, marveling at the discussions he'd had with the lost. Brilliant work the young man had done. Complete, insightful, using everything he'd learned about the emotional needs of extremists to connect with them, even through the looking glass of the Internet. He had been nearly a perfect spy for Henry.

He had wept twice in his adult life: first when his wife, and Luke's mother, died in a car accident that never should have been. Now he wiped a tear from his eyes when he thought about Luke.

Stupid weakness, he told himself. *You didn't even like him at first. Or his mother. You're weak. You cannot care, you cannot.*

But he did. Didn't the prince have a family? Didn't Mouser? Why should *he* be alone? It was unfair, just as so much of his life had been. A constant, unyielding thorn of unfairness.

On the ongoing television coverage, he watched the bodies lying forlorn in the streets of Ripley, film taken from helicopters, and he felt nothing. He saw a minivan crashed near the train depot, a boy's body a few feet from the wreck, and he thought of Luke.

He slept fitfully at his desk, the phone by his head. He forgot to eat.

When the phone rang, nearly a full day after the first ransom demand, he grabbed it so hard that he nearly flung it across the room. He forced himself to gain control before he spoke. "Yes?"

It was the hacker that he had asked to break into the GPS database. "Your son's BMW has been parked near the Dallas/Fort Worth Airport for the past day."

"Where was it before? From when it was at the Austin airport?"

"The GPS tracker followed it to Houston. It stopped at two addresses. I can give them to you. . . ."

Henry scribbled down the addresses. He called up the addresses on his computer while the hacker continued to talk.

"Then it departed to an area outside a small town in East Texas called Braintree. The coordinates match that of a rental cabin. Stayed parked there for nearly twenty minutes, then proceeded to the DFW airport, arriving at 6:07 A.M."

A nowhere town called Braintree. Why would a kidnapper after fifty million go to some rental cabin deep in the piney woods?

Stashing Luke, perhaps. Or killing him and burying him among the pines. The thought made Henry's throat go dry.

The addresses in Houston were for a parking lot and then a bank.

He thanked the hacker. The doorbell rang ten minutes later, as he hung up from talking to Mouser and giving him the information on the Braintree cabin.

Henry opened the door—to find a reporter and a television camera standing on his porch. The young woman shoved the microphone into his face and Henry froze.

"Mr. Shawcross, we need a comment from you. . . ."

9

Everyone was dead. Luke knew it as soon as he opened his eyes. He stood in the back of the private jet and began to walk through the small cabin. The whine of the engines, racing to nowhere, was the only sound. His father's friends lay slumped in their seats, faces blue, jaws slack. One had his fingers tucked into his collar, as though the fabric had strangled him with a nooselike tightness. Luke wasn't breathing either. He could see frost limning the inside of the jet's windows. He tried to wipe it away with his fingertips. If he knelt he could see out the glass, an endless smear of the Atlantic below, no land in sight.

The medal his father had given him, the avenging angel, burned with cold fury against his chest.

A ghost plane, everyone dead. A flight to nowhere. He walked away from the ice-shrouded window that looked out over the empty sea. The door to the cockpit was closed. Between him and the door stood a man, in a mechanic's uniform. Ace Beere. He was short, red-faced, pathetic. "You killed them all. You sabotaged the plane. You took my dad. For no reason."

"For every reason," Ace Beere said. He tapped his temple, marred by a bullet wound.

Luke pushed past him. His father and the pilots would be in the cockpit, they would be okay, not dead like everyone out here. . . .

He opened the door. "Dad?" he called.

The cockpit was empty, gone, the ocean rushing at him like a wall.

Luke jerked awake. He'd thought for a moment he was on that ghost plane, flying with its suffocated corpses over the ocean until its fuel was gone. But it was just a dream. He was in a far worse situation as he moved his arms and heard the clink of the chains and remembered he was bound to the cabin bed.

Trapped in a death, just like his father had been, far from everyone he loved, beyond rescue. Except his father had had no chance. Luke was going to have to make his own luck.

Betrayed. That son of a bitch Henry betrayed me. The thought cut like a knife in Luke's mind.

For most of the morning Luke had slept. Exhaustion, driven by the long dance with adrenaline, put a stronger claim on him than fear. He awoke in the late afternoon, bleary from his nightmare, twenty-six hours after Eric had kidnapped him, his stomach knotting in hunger, and thunder blaring outside the windows. He felt a childish urge to cry—a clutching in his jaw and his chest—and he kept it at arm's distance until it passed. He tested the chains again, as though their strength might have weakened while he slept, and then he dozed some more. When he awoke the rain had dropped to a steady hiss, a white noise that allowed him to think.

The chain cuffs were blister tight against his wrists and ankles. He found enough give in the chains to allow him to sit up on the mattress and stand up next to the bed.

He examined the room. The metal bed was pushed close to the wall and bolted to the wooden floor. The shackles were attached to the iron bed, not the wall. Under the bed sat a small plastic container. He opened it; it was a chemical toilet. It needed emptying but he felt a sudden relief that he wouldn't have to soil himself or his bed. Crumpled peanut-butter-cracker wrappers and an empty water bottle were also under the bed. Under the heavily draped window, a table stood. On it was a small lamp, casting an anemic glow on the hardwood floor. A plain wooden chair. Another door was in a corner, maybe leading to a closet. He couldn't get close to it.

Henry's betrayal echoed in his head: *I can't help you. I'm going to hang up now.*

Henry could have lied, he could have stalled. He hadn't. He had left Luke at his kidnapper's mercy. Henry was a Judas of the basest sort, and when Luke tried to summon an excuse for his stepfather, he could not.

So what would happen next?

The possibilities were few: The British woman, Jane, might come here. Either to get rid of him, or to try to force a change of heart from Henry. She might prove she meant business with violence.

The other possibility was that no one was going to find him, no one was coming, and a slow, lonely death from dehydration and starvation awaited him in the coming days or weeks. How long would it take him to die?

Luke had to find a way to escape.

He checked his pockets. He still had his wallet and he dumped the contents on the bed: Texas driver's license. Forty-one dollars. A Visa card he used often, another MasterCard for emergencies. A University of Texas graduate student ID. And against his chest, the cool of the Saint Michael's medal, his father's last promise of protection. So much for promises.

Nothing to use against the locks.

He got up from the bed and pulled hard on its metal frame. It didn't budge. He inspected the four legs of the bed. Three were bolted down tightly, but one—the left rear—was a bit loose. Barely. He noticed heel scuffs marring the wall.

Aubrey hadn't just lain here waiting for her knight to come rescue her. She'd tried to kick the bed loose.

Luke inspected the slightly loosened screw. She'd gotten it to give way from the floor just a hair. Not much. The screw was a crosshatch, Phillips-style. He put the corner of the credit card in it. Tried to turn, gently, so the plastic wouldn't shred. Careful. He felt eagerness, a cousin to panic, rise up his arm and he smothered the urge to hurry.

The screw wouldn't budge. The plastic wasn't stiff enough to turn it. He tried the driver's license. Same result.

He needed something stronger. He had to look at the room with new eyes—seeing everything as a potential tool—but there was nothing. Panic churned in him and then he noticed the lamp. Lots of parts: bulb, base, cord, plug. It was a good six feet away, and he could see where it was plugged into the wall. Luke stood and took two steps from the bed. That was close as he could get; so he needed to get the lamp closer to him.

He had an idea.

Luke tore the blankets and sheets from the bed. He knotted them into a long rope, with the care of a Boy Scout testing for a badge. He double-checked the knots, then slowly fed the improvised rope, thick and awkward, through his hands.

He lay on the chilly hardwood floor and stretched as far from the bed as he could. His feet remained on the bed; the chains would not give farther.

He whipped the sheet-rope hard toward the table. He wanted to snag a table leg, with the other end of the rope back in his hands. First try, it missed. He tried again, putting more snap into his wrist: missed. He realized he needed the heavier section—the blanket—whipping toward the table leg; the sheet was too light. He reversed his makeshift rope. His arms ached. He threw the rope again. Missed. Again. His arms felt dense as stone. Missed. Tried again. The makeshift rope caught the right front leg of the table, part of it U-turning past the leg, back toward him. But out of reach.

He got to his feet and picked up the little side table next to the bed. He smashed it against the wall and jumped on the legs, splintering them from the base.

He picked up a leg that had a bent nail sticking from its end.

Holding the leg, he reached toward the edge of the makeshift rope that was wrapped back toward him. He wanted to grab the blanket so he could pull the table toward him. He pretzeled his body to reach as far as the chains would let him. He turned the leg so the tip would face the blanket.

The cabin was cool from the rain, but sweat poured down his back; he didn't know how else he could drag the table toward him if this didn't work.

He aimed the leg, with its nail tip, toward the blanket-rope. The nail caught an edge of the blanket. He let out a tense sigh; he ached as though pushing a truck up a hill.

He began to pull the blanket back toward him, using the jerry-rigged table legs. The nail, trapped in the blanket, made a light noise as he dragged it across the hardwood. Soon he had both ends of the blanket-rope in his hands. Slowly he began to tug at the rope. The table, with the lamp atop it, began to inch away from the window. He drew the table three feet nearer and the lamp's cord went taut. He stopped.

He stood, holding the broken table leg with its bent crown of nail. He leaned as far as he could. The nail caught the edge of the lampshade and came free. He tried again, pulling the lampshade toward him, every muscle straining against his chains.

The lamp tottered and it fell to the floor.

Darkness. But he saw as the light died where the lamp had fallen. He groped in the dark, used the nail to catch the lampshade now on the floor. He could feel the countertension of the lamp's power cord, still mired in the outlet. If the lamp's cord broke, he was finished.

The lampshade crumpled, but he kept pulling on the top of the lamp. He heard the plug fall to the wooden floor. Breathless, he pulled the cord toward him.

His fingertips caressed the narrow edges of the plug's metal tips. Thin and strong.

Luke inched to the bed leg. Groping in the dark, he wedged the plug against the groove in the bolt.

The screw turned.

He fought down the hammer in his heart. He worked with the calm of a jeweler setting a tiny stone. *Don't rush, don't lose patience.*

He pulled the first screw free. It worked. Four screws on each base of the cot's legs. Sixteen screws total. Fifteen to go.

He worked steadily in the darkness, without panic. He unscrewed the first leg and worked the chain loose. Moved to the second. Now the back legs of the bed were both free. He started on the third leg. Then the fourth. His fingertips felt raw.

And with the last leg removed, he shivered in relief. He staggered to the far wall, the chains still on his ankles and wrists, but free from the bed.

The barest glimmer of light began to touch the edge of the curtains.

Flashlights?

Whoever was coming would hear him, running with the clinking shackles. He remembered Eric had taken the keys to unlock the shackles from underneath the flowerpot. God only knew if Eric or Aubrey had returned them.

If he went out the front door, whoever was coming would see him. He opened the room's door, shuffled toward the back door. He tested it. Locked. He undid the dead bolt, eased the door open, and waddled out, trying to keep the chains silent.

He closed the door behind him.

The night lay heavy and dark against the trees. The rain had stopped, and the wind hissed in the pines. Luke could hear voices and footsteps on gravel.

A man. A woman. For a crazy moment he thought Eric and Aubrey had returned. But too much time had passed, and they had been far too anxious to escape and leave him to his fate.

"Here's the problem with blowing up casinos," the man said, a bit of complaint in his voice. "It's mostly going to affect just one industry."

"No," the woman said. "It makes entertainment venues likely targets. There's a trickle-down effect, to theme parks, movie houses, resorts . . ."

They clearly weren't cops coming to rescue him. Blowing up casinos sounded like a plan hatched by one of his Night Road buddies. His heart boomed in his chest.

Luke heard another mumbled cursing—from the woman—and then the key working the lock, the front door opening.

Luke ran along the edge of the house, toward the front door, clutching the chains closer to him. He lay in the dirt close to the cabin. Risked a look around the corner. The front door was open and light came from the rectangle of the door. The flowerpot had been moved from its base.

Maybe the keys to the shackles were still there, waiting for Henry if he'd changed his mind about the ransom. He stood, slowly, trying to see if he could spot a silvery glint on the step.

"We're screwed," he heard the woman say. She had a low, raspy voice. "Or maybe he was never here."

"Someone was chained to that bed. He dismantled it. We better report in," the man answered in a heavy baritone.

"He's in chains, he can't have gotten far," she said. Her tone was like an echo in a cave of wet stone.

"Maybe someone came and collected him. Whoever grabbed him changed their mind, took him again."

"No, Mouser," he heard the woman say. "They would've just unlocked him or killed him on the bed. Luke pulled an escape trick." He heard a foot kick at the broken desk.

Mouser? And this woman knew Luke's name.

Luke put his eye back to the cabin's corner. It wouldn't take them long to search the upstairs and the downstairs. Maybe just a couple of minutes. He'd have a few seconds alone with the keys, if they were still under the flowerpot. Then he could run like hell, vanish into the woods.

The woman stepped out onto the front step. She was tall, thin, wearing jeans. From the light inside the cabin, he could see a crown of dyed white hair and a thin tracery of scar along her jawline. She held a gun in her hand and a flashlight in the other. She walked toward the woods. Away from him.

Luke would wait for the trees to swallow the woman, and then he'd hurry and retrieve the keys to the chains, if they were there. At least get his legs free. Then he could run.

She stepped into the heavy darkness of the trees.

He turtled toward the flowerpot, trying to move quietly enough where the crinkle of the chains sounded like the wind nuzzling the pines.

Luke knelt by the flowerpot. He heard the man call out from deep inside the house, "There's food in the fridge."

He tipped over the flowerpot. The keys to the shackles were gone.

Behind him the woman called, "You're not very smart, are you?"

"I guess not." Luke stood and faced her.

The woman wasn't even bothering to point the gun at him. She walked close to him, and aimed the flashlight into his face. "Don't take it the wrong way. I'm amazed you even got halfway free."

So close, he thought. He noticed she wasn't aiming the gun at him and wondered if she even considered him a threat. In a flash he thought: You've studied these people but you've never faced them. This is different from reading a book or a loudmouth posting on the Web. You can't analyze them, you just have to fight them. Because you know what they're like. Single-minded. Brutal. Reasoning hadn't worked with Eric; it wouldn't work with these two.

Luke felt the quiet scholar in him easing backward, something new and primal emerging.

"Mouser, he's out here. Still in chains. Looks like he's auditioning for *A Christmas Carol*." She laughed, a glassy sick giggle. "He looks like Jacob Marley. Or was it Ziggy? I forget. C'mere, Schoolboy."

Luke jumped at her, hammering into her before she could lift the gun, shoving the flashlight so it smacked her in the face. He fell to the grass with her and lassoed a length of the chain around her neck. She swung the gun at him, nailing him in the head, but he was tall and strong and desperate. He got her in front of him, the chain a choker across her throat. He knocked her down, pried the gun from her fingers as he yanked her back to her feet.

The man—Mouser—rushed into the doorway. He aimed his gun at Luke's head. "Let her go."

"No. She comes with me." His voice broke, like a teenage boy's. Luke put the gun on her head. The chain was a twisted braid in his left fist, the gun in his right hand. Don't think, just do.

Mouser lowered the gun and Luke saw the gesture for what the woman's laughter had been—a sign of contempt. This couple wasn't remotely afraid of him, not even with him having a gun.

"So you stay there," Luke said to him. "All right?"

"Luke Dantry," Mouser said. "We're here from your stepdad. Here to help you, find out who took you."

"You're not the police," Luke said.

"No, we're better. Don't be a stupid kid. Let her go and we'll call him."

But they'd been talking about bombing casinos and resorts. "I just want the keys to these shackles," Luke said.

"You don't know what a can of kick-ass you just opened up on yourself." Mouser sat on the porch step, with a sign of anticipation. Ready for the show to begin.

It was not what Luke had expected. "Where are the keys?" he yelled. The woman began to choke and he realized how tight the chain was across her throat. He eased his grip. But barely.

"I'm going to—*obliterate*—you," the woman said.

"Snow means what she says," Mouser said.

"Where are the keys?" Luke yelled again at Mouser. He tightened the chain again.

The woman pointed at Mouser. "His pocket."

"Toss the keys to her," Luke said.

Mouser didn't stand. "Snow? How you want to go here?"

"Give him the keys," Snow said.

"Whatever you say." Mouser lumbered to his feet, dug in his pockets, and tossed the keys. Snow caught them with a deft motion.

"Unlock me. The feet first."

"You think you're smart because you escaped from a bed?" She unlocked the chains binding his feet. Her skin was cool against his ankles. He pulled her back straight to him; she didn't resist. He kicked the shackles free.

"Be still and I'll unlock your hands," she said. "Then we'll play for real, Schoolboy."

If he lowered the chain from her throat she could fight him, even with the gun. Their confidence was daunting. He tightened the chain around her throat again, just enough to pull her close. "Not quite yet," Luke said. "Let's walk to your car."

"Mouser has the car keys."

"Car keys," he called.

"No," Mouser said. "Come on, Snow, enough. Let's get going before the sky opens up again."

Snow stayed still. "I just wanted to see what he'd try. What he'd do. It's like watching a hamster work a maze."

"I'm going to shoot you is what I'll do," Luke said.

"Then shoot," she said. Her calm was maddening.

"I—I need you alive for now. You come with me to the car."

"And we'll be hot-wiring it?" she asked. "You saw that in a movie, right, Schoolboy?"

"Come on." He gave the chains a harder pull than he'd meant to and she gagged.

"For every second of pain you cause me, I will give you an hour of it." The icy tone of her promise chilled his skin. He shouldn't be afraid of her but he was.

"Maybe he doesn't have the keys to toss me. Maybe you do," he said in a harsh whisper in her ear. "You. Mouse!"

"Mouser."

"Whatever. You stay on the porch. I see you come off, I shoot her."

"How you want to play it, Snow?" he asked. The rain started again, hissing in the pines, thunder booming in the distance.

"Do as he says," Snow called.

They hurried backward down the long path toward where he and Eric had come through the gate. The rain boomed out of the clouds, thick again. Mud sucked at their shoes, darkness drank them up except when the lightning flashed in the wet heavens.

Luke blinked, trying to keep sight of Mouser, looking back over his shoulder toward the gate. The metal chains grew slick in his grasp, from sweat or rain.

"Empty your pockets."

"I don't—"

"Shut up! Prove to me you don't have the keys. Pull out your pockets."

Snow made a little grunt of anger and jammed her hand into her pocket. She stumbled against the gun and he pulled it away from her head. Suddenly she lashed her head back to catch him in the face. He tottered and she pivoted and powered him into the mud. The hand holding the gun slid deep into the muck. She wrenched free of the chains, nearly breaking his arm. She aimed a brutal kick at his head but he rolled and caught it on the upper back. He raised the mud-glopped gun but she knocked it free from his hand, with a savage and precise kick. The gun was gone.

No gun. She was screaming for Mouser.

He lashed the chains at her face, she ducked back and fell, and he turned and ran. Away from the gate, from the glow of the automatic light. Into the rain-drenched blackness.

The grass rolled down a slight incline toward a dense grove of pines. He dodged around the trees; the faint glimmer from the gate lights receded.

He had no light for his path except the inconstant slash of lightning. He stumbled and fell, ran ten more feet into a pine, the bark scraping his cheek. Lightning again showed him an opening in the growth and he ran toward it. He spotted the silvery barbs of a wire fence. He eased below the bottom strand, sliding in the mud, slicking himself from head to foot.

Luke stumbled past the fence and back into a stretch of unpaved road. Roads led, eventually, to people. He tried to get his bearings. To his right, the road bent into the darkness where he'd run from. To his left the road went straight. Toward civilization.

He ran hard to the left, grateful for the clean, smooth, unobstructed line. He was tired of dodging pines.

He ran. Aware of nothing but the bright pain in his legs and the pounding in his chest and the chains weighing his arms down.

Suddenly headlights exploded into life behind him, a loud growl of tires speeding. Engine revving. The lights, low to the ground, cut across him, pushing him to run faster, as if the light had weight. The car accelerated toward him. He powered hard to the right. A gully cut down along the side of the road, topped by another wire fence. The car couldn't go across the gully.

He slid down into the mossy-wet ditch, hauled himself up the side, and skidded under another wire fence. The pine growth was heavy here. The rain strengthened, the wind rose. He bounced off the trees, trying to run as fast as he could. He roped the chain around his arms to silence their clinks.

He could hear the sound of pursuit behind him, moving past the trees, running. Suddenly a flashlight sparked on, caught his shoulders in its glow as he ran up to a jumble of fallen pines. He slid under the brush and where his leg had just been he heard a pop like a bullet. But it couldn't fly straight, not in this rain.

A scream gelled in his throat and he moaned it away. He scrabbled into the earth and slid under the pyramid of tumbled, fallen pine trunks—there was a narrow passageway, formed by nature. Hoping to God he wasn't barreling into a dead end, or a rattler's nest. He saw an opening, slithered through it, staggered to his feet.

He ran, for several more minutes, before he collapsed against a heavy trunk.

Gasping, nearly drunk with exhaustion, he heard an engine ahead of him.

Soaked to the skin, he followed the fading roar. A minute later he stumbled out into another road. Paved. A painted line gleamed on the center, under a heavy cover of incessant rain. A highway or farm-to-market road. In the far distance he saw red taillights, a car. Inching into another lane because of a dark shape huddled on the road's shoulder.

Someone pulled over because of the torrential rain. He ran toward the shape.

A semi tractor-trailer. He was twenty feet away when the truck's blinkers blinked and the truck inched forward.

Heading back onto the road.

No, he thought. He had to get out of here now or they would kill him.

The back of the truck read WINGED FEET TRANSPORTATION *Houston/Beaumont/Tyler.*

The truck's left wheels turned onto the asphalt.

Luke ran, every muscle in his body screaming. The truck's back was now ten feet away from him, the pavement slick. He stumbled, nearly fell, stayed on his feet. He grabbed the back door of the semi and hauled himself onto the heavy metal bumper. He stood on the bumper and looked for a way to open the truck's doors. He found the handle but it was locked.

It didn't matter—as long as he was getting away from his pursuers. He pressed his face close to the wet metal of the truck's doors, steadied his feet on the wide metal bumper that served as a step into the truck.

He looped the chains around the door's handle, an improvised safety belt. His arms felt like jelly. He considered signaling the truck—but then the driver would stop, and if they stopped, Mouser and Snow might catch them. Better to simply get away.

The truck eased its speed slowly up to a cautious forty—Luke guessed— and the wind and the rain plucked at him. His own breathing boomed in his ears; he shivered against the metal doors.

He heard a *whoosh*, then another, and the truck rocked in the wake of sudden hard surge of air. Two other trucks, passing in the opposite direction.

How many minutes had he piggybacked? Ten? Twenty? His legs ached, crouched on the bumper, lashed to the handle, trying to keep his balance. If he fell he'd break his neck.

Maybe his pursuers were still hunting him in the woods, blissfully ignorant that he was gone, speeding away on winged feet. His arms screamed in pain. He couldn't keep this up forever; maybe it was time to signal the trucker. . . .

He sensed the approaching lights behind him. He looked behind him and saw headlights—low to the ground, not a truck, a sedan. The lights were racing toward him, with the awful certain intensity of a snake slithering close, its unbroken gaze a hypnosis.

It couldn't be them, Luke told himself. At the worst the car's driver would signal the trucker and end Luke's free ride.

The sedan veered up close to the truck's rear, as though inspecting the odd big bug clutching the truck's door. A Mercedes.

The Mercedes swung up closer.

The pulse of the truck's brakes jostled him, the hiss of tires slowing on pavement. The trucker gave a warning tap on his brakes.

The sedan slowed a fraction, cut around the truck's corner, and sped up the side.

Through the curtain of rain as the car passed, Luke saw Snow staring at him. Smiling. Then the Mercedes was gone, out of sight, revving toward the truck's cab, veering into the opposite lane to pass.

They're going to cut him off, force him to pull over, Luke realized. But the truck was speeding far too fast for him to jump.

He inched along the bumper, trying to get a view around the truck's corner. The Mercedes winged close to the truck's cabin, Snow's window down, her hand waving at the trucker to slow.

The truck slowed, rocked, then picked up its speed.

Maybe the trucker didn't like what he saw. Snow looked crazy as hell with that sickening grin. Maybe he had valuable cargo and he just wasn't inclined to pull over in the middle of nowhere because another driver gestured at him.

He glanced around the corner again. The Mercedes swung out onto the opposite shoulder as another truck traveling the opposite direction barreled past, horns blaring over the growl of the storm.

Luke's arms seized in bone-deep cramps, his muscles knotted in pain. He eased the chains out of the door handles, held on to the handles themselves, and tested the locked doors again in blind desperation. If only he could have gotten inside the doors, squeezed inside, Mouser and Snow would have never found him. . . .

He heard the crack of a shot. The truck lurched, convulsed, and nearly threw Luke to the pavement. He gripped the handles and braced his feet hard against the bumper.

The truck veered off the road. It rocked and surged as pines and oaks snapped in its path. A thick trunk splintered, flying past Luke in a cloud of pulverized wood and pine needles.

The truck rocketed down an incline and to his left he saw the beginning of a bridge rising past him.

The truck plummeted, smashing down through the trees as the speed slowed. Luke put his face to the metal as spears of mud flew past him.

The jackknifing came with a wrench and if he'd kept the chains looped in the door handle the force would have torn his arms from his sockets. He tried to time the jump in a flash of pure instinct but the crash was chaos.

You'll be crushed under the rig, he thought, and then the rig broke free and threw him; he cartwheeled past the edge of the crumpling trailer.

Air. He opened his eyes, falling, and saw the swelling river beneath him, rushing toward him.

Water. Cold beyond reason and dark.

Earth. His shoulder scraped the river's stony bottom.

He kicked toward the surface, broke into air. Just long enough for a gulp.

Then the chains weighed him down.

Fire. Heat, surging through the river like a pulse. The current yanked him forward, the force of a blast pushed him into sweet oxygen again and he saw gray sky, dawn fighting to pierce the clouds.

Then the maddened river took him.

10

Luke kicked to the surface as the river swept him downstream, sinking again, fighting to rise. He rode the river's raging current for what seemed an eternity. It was a constant ordeal to keep head above water, to breathe. He gathered the chains close around him, terrified they would snag on rock or sunken tree and yank him downward to death. The weight of the chains was like hands pulling him down to the sleeping depths. A sudden bend in the river twisted ahead of him and the current battered him into the shallows, cypress and pine lining the banks. Then he spun away. He struggled, tried to swim. The river hurried him close to shore again, and he spotted a black shape, toppled into the water. A rotting tree. Branches stuck out like spikes.

Luke gathered the last of his strength and tossed the chain over one of the trunk's branches.

He stopped. He could breathe. He lay in the water, head above the surge, greedy for air. Slowly he pulled himself close to the tree. He used the chains to loop onto branches closer to shore and collapsed on the cold mud.

He became aware of a fresh onslaught of rain. The pain in his arms, in his chest, brought him back to his senses. He got to his feet slowly and staggered into the heavy growth along the bank. Arches of cypress and pine spread above him, sheltering him from the worst of the downpour. Behind him the river was sick with rain, beige with muddy runoff. Chunks of white floated in the brown water; packages of shrimp and fish, fresh from the Gulf.

The truck's cargo.

They'll be looking for you.

He hurried up the rolling incline that led from the river and staggered into the deep cover of the pines.

Please, God, he thought, *let the trucker have gotten out alive.*

Luke headed away from both river and road and deeper into the woods. As he walked he took an inventory of himself. Pants caked with mud. Shirt torn open, buttons gone, ripped by the force of the river. He glanced down: The silver of the Saint Michael medal glinted on his chest. Thank God, he thought, he hadn't lost it. He'd lost one shoe and sock but the mud felt soothing against his feet. His wallet and money were back in the cabin. His wrists were bloodied and scored raw from the shackles.

He walked. Listened for the sounds of pursuit but heard only the soft hammering of the rain.

Mouser and Snow were from the Night Road. It existed, as a vicious force beyond his database of potential malcontents. It was real. He was convinced of it. Their talk of casinos being bombed. His mind spun. They'd said they were from his stepfather. It didn't make any sense. They couldn't be from Henry and also from the Night Road.

The realization hit him like a stone dropped from the clouds. Could Henry be involved with the Night Road? It didn't seem possible. But Henry's refusing to ransom him hadn't seemed possible either.

Who is your client for this project? he had asked Henry. *What are you doing with this research?* Henry had smiled and dodged and maybe bribed him with a lucrative job offer to stop him from asking questions.

Luke had given him the discussion-group postings and the names, and a way to contact hundreds of people who might be extremists. He'd handed them to Henry on a plate. God only knew who his client really was.

He had to find a phone. Call the police.

Suddenly he stumbled into a clearing in the pines. A tidy little cottage stood in the glooming rain. White paint, a back porch that faced the river, a swing and wicker chairs, empty of cushions. A small fishing pier jutted into the river.

He ran to the cottage's back door and knocked, but there was no answer. The curtains were drawn on all the windows. He listened at the glass; no sound came from within. He walked around the porch; on the other side was a small one-car garage, a dirt road driveway leading down to it from a paved road, and a toolshed.

A lock bolted the toolshed door shut. He got a rock from the flower beds and smashed down on the lock with four jackhammer blows. But the lock held.

He ran back to the cottage. His conscience made him hesitate at breaking and entering. But he was desperate and this was his new reality. He had to adjust to it.

He broke the window. No screech of an alarm accompanied the tinkling glass. He fingered the lock, twisted it, and stumbled inside.

He shivered and turned on the central heating. It vroomed to life and the vents perfumed the air with a dusty burnt smell. The cottage was well furnished; someone's riverside weekend getaway, he decided. He wanted food, a shot of whiskey to warm him, and to be out of his filthy sopping clothes. But most of all he wanted to be free of the shackles. He searched the kitchen and in a drawer he found a ring of keys.

He hurried back out to the toolshed and experimented along the key ring. The third key opened the lock, chalked with dust from his earlier attempts.

The orderly wall held a nice array of tools. He saw what he needed—a power drill, nestled in its charger.

He inserted the drill's bit into the shackles' lock; he had to hold the drill at an awkward angle. It revved to life and bit into the lock's mechanism. Metal ground, shrieked, and began to shred. The shackles shook, dancing to the bit's beat, and the lock gave way. He uncuffed his right hand and felt the delicious relief of the weight dropping away. His skin under the cuffs was raw, bloodied, swollen. He freed his left hand in short order.

Luke put the tools back into place and relocked the toolshed door. He threw the shackles into the kitchen trash can.

No phone in the kitchen. He searched the rest of the vacation home, found two bedrooms, two bathrooms, and a den, and no phone. Bizarre. But this was a world choking on cell phones, so maybe the owners didn't feel the need for a landline for their weekend house.

He went back to the broken window. No sign of pursuit; no Snow or Mouser emerging from the dripping pines. He was safe, but God knew for how long.

He kept the lights off. He stripped off his ruined clothes and stood in the stinging spray of the shower. He scrubbed himself raw, hating to leave the reviving heat of the water. When he was done, he wrapped a towel around himself. In the master bedroom closet he found men's clothes. Luke was six two and the man's jeans were surprisingly a bit too long and wide in the waist. But better, he decided, than too small. He found a gray long-sleeve T-shirt and a flannel shirt, and a jacket. He found no shoes but galoshes; he put them on, with a pair of white socks he found, in case he had to leave quickly.

In the bathroom he slathered antibacterial gel on his hurt hands and wrapped them with gauze. He looked like he was hiding an attempt at slashed wrists. But he felt human again. The medicine cabinet held a few prescription bottles in the name of Olmstead. He was hiding in the Olm-steads' house. He hoped the Olmsteads were nice, understanding people. A sharp, sudden hunger—dulled for long hours by adrenaline—punched his stomach. He hadn't eaten since lunch the day he dropped Henry off at the airport, which felt like a lifetime ago.

He found scant offerings in the fridge—a jar of strawberry jam, expired containers of milk and sour cream, a few bottles of beer. In the pantry he found peanut butter and canned vegetables and soups. In the freezer were several packages of steak, a loaf of bread, and two vegetarian pizzas. The steak would take too long. He heated tomato soup and put one of the pizzas in the oven.

He stood over the soup, the mist of it warming his face, and in the distance, under the fading thunder, he heard the *chop-chop-chop* of a helicopter. There and gone by the time he got to the window.

He clicked on the television while he drank the hot soup, surfed to a twenty-four-hour Texas-based news channel. The heavy rains drenching East Texas and western Louisiana were the lead story. Apparently there'd been a derailment of a train carrying chemicals in the small town of Ripley and a massive chlorine leak, and the rainstorms had helped ground the poison. Thirty dead, hundreds hurt, the entire town and everything around it for twenty miles temporarily evacuated. But the storm had stopped the threat.

"Of course, whether this was an accident, or as some sources on the scene have suggested, a bombing of the rail line itself to cause the leak . . ."

A bombing. And here were Mouser and Snow, talking about bombings.

Luke sank to his knees before the TV, the soup tasteless in his mouth. The story went back to the wider effects of the wide-ranging rainstorms: two people drowned in Lufkin, another swept away in Longview, and a dramatic truck crash near Braintree—they went to an aerial shot of a semi, junked in an engorged river. The truck driver was missing, a search was under way.

Missing. *Please be okay,* he thought. *Please.* But he knew, from the shot, from the force of the crash, it was a dim hope.

He ran to the sink and waited for the wave of nausea to pass. He looked up at the screen as the anchor returned. "A brutal street shooting near downtown Houston is caught on an ATM camera, and the stepson of the leader of a prominent political think tank is implicated." Cut to a reporter, standing in the rain-soaked morning daylight of the bank parking lot where Eric had gunned down the homeless man.

Cut to a grainy tape aimed at the bank's parking lot. He saw his own BMW roar into focus. His own face closer to the camera as he slammed on the brakes to cut off the guy running toward the ATM. Then Luke lurched toward Eric, who could not be seen clearly. The BMW jerked out of the camera's shot, then returned as it exited the lot past the dead man, the license plate grainy but visible. The police must have enhanced the footage to read the plate.

"The car used in the shooting is registered to Luke Dantry of Austin, stepson of noted political think-tank president Henry Shawcross. Dantry is described as six foot two, brown hair, blue eyes, slim build, age twenty-four, a master's candidate in psychology at the University of Texas—"

The camera cut to his driver's license picture, a soft smile on his face. He'd never liked the photo but now he looked like one of those people who try too hard to look sincere and fail.

"The car was found abandoned at a parking lot near the Dallas/Fort Worth Airport. Dantry received a speeding ticket outside Mirabeau a few hours before the shooting, where it was reported by the officer that he was not alone in the car. Dantry's stepfather had this to say last night."

Then cut to Henry, gaunt and pensive, as though he'd aged ten years: "I hope my stepson will immediately turn himself in to the authorities. Luke is a good kid who has made a few unfortunate choices in his past. Luke, if you can hear this, just turn yourself in, that's for the best." Henry blinked wetly into the camera.

Then cut to some jerk who lived in the condo below him: "Dantry is kind of a loner. He didn't say much to people, didn't socialize, you know, but I guess I never thought he'd shoot someone." Then, with a shake of his head: "He should have been smarter not to do it in front of a camera. Grad students aren't known for common sense."

He had never liked that neighbor, a little snot who he'd had to ask to turn down his stereo several times. Being branded a loner on national television stung. It's what the commentators always said about the guys a jury would find guilty in five seconds. And Henry, talking about his past mistakes.

Not a single word that Luke had been kidnapped, or a ransom demanded for his return.

Not a hint that he was innocent.

Not a breath that Henry knew he was in danger—only an implication that Luke himself was guilty.

We're from your stepfather. Luke was sure now that Snow and Mouser had told him the truth.

The betrayal was complete. Not just abandoned, but framed. A rage rose in his chest. "I'm going to take you down, Henry," he said aloud. The words jarred him; he had never made such a threat in his life. In the quiet of the cottage the words sounded odd, even frail, lacking power. He didn't know how to start. But he was going to stop this, stop Henry, force him to own up to what he had done. The reason for Henry's betrayal didn't matter; Luke could not understand it. Only the reality of it mattered.

What had his father said? *You might be called to fight one day, Luke. Think of Michael. Think of strength and know you can win.*

One day was now.

He heard the anchor say that the homeless victim's name had not been released, pending notification of kin.

Eat, get your strength back, think, he told himself. Luke devoured the pizza. He knew if he went to the police, he would be arrested, charged at the least as an accessory to murder. Until he had information that could clear him, a terrible danger loomed in contacting the police or in asking Henry for help. And how would he explain the Night Road? He had, after all, helped put it together. Would anyone believe that he didn't know its true purpose?

Eric. Eric was the key. Eric had to know what was happening—why Luke had been grabbed to force Henry's hand, why the homeless man had to die.

Luke turned off the television. The weight of what he had to do hit him like an avalanche.

His only choice was to hunt down his kidnapper and force a confession.

The victim, going after the kidnapper. Alone, without the help of the police or anyone else.

Luke finished the pizza. He washed the plate and his cup. As he put them back in the cabinet, footsteps sounded on the porch.

11

He'd broken a pane of glass on the door facing the river to get inside the cottage. Assuming the owners hadn't ventured into the torrent to check their weekend property, this was either the police, a neighbor, or, worse—Mouser or Snow.

What would they have done when the truck crashed and burned? Run to the bridge to see if Luke was dead. Maybe they saw him surface, and then wash down the river. They could just have been following the river—which would have brought them to the cottage.

He slid open a drawer and found a steak knife, held it close to his hip.

Luke had never fought with a knife, but he'd kept a small blade on him during his runaway days. Knives were easy to come by, easy to hide. He'd only had to use it once, just to show to a tough kid in a Richmond alley who wanted his money, and then he'd run like hell.

It was clear he had been in the house: damp shower, his clothes and his shackles in the trash, the stove warm. He stepped back into the walk-in pantry, left the door cracked. He couldn't hide and hope they'd just leave. He'd have to make a stand.

A man's hand emerged from under the gingham curtain on the back door's broken pane, fumbled for the knob. Luke retreated to the kitchen.

The door opened, the volume on the wind rose slightly, then faded again as the door shut. No call of "Hello, anyone here?" that you might expect from a neighbor. The intruder stood still, as if listening for Luke.

He opened his mouth to silence the rasp of his own breathing.

He heard the sound of a foot on floorboard. Approaching.

"You must be scared to death," Mouser said from the hallway. "I sure would be. People only have so much courage"—a pause, and Luke could imagine Mouser swinging an open, loaded gun into the first bedroom's doorway—"and I suspect you've burned through all yours in one night."

All Luke had to do was reach the back door, on the other side of the kitchen, and run. In galoshes. Right. Mouser would put a bullet in him before he was down the driveway. "I just need to talk to you, Luke."

The shelves of the pantry pushed against his back. Mouser was silent. Luke felt the heavy weight of the cans. Thrown or bashed into a skull, they would hurt. They did not require the closeness of the knife. It would give him two weapons and maybe Mouser wouldn't think he had improvised more than one. He thought of putting the knife in the back of his pants, but there wasn't room in the pantry to reach. He carefully stuck the knife up the sleeve of his long-sleeve T-shirt, the blade's tip barely hidden by the cuff. Then he reached carefully above his shoulder and closed his hand on a large can of corn.

"So scared," Mouser said, like he was cooing to a child. "Holding on to that truck must've exhausted you—swimming in that hellhole of a river—" Then Mouser moved into view, across the lit inch of open door, one hand hovering over the stove, testing its heat.

Then Mouser looked right at the nearly closed pantry door. Raised the gun, and behind it he wore a smile. "I spy, with my little eye, a running boy. That was a merry chase. Come on out."

With one hand, Luke pushed the door open.

Mouser smiled. Now Luke could see his face clearly. He was bigger than Luke, a solid six foot six, body knotted with muscle. He had a boyish face—cheeks ruddy from the rain and wind. He wore a shirt streaked with dirt, jeans crusted with mud from the chase. His dark hair was cut in a burr, and his brown eyes held a sick amusement but no warmth. Bags under his eyes showed exhaustion.

"Drop whatever's in your hand, buddy," Mouser said.

Luke dropped the heavy can of corn to the tiled floor. It rolled to Mouser's feet. Mouser laughed at him. "Corn is a lethal choice. Step out slowly. Hands on head. So we can have a nice talk."

Luke shook his head. The steak knife, parked in his sleeve, felt looser than he'd like, as though it might just slip out of its hiding place. The blade lay cool against his skin.

"We need to have a nice calm talk. The trucker was . . . not planned," Mouser said, as if contrition would make moot the idea of murder. "My partner got overeager."

Luke said nothing.

"I want you to tell me who kidnapped you, Luke."

Luke said nothing. *Make him talk,* he thought. *Make him tell you more.*

"I don't repeat myself." Mouser slapped him. It was a hard, vicious blow that felt like it would part the flesh from Luke's cheekbones. Luke slammed against the refrigerator but steadied himself back onto his feet.

Now Luke spoke. "Murder's worse than kidnapping. You were going to kill me."

"Were we? I myself just wanted to talk to you. Now. Your stepfather wants you back in reasonably good condition. Don't make me pound the living hell out of you, boy."

"I'm sure Henry's worried I'm going to kick his ass when I see him."

"I hate family squabbles. So. Back to facts." He raised his hand for a second slap, fingers wiggling in anticipation, laughing when Luke flinched. "Who grabbed you?"

"I don't know his name."

"Just one guy?"

"Yes."

Mouser looked at him as though having allowed himself to be kidnapped at gunpoint by a single assailant was a moral failing. "Tell me what he looked like."

"Let's say I do. What happens then?"

"Then I don't beat your ass into the ground and I take you to your stepfather."

"You'll kill me. You already tried. I got shot at in the woods and that trucker got shot."

"Are you sure?" Mouser put on a hurt little frown. "That was sure a noisy storm. You're exhausted. You don't know what you heard."

Luke decided to give Mouser enough to maybe get him to talk, but not enough to make Luke expendable. He realized this was no different from the online prodding he'd done with the extremists. Except he was facing a gun instead of a computer screen.

Luke cleared his throat. "The guy grabbed me at the airport. Forced me to drive to Houston; he shot the homeless man." He paused. "Do you know who the homeless man was?"

Mouser said, "Keep talking, or I'll break your nose. With your can of corn."

First attempt deflected. "He made a phone call and we drove to the cabin. He took a photo of me, e-mailed it. We found a woman chained to the bed. He left me in place of her. Then he called my stepfather. Who stabbed me in the back."

"Yes, I'm aware of your Greek tragedy family dynamics. What else?"

"He's not my dad. My father's dead."

"I don't care. Everyone dies." Mouser slapped him again; the pain throbbed up his jaw, down his neck. He'd drawn close, his breath sour against Luke's nose. "Now, let's stay on topic."

"He got a call earlier in the day from a British woman."

Mouser frowned. "Who is she?"

Luke decided to keep Jane's name to himself. If he gave too much, he might not be useful anymore. "I don't know. He never mentioned a name."

Mouser tented his cheek with his tongue. "Physical description of your kidnapper." Now Mouser raised the gun. He didn't aim it at Luke, but he inspected it, as though admiring its steel.

Luke took a deep breath. Eric was tall; Luke said he was medium-height. Eric had dark hair; Luke said it was dirty blond and thinning. Eric had no accent, so Luke gave him a thick Boston inflection.

"I want to show you something." Mouser pushed him into a chair at the kitchen table. He reached inside his jacket and handed Luke a black-and-white picture, printed from a computer. It was Eric.

Mouser sat across from him. "Now. Revisit your description. Think hard. He look familiar to you?"

"No."

Mouser smiled. "You're a psychologist, right? You know there are physical clues to lying. A shift of the eye, a twitch of mouth. Especially apparent in the exhausted and overeducated." Now he aimed the gun straight at Luke. "Yes or no, you see this guy?"

"Yes." He stared at the gun, wondering if the answer was going to result in a bullet in his chest.

"Did he mention money?"

"Just the insane amount of money he wanted from Henry."

"Did he mention any names? Dates? Say anything about a road? Use the word *Hellfire?*"

This is where he decides to let you live or die, Luke realized. Luke bit his lip. "I—I can't remember what all he said, not with you pointing a gun at me. . . ."

"I'm going to let you live, Luke. Trust me. Henry's eager to see you, to explain."

Trust me. Fat chance. Henry had said the same to him the last time he'd seen him. Trust me, we can change the world. Eric had said it, too, assuring him that he'd be released if he cooperated. Trust was dead to him. "Tell me. Did I find you on the Internet for Henry?"

Mouser studied him. "I don't waste much time on the Web. Others, yes, not me. Now. What names did he mention?"

"Names. Yes. But . . . let me think for a minute." He could feel the weight of the knife hidden in his sleeve.

"Concentrate. You're supposed to be such a smart boy."

Luke hunched over the table. He dropped his arms and fake-shivered, and the knife began to work its way down into his hand, below the table's edge.

"He mentioned my stepfather . . . he mentioned a Night Road, but I didn't understand, it was a name I made up for Henry. . . ."

"He did?"

"Yeah, he said something about Hellfire. . . . Is that a code name?" That was a lie but it worked.

"Tell me what he said." The cool evaporated from Mouser's voice.

Under the table, the handle of the knife slid into his hand. And for a moment fear stopped him. *You have a knife, he has a gun. Seriously. How do you think this is going to end?* "Can I have paper and pen to write down everything I remember?" He put a tired whine in his voice.

Mouser stood and walked past Luke toward the kitchen drawers and

Luke drove the knife hard into Mouser's leg. The blade sliced through the denim into Mouser's flesh.

"Jesus!" Mouser screamed as he doubled over in surprise. His hand instinctively grappled at the knife's handle. But as Luke bolted past him, Mouser let go of the knife and got a steel hand on the back of Luke's neck. He worked his fingertips into a claw that pushed expertly against nerve juncture and artery.

The agony staggered Luke. He reached back and twisted the knife's handle and Mouser released him with a mix of roar and shriek.

Luke scrambled across the floor and he grabbed the heavy can of corn that he'd dropped and he lobbed it straight and hard at Mouser. The can nailed Mouser on the forehead as he tried to stand. Mouser collapsed to the floor again, staring at the tiles as though he didn't quite comprehend the past minute.

Luke wasn't about to risk getting close to the man again; he'd learned a hard lesson trying to fight Snow. He just thought: *Run.* He ran out of the cottage. No car. Which meant that Snow might be driving up and down the river road, hunting him same as Mouser.

He ran into the thickness of the pines.

12

The waiting was pure hell for Henry Shawcross. The police were gone, and he'd ignored the phone calls from the press following the brief statement he'd had to make on his front porch after the reporter showed him the Houston shooting footage. He was badly shaken; he hated to feel unprepared. He wasn't going to speak to anyone unless it was Mouser or Luke or the kidnapper, calling to arrange another deal.

He'd watched the coverage of the disaster in Ripley for five minutes with a coolness in his heart; the crushing rains had scraped the chlorine from the sky. But the damage was done, the fuse of panic lit in the American heart. Politicians were demanding, in gusting words, to know that the cargo railways of rural America were safe, that the chemical plants around the country where chlorine was stored were secure. Of course all they cared about was covering their asses, he thought. That was all any of those jerks cared about.

But they—his clients, and his soon-to-be clients—all wanted to know what would happen next. His dozen policy papers released in the past few weeks all outlined a variety of potential attacks, some inspired by overseas trends in terror, some inspired, privately, by the ambitions of the Night Road.

Success was simple. Predict the attack; then the attack happens, and you have the ears of the most powerful people in Washington. That was the kind of power, of respect, he needed to wield. His blistering, uncannily accurate paper on a possible chlorine attack had made the rounds of the Washington power brokers last month; his voice mail was full of inquiries from potential think-tank clients. From the government, from private industry. All wanting his insights, all wanting his opinion on what the future would hold now, where the terrorists would strike next.

It should have been his shining moment. But Luke's situation had tarnished it for him. The same pols eager to hire him would be watching the coverage of the shooting involving Luke, perhaps holding back. Which meant he had to both distance himself from Luke and get his next papers out quickly so he would still be seen as the main, most authoritative voice on the next stage of terrorism. He would be respected again. He would be close to the levers of power in Washington. Luke, on the news, would fade. The country would have much more to worry about in the days ahead.

Henry remembered, with a pang, a magician his mother had hired to perform at his sixth birthday party. *I don't want a magician, Mom,* and her answer had cut him to the bone: *Well, Henry, honey, it might make the kids want to come to your party.* She'd said it without thought or malice; she was possessed of a brutal honesty and a steady disregard of others' pain. Henry had inherited only the latter quality from her. So he'd sat on the cool cut grass, with neighborhood acquaintances who didn't much like him and who he didn't know how to make like him. While the kids who'd just come for the show and the squares of chocolate cake oohed and aahed, Henry drilled his gaze on where the cheap-rate teenage magician didn't want him to look: the hand in the pocket, the coin secreted between fingers, the intact paper curled up the jacket sleeve. He'd seen there was no magic, only distraction.

It etched a lesson on his brain.

Now Henry sat in his study in his Arlington, Virginia, home, the chessboard Luke had given him for Christmas five years ago on the table, the pieces locked in battle. Henry imagined Luke slumped across from him, sitting the way he always did when lost in the game, leaning hard to the left on an elbow, hand trapped in his brown thatch of hair, tongue tenting his cheek while he thought, humming some rock tune Henry didn't know. Henry played black against white, playing Luke's side in aggressive style. He moved his own pieces with the timidity of a mouse. Luke's bishops and knights closed in rapid conquest, his white queen shadowing Henry's black king, defeat three moves away.

Exactly what you deserve, Henry thought. *To lose and to lose badly. Just like how you lost Barbara. You're going to lose Luke. You already have.*

Henry rose from the chessboard, headed down the hall to get a cup of coffee. Steam danced above the mug. He added a dollop of milk. He took a fortifying sip. Mouser would find Luke, bring him to a safe place where Henry could question him and then make him understand. Make him see that the Night Road was the key to a golden future for them both—a road to respect, to power, to importance.

He stepped back into his study. From his left a gloved hand raced a knife to his throat, stopped the blade right above his Adam's apple. Hot coffee, sloshing from his mug, burned his hand. Henry froze and his gaze slid to the face of his attacker. He stayed still because he knew this man would kill him without a moment for mercy.

"Hello, Shameless," the man with the knife said. Henry hadn't heard that nickname in years. The man's voice was Southern-inflected, scraped from the bottom of an ashtray. "We need to talk."

Henry forced his voice to remain calm. "Drummond."

"Let's pour that hot coffee on the floor, please. I prefer you unarmed."

Henry obeyed. Then dropped the cup. It shattered on the hardwood.

"Good."

"You could have rung the doorbell." *He's here because he knows,* Henry thought, *he knows about the Night Road. And Hellfire. Convince him he's wrong or kill him.* "Put the knife down, for God's sake. Are you crazy?"

"When dealing with you, I prefer the direct approach," Drummond said.

"The doorbell would be direct. Hiding behind a knife is not."

"Goodness," Drummond said. "Did you grow a pair in the past ten years, Shameless? You're very steady. Ah, wait, now I see sweat making its debut on your forehead."

"Please put the knife down."

"Not yet. I'm not here for a casual reunion."

"The knife at the throat told me that."

"Your stepson killed one of our old friends."

Henry's mind went as blank as unlined paper. "What?"

"The man who your stepson shot in Houston was our old buddy Allen Clifford."

"What?" Henry didn't have to pretend shock; it thrummed through his body in a wave straight from his chest. "That's not—that's not possible."

"You are going to tell me what you and your brat are up to," Drummond said. "If you lie, you die. We clear, Professor?"

"Clear, Drummond."

Drummond lowered the knife. He spun Henry around and shoved him toward the table. "Sit down. Hands where I can see them at all times."

Henry sat on one side of the chessboard. Drummond stood on the other, the knife still in his grip. Drummond had always reminded Henry of a fireplug. Short, stocky, thick-necked, a flat bland face with a squarish nose. Drummond glanced around the study. "This used to be Warren's study."

"Yes."

"I remember, when Warren was working on a paper or a project, he would have those walls covered with sheets of paper, pictures, Post-It notes, like a blizzard of ideas."

"I keep my thoughts in my head."

"I'm sure that's a safer place for them." Drummond surveyed the walls: Henry's diplomas, pictures from his travels, framed medals from the Alexandria Pistol Club. "You still shoot?"

"Yes."

"You were always a crack shot, Henry, I give you that. Of course, I taught you. You teach Luke how to shoot? Maybe how to shoot from a car at a running man?"

"Warren taught him the basics."

Drummond jerked his head toward the interrupted game on the chessboard. "Are you still so friendless you have to play chess alone, Shameless?"

The old, undeserved nickname, a cheap variant on Shawcross, made the blood surge into his face. Humiliation. He hated Drummond with a loathing that went to his marrow, but he realized he needed him; he needed to know why his past and present were intersecting so violently. But he knew Drummond was trying to keep him off balance: the drama of the knife at the throat, then the offhand compliment about Henry's aptitude with a gun. Standard interrogation techniques, a constant shifting between threat and kindness. Henry kept a neutral expression on his face.

"I could hear the click of the pieces on the board from the hallway," Drummond said.

"Playing took my mind off my son." Henry cleared his throat.

"Your stepson, you mean." Drummond picked up one of the chess pieces—Luke's king—and inspected it, as though admiring the craftsman-ship. "You always did like to play both sides."

Henry crossed his arms. "You said Allen Clifford was the murdered man. Since when did he become a homeless street bum?"

"He wasn't. He was pretending to be."

"Pretending?"

"Allen Clifford was meeting with a fellow with ties to domestic extrem-ists who wanted to sell some information."

"Information?" Henry made his voice go weak.

"Yes. There's a black market, you know."

"And Allen Clifford was posing as a bum?"

"At the request of the guy he was meeting. Seller wanted to meet in the open; he wanted it to look like the meeting was just two totally harmless guys talking on the street. Very nervous. I assume he was worried about be-ing cornered in a room, or tape-recorded."

An extremist in Houston, selling information. Henry worried that the guy intended to sell his name. But no. The only ones in the Night Road who knew Henry's name were Snow and Mouser and Eric. Who could it have been? "How do you know all this? Whom was Clifford working for? Whom are you working for?"

"'Whom'? Oh, I've missed you, Shameless. Clifford and I both free-lance. He talked to me about the operation before he went down there. He was doing it alone; he didn't want the guy spooked. But clearly your stepson knew about this meeting. I want to know what he's been doing with his life since he lost his dad and"—here Drummond made a face—"got you as a replacement."

"Luke is harmless. He's just a psychology student."

"Harmless? The Houston police disagree. But I know even more than they do. I got access to his Internet records from his home account, Shame-less."

"Stop calling me that. You sound like you're in junior high."

"But you sure are pushing yourself today, aren't you? Shameless as ever. The amazing political seer, the Freud of the terrorist mind, the guy who claims to know the terrorists better than they know themselves." Drum-mond kicked the table aside, sending the chess pieces scattering across the floor. He put the blade up under Henry's jaw. "I call you exactly what I think you are. Your stepson's Internet records indicate he has been visiting hundreds of Web sites frequented by people with radical viewpoints. He's been corresponding with them through these sites, using tons of different e-mail addresses, sending them some rather fiery messages of agreement. Why?"

"He was working on a paper about . . . extremist psychology. He's been fascinated with it . . . ever since Warren died." That was true, and Henry stared hard into Drummond's ice-blue eyes. They reminded him of the hard blue of the sky beyond a mountain peak.

"So this reaching out to the fringes is for a research paper? No, I don't think so. He's compiled an avalanche of data, even for a master's degree. I think he's one of them."

"No. Not a paper; a book. He's working on a book." The lie wriggled, thick in his mouth. He had to convince Drummond, or Drummond would find Luke and kill him. Of that, Henry had no doubt. "He told me."

"Have you read or seen this book?"

"No."

"So he could have lied to you." He moved the knife off Henry's throat, let it dance along Henry's eyelashes. Henry bit his lip. "Does he know about us, Henry? You and me and Clifford . . . and his dad?"

"No. I swear. Luke doesn't know about the Book Club, I swear. I never told him. And even if I did, he wouldn't go after Allen Clifford or you or me. . . ." His voice trailed off. "He'd probably think we were all heroes."

"Heroes." Drummond snorted. "God. You did tell him, just to make yourself look smarter."

"No. I've never told Luke about the Book Club. Honestly, Drummond, why would I?"

"Bragging."

Henry gave a choked laugh. "Wasn't that our great failing, Drummond—not telling the world what we knew?"

"In your mind, Shameless, in your mind."

"We both know that if we'd been listened to, the world would be a very different place today, Drummond."

"I don't care to dissect history. I care about dissecting the present. You say Luke doesn't know about our past. But he knows about a meeting between Clifford and an extremist that is coincidentally scheduled to take place on the same day of a bombing that scares the piss out of the country. Maybe this extremist is one of Luke's online friends."

"No," Henry said. "I saw the video. Luke wasn't alone in the car. Someone else was in the passenger seat. Maybe Luke was forced to participate."

Drummond shook his head. "Hardly an acceptable theory. A trap was set for Clifford. And your stepson was the getaway driver."

Henry said, "Assume you're right." He could feed Drummond a bit of a line, see what Drummond was willing to share. "What was Clifford going to do with this extremist once he had him? Just how wide do your responsibilities range? Who was he going to turn the extremist over to?"

Drummond made a clicking noise, frowned. Henry could see him deciding to give a bit of information in hopes of Henry's doing the same. "Clifford would have hauled his ass out to a cabin in East Texas, up near Braintree, questioned him. With force, if needed. See how much he'd spill."

Henry blinked. The cabin. It had been originally intended for something other than Luke's kidnapping. An interrogation by Clifford. And the kidnapper had known that with Clifford dead, the cabin would be free to use for holding Luke hostage.

"Luke would not willingly participate in any crime," Henry said in an even tone. "Clifford, on the other hand, was contemplating the kidnapping of his source. You're here because you were working with Clifford. You're still nothing more than hired muscle."

Drummond let ten seconds pass. "Your defense of Luke is not convincing." Drummond shook his head. "His dad wouldn't be very proud of how his boy's turned out. You did a piss-poor job. I'm not surprised."

"Get out of my house, or I'm calling the police."

"No, you're not. How will you explain me?"

The silence stretched between them. Finally Henry said, "If you tell me what you know about this meeting, maybe I can figure out how Luke is connected. I might be able to find notes in his research to help you. I'll give you any information I find. But you have to promise me—you do not hurt Luke. I take your word as a fellow member of the Book Club that you will not harm him."

Drummond considered the offer for ten long seconds. "All right." The knife eased back.

"Who was the extremist? What's his name?"

"Jimmy Bridger."

Snow's old boyfriend, the one who had taken off a few days ago, a racist nothing. Snow had talked, and Bridger had looked to sell the information. Henry kept his poker face in place. "He wanted to talk and then he wanted protection."

"Who are you and Clifford working for that you could offer protection to an informant?"

Drummond didn't deny that he and Clifford shared an employer. "A private employer."

"A private employer who performs undercover operations that are clearly the purview of the FBI." Henry raised an eyebrow. "Are you telling me the Book Club is back in business?"

"The Book Club died with Warren Dantry and the others on that plane, Henry. Now all that's left of the Book Club is you"—he tapped the end of the knife against Henry's nose—"and me. Now that Clifford's dead."

"Are you working for the State Department?"

"I told you, the Book Club doesn't exist anymore."

"Okay." Henry thought, *So Drummond's working for someone who wants to flush out terrorists and for some reason is off the books. It could be the FBI, it could be CIA operating illicitly on American soil . . . what?* He didn't know. Drummond and Clifford had both been mercenaries at heart. "How did Clifford find this seller of information?"

"We'd been following extremist movements over here. Trying to apply pressure to people who want to leave the dark side," Drummond said. "Bridger mentioned to Clifford that he knew details on an impending attack code-named Hellfire."

The years of planning and waiting demanded that Henry not blink, not swallow, not betray the jolt of heat that pounded through his body and brain. This was not trust, Drummond sharing information. It was a trial by fire. He could feel Drummond studying his face for the merest reaction. He blinked, once, and hoped he had not betrayed himself. "Hellfire. Sounds religious."

"I don't think these are Baptist terrorists. If you know anything about this, Henry, whatever Luke's gotten involved in, you and I can deal. But now's the time."

"I don't know anything."

"The day after Clifford gets killed, a bomb goes off in Ripley, Texas. I'm sure you saw that on the news."

"Ripley was Hellfire?"

"Bridger made Hellfire sound much bigger than a single bomb. Much bigger. More than one city attacked."

"I can't help you. I know nothing, except that Luke is not a terrorist."

"No, Luke has just consistently reached out to freaks and people who hate. But he's not a terrorist, no." A smile flicked on Drummond's face. "What did you make him into, Henry? Now, Warren, he knew how to be a father. I think you just know how to be a screw-up."

"You judging me. Where were you again when our friends died? Those rehab places all sound alike to me." Henry kept his gaze locked on Drummond's eyes and to his satisfaction he saw he'd scored a hit.

Drummond lifted and inspected a photo of Luke, his mother, and Henry from the desk. A happier time, the photo taken at a vacation in Hawaii a year before the car crash that killed Barbara. Their smiles glowed. He set the photo down. "If you're hiding him, don't. Give him to me. If he's innocent or he's been pulled into this against his will, we'll help him and he'll go home with a clean slate. If he's guilty, then we find out what this Hellfire bullshit is and we stop it cold."

Drummond's tactic was nothing but playing nice cop before playing bad cop again. "I do not know where he is."

"The world you and your stepson are in is a little too small for my liking, Henry. You and Luke Dantry and Allen Clifford, all mixing it up years after we said our good-byes. Sit there. Move and you get cut." Then Drummond proceeded to search the study with a professional's keen efficiency. Henry sat, calmly, blanketing the rage inside him with a knowing half-smile. Nothing to link him to the Night Road, or to Hellfire, was here. Let Drummond look.

When he was done, Drummond stood. The frustration in his eyes was a knife that Henry could twist.

"You've kept Clifford's name out of the paper," Henry said.

"Yes."

"So you are with the government."

Drummond didn't answer but he wanted to prove his power, Henry could see. Proving his power, his superiority, had always been Drummond's weakness.

From his jacket, Drummond pulled out a photo and pushed it under Henry's nose. The photo appeared to be from a video camera mounted in a police car, aimed out the front windshield. It was a single shot, an officer talking to two men sitting in a BMW, a traffic stop. The ticket Luke had gotten in Mirabeau, Henry realized. He recognized the grainy profile of a man in the passenger seat. Eric Lindoe.

If he finds Eric, Drummond could find his connection to me, Henry thought. Keep the lies simple. "That's Luke at the wheel. I don't know who the other man is. Why hasn't this photo been released to the press?"

Drummond ignored the question and tapped the photo. "It's not a good enough shot to ID his face, but we'll find out who he is. I understand the last time you saw Luke was at the Austin airport. We'll nab all the video feeds from there as well."

He knew then that whoever was employing Drummond and Clifford would identify and find Eric Lindoe; it might just be a matter of hours. Maybe a couple of days. His world was unraveling. "This proves Luke is innocent. . . . He must have been forced—"

"Proves nothing. Innocent of pulling a trigger, perhaps, but Luke drove the car. Someone destroyed the Book Club before. Someone seems to be trying again. You and I shouldn't sleep too good at night. Maybe we're next."

"The plane flight—they were collateral damage. Ace Beere"—the private jet mechanic who had tampered with the flight system so everyone on the plane died from hypoxia—"he was trying to get revenge on his employer. Not the Book Club. We weren't the targets."

"Lucky, that you and Clifford and me couldn't make the trip."

"I always thought so," Henry said.

Drummond crossed his arms. "I need to understand Luke. Then I can figure out what his next move might be."

Henry saw that the sort of questions Drummond asked might reveal more than Drummond intended. He nodded. "What do you want to know? I'll tell you just to help Luke. You promise you won't hurt him?"

"I promise. After his father's death, Luke Dantry vanished for seven weeks."

"He ran away from home. He walked and hitchhiked south."

"His mother must have been frantic. Good thing you were there to comfort her." Drummond raised an eyebrow.

"A dear friendship and a good marriage came out of Luke's running," Henry said evenly. "Luke went to Cape Hatteras."

"It doesn't take seven weeks to walk or hitchhike from Washington to Cape Hatteras. Where was he during those seven weeks?"

"Mourning. Hiding from the world."

"He was living on the streets."

"He was only fourteen. But Warren had taught him to be rather independent. When the police found him he was sitting on the beach at the cape, staring out at sea where his father's plane went down. He'd been sitting on the sand for two days, watching the sea. Someone noticed him and called the police."

"Pining for the dead at this level doesn't sound quite normal."

Henry loathed Drummond's dismissive tone but he decided it might be a goad, a prod to make him talk more than he should. "Luke was extremely close to his—to Warren. You know how much everyone loved Warren."

"Didn't we all." Drummond tilted his head. "Luke never called his mom to say he was safe?"

"No. He should have. Luke had a tough time of it. He ran out of cash; he'd taken only a hundred dollars with him. His face was all over the Virginia papers then; people were looking for him. He figured out how to blend in, how to hide, how to survive on the run."

"I never thought of concealment as a genetic trait. His father was good at staying under the radar too." Drummond rested the knife against his leg. "This kid spent seven weeks evading the police and the detectives that your wife hired to find him. All without money or resources. And now he's hiding again."

Henry's mouth thinned. A twist of pride in Luke filled his chest. "If he doesn't want to be found, you won't find him." *I will find him first,* he thought. *And then I'll have Mouser kill you with your own knife, you insufferable bastard.*

"Are you using this kid to settle old scores? Let's be honest. You hated me, you hated Warren, you hated everyone in the Book Club."

"That's not true. . . ."

"Isn't it? We all thought you hated us."

"Hardly. I made the Book Club happen."

"Maybe. But Warren Dantry made it succeed."

Henry shook his head slowly. The words, and the truth, couldn't hurt him anymore. The Book Club was dead and he'd won. "Some success. A bunch of thinkers and thugs that no one paid much attention to in the first place."

"And now your stepson—"

"He's my *son*!" Henry snapped. An awful silence descended between the two men.

Drummond's lips curled in a sneer. "You really did step into Warren Dantry's life. His career. His wife. His son. My God, I guess you got over your hatred for him. How do Warren's shoes fit you, Henry?"

Henry breathed slowly, counted to ten, etched a half-smile on his face. He had never wanted to kill anyone as badly as he wanted to kill Drummond. He quelled the rage. "You know if I knew, I would tell you, because then I could help you find Luke. That's all I want. Luke to be found and home safe."

Drummond tented his fingers with the air of a man with a final card to play. "I'll find him. Before the police do. He's going to talk to me." Drummond stood. "It might be best, Henry, if you allowed yourself to be placed under my protection."

If he was kept under watch, the first wave of attacks might fail and then Hellfire would not happen. And no way he could find Luke or Eric Lindoe or the fifty million. "Some protection, you with a knife at my throat."

Drummond laughed. "Yes. But no one else would get a knife near you."

Henry swallowed down the tickle of bile at the back of his throat. "I stay here. If he comes here—my son needs me." A wave of dizziness flushed through his brain.

"Stay in touch, Henry. I will." Drummond handed Henry a plain white card, with a Manhattan address handwritten in black ink and a phone number below. "Henry. I don't want to see Warren's kid hurt, if he's innocent. But if he's not, if he killed Clifford, nothing you do can protect him. We just want to know why."

"I want to know why too." And it was true.

"Henry, this has just been great. I love reunions." He fixed a steely glare on Henry. "If you decide there's a greater truth you're not telling me, call me. Because I'm going to find this kid, and I'm going to find out the truth of what he's been working on. You don't want me pissed at you."

Henry said nothing.

Drummond left, this time out the front door. Henry slammed the door behind him.

Henry stayed at the front window until Drummond had driven away. *He isn't going to let this go,* he thought. He wondered who Drummond's boss was—a private employer, he'd said. What did that mean?

Henry dug out his cell phone and called the cabin rental number in Braintree, Texas, that he'd gotten earlier from Snow and Mouser. The number was posted on the gate to the road that led to the cabin. If Clifford had rented that cabin—if it wasn't coincidence—he had to find out who Clifford was freelancing for.

"Good morning, Braintree Park Rentals." A bright, cheery voice answered the phone.

"Yes. Good morning. A coworker of mine said he was renting cabin number three, I believe, and he's not been answering his cell phone, and I wanted to know if he had shown up there."

"Mr. Clifford? I saw him at the beginning of the week."

The very dead Allen Clifford had rented the cabin Luke had been taken to. "But not since?"

"People come out here to escape the world," the clerk said. "Maybe he just turned his cell phone off."

"Did he charge the cabin to the corporate card?"

"Yes, sir, but I can't give out details. I'm not allowed."

Henry didn't give up. "Did he give a billing address?"

"Yes. In New York. Who is this?"

"Oh. Was it this address?" He read off the address on the card Drummond had given him.

"Yes, sir, that's it." The clerk's hesitancy vanished. Henry could almost imagine him smiling.

"We have several firms under the umbrella, so to speak, which company did he charge it to?"

"Quicksilver Risk."

"Thank you so much."

"Did you want to leave a message for Mr. Clifford? I can go up to the cabin."

"No, that's fine. He's not supposed to be using a corporate card for his vacation but it's not a problem, we know he'll reimburse us. Thanks so much." Henry hung up.

Quicksilver Risk.

Henry glided back onto the Web and found the company's Web site. It was chrome-colored and discreet in the manner of the most expensive consultants. Only a mission statement and a trio of principals. Allen Clifford, hired muscle for the Book Club, was one. The other two were former professors, but with business backgrounds in risk assessment. They hadn't been part of the Book Club. No listing of clients. No listing of fees. No mention of ties to the government. It said that they'd helped Fortune 500 companies assess the risk of providing relief after the Boxing Day tsunami, after Katrina, after the chaos in a few African countries that had contested elections.

He tried the phone number. He got the voice mail, left a message for Allen Clifford. "Hey, Allen," he said to the dead man's machine, "it's Henry Shawcross, haven't talked to you in a while. I'd like to catch up. See what you're up to. Give me a call." He left a number. Hopefully someone at the firm would start returning Clifford's calls and he could ask more questions.

"What dirty work were you up to?" he said to Allen Clifford's photo.

The doorbell rang.

At his feet lay an overnight package, a large, thick plastic envelope. Luke's condo was the return address.

He weighed the package in his hand, he listened to every side of it. Light. No ticking sound, although that meant nothing with digital detonators. He carefully opened the box.

Inside was another package. It had been sent first to an American transport company for delivery in the United States, but had originated in France. Paris. An address he didn't recognize.

Without opening the inner package, he Googled the Paris address. It was a postal shop in the Saint-Germain district, the kind where you might rent a mailbox.

Inside was a cell phone. Plain, cheap, the prepaid kind. A card attached to it read *For Henry's ear only.*

He turned the phone on.

He very badly wanted a shot of whiskey. He was afraid what news the phone would bring. He was afraid of how the day could darken. But the phone had to be a positive, yes? It must be the kidnapper, reaching out to him. The phone was a blessing if Drummond was monitoring his calls. He had to assume Drummond was. Drummond knew how to tap lines, bug rooms—he'd done it for years when Henry worked with him.

He put the phone into his pocket and went to get his whiskey, his mind blazing with confusion. Things that should not be intersecting were. The Book Club, Luke, Hellfire, the long and still-hot hatred for Luke's father. A hatred he had worked hard to mask, every day, when he was around Barbara and Luke. It had been hard, keeping his acid loathing bottled up. Warren Goddamned Dantry. Warren was a know-it-all and a know-nothing, all at once. Even now the thought of Warren Dantry made Henry quake with fury, with disgust.

Warren had made the Book Club work, Drummond had said.

A lie. A complete lie. "I brought him in, I brought you all in," Henry said to the empty kitchen. His hand shook slightly as he poured, and the glass tinkled. He ran a finger along his neck, convincing himself that Drummond had left no mark. He would have to call Snow and Mouser, warn them that Hellfire—at the very least the code name—had been leaked, that if Bridger were found, Snow would be in danger of being exposed, and that Drummond was hunting Eric and Luke, just as they were. If they chose to withdraw, he could do nothing to compel them.

But then he would have to start the Night Road all over again. The Ripley operation's advantage of distraction would be lost, rendered to nothing like the chlorine in the rain. Or else he'd have no choice but to run, from the prince's throat-cutting wrath, since his fifty million was either locked in an inaccessible account or had been moved to Switzerland or had vanished into the ether.

Then he heard a quiet trill. He opened the phone.

"Henry Shawcross." It was a British woman.

"Yes?"

"You may call me Jane, for the purposes of our discussion. I thought given time to miss your stepson, you might reconsider my offer."

This woman was the mastermind. The boss. Relief flooded him; now he could strike a deal. "I want to know where Luke is."

"Shame on you, shoveling the blame on poor Luke. I suspected you were a truly despicable person and, my God, you didn't disappoint." She laughed. Laughed at him, a teasing giggle.

"You have made enemies with the wrong people, young woman."

"Have I? It's more that you have made the wrong friends. That nasty billionaire who played dress-up in the London park and offered fifty million to you while the pigeons danced for the crumbs at his feet. I heard your every word." She laughed again, silvery, and a cold fist closed on Henry's heart.

"What do you want?"

"Transfer the fifty million to a numbered account and you'll get Luke back."

She didn't know that the passwords to the accounts had been changed and he couldn't access the millions. Otherwise, she wouldn't have bothered with the call.

"I want to speak to Luke."

"I don't give the goodies without the cash. You can let him yell at you after the funds are delivered."

"No, now." Jane might be desperately bluffing, to get him to release the money that he couldn't touch. Nausea and rage swept through him. "Why did you have Eric kill Allen Clifford?"

"Oh, so many questions, so little time," Jane said. "I don't have to answer anything, love. That's what power is. Never having to explain yourself. Now. The money for Luke. Do I need to spell it out with pictures?"

"You'll kill Luke anyway." An ache suffused his entire body.

"Actually, we won't. We'll let him go. He'll be your problem, won't he?" And Jane gave the cruelest laugh he'd ever heard. "How exactly will you explain your refusal to help him? What you are, what you've done? Should we tell him to ask about what happened to his sweet mother?"

The unexpected words, delivered with a twist of steel, froze him.

"Barbara died in an accident. Anything else is a lie."

"She did, she did. A well-timed accident."

"It was an accident! It was!"

"But now he won't believe you, Henry. You're the nowhere man: always on the fringes, always laughing a bit late at every joke, who has to practice his smile. You finally get a family after years of being alone, one too good for you, and you toss it all away. I doubt Barbara Dantry and Luke ever quite recognized the stray dog they let in their house was a wolf."

Every word was a pile-driving fist, through bone and brain. Henry sucked in a harsh breath. "I'll give you the money. Please—"

"I want you to understand that if you don't transfer the money within thirty minutes, Luke is dead."

Oh, God. God, no, he thought. "Eric has the code for the accounts. Not me," he said. "Please don't hurt Luke. I'll find the money—"

"Eric *doesn't* have the money."

"Jane, he does. He's lied to you." And they would kill Luke now; he was useless to them. *No, no, no.* "That's why I couldn't give you the money before. Please. Believe me. Please—"

Jane hung up.

He fumbled on the phone. There was no call log; it had been disabled. No way to call back.

Henry drank the whiskey, very slowly. The shaking in his hands stopped. He drank another, neat. Then he poured the rest of the bottle down the sink.

She might be killing Luke right now. Right now, while you stand crying over a sink, whiskey on your breath, and you have caused the death of the one remaining person in the world that you care about, Henry thought.

The phone rang. The phone he used only with Mouser. Mouser's voice sounded raspy, hard, tinged with fury. "Luke identified Eric Lindoe as his kidnapper."

"Is Luke okay? Tell me you have him."

"Oh, I'll get him back for you. He stabbed me in the leg and he ran."

"Why did he stab you? I told you not to hurt him—"

"He knows we came from you, Henry, and you're on his shit list. Watch your back. Your boy is pissed and apparently able to fight."

The warning coasted over Henry's ears. Luke was alive. And out of Jane's clutches. Or maybe she had recaptured him after he escaped Mouser? "You sure someone else didn't grab him?"

"Not sure, but he was free as a bird last time I saw him."

Then Jane was bluffing. He had to fight back, he had to find this woman, find out who she was. And destroy her. "I don't understand. Why would Eric Lindoe turn against us and target Luke?"

"Luke says some Brit bitch used him as ransom for Eric's woman. She thought you could deliver the fifty million, but Eric must have already hidden it. If he hasn't given it to her, then Eric has it. We have to find him."

Henry wiped sweat from his jaw. "Eric lied to us all. Including this Brit. She made him kidnap Luke to force my hand, and he did it to cover up that he had taken the money. She must have asked him for it originally and he convinced her he didn't have the access. That I did." Oh, Christ, Luke's life destroyed by a single lie. "Eric hasn't given her the money. She just called me, thinking I could get it for her." Henry sank to the couch. "I don't understand. Luke stabbed you?" Luke, fighting two nutcase extremists with experience in murder and combat? He could not picture the scene.

"I wonder, Henry, how well you know Luke. He seems far more capable than you gave him credit for."

"I—I don't understand."

"It's simple. He's loose. He is a danger to us."

"No. I can take care of him." Henry thought quickly. "I'm going to put tracers on every friend Luke has, anyone he might turn to for help. . . . The police will do the same, but we must be smarter than the police. And faster. We have to find Eric. And we have to find Luke. I can make Luke understand."

"That I doubt."

"I can." Henry raised an eyebrow. "And if he's been as smart as you say, he might be very useful to us. Listen, I'm sorry he stabbed you. Are you all right?"

"Yes. But I'm not happy. Find where he's at and I'll bring him back to you. Maybe in one piece."

Luke, running. With Mouser and Snow and now that bastard Drummond all after him. What would he do? Come here? No. Washington was far. And he wouldn't trust Henry now, and he might believe the police were watching Henry, waiting for Luke to show. How else would he try to clear his name?

Eric. Eric, if forced to confess, could clear Luke's name of murder.

"He'll go after Eric." Just like he chased after his father's ghost, all the way down to Cape Hatteras. "We find Eric, we find Luke."

Henry felt charged with the fire of battle. He could win. He called a Night Road hacker, ordered him to find any records in the airline or credit-card databases that indicated where Eric Lindoe or Luke Dantry had gone. Over time, he had found hackers with back doors into such valuable databases. If they were not motivated by Night Road–style ideology, they were motivated by money.

His hunters, either on the ground, or electronic, would find Luke, and faster than Drummond could. He did not need to worry about warrants and permission. He did not want to think about Luke not believing him, and what awful sacrifice he might have to suffer. All he had to worry about was telling, and selling, the greatest lie of his life.

13

For twenty minutes Luke ran, walked, ran again, through the woods. He crossed open fields, cleared for cattle or horses, and he felt vulnerable and alone in the open. The pine trees, when he could stay in their dense growth, were like having a shield. He stumbled out onto a road, close to a bridge on the river. He had no idea where he was and he kept glancing over his shoulder.

He saw a teenage boy in a yellow slicker then, trudging up from the swollen riverbanks.

"Hi," the boy said. "Which search team were you with?"

"Oh," Luke said. "I got separated from my search team. I'm a friend of the Olmsteads', staying at their place on the river for a few days." He tried not to talk too fast or let his nervousness seep into his words. "Just thought I'd help. But I'm useless. I don't know the country around here."

"Well, I can give you a lift back to the search base."

"Thank you."

He followed the kid along the thin stretch of paved road, thinking, *If this kid's been involved in the search for the trucker, then maybe he hasn't seen the rest of the news with my face on it.* He couldn't dwell overmuch on the trucker. If he did, the guilt would overwhelm him and he'd make a mistake and be caught or dead. He could not bring the trucker back to life if he hadn't made it out of the river. But he could be sure that Mouser and Snow paid for what they did.

A red truck sat at the edge of the road. The kid offered his hand and said, "My name's Dumont."

"Hi, Dumont, I'm Warren," Luke lied. It was his dad's name and using it felt easy and right. He shook the kid's hand. They got into the truck.

"I feel bad for this gentleman's family. Wondering when we're going to find him." Dumont wheeled the truck south—away from the house where Luke had hidden. He tried not to sag against the door in relief.

"You look exhausted, man," Dumont said.

"Didn't sleep well. The storm kept me up all night." He stared out the window. Mouser was out of play for maybe just a few minutes, unless Luke had hurt him worse than he thought, but where was Snow? And how on earth was he going to find Eric?

They turned onto a main road that headed toward the town of Braintree, and a Mercedes shot by them. He could see snow-white hair at the wheel and thought she might notice if he ducked suddenly. So he stayed put and rubbed his face with his hand.

"You sure you okay?" Dumont asked. He sounded as though he were doubting his decision to offer this odd stranger a ride.

In the rearview he watched the Mercedes vanish over a rise in the road. No glow of brake lights, no indication she'd spotted him. "Yes, I'm fine. Just tired." He had to get out of this area now. He needed to know where Eric and Aubrey had gone. There had to be a clue in something Eric and Aubrey had said or done. Something he'd seen. He began to blink past his exhaustion and tried to replay from the beginning every nuance of the things Eric had said to him.

The truck pulled into a parking lot of a small motel, filled with police cars.

Police. His face had been all over the news, and there was probably an APB out on him.

To one side stood a news crew associated with a Houston station—a single reporter, a cameraman—interviewing rescuers. The media was more of a threat—they for sure would have seen his face on broadcasts.

"Thanks, Dumont," Luke said. "I appreciate the lift." He opened Dumont's truck door and stepped out into the rain.

The reporter, forty feet away, wiped rain from her face and raised a hand. "Hey! Y'all just get back in from the search?"

Oh, God, Luke thought. He turned and walked away, toward a tent set up for the search parties.

How the hell was he supposed to get out of here? Steal a car? He had no idea how to, and while breaking into a cottage for warmth and food after being starved for a day and surviving a cold river seemed forgivable, grand theft auto did not.

"Warren, hey man!"

He glanced over his shoulder and saw Dumont standing with the reporter, gesturing at him to join them.

Luke forced a smile, pantomimed a shiver and drinking coffee. He waved and kept his hand up by his face. Then, turning and pulling the jacket's hood halfway over his face, he ducked into the tent.

Coffee, bottled water, breakfast tacos, and doughnuts were being served on a short table. He snagged a cup of coffee, steaming and black, and collected his thoughts.

Nowhere to go and no way to get there. He watched a police officer speaking into a walkie-talkie. *Just turn yourself in,* he thought, with a sudden and deep ache of resignation, of surrender.

Find Eric. Find the answers. Don't you dare give up.

Braintree wasn't a big town and he walked down to the main street. He had no money, no way out of town. He checked his watch, a Rolex that his mother had given him when he graduated from college. That would be a source of cash, but he'd rather pawn it in a town where he wouldn't be remembered so easily. And he hated to give up a gift she had given him, but these were desperate times.

The library was open; it was just past ten in the morning. He walked inside, wandered the maze of the stacks. The smell and sight of books gave him a sudden comfort. They had been his friends after his father's death, after his mother's accident, and a library was a place he knew how to use. He went to an array of public computers, nodding at a tall blond woman who was working at the main desk.

He opened a Web browser and jumped to the *Houston Chronicle* Web page.

The chlorine bombing in Ripley still dominated the headlines. The rains had removed the immediate threat, and the ruptured tanks had been sealed.

Forty confirmed dead. Chemical plants around the country were on a massively increased state of alert.

The homeless man's murder was a second-tier story; but the report offered no picture of the victim, and no name. Except that the homeless in the area didn't seem to know much about the man. Several said he was a stranger.

That wasn't a mystery he could solve here. He had to find Eric and Aubrey.

Luke went to Google and entered *Aubrey kidnapped*. He found references to a soap opera character snatched as part of a story line, a Chilean activist who'd been missing since the Pinochet terrors, the sad detailing of a girl stolen in Oregon by her father five years ago. But nothing recent.

Maybe Aubrey hadn't been reported as kidnapped. Eric had gotten her home before anyone realized she was missing.

But missing wasn't the same as kidnapped. He searched on *Aubrey missing*.

Three results down he found it. A personal blog called "grace-a-matic," written by a young freelance designer named Grace in Chicago:

> My friend Aubrey (I did the logo design for her export-import business) is missing. She's not returning phone calls, she's not at home, she's not at her office, she's not updating her social networking pages, and no one has seen her. I called the police and they were useless. They said I have to wait twenty-four hours to file a missing persons report. That's insane. Her boyfriend, well, they just broke up a couple of weeks ago, but he said he doesn't know where she is. I don't know what to do omg I'm a little freaked out that the cops really do make you wait twenty-four hours.

Then two entries later:

> Update on my missing friend: Aubrey is no longer missing and apparently wasn't. She called me this morning to say she took a few days to deal with some personal issues and she's fine, thank God, and to please not blog about her life and I feel like fricking Chicken Little for panicking. The cops were right.

He went to Grace's portfolio and found the one logo she'd done for an export-import company. Perrault Imports, specializing in "artistic" imports from South America and Asia—modest pottery and wall hangings, sold in turn to retail outlets. The contact name was Aubrey Perrault.

Who, then, was Eric?

He risked signing onto the social networking site—he had an account there as well, as did most of his generation—and found a profile linked to Aubrey's. Ah, sweet, hello Eric, one of her top friends. Eric Lindoe. He jumped to Eric's profile. Thirty-five. Working at a private bank called Gold Maroft in Chicago. He Googled Eric Lindoe, found a few news stories, mostly tied to press releases from his employer about promotions. He had gone to University of Illinois on full scholarship. He had started in bank operations and moved rapidly up into overseas banking: for construction projects in Saudi Arabia, Britain, Switzerland, Dubai, and Qatar.

A man with so much to lose, committing kidnapping and murder—there had to be a reason.

He did another Google search, tying Eric's name with Henry Shawcross's. No results.

He had to get to Chicago. He had no money, no resources. And he couldn't turn to his few school friends; he couldn't put them in danger.

But he had people who wanted to be his friends. In the Night Road.

He remembered the other evening showing Henry postings from the one who called himself ChicagoChris. He went to his e-mail account through a Web site that allowed you to surf the Web anonymously. He'd learned about it in one of the discussion groups. Chris had sent him a phone number in one of his e-mails to Luke. He found it in an e-mail from two weeks ago and wrote it down.

Then he surfed to Twitter, the Web service that allowed you to send short updates and messages to all your friends in your network. His network included all his grad school friends, a few college and high school buddies. People he cared about.

He sent a message to everyone on his Twitter list: *I'm innocent*. In case he didn't make it out of this mess alive, he wanted to make that gesture, to give his friends reason to believe him.

Then he erased the browser's history and logged off the Internet.

He glanced up at the librarian, who sat frowning at a computer screen. He saw two volunteers murmuring over a book cart, sorting volumes. One laughed softly. The librarian stood and vanished into an office. The two women stepped toward the back of the library—Luke could smell coffee, hazelnut, on the air.

Luke looked over the counter and saw a purse. He peered inside and found a cell phone. He grabbed it and hurried to the back of the stacks. No one noticed.

He called ChicagoChris's number.

"Hello?" A young smoker's rasp, sounding tired.

"I hope this is ChicagoChris. This is Lookout. From TearTheWallsDown discussion group."

"Hey, man! Hey! How are you?" Chris sounded happy to hear from him, but it was the overabundant enthusiasm of someone who spent far too much time alone, and not happily.

"I hope it's cool to call. You sent your number."

"Sure, glad to finally talk." ChicagoChris painted himself online as a badass, a man who wanted to right the wrongs of the world by redistributing wealth on an extreme basis, a prescription for saving the world from over-industrialization, but he sounded like a giddy schoolboy. "You in Chicago?"

"Hardly," Luke said. "But I need to get to Chicago, and I need help. I'm getting hassled big-time."

Chris clicked his tongue in his mouth, waited.

"I wrote some truth on a board I shouldn't have, and the FBI's looking for me."

"You shouldn't say FBI on a phone conversation. The government picks up and records any conversation in the fifty states that mentions the FBI and it gets played back to the FBI. So if you say, fuck the FBI, they know you said it. They open a file on you."

"Sorry," Luke said.

ChicagoChris hung up.

Luke dialed again. Chris answered. "You have to be more careful. You don't want to trigger their monitoring software with a keyword."

Luke thought, in Chris's paranoid world *monitoring software* was probably a keyword, but he didn't want Chris to hang up again. "All right. I know you don't know me, but we're brothers in the struggle, aren't we?"

Chris was silent again. "Maybe."

"I need to get to Chicago. I need your help. But I can't travel on a charge card, and I don't have money."

"You want me to send you money." He sounded slightly incredulous.

"I swear I'm good for it." Most people would hang up. Help a friend you only knew from online? Not likely. But he was gambling on two things: Chris had sent him the contact information to begin with, because he liked Luke's postings to the group, and because Chris seemed needy for friendship. And the communities—even being online—still had the feel of closeness, of a bonded brotherhood. These people were so alone in their hatreds, they needed each other to reinforce their certainty about the world's wrongs. It was a key to terrorist psychology: Violence was a group decision. He had to play on that sense that they were partners. "Brother, I just need enough to cover a bus ticket to Chicago, and a bit for food."

"Where are you?"

"The library in Braintree, Texas." He fashioned a half-lie, one Chris couldn't resist. "I got information on that chlorine accident in Texas. That the government was involved."

"What exactly do you have?"

"Well, get me to Chicago, and I'll share the info with you. If the you-know-what with three letters doesn't grab me first."

"What's the info worth?"

"Send the money and I'll bring it to you."

"You could also be a cop, trying to trick me. The cops would love to get hold of me."

"I'm not. I can't e-mail you because I'm being followed. I've got to stay off the grid as much as I can. I'm making the call on a cell phone I stole from a lady's purse. So make your choice. Help me or don't."

Silence again.

"There's a bus station in Braintree," Luke said. "You can buy a ticket online for me."

"Do you need cash?"

"I have zero, Chris, so yes, please."

He heard the background clatter of typing. "I'll find a Western Union close to the Braintree library address, send you cash for food. If you don't pay me back"—his tongue made a click—"I'll find you and I'll destroy you."

He sounded different from Mouser. Erratic, not cool and focused. "No worry, I'm good for it. And thanks, man. Thanks so much."

"You're gonna pay me back," ChicagoChris said, and he hung up.

Luke erased the call from the phone's log. The volunteers had not returned from the stacks. He dropped the woman's phone back into her purse and walked out of the library.

Snow and Mouser knew Luke would be on the road, and all roads led to Braintree. Luke tried not to let the fever of paranoia build in his heart. He walked a half-mile and found the Western Union agent at a Price-Right chain store. Chris sent him $999—if he'd sent a thousand, Luke would have had to show ID. It said so on a sign behind the clerk's head. Luke couldn't believe the guy was actually doing it. And being smart.

"Lost my ID," Luke said as the customer service agent counted out the money. "Lost my wallet."

"That sucks," the agent said, not caring.

In the Price-Right store Luke bought a bottle of hair color. Blond. He thought: *When you've decided to color your hair, that's when you know you're in serious freaking trouble.* He bought a baseball cap and sunglasses; a small backpack, peanut butter crackers, bottled water, and apples; toiletries, sturdy sneakers, underwear, socks, and jeans.

It was just like what he'd packed when he ran away from home all those years ago, and Luke missed his mom and dad with a pain that cut to his spine. After leaving the store, he threw into the trash the galoshes and the oversized jeans he'd stolen from the cottage. He walked to a wireless dealer at the other end of the shopping center and bought a prepaid cell phone.

He hurried to the bus station. His online ticket, courtesy of Chris, had not been processed. He ate an apple and all the crackers. Fidgeting. Waiting for Mouser and Snow to walk through the doors as they shut off every route of escape out of Braintree.

A nerve-wracking hour later his ticket was ready, and twenty minutes after that the northbound Greyhound pulled out of Braintree.

Five miles out of town, Luke Dantry fell into a deep, desperate sleep.

The hacker's phone call came as Henry stepped out of the shower. He felt sick from lack of sleep and worry. *Please be good news,* he thought.

It was the Night Road hacker. "You wanted me to find Eric Lindoe. He and his girlfriend were on the passenger manifest for a flight from Dallas/ Fort Worth to Thailand yesterday." He fed Henry the details. Thailand. Of course Eric could run far; he'd taken the Night Road's money. It would be most difficult for Luke to follow Eric there, without cash, without a passport. Without help.

"What about breaking into Eric's bank?" Henry asked. It was their chance, without Eric, to find where the fifty million had been moved.

"I think your Eric screwed us and his own bank. I hacked into the bank's audit trail—the history of every transaction that's taken place this month. Someone inside looped the audit trail onto itself—there's dozens of gigabytes of transaction data more than there should be. It's a complete information overload. It's entirely disrupted the audit trail, destroyed its integrity. I expect there's a lot of upset people at Eric's bank right now. No one's going to be able to find what money went where for several days. Even their backups are corrupted. Eric knew exactly what he was doing."

Disaster. The Arab prince had given Eric to Henry as a contact. But Henry could hardly go to the prince and say, "Lost the fifty million somewhere in that bank. Could you lean on the bankers to cough it up?" Admitting failure would be a death sentence. And the bankers, if Eric had sabotaged their internal auditing system, would hardly be eager to admit they had a rogue employee; it would destroy their reputations. No. Henry would have to find the money without letting the prince know it had gone missing.

"I don't think I can risk a further hack at the bank. I set off intrusion alarms as it was."

Henry thanked the hacker and hung up. Then Henry's office phone rang. He hurried down the hallway, wrapped in his towel, to answer it. "Yes?"

A flat, cold voice he didn't recognize said, "You want your stepson back?" Not Mouser, not the British woman, not Drummond.

"Who is this?"

"You want your stepson back?"

Now he realized he'd heard this vaguely whiny voice before. Where? He couldn't remember. "Yes," Henry said. "Yes, I do."

"I'll call you back when I have him, and we'll make a trade." Then the caller hung up.

Henry checked the call log. The phone's number was not one he recognized, but the area code was for Chicago. Eric Lindoe's hometown.

Seventeen critical displays stood in the Braintree Price-Right store, considered vital because the Price-Right buyers wanted to measure customer response to price and product combinations. Twenty-four security cameras watched the store. Six of the cameras above the displays had been doubly purposed—not only for security, but to observe customer behavior. What path through the store did a customer who'd paused to look at the display take? Did they go first to clothing, then to toiletries, or electronics? What facial expressions did customers show at displays—smiles, frowns, shaking of heads, curiosity? How long did each customer study the display? Did they pick up and examine items, and for how long?

Tens of thousands of faces were captured at Price-Right displays in thirty-nine states every day. Each store's video feed went instantaneously to the corporate headquarters in Little Rock, Arkansas. There it would be run through a preliminary computer analysis, to provide the company's marketers with initial data to help them refine pricing and stock strategies.

But, for the past several hours, this film was also being siphoned off to another server, in the company's special projects division. This was done in response to a very quiet request from outside Price-Right. There, every face that had been captured at one of the monitored store displays across the country was compared to a photo. A photo of a young man, in his mid-twenties, light brown hair, blue eyes, with a defined and analyzed set of facial proportions, rendered into mathematical equations. The length of his mouth. The distance from lower lip to jawline. The angle of cheekbones. The distance between his eyes. The length and width of ear.

Every face caught at the displays was compared to the young man's photo.

Comparison number 10,262 found the closest match by far, a photo snapped when a young man bought a pair of shoes in Braintree, Texas. The server automatically sent an anonymous e-mail alert, snaking through the world and masking its traces, arriving on a screen in Paris, France.

The man who received the message studied Luke Dantry's face. For a long time. Then he picked up a phone, to order a search of all cellular calls coming in and out of the small town of Braintree, Texas, monitoring all communications, all financial transfers, all transportation records.

The man stared at the photo on the screen and thought: *They will kill you when they find you.*

14

Mouser had disinfected and bound the stab wound. No way he was going to let Snow know he'd been hurt. He'd explain the knife's rip in his jeans as a tear from running through the piney woods. He had called her to come pick him up at the cottage, but, Jesus, the pain was a hot bolt and the bandage didn't seem to be adhering well.

The little bastard. He would cut Luke's throat after he told them what they needed to know.

Snow was fooled for all of five seconds as he walked toward her car. "You're hurt." She turned him back into the cottage and sat him on the edge of the bathroom tub. She undid his zipper and slid down his pants—he didn't protest—and then she went and got a medical kit from her car's trunk. She tended to the wound with a brisk professionalism that startled him. Disinfecting and then suturing the wound.

"I learned to bind wounds at an early age," she said. "Had to."

"Same as your daddy teaching you to build bombs?"

"Uh-huh," she said.

"That must have been quite a summer camp he sent you to."

"Camp Life," she said.

"Tough life."

"I was a Child of the Lamb," she said.

He was silent, honoring her past. The Children of the Lamb had been a religious group, sheltering themselves away in a compound in Wyoming. The Beast had sent its army to flush them out—there had been lies about weapons being massed, and tax evasion, and child rape on the altars, and similar silky untruths that unfurled on the Beast's forked tongue. After a two-week siege, the Feds had laid waste to the compound, killing thirty, leaving a dozen survivors. It had been ten years ago.

"I see," he said quietly. With respect.

"One of the four kids who survived the siege," she said. "I was fifteen."

It explained the burn scars. "Your parents?"

"Dead. Burned up. Daddy shoved me out the window. His hair was on fire. I ran but the agents caught me, wrestled me to the ground. I watched our temple burn. I saw my people rise, in the smoke, to God." She focused on his bandage.

"I'm sorry," he said.

"I'm not," Snow answered. Now she looked up at him. "It made me who I am, and I like myself just fine."

He put a hand on her shoulder. "We're gonna beat the Beast together. We'll find Luke. Hellfire will happen."

"Yes," she said.

He picked up his phone, rang Henry, talked, listened. He hung up. Snow still sat on the tile floor, looking at him, seeing a rising mix of judgment and anger in his eyes. "Your old boyfriend, Bridger, he tried to talk. He told some group called Quicksilver about Hellfire. At least its names—he was holding out on the details for money. But we got to move fast. How much does the bastard know?"

"I'm sorry," she said. "I never told Bridger a word. Maybe he heard me mention the word on the phone when I spoke to Henry about how to make all the bombs. But I never told him. But I can't guarantee he didn't spy on me."

"Does he know where the bombs are? Does he know our targets?"

She didn't answer right away, and he could see she was flipping through the pages of her memory. She did this with care and he believed her now, completely. Instead of reaching for her neck to strangle her, he barely touched her hair with his fingertips. "No. He doesn't know where they're stored, he doesn't know the targets. About that, I never told him, never wrote anything down he could find." She spoke with such calmness, there was no room in her words or her breath for a self-serving lie. But she ducked her head. If he wanted to kill her, he could, and he realized she would accept her fate like a soldier. He felt his heart shift in his chest. He pulled his hands away from her head, folded them back in his lap.

"Okay," he said. His voice was hoarse. "Where will Bridger hide?"

"His family's from Alabama. He might go there. Or he might stay in Houston. He's not real bright."

"We'll get the Night Road looking for him. We'll find him and he can tell us who these Quicksilver assholes are."

Now she looked up at him. "Why do you hate the government?"

"I just do."

"I told you my reasons. Tell me yours." She leaned toward him, their faces an inch apart. "Please, Mouser."

For a moment the words, hanging in the wet air between them, were more intimate than a kiss.

"I prefer not," he said.

She leaned back and closed the medical kit.

"Thank you for tending me," he said. "You could have been a doctor or a nurse."

"No. I don't much like people anymore."

He knew how she felt.

"What now?" she asked.

"Luke might be in the town nearby."

"Or hitchhiking up the highway. He seems to like trucks."

"Then we better get resources on our side. He's going to stick his head up and we need to be ready."

"How's the pain?"

"Tolerable," Mouser said. She'd given him a woozy shot of relief from her medical bag.

"Let's see what's tolerable." The wound was low on his leg, above the knee. She reached out to touch it but her hand slid up past the bandage to his underwear. She reached inside the opening of his boxers, closed her hand on him.

"What?" he said in utter shock.

"It's a lonely life, isn't it, Mouser?" she said.

It had been four years. He had the mission, he did not need women. But his hands didn't rise to push her away and her mouth was a warm buzz against his lips. The pain seemed to fade for him, when she slid his jeans off all the way, there on the cool bathroom floor. An hour later they left the cottage and he thought: *Damn, you don't let feelings get in the way of fighting the Beast. Should have been chasing him. Not chasing her.* He was ashamed of himself.

When he called Henry again, he got a surprise.

"I want you two to go to Chicago," Henry said. "I have reason to believe Luke is heading there."

15

The hand shook Luke awake and his first thought was, *They've found me.*

He opened his eyes to see the kind face of an elderly woman who had been sitting across the aisle from him, working a pencil patiently through the pages of a crossword puzzle book.

"Texarkana, honey. We got a dinner stop and layover here if you're going farther."

He blinked and thanked her in a broken mumble. She stepped back with an uncertain smile and waddled down the aisle.

Luke stumbled off the bus. The air was cool and humid, the rain past. He started to walk down the street in search of food.

A four-hour layover before his ticket took him onward to Little Rock, Memphis, and then Chicago. He devoured a double hamburger at a fast-food chain, careful not to meet anyone's gaze. He walked down a couple of blocks to a bar, slipped inside its welcoming darkness, and ordered a Coke.

The television was on, the early news reporting that the demolishing rains that had moved up from the Gulf had begun to subside. Confirmation from a reporter outside Ripley that the rail yard disaster had been a bomb. Not an accident. The bar hushed as the reporter described how the FBI was trying to determine if this was a jihadist attack or a domestic enemy's. The screen went to a commercial and the conversation of the beer drinkers resumed, although subdued. Luke sipped his soda. The news came back on, covering the bizarre shooting of the homeless man again, Henry speaking on camera once more, the betrayal repeating itself. Luke's face was on the screen. The few early drinkers were lost in their conversations, studying their beers, or clicking billiard balls. Luke kept his sunglasses on.

But now there were new reports. Luke saw a shot of a friend's cell phone, with the message Luke had sent to all his friends on Twitter. *I'm innocent.* And one of his grad-school friends, rising to his defense, blinking into the camera said, "If Luke Dantry says he's innocent, I believe he is. What motive does he have to kill a homeless stranger? None."

But then the reporter went back to Luke's past. A runaway, a couple of run-ins with the law as a kid. Enough to confirm to the casual viewer that Luke was trouble, reinforced by his stepfather's pleas to surrender.

The barkeep let two more stories play out on the news, and as a steady stream of customers began to enter the bar he clicked over to ESPN for the Dallas Mavericks game.

Luke left a dollar tip and walked a half-mile until he came to a larger gas station, one with a sizable convenience store attached. He bought a pair of nail scissors and went to the bathroom, locked himself in a stall, and read the hair dye directions. He faced the mirror, applied the hair dye quickly and a little sloppily. He returned to the stall, sat, waited, while a few customers came and went. After thirty minutes, he rinsed the gunk from his hair quickly in the sink, dried it with a paper towel. Then he took the scissors, clipped his hair close to his head. Messy but now blond, and he covered most of his new hair with his baseball cap.

He tried Chris with his prepaid phone but got no answer. He felt tense, restless. He walked back to the bus terminal and kept his back to the passengers.

He heard the call for the bus servicing Little Rock, Memphis, and Chicago. He boarded—the bus was more crowded than he'd expected. Not good, but it was easy to be as anonymous as you wanted on a bus, especially at nighttime. Luke settled into a rear seat, kept his sunglasses on, his cap low. He dozed, on and off, and as the bus made its stops and brief layovers in Little Rock and Memphis and a dotting of towns in between, the long night and his clear lack of interest in chatting kept him in a cocoon.

When he didn't sleep, he thought about Henry. He didn't truly know the man who had helped raise him since his father's death. The man who had barely survived the crash that killed his mother. The realization sent a twisting chill down his spine. After his own dad died, Henry had been a rock of constancy in his life. Strong when Luke was weak, focused when Luke drifted. He was the one who always believed in Luke; the gentle man who'd married late in life and seemed both surprised and grateful to fate for having given him a special friend, and son, in Luke.

Had it all—every sign of support, every gesture of kindness, every encouragement—simply been the cruelest and most calculated of lies? What kind of monster was Henry?

I'm going to uncover the truth about you, Luke thought. *Every awful truth.* No matter what it would take, no matter what he would have to do.

The next day, he arrived in Chicago at three in the afternoon; the bus had been delayed extra hours in Memphis. Luke felt exhausted and grimy. The bus station near downtown Chicago was busier than Luke had expected. He saw young mothers, soldiers, older couples, single men. He could vanish into the crowd, get his bearings. Then figure out a way to find Eric and to see if he could learn anything useful from ChicagoChris.

His nerves felt as taut as a violin string. Now he would be playing someone he knew to be dangerous, maybe even homicidal; possibly someone who was part of the Night Road. This could be a lion's den. It could be a trap. He felt almost like bouncing on the balls of his feet, getting into a fighter's stance, trying to cut past the fatigue to force himself to be smart.

Luke headed toward the doors on Harrison Street, navigating through the crowds of people arriving and departing, and a hand closed around his arm. He jerked away, nearly falling over. The man who held his arm was young, head shaved bald, an intense glare burning behind his clunky glasses.

"You're Lookout." He steered Luke out into the bright sunshine of the street. ChicagoChris was shorter than Luke, with a brow furrowed as if in constant worry or anxiousness or anger. Pale lips and eyes of light hazel gave his face an unfinished look. His teeth shone, tilelike, in his tense grin and Luke thought, *I bet you got teased about that grill.* He wore a black leather jacket and a black T-shirt with a raised fist in gaudy red. "You made it!"

"Um. Yes." Luke had not expected him to show up at the bus station, but why shouldn't the guy? He'd paid the ticket, he knew the itinerary, he'd been promised information in return.

"I'm glad my money was helpful."

"I'll pay you back as soon as I can."

"Your face is all over the news, Luke. You can't be out here. Let's go."

He knows you're Luke Dantry. Luke didn't want to go—he wanted to find Eric and Aubrey's trail. His reluctance must have shown on his face because Chris unveiled a harder diamond smile and said, "Of course, I could scream out to all these nice people that I found you. The cops would be here in no time."

"That's not necessary," Luke said.

"Glad we agree. Let's go. I've got an art studio over in Wicker Park. We can talk there."

"Wicker Park." He had heard of it. "Very hip, right?" If this guy had a high-end address and money to risk sending to online friends, he must be a successful artist. So why would he be spending his time posting hate and anarchy and revolution? What was he so angry about?

"Wicker's so ancient now," Chris said. "It's all going corporate."

Feeling like he had no choice, Luke followed Chris to a car. A polished new Porsche. They pulled away from the bus terminal and headed north, past downtown. Luke stayed low in the seat, wondering if Chris was the only extremist he'd found who drove a rich man's car.

The Texarkana barkeep finally said to his wife, over cigarettes and coffee, before going in for his next evening's shift: "That young man on TV. The one who shot the homeless guy down in Houston."

"Who?" She did not follow the news much; she found it depressing, and the recent chlorine attack in Ripley had only confirmed her pessimism.

He told her what he had seen on the news and that one of his customers from a day ago sure looked like that young man. "He wore sunglasses inside. Weird unless you're blind."

"Maybe he was blind."

"It's preying on my mind, I should call the police," the barkeep said.

"I seriously doubt you saw a fugitive," the wife said. Her practicality was a gift to the marriage. "I mean, all the bars in the world, and he comes into yours. While there's a news story on about him. Please."

"He's got to be somewhere when the news is on. I can't quit dwelling on it. He had a knapsack. We get business when the buses come in the late afternoon."

"A fugitive on a bus. I thought they always stole cars."

"That's the movies. Do I call the police or the FBI?"

"The FBI," she said. "If you saw him, he's already crossed a state line. No one runs to Texarkana and stops." She lit another cigarette, watched him stand before the phone as though deciding on a vote. She gave him a gentle nudge, for the sake of family peace. What harm would a phone call do? "If you're right, and they catch him, you'll be on CNN this week. Of course, there'll be no living with you then." She loved him a lot and she smiled.

The idea pleased the barkeep, but he just made a grunt, and he picked up the phone and opened the phone book. "I'll call the cops first. Out of respect. Cops come into the bar and I've never seen an FBI agent there."

The wife shrugged, went back to proofing their teenage daughter's essay on *Alice in Wonderland* for her English class, only half listening to her husband start to tell his silly, overwrought suspicions.

16

Chris worked near the heart of Wicker Park, not far from the Damen train station, in an old building converted into retail on the first floor and office and loft space above. The exquisite ironwork sign mounted on the brickwork read BENNINGTON GALLERY. Next door stood an open-air coffee shop, with idlers on laptops soaking up the nice sunny day. On the other side was a high-end martial arts center that looked like a Japanese spa. Behind the building, Chris eased the Porsche into a reserved parking spot below an old iron fire escape. As they walked inside a nervous doe of a woman hurried toward them. She was in her forties, dressed all in black, skinny as a teenager, with an elfin face that looked like a kinder version of Chris's stony stare.

"Hi, Chris, sweetheart," she said. "Is this a friend of yours?" She gave Luke an uncertain smile that seemed to beg him to be Chris's friend. But almost like she wasn't sure she wanted to meet any friend of Chris's. A conflict of emotions swirled on her face.

Chris's eyes hardened at the word *sweetheart* and he said, "Yeah, he's a friend, and fuck the hell off, Mom."

Luke froze. He had fought plenty with his mother through the years, but he never would have dreamed of speaking to her that way. Chris's mother's smile wavered and then withered but didn't entirely vanish. Chris gave his own little smile as if to say: *Just what I expected.*

"I'm sorry," Luke said. He didn't know why he was apologizing, but he felt someone must. "I'm Warren, it's nice to meet you." He gave his father's name again.

"Nice to meet you," the woman said, and hurried off, toward a wall of multicolored smears of abstract art. No customers were waiting. She'd simply retreated from her son's ugliness.

"She's useless," Chris said. "Come on. My studio's up here."

"This is your mom's place?"

"Yeah," Chris said grudgingly.

The irony that she was providing Chris studio space above her gallery, when it could probably command a substantial rent, was not lost on Luke. The whole interchange had the feel of a high schooler mouthing off to his mom, trying to look cool in front of a new friend and revealing that he was simply an insecure jerk. But Luke said nothing.

Chris had five locks on the door and it took him a minute to work all the keys.

Five locks, Luke thought. *What are you up to that you need five locks?*

Inside, the studio—which doubled as a living space, with an unmade bed shoved in a corner—smelled of paint, of stale coffee and weed, of unwashed shirts. Exposed brick walls and clean skylights were the best features. It was expansive, room for a big talent to spread its wings, but the art Chris painted was very bad. Angry. Smears of red and black, a brown earth hanging above a closing red hand, penciled figures of suburbanites running from flowering napalm fires. Ugly, Luke thought. Another painting showed an array of fists, connected with a spider's web of lines, flame arcing along the threads. A graffiti swirl of paint, spelling an obscenity in cheerful rainbow colors, in a font favored for children's books. A final one, two teenagers, scowling, fire erupting from their heads as though they were volcanoes. The two painted faces looked vaguely familiar, but he couldn't place them.

"Nice." Luke didn't know what else to say and he was afraid to make no comment at all on the art. How did one compliment death? Did this crap sell?

"*Nice?* It's not at all supposed to be . . . nice." Chris's face reddened.

"I'm sorry. I meant to say it looks accomplished. Insightful. Compelling. Forgive my exhaustion."

Chris took a deep breath, as if drinking in the praise through a straw. "I'm influenced by the photojournalism of war, and I transpose that on an American setting."

"I'm sure they must sell well," Luke lied.

"Hell, no. They'll never sell. They'll be recognized as great art one day, but not while our diseased culture remains."

"How do you pay the bills?"

"My dad builds homes. Thousands of them." Chris smirked. "You can't believe the waste you see in the modern suburban home. The sheer extravagance of it all. Money that could feed half the world." He shook his head.

"Well, but people need houses," Luke said.

A light flared in Chris's stare. "Build large apartment buildings. Much more convenient, much less ecological impact. Burn the cities to the ground, man, and stack the apartments high. Much less waste."

"That's grim," Luke said. "You would have been a good architect in the Soviet Union." He wandered past the paintings and as he turned back to Chris, Chris was less than a foot away, a devil's curling smile on his face.

"After I help you," Chris snapped, "are you laughing at me?"

"No. Not at all. I'm sorry." He'd made a misstep. Chris didn't carry the single-minded stare that he'd seen in Snow and Mouser. The light in his eyes was something entirely different in its heat. He had to make Chris tell him what he needed to know, but carefully. "I'm really surprised you trusted me with the money. You don't know me."

"I know your words. That's the same, to me." Chris lit a cigarette, offered the pack to Luke, who shook his head. His anger seemed gone, as quick as a snap of fingers. "So. What's the information you have about the wreck in Ripley?"

"It was a bomb."

"Old news. Next?" He smiled. "I bet you know who put it there."

"Yes," Luke lied. "The government." He thought this story was exactly the kind of meat that Chris liked to chew.

"Ah. And you have proof of this, in exchange for my many kindnesses to you?"

"I think I can find the proof. If I had the right kind of help."

"Help."

"I need to know if you're part of a . . . group that can help me."

"Group."

"The Night Road."

"You want to know if I'm part of the Night Road." He looked, to Luke's astonishment, as if he might laugh.

"Yes."

"That's a really good lie," Chris said. "Better than I expected."

"I'm not lying. I—"

"I want in."

"In what?"

"In whatever group you're a part of. Is it called the Night Road? I like it, kind of a twist on the Shining Path. The Peruvian terror group. They've lasted a good long time."

Luke blinked. He'd made a misstep. "I'm not part of any group. I thought your group could help me."

"I don't care for liars. You know what I mean. The group your stepfather is putting together."

Luke crossed his arms. "You *know* him?" Oh, God, what if he'd contacted Henry, told him Luke was coming here?

"Yeah." Chris exhaled a stream of smoke. "I joined the online groups because no one believed as I did. None of my family, none of the people I tried to be friends with—" He caught himself and said, "None of my friends. But you don't really belong to anything in this world. The people in the Internet groups, they're nothing but talk, sound and fury, signifying very little indeed." He pointed out the painting of the fists connected by lines of fire. "That's what the online communities should be, fire and action and burning this dirty nasty world to ash so we, the right and noble people, can start again, but they aren't." Now he turned his gaze to Luke and Luke's blood chilled. This guy, he realized, wasn't just angry, he was clinically crazy. The triumph in Chris's eyes was bent, wrong, ugly. "The new group you're in, you're shutting me out now. That just won't do." The smile slid back onto the white mouth.

"I told you, I'm not part of any group." He was suddenly more scared of this guy than he had been in the cottage kitchen with Mouser. Chris's soft, false grin was a mask for a different, twisted darkness.

"Your stepfather contacted me, Luke. A month ago. Wanted to meet me for coffee near the airport. I recognized him from CNN yesterday, talking about you."

A thrum of horror touched Luke's chest. "Did he say why he wanted to meet you?" This was it, proof that Henry had taken Luke's research—and personally reached out to the extremists. And he'd pissed this one off.

"He found me through the IP address I used to post from. He said he admired the beauty and logic of my arguments. My passion. It's not the kind of invite I get every day. I went and I had coffee with him. He wore a heavy cap, and different glasses, and he spoke with a Southern accent he seems to have lost when on television. But it's him."

"But it didn't go well."

"I can see judgment in the eyes of lesser people. I'm a threat to folks, their sense of security. Because I'm smarter and more talented. Mother tells me everyone's jealous. It explains a lot. But I wasn't good enough for him." The awkward happiness he'd shown earlier was gone, replaced by a simmering fury. "Can you imagine?"

He was a threat because he was crazy, Luke realized. Not focused, not disciplined like Mouser or Snow. The army doesn't want the crazies, neither does the Night Road. Crazies are a risk.

Chris had not been invited to the party.

Luke looked past Chris's shoulder, searching for a weapon, a way to defend himself. His gaze fell again on the paintings: the fists bound in a web, the two sullen teens. With a wrench of his gut he recognized their faces. The Columbine gunmen. "Maybe my stepfather didn't properly assess your potential contribution."

"He wanted to know if I'd ever thought of turning my words to action. Did I have computer skills? Was I able to get money easily? Did I have contacts in the drug world? Please. I don't cloud my head with drugs. I'm a decent guy who's just sick of hypocrisy. And I guess being a painter just isn't enough." The sneer deepened. "I never heard from him again. If he was contacting me about world-changing work, it stands to reason he was contacting others. People he'd found on the discussion boards who can make a difference. So."

"So."

"You're valuable to him. You're my invitation into his private club."

Luke took a step backward. "You're wrong. Dead wrong."

"You beg me for help, and now you won't help me. Story of my life." His anger turned into a pleading whine. "I could be of real value to you guys. I can help you change the world. I could finally . . ." He stopped and in Luke's head he heard the sad simple truth: *I could have friends.*

What was it like when even the fringes rejected you? He saw an abyss in Chris's anguished stare.

"I am really, really tired of being told I'm not good enough. I caught you when no one else could. So let's you and me call your stepfather, and see what we can work out."

Luke closed the three steps and he slammed his fist into Chris's jaw. It surprised them both. Chris crumpled and the pain from the blow rocketed up Luke's arm. "Did you tell my stepdad I was coming here?" Luke yelled.

Chris fingered blood from the corner of his mouth. "You hit me. You *can't* hit me." He sounded like a first-grader, outraged by a breach of playground etiquette.

"Answer me."

"Yeah. I sold your ass. I give you back, I get in the Night Road, I get to show how I can shine." He glanced at his watch. "They should be here for you soon. I just wanted you to know I'm much smarter than you. Much smarter than they are."

"You're insane."

Slowly Chris got to his feet, as though feeling his arms and legs for the first time. "The martial arts studio next door. They teach krav maga. You know the beauty of krav maga."

"Now you're raving."

He gave a disgusted huff. "Krav maga is Israeli self-defense. I joined because when the war comes, I wanted to be ready. People said I fought like I enjoyed it too much. They kicked me out." He rolled his eyes at this bit of insanity. "But I learned enough to break your bones. You're not going anywhere."

And he rushed at Luke.

17

The first series of precise blows sent Luke reeling across the scattered sketches on Chris's table. His face, already bruised from Mouser's blows, hurt bone-deep. He was going to get the snot beaten out of him by this freak.

"No quarter is given in krav maga," Chris said, with the calm of a lecturer. He paused to pick Luke up, hammer his chest and face with a flurry of fists, and shove him hard toward the scrawled paintings.

Luke crashed into the bad art and a table of paint supplies. He blinked past the pain in his jaw and his chest, and saw Chris sauntering toward him, snapping fingers, dancing on the balls of his feet. Luke's hands fumbled for an improvised weapon. His fingertips roamed across brushes, spilled water bottles, a dried, dirty palette. His hand closed on a metal canister.

A spray paint can.

"I'm necessary," Chris said. "To be given a high place in the emerging order. Everyone then will know my name. Know my art. Know my—"
Luke's back was to Chris and as Chris lifted a foot to hammer a kick into Luke, Luke spun and fired a jet of red. A scarlet mist caught Chris in the face. He howled and lurched back. Crimson frosted his eyeglasses and Luke slammed a chair into his chest. Twice, hard. Chris fell.

"They'll know," Luke spat, "you don't know when to shut the hell up." He ran for the door with the five locks. He pulled on the knob, but it held fast. He had to get out of here. This guy was nuts and maybe Mouser and Snow were on their way.

Looking at the garish paintings, he hadn't noticed Chris lock the door behind him. He flipped the dead bolts. Still the door was locked. It required a key.

"You're not leaving." Chris staggered to his feet. Bleeding hard from his nose, like Luke was. Smiling through blood and red paint. "Not when you're my ticket to glory, man."

"Give me the keys," Luke said.

Chris fell against a table and Luke could see a huge splinter from the chair lodged near his ear, creating a bloody mess.

Luke charged toward him.

Chris yanked a drawer open.

Luke thought it would be a gun. Chris wouldn't rely on fists now that he'd been hurt. Luke saw the fire escape on the other side of the window and ran for it.

A trio of shots shattered the open window seconds after he stepped out onto the fire escape and bounded down the stairs. Glass hit his hair. The sound was loud, bright in the afternoon air, cutting through the hubbub of traffic sounds of Wicker Park. He clattered down the fire escape and dropped onto the hood of Chris's Porsche, denting it with his weight.

He heard Chris howl above him like a wounded creature.

Luke bolted out into a wide street, stumbling into the path of a taxicab, which berated him with a long-drawn honk of the horn. He broke into a hard run. He had to get off the street before Chris saw him. He ran behind another squat building, decorated with garish neon, into a web of alleyways. Turn right, turn left, he came up behind a bakery that gave off a motherly scent of chocolate and almonds and a corner bar, open early for happy hour.

At the end of the alley was a construction fence. Luke scrambled over it and he heard the wail of a siren. Police. Fear opened like a fist in his chest. Someone had called, probably reporting Chris's shots.

He ran through a passageway that backed a block's worth of restaurants and storefronts. He thought of hiding inside a Dumpster, but hiding might mean capture. He had to get free and clear of the neighborhood.

At the end of the alley, fronting onto a quiet street, a police patrol car wheeled past. Luke ducked behind a Dumpster. Peered around its edge.

The police car was gone.

He ran from the Dumpster's shadow and tried a doorknob. Locked. He ran down to another door. Tested it. It opened onto a small kitchen way. Two men, short, Latino, glanced up from scraping a grill. Hamburger perfumed the air and he heard a radio playing a murmur of Spanish music.

"Sorry, sorry," he said, sidling past them, and one of the cooks said, "What the hell, this isn't the front door," in rapid Spanish.

Luke ignored him and hurried out onto the dining room floor. The restaurant was a small, spotless diner, a few tables, a chalkboard announcing burgers, sandwiches, a lunch special of meat loaf and garlic mashed potatoes. A few late lunchers sat huddled at the tables, including most of the waitstaff. A waitress was erasing the boards to write the dinner specials.

Luke ran past her and the smells of comfort food and out onto a street. This avenue was busier, filled with cafés, a scattering of funky clothing shops, an Irish pub.

The police car turned back onto the street, toward him. He stepped into the nearest business, a small flower shop. The air was thick with the smell of blossoms and clean water. No one stood at the counter but the door's attached bells jingled his arrival.

He saw a heavy plastic curtain—behind it were large plastic containers of cut flowers. He moved past the curtain, headed toward the back door.

The front door jangled behind him.

"Hi, Officer, can I help you—" he heard a voice say on the other side of the curtain. Then silence.

The police had seen him come in. They were looking for him. Or his movements had incurred suspicion. He reached the back door, eased it open, closed it behind him. Through a small window he saw the officer move into position on the other side of the window.

He stumbled into the alley; it was already shadowed, the afternoon light dying in the narrow passage.

"Officers!" Chris practically screamed in his ear. "Here he is!" His face was red with the slash of paint. He closed arms around Luke.

"He shot up my studio, he's nuts!" Chris screeched through his painted clown's grin.

"Police! Stop!" The cop hurried out into the alley.

Luke froze. "Help me," he said. "This guy tried to shoot me."

The officer took a measured look at Luke's face, seemed to study the hair, the bruises. "Luke Jameson Dantry. On the ground, now." The officer barked his orders.

Luke obeyed. "I'm unarmed," he said. "He fired the shots, sir, not me."

"Just like a criminal," Chris said. "He's lying. I caught him."

"You on the ground too," the cop ordered.

Chris obeyed.

Luke felt the officer patting him down, heard the clink of cuffs being removed from a belt. It took him back to the horrors of the bed in the cabin. "No, I don't want to be handcuffed. Please, please don't, I'm not the bad guy here." His voice rose into a yell. He yanked one hand away, buried it under his chest.

The officer fought to regain control of Luke's arms. "Stop resisting! Are you Luke Jameson Dantry?" the officer yelled.

"Yes, sir, and I have information on a dangerous group of people. Please don't, please don't cuff me, please—"

The officer started yelling into his shoulder mike, still trying to slap the cuffs on Luke while Luke bucked and kicked. Luke turned his head and saw a figure at the end of the alley.

Snow. Smiling at him.

Luke screamed, "Officer, look out!"

Her hand came up and Luke didn't see the gun, but the short sharp *th-weet*s were loud in the shadowed alley. The cop dropped midsentence, two holes painting his face. The blood hit Luke's hands and he retreated behind the trash cans.

Done, a snap of the fingers. Luke could hear her walking toward him, the click of her boots on the pavement. Not rushing, because she didn't know if Chris was armed. He felt he could read her mind, understand her approach.

"You're Chris, right?" he heard Snow say as she came forward. Friendliness in the tone.

"Yes, I am." Chris stood, with ugly triumph. His genius had finally been recognized. "Are you here to help me?"

"Baby, I am," Snow said, and she shot him.

Chris collapsed against the Dumpster. As he died the surprise faded from his eyes, replaced by the blankness of a world without anger.

"Come on, Schoolboy, time to go home," she said as she approached.

Luke saw the policeman's service piece, still holstered, and yanked the gun free.

He fired a blast at Snow, wide, then fired again as she took cover behind a pile of discarded pallets. The second bullet caught her—he saw her shoulder jerk, saw a stain on her jacket. She didn't scream. She gritted her teeth, like he'd only dealt her a wasp's sting. He aimed again, fired, and turned and ran down the alley. He vaulted a fence to the other side of the street.

Her bullets powered into the fence, a bare inch from his hands as he went over the top.

He fell onto the wooden fence's other side and ran.

He kept running, for six more blocks. No sign of her. He'd wounded her so badly she couldn't give chase.

Sirens pierced the air. In a deserted alley Luke threw the policeman's gun in a trash can. If he got caught holding a dead cop's gun . . .

He found a discarded newspaper and wiped the blood from his hands and his face. He could hear the rumble of an elevated train—Chicago's answer to the subway—and he ran until he saw the Damen station.

He fed money into a machine and it spit a card pass at him. *My God. She killed a cop. I hope I killed her.* The realization cut past the pain from the shrapnel. *The officer radioed they had me—knew my name—and now he's dead.*

Luke stumbled onto a Blue Line train headed toward the Loop. Insanity. The officer was just doing his job. The entire city's police force would be hunting Luke with an intensity he could barely imagine. He could not long evade their search. He sat down and studied the train's map. His hands shook and he thought he might vomit when the train braked and then lurched back into motion. He tried not to look at anyone. No one seemed interested in him. He looked a little rough and grimy and no one wanted trouble, avoiding eye contact with him.

What now?

He had one choice, and he had to get there before Snow and Mouser. Eric Lindoe. He had to find him.

Luke did not know Chicago well and he was unsure how to reach Eric's bank. He got off at a station downtown. He wandered into a bookstore and used the coffee bar's Internet connection to find Eric's business address at the private bank. It was on LaSalle Avenue, in the Financial District.

Ten minutes later, he stood outside Eric's office in the fading sunlight. A news vendor nearby had a radio playing, and Luke drifted close enough to hear a report of a police shooting. An officer and a civilian down.

Only two. Chris was for sure dead. Which meant that he had only winged Snow, and she had slipped away. Every inch of his skin went cold. He kept seeing the officer's face, a man just doing his job, and now dead for it. He pulled out the cheap cell phone he'd bought in Braintree, called 911, gave the operator a brief and precise description of Snow and Mouser as the shooters. Then he dismantled the phone, dropping its guts into the trash.

I'll make them pay for you, Officer, Luke thought.

Luke's stomach rumbled. He bought a mustard-smeared hot dog and an apple juice from a street vendor and he ate the food without tasting it. Three bites into the dog, Eric Lindoe—kidnapper and murderer—hurried out of the high-windowed glass lobby of the skyscraper, glanced at his watch, and walked away. He wore a long coat, a cap pulled low over his face, dark glasses, and a look of utter guilt.

Luke followed him.

18

Eric Lindoe stepped onto the third car of a Brown Line train. Staying well back, Luke stepped onto the fourth car, nestled close to the doors. He hoped that at each stop he could step out to see if Eric disembarked.

The first stop Luke eased out a foot onto the platform, pretending to make way for departing passengers, holding the door. He got a couple of thank-yous, which was more attention than he liked.

Eric stayed on the car. So did Luke.

More stops; the train headed north. The woman next to him had a smartphone; she was reading CNN's news feed on it. Luke glanced at it over her shoulder. All bad news but worse than usual. An explosion in Canada had ruptured and shut down an oil pipeline. A recall of a million pounds of ground beef from a plant in Tennessee after several people in twelve states got sick yesterday with *E. coli;* a note sent to the local paper claimed the poisoning had been deliberate, an attack on the American food system. Authorities said they had no proof, yet, of malicious intent. A young actress of note was in rehab. The "Houston hobo" shooting, with its unexpected tie to a Washington power player's son, remained unsolved. A Chicago police officer and a bystander had been shot and killed an hour ago in Wicker Park.

His story.

The woman kept her back to him but she sensed his uncomfortable closeness and he saw her back stiffen. He moved away, locked his gaze to the floor. The police would dig into Chris's mess of a life, and find that Chris had sent money to buy a bus ticket, and the authorities would figure out the recipient had been Luke. Chris's mother would not remember her son's cruelties, but rather Luke's face. And Chris and the officer lay dead together in an alley.

He could not let Eric slip through his fingers. He had to force him to tell the truth.

Because, Luke knew, his life was *gone*. Destroyed, mangled in a way that could not be set right again. If he had self-destructed—turned away from a woman he loved, become a drunk, lost himself in work and neglected the rest of his life—then the fracturing of his life would have been easier to accept. But this? He had no idea why he had been destroyed. No idea why a man who called him son had used him and betrayed him so deeply. He had no trail to follow except Eric's. If he lost Eric now, in the crowd, or because someone recognized Luke and grabbed him, he was finished.

The train stopped at the Armitage station. Eric rushed out, surrounded by a pool of other commuters, from the third car.

He would have to walk past Luke to reach the ground exit.

Luke hung back and followed, letting Eric storm a good ten feet ahead of him. The flock of commuters marched from the elevated platform to a metal stairway. Eric headed down and Luke risked drawing closer—only five people separating him from his kidnapper. If Eric glanced over his shoulder he would see Luke.

Eric reached Armitage Avenue, went through the exit gate. Luke stopped behind a pillar and waited, watched Eric hesitate—and then Eric crossed the street, under the elevated rails, dismissing the jeer of annoyed car honks with a polite, gentlemanly wave of his hand.

Luke followed, staying on the opposite side of Armitage, trying to keep him in view, trying not to be noticed. Thin trees stood on his side of the street and he tried to stay close to them, not be noticed, feeling vulnerable as he tracked Eric.

Lincoln Park—banners on the streetlights announced the neighborhood's name—was a well-heeled neighborhood, high on the charm factor. Storefronts, nice retail and restaurants, with apartments and offices on the higher floors. Eric turned into a small candy shop. Luke fought the urge to stop. He walked on, risking a single glance back. No Eric. Luke stopped at the end of the block. He felt horribly conspicuous just standing there. Five minutes passed. He walked back another half-block toward the candy store, paused to study the posted menu on an Italian bistro. When he dared a glance over his shoulder he saw Eric six steps out from the candy store—*Thank God I didn't cross the street,* Luke thought—heading on his original course. A bag of candies in his hand. Eric walked, glancing down at his phone, tapping out a number with his thumb. Luke let him pass his position, careful to keep his back turned.

When Luke turned back, Eric was gone, as though the street had swallowed him whole.

Panic clutched Luke's chest. He scanned the street again. Eric was tall. He couldn't have vanished off the street.

Luke scanned the storefronts. A wine store, a small bookshop, women's clothing boutiques, a fancy kids' clothing store. Eric could have gone into any of them. He could be watching Luke from any of them.

Luke retreated into the doorway of a small bar. He could hear the thrum of music. He checked his watch. Two men moved past Luke, laughing, and opened the bar door, letting a blast of sound, a jangle of folksy guitars, and laughter rise from inside.

Eric stepped out of the wine shop. A neat paper bag in his hands. He didn't glance over at Luke; he was fifteen feet ahead of him and across the street.

Candy and wine. Luke wondered if Eric was going to spend an evening with Aubrey. Had he simply stepped back into his normal life after murder and kidnapping?

Luke walked slowly, trying to keep a few cars in the diagonal angle between him and Eric. He crossed the street, dodging traffic. He gained on Eric, hurrying now, not running.

He got up five feet behind him, but he couldn't grab him on the street. People would notice. And maybe he still had the gun he had kept at Luke's throat and ribs.

Eric spoke into his phone. "Yeah, a large vegetarian, thin crust. Yeah. For Crosby, Grace."

Grace Crosby. Luke remembered the name—the young blogger who had raised the alarm that Aubrey was missing; it was the clue that had led him to Chicago.

Eric turned into a side street and Luke dropped back, let Eric walk ahead. He had gotten too close. A gaggle of young women—early twenties, loud, laughing, stylish and they knew it—walked between him and Eric, and he used them as camouflage crossing the street. The women peeled away, heading down Armitage toward an Italian restaurant.

Eric walked up a stone flight of stairs into a condo building.

Luke followed.

Eric vanished into the entryway. Luke hurried to the bottom of the stairs and counted to ten. He walked up slowly. He couldn't see into the building's entryway; the glass was leaded and shaded.

An array of buttons announced the residents' last names. Crosby was listed.

He could buzz in twenty minutes, pretend to be the pizza guy. But if he timed it wrong, if the pizza guy arrived while he was heading up the stairs or trying to find the right condo . . . he considered. He might not have enough time to make it. Then Eric would be on guard. Better to wait, not get caught in a time trap.

The pizza guy came up the side street twenty minutes later. Indian, looking harried, snuffling like he was losing a battle against a cold.

The pizza guy hurried up the steps and Luke took a chance.

"You got a pie for Crosby?"

"Uh, yeah."

Luke flashed a twenty and a ten. "It's mine."

The pizza guy looked again at the slip. "You don't look like a Grace."

"I'm a Greg. They keyed my name in wrong and they've never fixed it. How much?"

"I'm supposed to deliver it to the door."

"Well, then, you can follow me on up. I called it in on my way home, got scared you'd beat me here." You're talking too much, Luke thought. He stuck the money out.

The pizza guy took it, started digging for change.

"You can keep it," Luke said. "And tell them it's Greg, not Grace."

"Sure, sir, thanks." Luke made a show of opening the box, inspecting the pie. A waft of fragrant steam stroked his face and he breathed in the scent of mushrooms, olives, and garlic.

The slip read CROSBY GRACE APT 404.

He glanced over his shoulder, made sure the delivery guy was hurrying back to his car and was out of earshot. He pressed *Crosby* on the callboard.

Long silence and then Aubrey's voice, burned into his brain, the voice that had bugged Eric Lindoe to spare his life. "Yes?"

He glanced at the slip. "Romano's Pizza, ma'am."

"Come on up." She sounded tired. The door buzzed and he pushed his weight against it.

The foyer was tiny and tiled and the only sound was the huff of his own breathing.

He ignored the small elevator and headed up the stairs, considering his plan of attack. His hair was a different color; he wore sunglasses. Through a peephole, expecting to see a pizza deliveryman, would she recognize him? He thought of holding the pizza box at such an angle that it masked part of his face, but that would look suspicious. And if Eric came to the door, he'd recognize Luke, no doubt. They'd spent far too much time together.

He kept up the stairs, reaching the fourth—and top—floor. The hallway bent in regular ninety-degree angles. The walls boasted new paint but the carpet appeared worn. From behind the door of the apartment closest to the stairway he heard a low thump, then a woman's voice saying, "Turn it off, boys, dinner's ready." He found 404. He crept up to the door and listened. He heard the soft murmur of the television, turned to local news—no sound of conversation. It was one of two apartments tucked into the corner of the hallway. The irregular grouping of doors suggested some apartments were larger than others.

It gave him an idea.

The closest apartment to 404 was 405 and he tiptoed toward the door. He pressed his ear against the wood and listened hard. No sound of television, music, or movement. He knocked, lightly, hopeful that neither Eric nor Aubrey would hear.

No answer.

He risked a louder knock.

No answer.

He stationed himself leaning against the wall. Back toward 404, slouching a bit, pizza held aloft. "Piz-za!" he announced with a louder knock. "Piz-za, hello!"

No answer, but he heard the door to 404—ten feet behind him—creak open.

"Hey, that's ours." Eric. He sounded tired, too.

"Piz-za," Luke repeated, keeping his back to Eric, slouching against the door frame. He cussed softly in garbled words, hoping he sounded vaguely Russian or Serbian. He wanted Eric to think he was a confused immigrant, new to making deliveries.

He heard the whisper of feet on carpet. "You're at the wrong door, dude, that's our pizza," Eric said.

Luke turned and let the surprise dawn onto Eric's face.

Then he powered his fist into Eric's gut. Hard. Eric bent, stumbled onto the dropped pizza box, and Luke hit him again, square in the jaw. Pain bit into his fist.

Eric staggered back and aimed his own fist at Luke's face. Hit Luke's jaw. Luke fell against the wall, heard shattering glass. He reached into the broken fire-extinguisher holder. He pulled out the extinguisher and slammed it into Eric's face, heard the crunch. Eric fell back, blood gushing from nose and mouth. Moaning.

Luke seized him by the throat and bum-rushed him into Aubrey's apartment. He kicked the door closed.

The condo was small and neat. Most of it had a minimalist, sleek feel— clean woods and chrome, a geometric rug on the floor, blotchy modern art on the walls. A framed photo on the mantel of a couple, not Aubrey and Eric. Across the living room was a small kitchen and Aubrey stepped into the doorway, a glass of red wine in her hand.

She dropped the glass; it shattered at her feet with a plum spray.

"You scream or run and I swear to God I'll bash his head in." Luke still had the fire extinguisher, and he hoisted it to club Eric.

"Don't hurt him," she said. "Please." Fright whitened her cheeks. "What the hell are you doing here?"

"Who else is here?" Luke asked.

"No one," Aubrey answered. She looked tired but lovely, the grime of her ordeal gone. She wore jeans and a black sweater and her dark hair was pulled back into a ponytail.

"Where's Grace Crosby?"

"With her husband; he's a lawyer. At a conference in Detroit. Gone through the weekend. We decided to hide here."

Hide. "Where's Eric's gun?"

She glanced at Eric. Her voice had a warm rasp to it. "Chicago River. I made him get rid of it."

"Please," Eric said. "Please just leave us alone."

"You have to be kidding me. Leave you alone?" Luke forced Eric against the wall, frisked him under the suit jacket. No gun.

Eric tried to jerk away. Luke swung the extinguisher and it caromed hard off Eric's head, into the wall, and back against his skull. Eric fell into a crouch, clutching his head.

Luke glanced up. Aubrey was gone. He bolted through the dining room and saw the bedroom door starting to slam. He kicked it open; the wood splintered above the knob. But she didn't fold, pushing the door back toward him. He squeezed through, grabbed the back of her sweater as she lunged for the phone.

He clamped a hand over her mouth to keep her scream locked in her jaws.

"Eric kidnapped me," he hissed in her ear as he hauled her, kicking, back down the hall. She was wiry-strong, determined, and she knocked him against the wall twice before he got the leverage to muscle her down the hallway.

Eric still was in the apartment. He could have run and he hadn't. Not without Aubrey, Luke saw. Eric stood on unsteady feet and raised a bloody hand. "Don't hurt her."

"I don't want to hurt anyone. Aubrey!" Luke yelled; she'd nearly wrenched loose from his grasp. "Stop it—you *know* he kidnapped me to rescue you. I was your ransom."

Now she grew still.

"You know what else he did?"

Eric wiped his face with the sleeve of his suit. "Aubrey, he's a liar. I told you what kind of guy he is. You know how much I risked to save you—"

"He grabbed me at the Austin airport. He threatened to shoot a family if I yelled for help. Forced me to drive to Houston and he shot a helpless man dead in the street. Shot him in cold blood"—Aubrey moaned into the cup of his hand, started struggling against him—"and *then* he got a phone call telling him where you were. And you know he left me in your place."

Aubrey went still.

"Aubrey, don't listen. . . . I did it all for you." Eric's words cracked like falling china.

"Yes, he did. He did it all. Every rotten thing I've described."

"You know what he is, Aubrey!"

"Tell me, what am I, Aubrey?" Luke's palm was just above her mouth and the feather of her breath tickled his skin.

"I don't know anything—he didn't tell me anything—please just leave us alone."

"I know you think he saved you," Luke said. "Fine. He's your hero. I don't care. But he has to tell the police about what he did. . . ."

Eric started shaking his head, fury and hate in his face.

"You have to. We go to the police together, we tell them everything about the Night Road. I've been running like hell since I got away from that cabin. And I'm done. This is the only way to save us both, Eric. We're going to the police. Together."

"No. No."

Luke glanced at Aubrey. "Did he tell you why you were kidnapped?"

Aubrey nodded. "A woman wanted access to money from accounts he controls. But he doesn't control the money, your stepfather does."

"Money. Fifty million dollars that belongs to some very very bad people. They're tied to an extremist network that might be responsible for the train bombing down in Texas."

"He—he . . ." Aubrey blinked, glanced at Eric.

"It's okay, baby." Eric put his bloodied face in his hands.

"Don't call me 'baby.'" she said, and Luke saw her words sliced into his heart.

Luke knelt by Eric. "This Jane woman—who is she, how does she know about you and my stepfather?"

"I don't know, obviously, or I would have called the police. She said Aubrey would be killed if I didn't do what she said, and I'd do anything for Aubrey. Anything." He shoved his whole world into that word. *Anything.*

Aubrey stiffened under the grip of Luke's arm. She looked confused. Eric had lied to her to protect himself as her rescuing knight, and Luke was going to have to destroy the illusion.

"Aubrey"—Luke made his voice quiet—"I don't want to hurt you or even him—"

"Just—leave Aubrey out of this. I'll go to the cops with you. I'll talk. Just leave her out of this." All the threat, the bravado, seemed gone from Eric. As though, in the time he'd had to contemplate his crimes, shame had found a home. But that didn't mean he still wasn't going to run. Especially if he'd tapped into that fifty million. He would have the resources to vanish and Luke might never find him again.

Don't be fooled, Luke thought. *He is a dangerous guy and now you've cornered him.* "No. She's a witness. She talks too. Otherwise we're the two assholes in a Beemer who killed a defenseless street person and no one can corroborate our story."

"Would you please let me tend to him?" she said.

"No. Talk first. He answers my questions before we go to the cops."

Eric got up from the floor, sat on the sofa, took off his suit coat. He folded the fabric carefully, put it against the blood welling from his face, although the flow had stopped. "I'll buy your friend a new couch, Aubrey, if I get blood on this one."

"For God's sake, Eric." Luke heard a resignation and a soft, quiet grief in her voice. An impatience that he didn't understand. "Just tell him what he wants to know. For my sake."

Eric blinked.

"How are you and my stepfather connected?"

"I got a call from a friend of mine to provide private banking services, to move some money in from overseas. I had no idea it was connected to anything criminal."

Luke wasn't sure he believed that, but Eric wasn't about to damn himself further in Aubrey's eyes; Eric was watching her reactions as closely as he was watching Luke's. "Your stepfather was the contact."

"But you disguised your voice."

"I was ordered to do so. The voice modulator came with the phone Jane sent me after Aubrey was kidnapped."

Why would it matter that Henry not recognize Eric's voice? The reasonable answer was there was an advantage for Jane if Eric was not identified as his kidnapper. Why would Jane care if Eric was known to be the kidnapper? Was Jane now somehow protecting Eric? Who was this bizarre, mysterious woman?

"Aubrey, who grabbed you?" Luke asked.

Aubrey sat next to Eric, put an arm around his shoulder. "I never saw a face. I was leaving my office—working late on my own—and suddenly a burlap sack—it reeked of onions, it's all I really remember—yanked over my head and I felt a needle go into my arm. I woke up tied up in the trunk of a car. Blindfolded. I think I had been unconscious for a very long time. The car stopped"—she hesitated, touched fingertips to temples, as though in pain—"someone dragged me inside that cabin down in Texas, chained me to the bed. The kidnapper left without saying a word. I managed to get the hood off my face. I lay there for—I don't know, maybe a day and a half before you and Eric came. It felt like forever."

"Was the kidnapper a woman, maybe?" Jane might have done her own dirty work.

Aubrey glanced at Eric. "Maybe. I don't know."

"Are you two married?"

Aubrey shook her head. "We'd been dating for several months. We broke up late last week but I guess the kidnappers didn't get the memo."

"We're back together—" Eric started.

"Eric." The word, short and sharp, was like a closing door.

"I never wanted you hurt, or involved," Eric said.

"I never really knew you," Aubrey said. "That's the worst. I never knew what you were capable of."

"You proved your love and lost it all at once." Luke realized that perhaps the same trap had been intended for Henry. The kidnapping had exposed Henry's crimes to Luke, destroyed his vision of his stepfather as a decent man. The ugliness of the truth he'd spoken hung in the air between them.

"Don't whine," Aubrey said. "You can still have my respect, if you'll just be honest. Please. Tell him about this Night Road."

Eric frowned, letting the weight of the world settle on his shoulders. "I don't know exactly what they are. A group of people. A client at the bank ordered me to set up several accounts for them, at different banks around the country. I did so. But Jane wanted all those accounts closed. That was the first part of the ransom, close the accounts. Second was killing the man in Houston. Third, and last, was grabbing you."

He was lying, Luke was sure. "Jane didn't ask you for the money?"

"I didn't have the money yet. Your stepfather controlled it. That's why Jane asked him for it, not me." Eric turned the knife. "You heard him say no, Luke. He put the fifty million ahead of you."

Luke ignored the jab. "Who's this client who had you set up these bank accounts?"

"A company called Travport. They're a cargo aviation firm; they fly all over the world. Entirely respectable."

"Where are they based?"

"Dubai. But owned by Saudis."

Fifty million dollars. For the Night Road. To create chaos and further their agendas. Through violence. Through fear. Through their little wars, and wars needed money like the body needed blood.

For attacks like Ripley. How much terror could fifty million dollars buy? He'd sent Henry six thousand names from his online research. If Henry recruited fifty dedicated radicals for the Night Road, they could each receive a million dollars. How many guns, how many payoffs, how many weapons and explosives, could all that buy? Terrorism was relatively cheap. A million could fund a huge string of attacks. And added all together, fifty million . . .

Horror swept up him like a flame in his gut. "If you were getting accounts ready to put this fifty million in, you must know where the cash is coming from." He was suddenly sure of it. What had Henry said first? "I will not pay." Not *cannot*. I *will* not. "You convinced Jane you didn't have the access, that my stepfather did."

"Henry's the big dog. I'm just hired help."

"Where's the money, Eric? Where's it coming from?" Who would just give fifty million dollars to a bunch of American extremists?

"If I know, then that's my insurance, isn't it? No one can touch the money but me." Eric lifted his chin in defiance.

"You have the money," Luke said slowly.

"Yes. I have it. We can hide anywhere in the world. I'll give you a slice, Luke. We'll all hide. We'll all have a real life again."

"Oh, God, Eric." Aubrey put her face back in her hands. "Just tell us where it is."

"The one thing the money won't protect you from is a murder charge," Luke said. "I can testify you killed that man under duress."

Eric shifted in his seat. "I'm not going to tell you where the money is. You don't need to know."

Luke tried another tack. "Who was the man in Houston you killed?"

"His name is Allen Clifford. I don't know anything else about him. I was just told where he would be, what he would look like. Jane e-mailed me a picture."

Allen Clifford. The name meant nothing to Luke.

He tried to think how Jane could have entered this picture. An extremist network created by Henry, funded by Eric's mysterious corporate client, with the money handed out by Eric. Jane was ruining the Night Road's plans. But who was she? Who else would know about the existence of the Night Road—except people like Chris, who'd been approached and rejected?

Who was Jane?

Luke said, "Give me the phone Jane sent you." Luke held out his hand.

Eric hesitated. "Give it to him," Aubrey said. "Please. He's smart. He's gotten this far, maybe he can figure out who's after us." Eric tossed it to him. Luke caught it.

"I want to know why you haven't already run and hid with this fifty million," Luke said. "You could buy a lot of protection with it. You could cut one of those deals you loved to mention." Luke stopped. "Maybe you already have."

Eric stared at him, an answer starting to form on his lips.

The lights went out.

19

It took three phone calls for Mouser to find the right kind of doctor for Snow. He called Henry and screamed into his voice mail while Snow bled in the backseat. Snow kept laughing.

"I never saw one die," she said. "Bombs put a distance between me and them. But the gun, Jesus, that was cool. I saw it happen!" Then she would scream and laugh and clutch at her shoulder. She never complained.

Quickly, Henry called back, steered him to a doctor on the western edge of downtown Chicago. The doctor's medical license was long suspended because she'd burned through too many prescription pads in a year, and once paroled she was a resource for the gangbangers and the mob when they needed needles and sutures. The doctor worked at a shoddy sandwich joint on a narrow street. Her apartment was above the shop. He carried Snow up the stairs and the doctor met him at the door, still with a hairnet on her head and hands bright with vinegar and oil.

But her demeanor was brisk and efficient and the apartment was spotlessly clean. The doctor helped him get Snow into a small bedroom stuffed with medical gear.

"Outside," the doctor ordered.

"It's gonna be okay," he said to Snow. "I'm going to kill him for you."

"No. I'll kill Schoolboy for me," she whispered.

"I don't wish to hear these promises," the doctor said. "Outside, please, sir."

He realized that he could care about Snow. It was unsettling. He sat on the couch in the apartment and an hour later the doctor emerged. He had been watching the news accounts of the shooting—no mention of Snow or him or anyone fitting their descriptions fleeing the scene.

The doctor dropped a bullet in his hand. "Since you seem sentimental about revenge. She asked you to keep this for her."

"I'll bet she did." Mouser closed his fist around the bullet.

"She needs rest but she will be fine. Bullet in the meat of the shoulder, didn't hit anything major but she's going to be sore for several days. I'll give you a couple of bottles of painkillers and gear to tend the wound. You know how to change a dressing?"

"Yes, ma'am."

"I gave her blood. I keep a stash. Rest will set her straight. Good luck."

"Can she stay here while she recovers?"

"Let me suggest a motel nearby. You can recover in privacy and I'm close enough to come tend to her if needed."

He felt a surge of gratitude. This was why he was glad to be part of the Night Road; it had gotten him this doctor. Without the Night Road, he would have had nowhere to turn. "Can I see her?"

"Yeah. I'll get your goods ready. Then I will look at your leg, change the dressing. She told me you needed care as well."

Snow lay in the bed. She seemed smaller. She stared at the ceiling. The room smelled of blood and chemicals and wet paper. He took her hand; she pulled free from his fingers, which surprised him more.

"Don't be mad," he said.

"Schoolboy's gotten away from us three times now. It's embarrassing. He's a nothing."

He crossed his arms. "Did you have to kill the cop and the little freak?"

Her eyes, half-lidded, opened widely. "Yes. The cop was the greater threat. The little freak would have been stuck on us like a flea on a dog, wanting to be our new best friend, according to what Henry said." She put the flat of her hand over her eyes. "The nerve of that bastard. Shooting me."

The doctor came in, clucked over Mouser's stab wound. She changed the bandage and told Snow she'd done a good job tending to Mouser. Snow thanked her. They left and got settled into a cheap motel. The room was clean, smelled of disinfectant, and the cable TV worked. He tucked Snow into bed, gently.

She watched him. "Don't get all sweet on me," she said, sleepy from the medications.

"I don't do sweet."

She gave out a soft growl of a laugh. She touched the back of his hand, tenderly. He didn't know what to say.

His phone buzzed.

"Mouser? Henry asked me to call you. We have a lead on your targets." One of Henry's friends, another member of the Night Road, he thought; the voice was dry, Southern.

"A lead."

"On Eric Lindoe and his girl."

"They're in Thailand, according to Henry."

"No. They were ticketed on the flight but they were not, repeat not, on the arrival manifest. They didn't get on the plane. No charges on their cards in Thailand, no records of their passports going through Thai customs. We cracked the relevant databases fifteen minutes ago."

"Where are they?"

"They might still be in Chicago. No one's looking for them there."

Oh, yes, please, he thought. "Where in Chicago?"

"They have not used credit cards. They could be staying with a friend. We checked Aubrey's phone records and several of her calls are placed to a woman named Grace Crosby. I did a cross-check and Grace Crosby's credit card was charged in Detroit today. So Crosby might have let them stay in her apartment while she's gone."

"Where is this apartment?"

The voice fed him an address in Lincoln Park.

"I can be there in twenty minutes."

"Call me when you get there. I can give you a gift."

"What?"

"I can cut the power to the building. Another friend gave us a tap into the power grid. I can kill the power in the whole neighborhood. We mastered how to do this in preparation for Hellfire. Make the overall situation during the attack worse, you know."

He thanked his fellow Night Roader and hung up. Wow, work as a team effort. Hope stirred in his chest. This would all be resolved soon. The loose ends tied into neat knots, the money in the right pockets again. Mouser leaned close to Snow. She was fast asleep. He risked the slightest kiss on her forehead. She didn't stir. He headed for his car, the warmth of her still on his lips.

20

Luke froze in the darkness.

Silence hung between the three of them and then Eric said, "This isn't coincidence. No way. You were followed."

"Me? No, I followed *you*. I wasn't—"

"You don't know what these people are capable of," Eric said. "You've just killed us all. They found us. We had them tricked into believing we'd gone to Thailand."

"It's just a blackout." It had to be. "The Night Road couldn't control the power to a city utility."

"You're an idiot. You found these scumbags for Henry and now you're going to underestimate them? They've put major plans into place for a massive attack. Screwing with the power grid is entirely possible for them." Terror wrenched his words into a half-scream.

Aubrey said, "We have to get out of here." Now steel calm coated her voice.

Luke went to the window. "They can't have killed the power to the whole neighborhood." But he could see light only in a distant gleam, several streets away. Holy God. His surprise was eclipsed by an immediate sense of danger.

In the hallway, they could hear rumbling, voices calling out to one another, neighbors hailing neighbors.

"They could be waiting for us in the hallway," Luke said.

"There's no fire escape," Aubrey said.

"The ledge is wide enough—maybe—" Eric started.

"Are you insane?" Luke grabbed his arm. "We're not climbing the outside of the building."

"You don't know what we're up against. These people—they're brutal."

"Let's go, please." Panic now creeping into Aubrey's voice.

"Take her with you," Eric said. He went into the; kitchen, rummaged in a drawer, and produced a flashlight. "They want me; they want the money. Take her with you. Let them chase me."

"No. You come with us," Aubrey said. "I'm not leaving you." She sounded outraged at the suggestion.

"I can't. I'll stay here, make a deal with the Night Road."

The money was key to the Night Road's survival, Luke realized. It had to be, funds for a cataclysm far bigger than the train bombing in Texas. It couldn't fall into their hands, so Eric had to come with them.

"Forget it, Eric, we're sticking together." Luke opened the door. Most of the neighbors were huddling in the hallway, a few with flashlights. Luke heard laughter, the pop of a beer can opening, people making the convivial best of the blackout, not wanting to sit alone in the dark.

Luke grabbed Aubrey's arm—she was the only way he could ensure Eric stayed with them. She didn't pull free as they wound through the hallway.

"The stairway's ahead to your left," Aubrey said.

His circle of light found the door. He eased the door open. The stairway was pitch-dark.

Luke had to assume the worst. Where would they strike? The stairways and hallways were crowded right now, and Mouser and Snow would want privacy to kill him. The staircase would spit them out into the foyer. He pictured the small lobby in his mind—the staircase on the far left side, the old-style tile flooring, the dimensions of the room. If you wanted to ambush someone—it was close to a front exit. In the confusion Snow and Mouser could be out in the street and gone in seconds.

He stopped and Aubrey ran into his back.

"Stop at the second floor—we're not going out into the lobby."

They went down the stairs and opened the second-floor door and the hallway was empty.

"Is there an exit to the back?"

"Only through the lobby. Not from the residential floors."

"Hold on a minute," Eric said. Luke pulled the light toward his face and Eric blinked.

"I'm going to talk to whoever's after us. I'll make a deal." Eric sounded confident again.

"They won't talk."

"They will with me. I'm calling the shots, Luke. I'm sorry."

"Talk later, move now. Please," Aubrey said. Then she gave a gasp and in the disk of the flashlight's glow Luke saw the pistol in Eric's hand.

21

Waiting in the lobby for his targets to emerge, Mouser had not foreseen a big problem.

People with flashlights in a darkened building tend to shine the circle of light square in the faces of people nearby. They expect to see neighbors, and maintenance men, and they have a sudden bright suspicion of people they don't know. Mouser edged back toward a column.

Two older women were standing in the lobby, miffed at the inconvenience of ruined dinners, and one kept pointing a light in his direction.

"I'm sorry," she finally said. "Do you live in the building?"

"No, ma'am, my friend does and she asked me to wait in the lobby."

"Who's your friend?"

"Grace Crosby."

The answer seemed to satisfy the woman. "Well, they better get the power back on. We got half-cooked pork chops sitting in a skillet."

"Told you we should have baked them," the other woman said. "Oven would have finished the job, kept 'em hot."

The first woman growled in annoyance and agreement. But she performed a valuable service for Mouser—she flashed her light toward every entrant into the lobby from the stairwell, as regular as a sentry. So he would see Aubrey and Eric before they saw him, and they would be blinded for a second or two. His hand in his coat pocket held a Glock 18. He could kill the woman immediately, hustle Eric to a place where he could be questioned, and find the missing money. If the two elderly women got in the way, too bad. Darkness and chaos would give him cover enough to escape with Eric.

Then the job would be done and he could take Snow someplace safe. They would have their reward; they could start to reshape the world. Make Hellfire happen and begin to truly kill the Beast.

Sooner or later, his targets would come.

Ten minutes went by and they hadn't appeared.

The stair door clanged again and the old woman shone light against unfamiliar faces and he knew he'd worried too much about extracting Eric quickly onto the street. Wrong approach in the blackout. He headed for the stairwell.

22

When Eric got the flashlight, Luke realized—Aubrey had a gun hidden in the apartment and Eric had grabbed the gun when he got the flashlight.

"Aubrey, come here," Eric said.

Aubrey stayed put. "This is insane, Eric. Just—stop it."

"He's going to force my hand. I'm not going to the police. Neither are you. If he's gone, we're free."

"Free?" Luke said.

"They're not here for us. They're here for him."

"Bull. They're here for Eric and their fifty million bucks, and he knows it," Luke said. "That's why he offered to go talk to them. Unless that was just his way of abandoning you, Aubrey, and he was going to run for his own sorry life once he hit the front door."

"That's a lie!" Eric snapped.

"Eric, stop it," Aubrey said.

"Don't you switch sides on me, Aubrey, not after all I did for you."

Luke shone the light on her face and her expression had turned angry. "You're an asshole," she told Eric. "I should have broken up with you ages ago. You are not a hero."

"Stop this, we need each other," Luke said.

"Spare me the idiotic let's-work-together sentiment," Eric said. "Aubrey. Move away from him."

"And go where?" Aubrey stayed at Luke's side. "Where are we supposed to hide? How are we supposed to live that way? There's no rock quite big enough for us to set up housekeeping."

"I could have left you to die, Aubrey." All the warmth bled out of Eric's voice. But it wasn't replaced by anger. Luke heard anguish and bitterness. "I gave up everything for you. Even after you dumped me."

"Eric, it's not too late."

"I killed a man for you! Jesus, you don't get a do-over. I killed him."

"Under coercion. Under stress." Aubrey's voice went soft, cajoling. "You could get everything back, but this is not the way to save our lives."

"Give me the gun," Luke said.

"I know you're a good man at heart, Eric," Aubrey said, "I know you're scared. I know what you wanted for you and me. But this isn't the way. . . ."

Luke moved the light toward Eric's face, thinking he could blind him, break his resolve. "We have to get out of here. Assume they want to flush you out of hiding, force you to tell them where the money is. That means they might be waiting down in the lobby, or the street." It wasn't so different, he thought, from when he'd stolen food in his runaway days. If you had to hide, you did not hide in an obvious place. "We need another way out; we need to hide where they won't expect us to be."

"I have an idea," Aubrey said.

23

Mouser hurried up the stairs and as he hit the door the lights surged back into life.

The power company had overridden the darkness he'd been promised.

No matter. He reached the Crosby apartment, tested the knob. Unlocked. He opened it, scanned the room with his Glock, moved from room to room. A shattered glass, a gush of red wine, a fire extinguisher, blots of blood on the carpet.

The apartment was empty. They had not exited through the lobby; he'd have seen them in the windows as he approached. They must still be in the building.

So where would they hide? A neighbor's? Unlikely—this wasn't Aubrey's and Eric's real home; they wouldn't know the neighbors. So they had to be on the roof or in the basement.

The roof would be a dead end. The basement would offer service exits. Maybe onto a back entrance or alley.

Mouser hurried down to the lobby, then across it till he found the basement entrance, and headed down the stairs. A faint red glow from the emergency lights led downward, the red gleam like a mockery of hell.

"Trust me, I can cut a deal," Eric said. "I can reason with them. I've been planning on it."

Of course he was, because he was treating the money like a bulletproof shield, Luke thought. "They don't want to negotiate. They'll force you to hand over the money and they'll kill you." Luke pushed him along into the depths of the basement. Part of the floor was being renovated into ground-level units, but an open stretch of space at the back contained electrical equipment, a nesting of pipes, and a set of industrial water heaters. The disorder created a maze of construction junk, half-walls, and maintenance equipment. They'd lucked out getting here; no killers waiting in the stairwell.

The power surged back on.

"Maybe he's gone," Aubrey said. Luke reached to the switch and killed the lights again.

"Let's see if we can wait him out. Eric, give me the gun," Luke said.

"No."

"If this is the same guy who's after me, if he sees you with a gun, he'll just shoot you. No time for a deal," Luke said.

"I know what I'm doing. I'm keeping the gun. I'm not going to let them hurt Aubrey."

Luke heard a door open above.

They hid in the labyrinth of pipes, kneeling to the cool concrete floor. In their hiding place Aubrey was farther back, then Luke, then Eric, close to the front. Luke raised a finger to his lips.

Luke listened. Hard. A footstep. Another.

In the trickle of the light he peered between the pipes and a black form passed between the far wall and a table of tools. Stopped. Listened.

In the thin red light Eric stood and came out from the hiding place and walked toward the figure. Luke went still. If he yelled he would betray himself and Aubrey. But Eric was already betraying them.

"Hey," Eric said quietly. "Night Road?"

The shadow gave no answer.

Luke stifled the urge to run in blind panic. Eric was going to either save them or hand them over to this enemy.

"I'm Eric Lindoe."

"I know who you are." It was Mouser. "I've been carrying your picture in my pocket. I thought I was gonna get a nice vacation in Thailand, chasing you down. How you doing?" His tone was relaxed, friendly. "You look beat up."

Aubrey closed her hand over Luke's arm.

"I'm okay," Eric answered.

"Where's your girlfriend, Mr. Lindoe?" Mouser asked.

"She's someplace safe. You don't need to worry about her. She'll stay quiet about this mess. But Luke Dantry's gone."

"Excuse me?"

"There's an alley exit—for maintenance delivery—on the other side of the basement. He went out the door."

"Luke Dantry was *here*?"

"Yes."

"How long ago?" Mouser was already turning to run.

"Five minutes. I doubt you'll catch him."

Silence again. Luke's heartbeat rattled like wind in a chimney.

Mouser said, "You have a lot of explaining to do. You have our money."

"Yes, but I've kept it safe for you."

"That's a piss-poor interpretation of the situation," Mouser said.

"I know where the money's hidden. I'd like to trade that information."

"Fine. Trade it for your continued breathing. Where's our money?"

Eric made no answer—there was only the creaking of the building, its bones settling and stirring, the outside hum of traffic, the distant murmur of voices. Luke could feel Aubrey's breath against his shoulder.

"Let's make a deal," Eric said after a deep breath. "If I give you the money, then you let me walk away. Because I'm done with the Night Road. I want out."

Mouser's voice devolved into a low hiss. "We're not negotiating. You tell me where the money is. Or you die. Five. Four. Three."

"Okay. Here's the deal. Immunity for me and my girlfriend, from Henry, from the Night Road. All I did was cause a hiccup in the plan, just to get my girlfriend back. I give you the money. We walk away from each other. I just want out, free and clear."

"Except I need more than the money."

"What?"

"This British woman, this Jane. She's the Night Road's enemy," Mouser said. "We need to find her, find out how she knows about us. Because that's the ticket—ain't nobody supposed to know about us, about what we're planning, about Hellfire."

"I have no idea who she is. All I can give you is the money." And then the knife twisted. "Luke Dantry knows. He's figured out you're the people he found for his stepfather. He won't stay quiet."

"We'll call Henry; we'll talk to him on the phone together."

Between the pipes Luke saw Eric sag in relief.

"Except." The word hung in the air like a sword ready to slash. "I would like to know a couple of details."

"What?"

"You and your lady friend were on a flight manifest to Thailand. Now. How the hell did that happen if you didn't get on the plane?"

Eric was silent.

"You buy a ticket?"

"Yes. But we didn't use the tickets."

"But you don't get on the manifest unless you use the ticket. How did you get on that list?"

"I don't know. Clerical error. What does it matter?" A panicky edge touched Eric's voice.

"It matters. Somebody's trying very hard to protect you, Eric. Somebody with the rather impressive power to alter a flight manifest. Tell me who's protecting you, Eric."

The silence from Eric told Luke that Mouser had hit a nerve, had seen the key in Eric's deceptions. Finally Eric said, hoarse: "No one's trying to protect me."

"You cut a deal with someone else. Maybe with someone powerful who'd hide you if you betrayed the Night Road, whispered all our secrets in their ear. Maybe let you keep a chunk of our fifty million."

"No." But Eric, pushed to the limit, sounded as though he were about to cry.

"Did that same powerful someone offer a deal to Luke Dantry? Does Luke know where the money is?"

"No."

"I want a name, Eric. Who is protecting you?"

"No one."

Luke peered through the pipes and saw Mouser toss an object to Eric. Eric caught it deftly in one hand.

"What's this?" Eric asked.

"PDA with Internet capability. I'm assuming you aren't hauling around fifty million in tens and twenties. You've got the money parked in an account somewhere. Prove it to me that you've got it, show me the account balance online, and we can deal. Show me the money, bud."

Eric held the phone, looked at the screen. "I—I . . ."

"What are you waiting for?"

"I'm not going to show it to you."

"I need proof that you've still got the whole fifty million."

Eric didn't look over toward Luke, but he raised his head with a slow dignity. A decision made. He tossed the PDA back to Mouser, who caught it one-handed. "I've got it all, but I'm not showing you the accounts. I have no reason to lie."

The sound of the shot was a hard slap in the close air of the basement. Under his hand, clamping over her mouth, Luke felt Aubrey choke down a scream.

"Not anymore," Mouser said as a soft eulogy.

Luke did not risk peering through the pipes. He tried to breathe silently, through his mouth. Mouser had killed Eric. Just ten feet away from them.

He heard footsteps. A clanking of metal—the unused basement door. The cool night crept into the basement.

Aubrey pressed her face into her elbow, curled on the concrete.

The door clanged shut. Mouser was in the alley.

The gun. Eric still had his gun. In his jacket.

Luke moved from the web of pipes and didn't even glance behind at Aubrey.

Eric lay dead on his back, a Rorschach blot of blood on his forehead. Slackening astonishment on his face.

Luke glanced at the door. It began to push open again. Too soon to be anyone but Mouser.

Luke ran and shoved the door hard, kicking his heels against the concrete floor.

A bullet tore through the thin metal, ricocheting into the air an inch from Luke's scalp.

He slammed the door fully shut, slid the dead bolt.

Luke was running now, yelling for Aubrey. She crouched, shivering over Eric's body, her mouth trembling, her skin pale as moonlight. He knelt, grabbed the gun from the jacket, a sheaf of papers, a key ring and cell phone from the pocket. A miniature basketball on the key ring bounced against his palm. Luke grabbed it all, put the gun under his own coat.

Luke and Aubrey ran up the stairs, into the small crowd in the lobby, out into the cool of the wind-blown street. They took a hard left and ran onto the busy sidewalk. Cars zoomed past, headlights painting them in whites.

It would be only a minute before Mouser was on the street.

People crammed the sidewalks, thronging from the restaurants and stores. Luke and Aubrey ran and he looked ahead and to the left, at the upcoming intersection, and he saw Mouser scanning the street, suddenly raising his hand. Running after them. They dashed out onto Armitage Avenue. Mouser closed fast on them.

In the street they were caught in a wash of lights, a roaring peel of brakes. A Chicago Transit Authority bus honked, veering to avoid Luke and Aubrey. He saw the lighted windows of the bus, commuters standing and sitting, just wanting to get home to their safe cocoons, frightened and gripping the seats and one another as the bus driver hammered its brakes, spun, crunched into cars parked along the avenue.

For a moment Luke thought the bus would either topple on them in its skid or simply run straight over them. But they dodged out of its path, Luke glancing back, seeing Mouser vanishing as the bus blocked Luke's view. A car rammed into the side of the bus.

They ran. Luke heard the squeal of brakes from a truck trying to avoid them. Aubrey grabbed his arm and they ran down a side street. Luke glanced back, didn't see Mouser in the chaos of the braked cars, didn't hear the crack of another gunshot.

They ran back toward the elevated train station. They fed their cards into the ticket reader and hurried up the staircase.

They stood at the end of the platform, waiting for the rumble of the rails. Aubrey leaned against him, panting. If Mouser made it up the steps . . .

"Go," he said. "Go to the police."

She looked at him and a toughness in her that he had not seen before settled in her eyes. "I'm not sure the police can protect me from people who can kill the power grid. You took his keys?"

"Yes."

A train, bound for the Loop, rumbled into the Armitage station. "Let's go," she said.

They stepped onto the train. The crowd mixed, doing the dodge-you-first dance, jockeying for seats and stands near the door. The train was less crowded than he'd thought it would be. Businessmen, rough-looking kids, a group of women chattering in Spanish. Luke and Aubrey sat down, as far from everyone else as they could.

Aubrey huddled close to him and shivered. "I might be sick."

Awkwardly he put a calming hand on her back. She breathed hard. "Oh, God. Oh, God. He did it to save us."

"To save *you*. He was definitely not trying to save me. He painted a god-damned target on my back."

She looked up at him; her eyes were wet but she blinked hard as though unwilling to risk a trickle of tears. He saw the strength in her face. "He was wrong to do that."

Luke watched the train speed past the lit buildings, a mist starting to fall, the light smeared and dreamy.

This money was the key, to stopping the Night Road and perhaps finding out who Jane was—the architect of his destruction. They had to find where Eric had hidden it.

"Where's Eric's apartment?"

"Near downtown, River West area."

The train huffed into the station. People shuffled on and off. A trio of homeless men boarded, along with an elderly man in a neat suit, with a frown on his face and a newspaper tucked under his arm.

"How many more stations?" Luke did not like sitting still, where some-one could study and remember his face from television. "Where should we get off?"

The homeless men laughed at a private joke among themselves. The el-derly man sitting across from Luke and Aubrey inspected them as though measuring them on a finely tuned secret balance. He opened and began to read a newspaper.

Luke saw his own face—the image captured on the ATM camera—on the front page. A headline read SUSPECT IN HOBO KILLING MARKED BY TRAGEDY. Probably an account of his father's death in a bizarre plane crash and his mother's death in a car crash. The twin blots of sorrow in his life.

Aubrey saw the headline and touched Luke's hand. She pulled on his sleeve and he stood, getting away from the newspaper, following her toward the homeless guys, who had staked out the center of the car as a temporary turf. The rest of the passengers gave the trio plenty of space.

Luke and Aubrey stood near the door. Luke kept his face toward the window. The great city lay beyond the glass. He wished he could enjoy the view.

He glanced back at the man.

The elderly man had turned to the first page of the paper. It lay folded on his lap, Luke's picture above the crease.

24

Mouser watched the train arrive to sweep them away—
no way he could reach them in time. So he stopped running.

Eric had been lying. He was sure they'd been the ones to lock him out
of the basement. Which meant Eric had died shielding them. So. They
must know where Eric had hidden the money. It was the only reasonable
explanation.

He turned and headed back to his car, parked at a pay slot. A slow heat
warmed his skin. His phone rang as soon as he reached the car.

"Did you get them?" Snow sounded tired.

"Not all. Just Eric. Luke is with Eric's woman. I think Eric's told them
where the money is. He wanted to save that girl something fierce."

"I can help. Where are you going now?"

"Don't you worry. I'll be back at the motel soon. It's going to be okay."

"I can meet you. I have a car."

"You have a car."

"I did not like that doctor. I borrowed her car when she came over to
check on me." Then a hint of crossness in her voice. "She shouldn't have
tried to stop me."

"What did you do?"

"It's not like she was a *real* doctor."

He did not feel a shudder or coldness to her announcement of murder;
just a disappointment. "You don't treat assets that way."

"She'd seen our faces."

He didn't want to argue with her. "Just find a motel. Check in. Rest. Call me later. Do not hurt anyone else."

"We got to stick together."

"Help me by doing what I'm asking. I will find them."

"Please, meet me somewhere."

He couldn't have her wandering Chicago, so he told her to meet him at Navy Pier, on Lake Michigan; it was an easy landmark for her to find, with its giant Ferris wheel. He hung up. He was annoyed and it did not occur to him that being wounded, she might be frightened and afraid of being alone. He thought only of the mission. The phone rang again. It was Henry.

"How is Snow?"

"She'll be okay. Eric's dead. Luke got away. I am going to put some hurt on him. Don't tell me not to. He deserves it. You know it, I know it."

Henry heaved a long, broken sigh. "Do you have the money?"

"No."

"What about Eric's girlfriend?"

"She's with Luke. I believe they might have the information on where the money's hidden." A misery crept into his flesh, his mouth.

"Odd Eric would offer help, since he kidnapped Luke."

"They must have made an alliance."

"Mouser, tell me why I shouldn't unleash the Night Road against you for failing. I have a long list here of people who might do a better job than you in finding our funds."

"Because admitting failure shows you don't have control of this situation. Of *their* money. Which might make them all quite nervous about you running the show. You could be replaced." He knew from the silence he'd scored a hit. "Let me and Snow finish. They have to still be in Chicago."

The only sound Mouser could hear through the phone was a ticking of clocks.

Henry said, "You aren't just failing me, but failing the entire Night Road."

Mouser didn't care much about what other people wanted, but the rest of the Night Road could be useful to him. "If they will help me—I won't fail them." He decided this was the most diplomatic thing he could say.

"Then the Night Road will help you. As long as we don't give them details on the current difficulties. I don't want the rest of the network to panic or decide to leave us." Henry was offering a truce between them; they would not alert the rest of the network to the problems they faced.

"I agree," Mouser said. "The first step is to find a way to track Aubrey Perrault. Maybe her car has GPS. They took off on the train but she must have a car. And we need an eye inside Eric's bank. Trace where he moved the money, because he had to have stashed it where he could get it quickly."

A pause. "Luke. He was all right?"

"I saw him running. He appeared fine." *He shot Snow,* he wanted to say. *Who cares how he is?*

"You didn't hurt him."

"No." *Only because I didn't get the chance,* he thought. Henry's concern for Luke enraged him. The mission, the mission, one could not be distracted from the mission. Henry was becoming a liability. But he remained silent.

"Oh, how was that doctor for Snow?" Henry asked.

"Fine. Just fine," Mouser said.

The elderly man stared right at Luke. Luke glanced at the grime on the window. Out of the corner of his eye he saw the old man unfold a cell phone from a pocket, dial it, and speak into it. His calm—his certainty—was somehow more frightening than if he had produced a gun or a knife.

"We're almost to the next station," Aubrey whispered in Luke's ear. He kept his face neutral, calm, seemingly uninterested in what the elderly man was doing.

"He's the kid in the paper," the man announced to the train. He closed the cell phone. "The Houston kid who killed the homeless guy." He tapped the paper.

"You're nuts," Aubrey said. "Leave my brother alone." She was a quick liar.

"I called the police." A smugness filled his voice. "Killed a homeless guy," he said to the trio of street guys.

One of the homeless men—gaunt, fortyish—reached out and grabbed Luke's arm.

Aubrey pulled the homeless man's arm from Luke. "I said to leave him alone."

"Don't let them get away." The elderly man raised the folded paper like an accusing finger.

They all swayed as the train braked to a stop, and suddenly two of the homeless men hammered Luke into the wall. They smelled of wine and of sweat fermenting too long in wool and as the doors whooshed open, Aubrey and Luke fell out onto the platform in a tackle of legs and arms. Luke threw a hard punch into the matted beard of one of the men. His fist scraped dirty teeth and a rubbery lip.

Aubrey grabbed the other man's greasy hair with a twisting yank, started to scream for help.

The other men grabbed Luke's arms, hauled him, and slammed him into a concrete column.

"Stop it!" Aubrey yelled.

And now the crowd moved, three young men rallying to their defense, grabbing at the ragtag accusers. Aubrey seized Luke and they ran. They stopped running at the bottom of the stairs as a policeman hurried past them.

They vanished into the mist.

25

"Where would he have hidden the money?" Luke and Aubrey were walking the streets of a quiet neighborhood north of downtown. Aubrey kept glancing over her shoulder. *Keep moving,* Luke thought. "He worked for a bank. . . . Wherever he put the money, he was willing to die to keep it a secret."

"Which means he could have hidden it anywhere," she said. "But I'm guessing he stashed it in another account, probably another bank, that wouldn't be so obviously tied to him." Her voice broke. And he could sense her drawing away from him.

"I know you cared about him. I'm sorry, I'm really sorry."

"Are you?" She studied the sidewalk. "He's the reason you're in this mess."

"No. He was a pawn, just like me, just like you. Even the people chasing us aren't much more than pawns. The king on the chessboard is my stepfather. The queen is this Jane bitch. She has to be crazy, trying to extort money from terrorists."

"I don't like chess and I don't like being a pawn." She raised her head, looked at him with a mixture of defiance and grief. "It makes me mad."

"Mad is good. Mad might help us stay alive."

She started to walk again and he fell in step with her. "I can't believe he's dead. He was just so desperate to convince me he was on the side of right. He just kept talking about all he'd done for me, risked for me. . . ."

"He was leveraging your kidnapping to bring you back to him."

She nodded in shame. "It sounds horrible. But he wanted us back together." She glanced over her shoulder again. "I'm really not so special. I don't know why he couldn't let me go."

Luke thought of her calm, her brave pleading with Eric not to leave Luke chained to the bed, her resourcefulness in the elevated train in fending off the mob. He knew exactly why Eric would not let a woman like her go easily.

"How did you meet him?"

"At his bank. I set up my company accounts there. He handled them."

He remembered Aubrey's export/import business now, from her friend's blog.

"I bought an import company a few months back. From a friend. Pottery from South America, African décor and jewelry, crafts and furniture from Mexico and Eastern Europe, not expensive stuff. But you have to watch your expenditures, deal with making payments overseas, receiving payments from overseas, it's a hassle. Eric helped me sort it all out. Then he asked me out to dinner. . . . I thought he was a good guy. I don't often choose well."

"Did he have a chance to win you back after he saved you?"

"I don't know. I was furious with him and grateful all at once. But once I saw the footage on TV—I recognized you—I knew he was involved in killing that man. To *save* me. It was going to bind me to him forever and I was very afraid. Whoever's after him isn't going to give up."

They passed a nearly empty diner and she glanced at the menu in the window.

"Are you hungry?" he asked. He realized he was starving but suggesting dinner seemed bizarre.

"We never got to eat our pizza." Aubrey rubbed her temples. "I'm horrible to even think of food right now." Her stomach growled.

"It's okay. We're in survival mode."

"Weird. And everything else seems so ordinary." She crossed her arms.

"We're different, the world isn't."

Warm light filled the diner and the few customers laughed over coffee and sandwiches and blue-plate specials. They went inside, Luke's skin prickling at the thought of sitting still in public. They took turns going to the bathroom and washing faces and hands and Luke thought she might bolt, but when he came back to the booth she was sitting there waiting. They ordered scrambled eggs, bacon, toast, and hot coffee, which sent a welcome jolt of heat through their bodies. She stared at the mug. "I should be a mess. But it's a luxury, isn't it, to be a mess. In the worst of times you just have to forge ahead."

She was right. They had to keep moving, and they had to find the money quickly. "The luxury we don't have is time."

"What do you mean?"

"These people expect this money soon. It's tied to a bigger attack—even bigger than the bombing in Texas. Mouser called it Hellfire. We have to find out what it is, and I'm guessing from Mouser's tone that the attack is very soon. Within a couple of days."

She said nothing for thirty seconds, frowning in thought. She waited for the waitress to refill their coffees and leave their corner. "It won't take the police long to find Eric."

"No."

"And they'll look for me."

"Yes."

"And whoever this Mouser man works for, they'll be looking for me too."

"Yes."

"If the police find me, then Mouser finds me."

"Well . . ."

"They killed the power, Luke. They're more capable than I ever imagined."

He sipped coffee. "If you talk to the police, you can clear my name."

"What will clear your name is finding this money. Prove the motive Eric had to kidnap you. Then you give the money and all the information on the Night Road to the FBI."

Give it all to the FBI. The fifty million. And his traitorous stepfather. He didn't want Henry in jail. He realized, with shameful anger, he wanted Henry dead for the hell he'd created for Luke. No. He put his face in his hands, let the wave of hate pass. "You don't have any idea what you're signing up for, Aubrey."

"I can't tell the police anything more than I told you. I think we should stick together."

The sense of responsibility weighed on him. He had barely survived his encounters with the Night Road; she had no idea of the brutality they would have to confront. But he saw the resolution in her face and he decided not to argue with her. She wanted to hide; he didn't blame her. She wanted to help him, for Eric's sake. "So the two kidnapping victims are stuck with each other."

"Yes," she said quietly. "I don't know how to fight, but I'm not going to let these people get away with what they've done, to me or to Eric or to you."

Her resolve strengthened him. "What I don't understand is—why didn't Eric just hide with the money? Why not go to Thailand, take the money, run with it?" he asked.

"He said tonight that he had made a deal that would save us. Right before you got there. We were having a wine to celebrate but he hadn't told me the details yet."

"A deal."

"A deal where someone powerful would protect us—just like that Mouser man said before he shot Eric." She cleared her throat, rubbed at her eyes. "I was furious with Eric for getting me involved in this mess. I wanted out and he was trying to convince me I didn't have a way out except through him."

"Who was going to protect him? Maybe they could protect us."

"Maybe," she said. "But he called it a deal. He had to be giving something in exchange."

"The fifty million," Luke said.

He remembered the pages he'd pulled from Eric's jacket when he'd gone for the gun. He removed the papers from his back pocket and smoothed them out on the table.

"What is that?" Aubrey asked.

"Papers Eric had in his pocket." Each separate page was a printout confirming the opening of an account at a bank. The banks were scattered across America: Tennessee, New York, California, two in Texas, Minnesota, Washington State, Missouri. He didn't recognize the bank names: They all appeared to be regional banks, not large chains. "These must be the accounts he set up for the Night Road."

"How would we check to see if they're empty or not?"

He looked up at her. "You think he stashed the money in them?"

"It would make sense. Maybe he opens the accounts, deposits the money, but he hasn't given the account information yet to the Night Road. That way, he can still reach the money, even if they can't."

"We can't go to them; they're all over the country," he said. "You have to have a password to access information online or over the phone."

"Then step one is finding where Eric hid those passwords," she said.

"Might've just been in his head."

"That many accounts? No. He was the kind of guy who wrote everything down."

Two policemen walked into the diner. The two officers gave the restaurant a cursory glance; Luke had his back to them. He sensed the momentary weight of their stare. Aubrey and Luke studied their coffee cups, waiting for the policemen to slide into a booth on the opposite side of the diner and to lose themselves in the study of the menu.

"We need to go. Now," Luke said. Sweat coated his back.

He unfolded money for the bill and they got up and left. Aubrey leaned on him hard, rubbing his back, her pretended affection camouflage. He didn't look like a cop killer on the solitary run. Luke was careful not to look toward the officers.

When they were out of the diner, she stepped away from him, crossing her arms. They walked for three blocks, found a bus stop, figured out the route to get back to Lincoln Park, where Aubrey's car sat on a side street. The car was a late-model Volvo, and he checked its underside.

"Do you know what you're looking for?" she asked.

"Not really," he said. "A gadget that could track you. Like I'm going to recognize that." He risked a grin and she smiled, barely, back.

"Or blow us up. Aren't I Mary Sunshine?" Exhaustion cramped her voice.

Luke slid out from under the car. "I don't see anything there that looks totally foreign."

"All right." They got in; she drove into the dark street.

"Where to?"

"Someplace we can plan. I need sleep." Luke's fatigue was overwhelming. His body had no adrenaline left. He felt like he had been running forever.

"Someplace cheap," she said.

"Someplace cheap," he agreed.

"Eric lied about his whole life," she said unexpectedly, and tears spilled from her eyes. But not sobs. The tears were steady and controlled and she wiped them off her cheek with the back of her hand. She kept driving and Luke didn't know what to do until he put his hand over her hand on the steering wheel. Just for comfort.

Neither of them noticed the traffic camera perched on the closest intersection, watching them with its uncaring eye as they pulled away from the curb and drove into the night.

26

Snow slept in the motel bed, exhausted from her mending shoulder and her ill-advised murder. Mouser opened his laptop and took a walk along the Night Road.

He felt lonely much of the time, but signing on to the Night Road's private Web site was like slipping into a warm bath. Happiness, comfort, knowing you belonged. It was a rare sensation for him.

It was not a single Web site, but rather a fortress of several linked sites, hosted on a Russian server. The sites appeared innocuous—even boring—until you entered a password, and their delights opened up to your eyes. You could not get a password without being cleared by Henry Shawcross. Very few in the Night Road could name, by true identity, another member. He glanced at Snow; he still didn't know her real name. It was better that way.

He sighed, with relief and pleasure. He read the fresh postings on the site—encoded in Night Road parlance. Celebrations and congratulations on the oil pipe explosion in Canada. A Night Road member had managed to inflict millions in economic damage on both Canada and the United States for the tiny investment of five thousand dollars for plastique and transportation costs. Electronic versions of high fives floated in the postings. The *E. coli* meat poisoning scare from the Tennessee food plant was also mentioned as a triumph, the combined work of two members who hadn't known each other before being introduced via the Night Road and had pooled resources and knowledge to infect the processing plant and send a wave of panic across American tables. Low cost, high impact.

A select few, proven the most capable, would take part in Hellfire.

He moved past the accolades. Someone in Alabama wanted training in explosives and wanted a new source for firearms. A man in Los Angeles was looking for other groups to network with to disrupt highway traffic on the Fourth of July. Another poster in Belgium had lifted a large number of credit card account numbers from a U.S. Army depot and was selling them.

Mouser paused at one posting—a British hacker had dispersed a Trojan horse via a porn site out of St. Petersburg and the Trojan had begun a rapid propagation around the world; the hacker announced he was ensnaring a thousand unsuspecting PCs a day. The Trojan malware would serve up all passwords and credit card information stored on the infected computers. Blocks of one hundred systems were available for sale; bidding was intensifying.

Mouser considered. He'd funded his last three operations against the Beast—ammunition, travel, and lodging—by buying a block of infected systems. It was like buying a mutual fund; some hijacked systems could deliver hugely profitable information; others—usually owned by teenage boys—would produce slim to none. But nice clean identity and account information was valuable—and given how badly the past couple of days had gone, he and Snow might need clean names to step into, for a short while. Until the dust settled. And if the payments he'd been promised fell through, then he could use the financial info to resell down the chain. He knew of Serbian crime rings and one ever-desperate Muslim terror cell in France who would buy nearly anything.

Mouser put in a bid on two blocks of machines and then posted his own request.

Need access to Creeps full-blowns for P24. Only 2. 1 GPS.

In Night Road tongue, he was asking for access to all credit card databases for charges paid in the past twenty-four hours, for two names, and GPS information for one car—Aubrey's. He waited.

Five minutes later, a voice elsewhere in the world replied:

Might can do. Offer?

Mouser responded: *Can trade skills in US.*

Skills was a code word for "kills"—he was offering to kill someone in exchange for the data he needed.

The reply: *Not in US. Sorry. Good luck.*

Then another offer appeared: *I can help. Post details at skeech@netter.net*

This e-mail address was an established blind—clicking on it took you to a legitimate computer Web site, a discussion group for American movies and TV shows owned by one of the same holding companies that owned Travport Air Cargo. The discussion group was in Malaysia, and the postings ranged from fluent English to Malay to badly broken English—perfect for shorthand cues. The site was again hosted out of Russia and when needed, postings by Night Road members were automatically purged from the system. It was not perfect anonymity but it was close.

He slipped into the forum, created a new user ID, and signed on. He posted a new topic, asking in broken English about an upcoming DVD release with the word *skills* in it. A moment later another poster responded with a long answer written in a motley, text-message-style shorthand.

They chatted, continuing the camouflaged dance, until the respondent gave an encoded answer that contained a phone number with an area code in New Mexico.

Mouser called the number.

It was answered on the third ring. "I'm your new friend," Mouser said.

"I can get your information." The voice was baritone, Spanish-flecked, tobacco-hoarse. "But it will take a few hours."

"I need it now."

"Your need is irrelevant. It will still take a few hours."

Mouser sighed. "And you can guarantee continuous reading of the car's location?"

"Until my path into the database is discovered. No guarantees. But you should get a solid read on where your target is."

"Who do you want handled as payment?"

"You take out a cop and we're square."

"You mean just any cop at random?"

Mouser considered. Police officers were servants of the Beast. It was strangely thrilling to know a police officer was going about life, unaware that he or she would soon die so Mouser could buy information. "All right."

"What's your car registrant's name?"

"Aubrey Perrault. She drives a Volvo, license plate F52-TJR, Illinois. Tonight she would have been parked in Lincoln Park, off Armitage."

"I have a friend who has a back door into most of the major metropolitan traffic camera feeds. I can see if she's popped up anywhere in Chicago—it would help narrow the search—in the past few hours and contact you via the site." They would not use these phones again with each other; they were prepaids, to be destroyed and disposed of when their business concluded.

Mouser thanked him and clicked off the phone. He signed off the Malaysian site and returned to the Night Road site. So many people, all with their own agenda, their own skills, their own cause, trading their brilliance and their resources, ready to strike against the far wider world. An army, hidden in the shadows, and waging a war that would change the world. A Night Road, built by Henry Shawcross out of the bricks given to him by Luke Dantry. A scary, and a beautiful, creature, a beast of justice, was being born.

With Hellfire as its birth announcement.

Out of his window, Mouser looked up into the starry night and wondered if he could see the GPS satellite far above, which would tell his new buddy exactly where Aubrey and Luke were. He wanted to blow the distant eye a kiss.

27

Luke and Aubrey drove to a small chain motel on the outskirts of Chicago, on Interstate 55 toward St. Louis, and checked in—one room, two beds. Aubrey paid cash; Eric had given her money that afternoon, since they couldn't use credit cards.

Exhaustion threatened to swamp Luke's brain but he sat on the bed and studied the list of states, banks, and accounts. He didn't know where to start. There were no names on the accounts, no passwords, no identifiers beyond Eric's notes. Any other information he needed had died with Eric. And if these were the closed accounts—they were useless.

Unless they could give him hints about which Night Road member each account was intended for. Presumably these people were scattered around the country, like Snow and Mouser. The bank with their Night Road funds would have to be close to them. It might help find them.

Aubrey showered behind the closed door and he kept his back facing the bathroom. He lay down, and fell asleep almost instantly. In his sleep he stood and he was back on his father's flight. The man who had sabotaged the plane was gone, but he could see, from behind, his father's body, slumped by a window.

Dad, he called. His father's hand lay on the frosted window, the silver Saint Michael's medal dangling between his fingertips.

He touched his father's shoulder.

Turning, standing, the dead man was not Warren Dantry but Henry, his face blue, his lips gray, reaching for Luke's throat.

Luke sat up, mouth dry, skin clammy with sweat. Aubrey, dressed in her clothes again, hair wet, sat watching him from the other bed. She had turned on the television and as he looked at the screen he saw the pictures of the two dead men in the alley. Chris and the poor officer.

He reached for the remote, turned up the volume. No arrests in the double shooting. No suspects as of yet.

"I'll be back in a few minutes."

He walked down four streets and, at a busy intersection, found an ancient pay phone in front of a convenience store. But it was too close. He took a bus a few miles away, found another convenience store with a pay phone. He fed it quarters and dialed 311, said quickly and clearly, "I called in earlier the tip on the murdered police officer. The two people responsible for shooting him may also have a connection to the train bombing in Texas, and they are working on a bigger attack called Hellfire, but I don't know what it is." He hung up. He could have said something about Henry; he hadn't. Why? He owed Henry no loyalty. But his mouth had not been able to form the words, to say what he believed about Henry as an absolute truth. He picked up the phone to dial it again, then slowly hung it up.

He knew the awful truth: He wanted to deal with Henry himself. He wanted Henry weak and vulnerable in front of him, to be forced to admit he had used and betrayed Luke. To be made accountable, if for only a few moments, for having taken Luke's well-intentioned work and built an obscenity from it. It was a disquieting realization, and it gnawed at his heart during the trip back to the motel.

By the time he returned, Aubrey had turned to another news channel. Authorities in Alaska were reporting that a trio of Seattle men had been arrested trying to sabotage an oil pipeline near Sitka. They had been caught with a few homemade bombs, devices powerful enough to have torn an expensive hole in the pipe and shut down delivery capacity for days. The men were allegedly ecological extremists; but the stock market had reacted to this late-afternoon news with a feeling of havoc narrowly averted, especially after the week's earlier pipeline blast in Canada. Oil prices soared to new records and the rest of the market cratered for the day. Millions vanished on paper.

"Seattle," Luke said. "I found some extremist environmentalists in Seattle that I handed over to Henry. This could be them."

"Or not."

"I can't hear about an attack, or a political crime, and not think it's connected to the Night Road right now. My God, I gave him so many names. Even if there were only fifty or so that were serious, that's a million per terrorist."

"Life has a soft underbelly," Aubrey said. "I mean, if just a few people wanted to wreck the economy, they could, with surgical precision. Just by hitting us where we're vulnerable. Our energy. Our food. Our communications." She looked at him, sadness in her eyes. "If they scare enough people, they will change how we live."

"Yes," he said. "Look at September eleventh, what a few people can do with so little. Nineteen guys. The whole operation cost a half-million. These assholes could cause so much more suffering with so much more money. Not just one big attack. Maybe a whole long series. An onslaught of terror."

Then the next story was about Eric, but it did not mention his name. The screen showed police tape cordoning off the condo building on Armitage. No witnesses, no description of a shooter, except three people—a man and a woman, pursued by another man—had run into traffic, nearly causing a major bus crash. The anchor said, "We're told the power across the Lincoln Park area had failed due to a computer glitch, although no problems elsewhere in the power grid have been reported, and ComEd is investigating the situation. . . ."

She smoothed her damp hair back from her head. "You sort of stink, Luke. You might want to shower."

He hadn't gotten clean since the cottage near the flooded river. He ducked into the bathroom, stood under the stinging spray, lathered his body with soap. A warm gratitude dawned in his chest that she was sticking with him; he didn't want to be alone. He didn't like putting his grimy clothes back on but he had no choice. He'd lost his knapsack with his clothes at Chris's studio.

Aubrey lay curled under the sheets. Dozing. He moved to his own bed and doused the light. He realized he'd left the bathroom light on. He got up, switched off the light, and, walking in the darkness back to his own bed, inadvertently hit his shin against her mattress.

She sat up with an abbreviated scream.

"Sorry," he said. "Sorry, Aubrey."

"I'm okay. I thought—I dreamed I was back in that cabin. . . ."

"It's okay." He sat on his bed. "I had a bad dream earlier." He could hear, in the dark, the rustles of the sheets on her bed as she eased back down on the mattress.

She said, "I was sure—when I was chained to that bed—no one was ever going to find me. I was going to starve to death. Or die of thirst. An ugly death alone. I don't even like to eat lunch alone."

He laughed, very softly, and she sighed and then she cried, for Eric, for the life he had robbed from her.

Luke watched a thin crease of moonlight that came into the room through the barely parted curtains. He looked over at Aubrey and for a moment he didn't realize that she was holding a hand out toward him.

He took her hand.

"Just for now," she said. He knew. He understood.

"I thought I was going to die in that cabin too," he said. He closed his hand around hers. His breath seemed to pause. She drew him to the bed. They nestled together, both hungry for warmth, both exhausted, hearts and minds tattered by crisis.

Then her mouth turned to his, needy, hungry, a kiss that said, *I'm just so thankful to be alive.* He covered his mouth with hers, slowed the kiss, broke it. Her lips tasted of coffee.

"Bad idea," he said.

"I don't care. I've been living a bad idea for days. I didn't love him anymore. He's ruined my life. I can't . . . I just need . . ."

He knew. The need to feel alive, to not be deadened by the horror. She withdrew from the kiss, almost shy, and then he touched the hem of her T-shirt, felt her lift her arms, wanting to be free from the fear. He tugged the shirt off her head and eased off her bra. He pulled off his own shirt and leaned in close to kiss her again. The silver of the Saint Michael's medal touched her naked breasts.

"What's this?" She fingered the medal, the angel's wings.

"Saint Michael. My dad gave it to me before he died. He's supposed to keep me safe, he said." Aubrey studied the medal in the cold bar of moonlight from the window, cupping it in her palm; then she ran the medal along the silver chain and put the angel on Luke's back.

"It tickles me," she said.

"Okay." She closed her eyes and Luke felt her fingertips begin to push his boxers from his hips.

The lovemaking was gentle and comforting and good and they both slipped into warm sleep. In the deep of the night Luke awoke at the sound of a door shutting down the hall. He thought he should stay awake, stay on guard in case Mouser and Snow worked more sick magic to find them, but he knew they couldn't, that he and Aubrey were safe, they were invisible. But he stayed awake for a long hour, thinking not of the woman curled in the shelter of his arms, sleeping in abject relief of momentary safety, but of Henry.

Thinking of what he would do when he saw Henry, the king of lies, the false face, the betrayer, the serpent who could say *Trust me* and turn the words to poison.

Luke was steeling himself, he realized, for murder.

28

They both slept until late in the morning, the sunshine crafting through the windows. Luke awoke and she lay next to him, watching him.

"Shouldn't have," she said, but she offered a shy smile. He saw what he thought was regret in her eyes. She blinked it away, as if she knew it lingered, and gave him a warm kiss on the mouth, followed by a chaste kiss on the forehead. She kept her hand on his flat stomach. "But I'm not sorry that we did."

"Shouldn't, couldn't, wouldn't," he said. "I have no regrets either."

"You're a good guy."

"So are you. Not a guy. But good." He had never been deft at the morning-after chatter and he saw he wasn't improving now. He felt a pang of regret, because this was going to change or complicate an already tough situation between them. He couldn't deal with another problem. But if he was going into battle, he wanted her: a smart and brave partner.

"Are you all right?" she asked.

"Yes. You?"

"I'm sad for Eric. I can't help but feel that way."

He said nothing.

"But we . . . we can get out of this mess," she said. "Get our lives back."

"If we find who he made the deal with, where he hid the money."

"Where do we start?"

"We start with his cell phone." He opened up the phone he'd taken from

Eric's pocket, searched the call log. Aubrey leaned over his shoulder. There was only one number listed on the log. An international number.

"I know that international code is France," Aubrey said. "Eric and I went to Paris a couple of months back. He had business and I'd never been."

"Business," he said. "What kind?"

"Banking stuff, I don't know."

Luke pressed the callback option under the number.

"Um, is that smart?"

"Let's see," Luke said.

Four rings, and then: "Hello?"

He recognized the British woman's voice. "Hello, Jane," Luke said.

She didn't seem shocked at the use of her name. "This isn't who I was expecting."

"No. Eric Lindoe's dead."

"Sad. I thought he'd make it through the weekend, at least. Let me guess. Luke Dantry, running man?"

"Why did you want me kidnapped? Why have you involved innocent people?"

"Nothing personal, darling," she said.

"Bitch, it's personal," Luke said. "Why did you do it? What did I or Aubrey ever do to you?"

"Nothing. Hence, not personal." Her voice was cool, as crisp as a breeze caught in linen. "You're not going to find me. You can't hurt me."

"I have a question for you. You knew about the fifty million. So who the hell's giving it to the Night Road? Where's this money coming from?"

"Some secrets, sweetheart, go to the grave. My lips are sealed."

"This fifty million you want so badly? I'm going to find it before you do."

"That, darling, I seriously doubt." Then he heard a click, Jane hanging up.

He tried the number again. No response. "Why would a British woman in Paris be using us as pawns?"

"Insulting her wasn't exactly productive."

"Aubrey, this woman isn't going to negotiate with us. Not until we find where he hid the money. Only then could we maybe lure her into the light." He shook his head. "I want to know where this money is coming from."

Aubrey bit her lip. "I do have a thought about a potential hiding place for the money."

"Where?"

"Eric's childhood home. We stopped there on the way into Chicago after we ditched your car in Dallas. Eric was getting his stepfather's gun. The house is empty; Eric's stepfather died recently and he hasn't sold it." She swallowed. "Maybe he did more than get the gun. Maybe he left something behind."

The house was a few blocks off Cicero, not far from Midway Airport; in a neighborhood that looked like its better days were more myth than memory. Narrow brick houses were jammed close together, as if sharing secrets. Some of the houses were maintained with pride and care; some were not. People idled in yards, on corners, bored, laughing, arguing. They drove past a trio of teenage boys who looked at them with a mix of calculation and studied disinterest. Luke parked in front of the old Lindoe house. The small yard needed a mow. Every window was darkened. The Lindoe house looked like the shy child on the block.

"Eric paid off the house for his parents when he made real money," she said.

Luke thought if he'd made serious money he'd have bought his parents a nicer place, but who knew the calculus of relationships in the Lindoe family? Maybe this had once been a happy home, one worth staying in for memories alone. Why would a wealthy, successful guy keep this house? Sentiment? Or maybe because he was involved in dirty dealings? After six months, had the will even been probated? The property would still be in his stepfather's name. It was a perfect place to hide.

They used a key on Eric's ring to get inside the house. The house smelled slightly musty.

"He's not here much," Luke said.

"Yeah. His mom died of cancer two years back. His stepdad passed about six months ago—heart attack. Not long after we met. Eric said his stepdad didn't want to live without Eric's mom."

"Yeah. My own stepfather said the same thing after my mom died."

"I'm sorry, Luke. How . . . ?"

"Car accident. She was driving. Rainy night. They hit a skid, went through a guardrail, tumbled down an incline. She died, he lived."

Aubrey opened her mouth and closed it. The silence grew heavy.

"But because of what you know about your stepdad now . . ."

"I wonder if it was really an accident." He shook his head. "Henry nearly died. It took him a long while to recover. I don't know. I thought he adored my mom. But he's the king of lies. Maybe I'll never know."

Aubrey took his hand, gave it a kind squeeze.

He switched on the kitchen lights.

"Eric made me hot tea and told me to sit here and wait," she recalled. "I was still so rattled by what had happened and what we were facing, I don't know what he did while I waited for him."

"Where did he go?"

"In the back."

They walked to the end of the hallway and found a master bedroom, the cheap furniture shrouded in plastic, as if trapping memories in a clear amber. Dust covered the plastic.

They backed up to the next bedroom. Eric's bedroom. A flicking-on of the light showed a room little changed from when Eric had taken his scholarship money and headed off to the University of Illinois. Clippings of his achievements dotted the wall—from high school through college, and then after, a shrine of proud parental hopes. A son who'd made nothing but good choices and then made a very bad one.

Luke studied the clippings. "He was president of an honor society, and he ends up a killer and kidnapper and a money man for extremists." He ran a finger along the frames: Eric's first letter offering him a banking job, in the operations division of a national bank; Eric in the sands of the Middle East, at a construction site, shaking hands with an older, elegant Arab businessman; in London, standing stiffly with other bankers; on a windswept beach, a borderline between desert and sea, watching the skeleton of a resort take hold.

"He really did spend a lot of time overseas. Did he ever talk about it?"

"No." She paused for a moment, looking at the smiling Eric beaming in the desert sun. "At my import company, I bought these really unusual pots from Papua New Guinea. There's a face on each side, like a totem. Eric thought they were cool. Maybe he liked them because they were two-faced, just like him."

"He's like Henry, in some ways. Henry loves his photos of himself at work, surrounded by powerful people. I don't understand why Eric and Henry got involved in this. Why? Why risk it all?"

"Some men can never have enough—money, pride, power," Aubrey said. "Name your poison and it will have an addict."

He peered inside the closet. "Help me look."

"What are we looking for?"

"What shouldn't be here."

She found the laptop three minutes later, tucked behind a stack of worn paperbacks on the top shelf. An old, cheap subnotebook, paired with a power cord.

Luke plugged in the system, started it up. It presented a password prompt.

"Any ideas?" Luke asked.

Aubrey rubbed a finger against her lip. "Let me try." She sat and tapped words on the keyboard. "I'll try words that mean something in his life." Luke continued searching the room. He found two guns—Glocks with ammunition. The serial numbers had been filed away. All was hidden in a box under the bed, camouflaged by a scattering of old Hardy Boys paperbacks. And money. Five thousand in cash.

Not fifty million, which would take up a considerable amount of room.

Luke put the money and the weapons on the bed.

"Nothing is working," she said.

"Stop and think for a minute. You said he set up your bank accounts. Did he set up your passwords at first?"

"I kept the passwords he used," she said. "They were more secure than what I would have conjured up. I would have used my name or my phone number or my first cat's name. He came up with passwords you could remember but that were hard to break."

"How?"

"Well, he always said to use words with letters you could easily replace with numbers and it would look kind of the same in your head. Like a word with E's, replace the E's with 3's. Or L's, replace with 1's. He said it was much more secure than the word itself, and still easy to remember."

"What did you choose for your passwords?"

"*Aubrey,* but with a 3 replacing the *E*. And another one, for an account he set up for me after we got back from Paris, was *Paris,* but with a 5 instead of the *S.*"

"Where did you go in France?"

"Mostly around Paris. Montmartre, Saint-Germain, the Louvre. All the tourist spots. We also went to Versailles and we went to Strasbourg for a couple of days."

"Did you go on any other trips with him?"

"No."

"Let's write down every shared interest you had, every place you went together."

"Just because he gave me passwords that meant something to him doesn't mean his passwords will also tie back to me."

"Maybe not," he said. "But you were his priority. He put everything on the line for you, Aubrey. I am willing to bet you were in the forefront of his mind when he was hiding this money. It was a ticket for the both of you."

He found a piece of paper and wrote down all the various neighborhoods and sites they had seen, all the common threads she could think of—their gentle rivalry of Cubs and White Sox, his obsession with Bulls basketball, his few favorite music groups and TV shows and movies, their preferred restaurants, a wine they drank on special occasions, the places they'd traveled together. Luke felt they were conducting an autopsy on the happier moments in Eric's life. Then they started playing with the words, replacing letters with numbers in Eric's style, turning *E*'s and *B*'s to 3's, *L*'s into 1's, *S*'s and *G*'s into 8's, and *P*'s into 5's. The list grew into dozens of permutations.

He became conscious as he scribbled with the pencil that time was passing. Maybe a neighbor would knock on the door, wondering who was parked in front of the empty house. Maybe the police would come, looking for evidence as to why Eric had been murdered. Sweat formed along his lip. He pushed a piece of paper at her. "Start entering these, please."

She typed, fingers pistoning on the keyboard, working through each possibility. "No. No. No."

After the tenth no he said, "You're being negative."

She hit it on the forty-second try. "This laptop," Aubrey said, "is officially our pet bitch." She turned the screen toward him. Unlocked, it showed a normal desktop.

"Which word?"

"It was *versailles*, except with ones instead of *L*'s. I should have guessed.

We had a really nice day in Versailles. He wondered aloud if you could get married there."

An awkward silence filled the room and Luke broke it. "Thank God for the consistency of bankers."

She got up and he leaned over the laptop. He started to search through its files. A few text files, an e-mail program and a Web browser, nothing else installed. Luke opened one of the text files; inside were listed the same accounts as on the piece of paper. Beside each account was a regional bank and a password, and a business name. The companies carried names that spoke of vague occupations—Lionhead Consulting; Three Brothers Partners; Jester, Inc.—nothing that hinted at what exactly they did. He counted a dozen of them. "He established a bunch of accounts for different companies."

"Try them. See if the fifty million is in those accounts." He could hear the urgency in her voice.

Luke surfed to each regional bank's Web site, entered in the account info and the password. He could hear Aubrey holding her breath, her mouth close to his ear.

But each account held only a hundred dollars, probably the minimum to stay open.

"These must be accounts he set up for the Night Road," she said. "For them to access money." Her sigh tickled his shoulder.

"He hid the money somewhere else. He could have tucked it into an idle account at Marolt Gold, changed passwords, opened up new accounts under false names. He started in bank operations, I saw it on his bio. Which means he's technically adept. We may never find it." A wave of despair washed across him.

Luke did online searches for the various company names. They did not have Web pages. "These are all dummy corporations. Another dead end."

"Luke, we have to find this money." Frustration filled her voice.

"Let's see where else he went the last time he was online." Luke looked in the browser's history window, which told him every site Eric had accessed. Aside from the banking pages, Eric had visited only one other place on the Internet: a Web site about TV shows.

"That's odd." He clicked to the Web site. A password page opened for him to log in.

"Why would you need a login?" Aubrey asked.

"I don't know. Was he a big TV fan?"

"Sports, mostly. The Bulls games."

Luke remembered the toy basketball on Eric's key ring, with the Bulls logo. "In the middle of hiding millions from killers, he goes to a foreign-based television fan site. It's like getting a haircut in the middle of a funeral, it makes no sense."

"Log on, see what happens," Aubrey suggested.

He tried the *versailles* password but it didn't work. He pulled the password sheet close to him and began to key through the possibilities again. All failed.

"I can't take another dead end."

"If it's not a password that connects to his life with you . . . what else in his life?"

"Well, his secret life."

"The Night Road." He entered the term, plain. It failed. He entered in variants, using the same number-replacement key as before.

The first few variants didn't work; then he tried *Ni8htRoad*. The password was accepted.

The dark world opened before him.

He scanned the newly loaded page and saw a long list of postings. Some of the posters used the same login names they had used on the Web sites where he had found them weeks ago. Their postings inside the Night Road were calmer. Offers for advice on cleaning funds through cheap insurance policies, requests for help on how to use automatic rifles, suggestions on how shrapnel could make a real difference in civilian deaths. Trade in murder, in secrets, in stolen identities and credit cards. Celebrations over the bombing of the rail yard in Texas, the pipeline in Canada, the *E. coli* food scare that had spread from Tennessee across the nation.

A bazaar for violence, a marketplace for twisted ideas. Horror braided his guts. He had found these people, given them to Henry as abstract bits of psychological profiling, and now they were a *community.* Worse. A secret army, readying for battle at home.

"Oh, my God," Aubrey said.

He did a search on the discussion forum for Henry Shawcross. For Mouser. For Snow. Nothing.

Then on Hellfire.

Nothing.

"They're celebrating the recent attacks, but they're not talking about this Hellfire thing," he said. "Hellfire must be separate and distinct from the current attacks."

"Maybe they canceled Hellfire, if they don't have the money."

"They don't seem like the canceling type. Or maybe the whole group's not involved. Only a few." Luke logged out from the discussion group.

"Why did you do that?"

"They could have software recording every account that enters, every address, every password. I don't want them to know that I'm here." He wiped his mouth. "I read about another community like this, set up in the Mideast by a weapons dealer to move explosives around the region. They could shut down, move their database and server, and the authorities couldn't find them again."

"So take it to the cops."

"I will. When we know where to find a member who will talk. Otherwise they'll just vanish into smoke."

He opened the e-mail program. Everything had been cleaned out, except one e-mail. It read:

> Your kind offer is accepted and protection is extended. Meet LAP,
> 23rd at 7 p.m. for your getaway.—Drummond.

"Do you know this Drummond?" he asked. The message had been sent from a common online e-mail provider, the kind of account you could set up in thirty seconds. The twenty-third was today; the rendezvous was in two hours.

"No," she said.

"*Protection is extended.* This is the deal he told you about, for protection to save you two," Luke said. "We have to find out who this Drummond is."

"So we can make the same deal?"

"Absolutely. I very much would like some protection now. Maybe Drummond can help us. We figure out who or what LAP is and get there in the next two hours."

Luke accessed the Internet, searched on *LAP CHICAGO*. He found references to a lawyers' assistance program, lap dancers, and a Lakefront Air Park. A private air park for general aviation.

Luke said, "This is the answer."

"He's meeting someone at an air park?"

"If he made the deal, part one is an escape route. Let's go."

She got up, touched a photo of Eric Lindoe, the bright-eyed boy with a wide smile and brilliant future awaiting him. She kissed her fingertips, pressed them to the photo, and then turned away.

They took the laptop, the money, and the guns, and headed north toward Lake Michigan.

29

The Lakefront Air Park's office was small, low, and sleek. The chrome and glass gleamed. They'd had to drive through long stretches of Chicago rush-hour traffic, and the setting sun burned the sky orange. The light reflected hard off the mirrored glass.

They'd parked Aubrey's car in the small adjacent lot. "This is certifiably insane," Aubrey said as they walked toward the building. The wind, which had been cooling all afternoon, bellowed, and they drew closer together, without thought.

"You're right," he said, "so no one will be expecting it."

The air park's offices were dim and, surprisingly, slightly shabby, as though all the money had gone into the architecture and design and there had been only stray pennies left for the furnishings. At one desk, a man in his thirties sat peering at a computer screen. He was of Asian descent, compactly built, a thin scar marring the corner of his mouth. He frowned at the screen—which Luke could not see—as though puzzling over bad news.

Luke took the lead. "Hey, I'm Eric Lindoe. I had a flight chartered for today."

"With who?" The man cranked a crooked smile.

First roadblock. "Mr. Drummond."

"Hi, Mr. Lindoe. I'm your ride." He offered his hand. "Frankie Wu."

Luke shook what he hoped was a dry hand with Wu's. "This is your other passenger, Aubrey Perrault."

"Hi."

Wu shook hands with Aubrey. "You're shivering, Ms. Perrault. You scared of flying? Don't be."

"Terrified," Aubrey said, with a glance at Luke.

"You and my wife. Actually she's more scared when I'm driving. You're in excellent hands."

Aubrey offered a smile. "I feel better already."

"We're fueled up and ready to go, Mr. Lindoe."

Where the hell are we going? He wanted to know. But he could hardly ask.

"You don't have more bags?" Wu asked, glancing at their cheap knapsacks. They'd stopped and bought a couple of changes of clothes and nothing more. Luke had the gun and the laptop and the money they'd taken from Eric's house in his pack, Eric's key ring jangling in his pocket.

"We travel light," Aubrey said.

"Please explain that virtue to my wife." Wu shut off the computer, scribbled a note on the clipboard.

"I only hope I brought the right clothes," Aubrey said. *Good,* Luke thought.

"The weather in New York should be fine. Paris might be rainy by tomorrow."

New York. Paris. Not one destination, but two. Was someone joining them in New York to go on to France? Luke felt a surge of panic—neither he nor Aubrey had a passport. Paris wasn't going to happen.

Paris. Where Jane was, the mastermind behind their kidnappings. He glanced at Aubrey; she gave the slightest of nods.

As he and Aubrey and Wu walked outside, across the tarmac to the waiting plane, he thought: *Don't do this. Turn and run. Aubrey's right, it's crazy.*

He kept walking toward the plane.

If he turned and ran, he would never know why the man he had thought of as a father had betrayed him. He'd never know who was after him; he'd be forced to live a half-life, always afraid, branded a murderer. No more turning or dodging. This lavish, expensive plane that was a dead man's escape route was going to take him straight into the heart of the matter.

His throat tightened as he looked at the plane. A private jet. Much like the one his father had died in. A swirl of painful memories churned in his head: the rainy night in Washington, hugging his father good-bye and breathing in the Old Spice scent of him; finding his mother red-eyed at the breakfast table the next morning, bearing her grief alone because she wanted Luke to sleep through the night; the letters pouring in from the universities where he had been a guest lecturer—Cairo, Bonn, London; the news footage of the salvage ship off the North Carolina coast, hauling the wreckage aboard out of the gray depths a week after the crash. The eulogies about what a wonderful teacher his father had been, listening to them, his mother holding his hand so tight he could feel the skip and beat of her pulse under her skin.

And Henry, introducing himself to Luke at the reception, a plate of chicken and salad in his hand, offering the other cool palm to Luke to shake, saying how much he had admired his father. How much he would miss him. As if anyone could miss him more than Luke and his mom.

He wondered, with a jolt, how life would have been different if he had not run away three days after the service. He had given Henry an easy, sympathetic key to wriggle his way into the family. If he had stayed home, maybe his mother would have never become friends with Henry Shawcross.

They followed Frankie Wu onto the plane. The Learjet was larger than Luke had expected, with a private cabin and cockpit. The cabin seated ten. A small galley was at the front of the aircraft. Aubrey sat down and he sat next to her, his heart thrumming in his chest.

Wu completed his final inspections, walking around the plane. Aubrey and Luke waited in silence. Wu walked, a cell phone pressed to his ear. He said a few words, then listened while he completed the inspection.

"He's letting someone know we've checked in," Aubrey said.

"Maybe," Luke said. He wasn't sure what he would say if Wu asked for Lindoe's ID. Say he'd lost it. A bead of sweat trickled past his ear.

"What's wrong?"

"My dad died in the crash of a plane like this. A mechanic named Ace Beere worked for the charter service. He had extremist views he shared at work; he found out he was going to be fired. He sabotaged my dad's flight. Him and several of his professor friends, they were flying down to Cape Hatteras for a retreat and some fishing. I'd wanted to go; he said no. Beere damaged the plane's systems so it lost pressure midflight. Everyone on board suffocated, died from hypoxia. The plane kept flying, far past the coast, until it slammed into the Atlantic." He glanced around. "Yeah, this plane's real similar." His throat tightened.

"Oh, my God, I'm sorry. Are you going to be all right?"

"I'm okay." He gripped the seat. Suddenly his father was like a physical presence in his chest.

"You're pale."

"I'll be fine."

"Tell me about your dad. What made him cool." She put her hand on his knee.

He savored the strength in her grip. "He always listened to me. He always had time for me. He was gone a lot, teaching overseas, and we didn't always get to travel with him. But when he came home, I felt like the most important person in the world. Like he breathed in every word I said. He took me fishing, shooting—old-school stuff that dads don't do much with their kids anymore. He always expected the best from me. That was a kindness, not a cruelty." He stopped, embarrassed, closing a hand around the Saint Michael's medal on his neck, hidden under his shirt. "The man who killed him, I always wanted to understand why. How do you just snuff out innocent lives, how do you justify that decision? He committed suicide, so I could never know. But that shaped my life. My career. If I hadn't been interested in the psychology of violence . . . I never would have been able to put together the Night Road for Henry. It all comes back to my dad's death. It's everything that has made me, shaped me."

Wu stepped back aboard. He flexed the smile back on. "Looks like all the masking tape and glue is in place."

"Ha-ha," Aubrey said.

"Did you check the baling wire?" Luke asked.

"Sealed it with spit," Frankie Wu said. "We'll depart in just a couple of minutes." He vanished into the cockpit and shut the door.

Luke leaned into Aubrey's ear and whispered, "He may be able to hear us over an intercom."

Aubrey nodded. She said, in a clear voice, "Eric, hold my hand. Mr. Wu might not have checked all the masking tape."

Luke took her hand. It felt strange and right all at once. He was Eric Lindoe, at least for the next few hours, until he met his kidnapper's benefactor.

Ten minutes later they arrowed into the night and blasted toward the east.

*   *   *

She slept and Luke watched her. He wanted to sink into the warmth of sleep but he couldn't.

New York. Paris.

He looked out the window, past the thin haze of clouds, over the glow of heartland light, as Illinois became Indiana, the diamond towns and the clouded black spreading beyond to Ohio and Kentucky. The low hum of the plane lullabied him.

He went to the cockpit and opened it. Frankie Wu was speaking softly into a radio and stopped, turned with a smile.

Luke asked, "Can I use my cell phone on this flight? I didn't know if the rules were different for private jets."

"There's a phone in the cabin you can use, yes."

"But not mine."

"No. I'm surprised you'd be wanting to call anyone, Eric." Like he knew Eric was running, Eric was in trouble.

Luke said, "I need to tell someone good-bye."

Frankie Wu turned back to the controls without comment. Luke shut the door. He had no intention of using the cabin phone; it could be monitored and he didn't want Wu overhearing this call. He sat at the back of the cabin and opened the phone he'd taken from Eric, the lifeline to Jane, and dialed Henry's number.

"Hello?" Henry sounded exhausted. The reception was spotty.

For a moment he couldn't speak. He listened to the sound of Henry's breathing.

"Hello?" Henry repeated. He sounded nervous.

"You sorry-ass excuse for a human being."

"Luke. Thank God, thank God, you're alive."

"I am never, ever going to forgive you for what you've done to me."

"Luke. Listen to me. I can help you. I'm your best hope."

"You sorry bastard. You knew I had been kidnapped, you listened to me beg you for help and you hung up the goddamned phone. I saw you on TV—"

"My clients—they're not who I thought they were. They used us both. And they wouldn't let me do anything but damn you to the public. But meet me, we'll figure out how we can both get out of this mess."

"Mess? This is beyond a mess. You sent Mouser and Snow after me like dogs to hunt me down. They tried to kill me. They've killed people, trying to kill me." His voice broke. "Well, I shot one of your dogs and stabbed the other, and I'm going to do the same to you."

"Don't cut me out. Don't. Tell me where you're at. I'll send you money; I'll send you whatever you need to hide. Mouser was only supposed to find you and bring you to me. So I could make you . . . understand."

"Understand what? That you used to me to knit together a terrorist network? Are you kidding me? What do you think I'm supposed to understand?"

"I can deal with Mouser and Snow, and anyone like them who bothers you. But there is another man who's hunting you. Drummond. Stay the hell away from him, from anyone connected to him or a group called Quicksilver."

The breath gelled in Luke's chest. "I—I don't believe you."

"Listen carefully to me. The cabin where you were held, it was paid for by a company called Quicksilver Risk. Stay away from them. I am begging you to listen to me. I know I screwed up but I never wanted you hurt. Ever."

"I hope you die, Henry, and I hope I'm there to see it."

"For God's sake, Luke." Henry's voice rose. "I have been your father for ten years."

"You're not fit to say the word *father*," Luke said.

Henry forged ahead as though Luke's contempt was mist. "I am not trying to get you killed, I'm trying to save you. I'm trying to find out who's attacking us, who's using us. Quicksilver is behind your kidnapping. Stay away from them." Then a pause, while Luke's head spun. "The man in Houston who was killed. His name was Allen Clifford. I knew him. So did your dad. We once worked together. On a special project for the government. Everyone who died on your father's plane, they were part of the project. It was called the Book Club."

"What do you mean, worked for the government?" The air left Luke's lungs. "He was a history professor, for God's sake."

Henry's words burned as unrelenting as a fuse. "After the accident, there were only three members of the Book Club left. Me. Allen Clifford. And Drummond."

"He was a teacher. A scholar. Just more lies from you—"

"Every word is truth," Henry thundered. "Drummond thinks you're part of the Night Road. He blames you for his friend's death. He came to me, threatened me if I didn't turn you over to him. He has significant resources to find you. And I know this man, when he finds you, you will vanish forever."

"You can't tell me all this and expect me to believe it." He stood, went to the back of the plane, fought down the scream that wanted to roar up from his lungs.

"I'm trying to show you I'm on your side. Son, please."

"Don't you call me *son*. I'm not your son. I never was. If you were on my side, you never would have gotten me involved. I was your needle and thread. Stitching together a whole bunch of killers and freaks and fringers for you. I met your buddy Chris. You actually went and shook hands with these guys who think an American al-Qaeda's a great idea, met them with open arms, planned to give them money." He leaned his head against the plane's wall. "You are funding terrorists to the tune of fifty million dollars. You are such a piece of shit."

"I didn't lie to you. My clients lied to me. They are using the research in ways I didn't consider. I need you to meet me."

"No, Henry."

He heard a long intake of breath. "I love you like you were my own child. I didn't at first, because you were such a pain. Spoiled, contrary, too smart for your own good. But I grew to love you as much as your own father did, Luke. I have tried only to protect you. To do right by you. Meet me at a place of your choosing and we'll work out a plan to get your name clear and you safe. Together."

"You weren't brave enough to help me. You could have gone to the police, to the FBI, and you didn't. You left me to die."

"I am trying to save us—"

"Prove it. Hellfire, Henry. What is it?"

Silence.

"Tell me what it is, give me your greatest secret, and I'll believe you want to help me. I know it's separate from the attacks that are happening now. It's bigger, isn't it? What is it? Bombs? Airplanes? Bioweapons? God help me, is it a nuke?"

A silence again, a stillness heavy enough to crush a heart, to flatten a family. Then: "I don't know that term *Hellfire*. I swear to God I don't know."

"Good-bye, Henry."

He took the phone and he broke it apart, scattering its components on the floor. He saw no point in talking to Henry again, no value in talking to Jane. What was he going to do: beg them for his life back? Screw pleading and begging.

A rage and a despair he had never felt before filled him. He imagined what it would be like to kill his stepfather. But the image of Henry's face, distorted in fear and remorse, the thunder of Luke's own heartbeat in his head—vanished in a snap.

You can't kill him because then you're him.

He stood over the broken phone and the rage changed to a hardness in his heart, a welcome toughness.

While Aubrey slept, he sat on the floor in the back of the plane, knees drawn up to his chin, wondering what darkness he was flying into, salvation or death. For a moment his hand closed on the Saint Michael's medal. Strength, the ability to face and overcome evil of the basest sort. He had to find his courage, fan its flame, keep going. He slipped the medal back under his shirt. The hum of the plane worked through his exhaustion and he closed his eyes to ponder his next move.

30

The Night Road was cutting its path through the heart of America, as Luke headed toward New York.

The high school football game in suburban Kansas City had been targeted because the attacker was a neo-Nazi and the high school had been named for a soldier who died early in the war in Iraq. The soldier was Jewish. The neo-Nazi hated seeing the Jew's name on the sign when he drove past every morning on his way to work.

The football game was a close one, and the neo-Nazi sighed in relief: A rout might have led to more people leaving earlier. Instead the game—he could hear the distant rumble of the announcer, voice tense with excitement—had been decided in the final three seconds by a field goal. The target school's team had won. The neo-Nazi rubbed at the dark tattoo across his neck—a highly stylized swastika—gritted his teeth, and thought: And no one will remember that. As the crowd spilled out into the lot, waving flags, banners, girls laughing and clutching at boys' arms, he pressed the first button.

The trunk of the car he'd parked in the middle of the lot popped open.

He saw a white girl, holding on to the arm of a boy who looked Mexican, glance over at the popping hood. The neo-Nazi gritted his teeth again. The world would go mongrel in two generations, if people didn't realize they just couldn't do what they wanted, he thought.

He waited until a bigger mass of people had spilled out into the lot, but before many of them had gotten into the protective cocoons of their cars.

He pressed the second button.

The bomb was not big; it had been built the month before by Snow. The neo-Nazi, who had picked it up from her last week, packed her creation with nails, bolts, and screws.

Chaos. A flash that burned his eyeballs. Screams and a distant heat and, he imagined, the whistle of thousands of flying blades whittling through flesh and bone. And then he heard the screams, much worse than even he had dreamed they would be. A glimpse of hell.

He got into his car and drove away, careful to stick to back roads. The emergency responders would be creating a traffic headache. He drove south and dialed a phone number. "Mine is done with success," he said by answer. "I get to be in Hellfire."

Henry Shawcross—but the neo-Nazi did not know him by this name— said, "There has been a change in plans."

"Is Hellfire canceled?"

"No. Check the following e-mail account." Henry gave him a Gmail account name and password. "It will contain the name of a city. Drive there, call on a fresh prepaid phone when you arrive, and await further instructions."

"When do I get my money?"

"Follow instructions." He hung up.

The neo-Nazi bit his lip. Not even a word of congratulations? His contact sounded like he'd lost the stomach for this battle. The neo-Nazi did not like that answer but what could he do? Complain? The mission first, that had been driven into his brain ever since he'd met the man with glasses and the rumpled gray suit at a coffee shop. He'd spent so much time on Web sites complaining about the damned Jews (and various other groups) and their plots to eviscerate America, it had felt good to meet with someone who recognized his unique potential. And with the first wave of attacks nearly done, now they could truly hurt this hated world. Feeling the need to put distance between himself and the school, he drove ten miles before stopping at a suburban coffee shop that offered free Internet access. He opened his laptop, checked the account.

The e-mail account's one message simply said: CHICAGO.

He checked the news Web sites. The bombing was, of course, the lead news story. A smile, a bubble of laughter, rose from his chest and heat traveled along his skin. It felt good to make a fist for justice and throw a hard, savage punch. And Hellfire was going to be so much more than a little punch. He trembled with excitement. With his promised cut of the money, he could recruit new adherents. Buy automatic weapons. Buy better material for bombs, higher-quality explosives, and much more of them. He could set up operations throughout the Midwest.

He could be somebody who shaped the world.

He was tempted to go onto the Night Road site, but no. Not now. Not here. There were a few patrons lingering over their lattes. And the barista, she looked Jewish to him, and she kept trying to see what the sharp-edged tattoo on his neck was. He suddenly didn't want her looking at him.

He got back in his car and drove north toward Chicago in the long sprawling night, the screams playing in his head like a symphony he'd written himself, a masterpiece.

The second attack took place in Los Angeles, California, outside of a small restaurant off Sunset Boulevard. It had, unusually, been a stormy day in Southern California. Rain fell in broken windblown curtains and the wind hissed like steam, and the young man in the car waited on a side street. He had never killed before and his hands shook with fright at the thought of what he was about to do. He opened the file folder next to him, although he had studied it for hours in the past several days, when he wasn't praying at the mosque or trying to hide his activities from his mother and his father, who would disapprove.

The target's picture had been torn from one of his book jackets, which outlined how the war against Islam must be waged, and sold in the hundreds of thousands to the unbelievers. His advice was being cited in Washington; he had the ear of powerful people who might act contrary to Allah's will. He was a history professor at UCLA, a specialist in terrorism and the Middle East, an educated man who apparently knew nothing. His words could not be allowed to continue, and he had been talking and writing more and more about the possibility of American Muslims being seduced into violence, as had happened in France, Germany, and Britain, becoming homegrown carriers of terror.

Then the young man saw the professor. Walking with his wife and his teenage daughter, hurrying, huddled under an umbrella. The rain had eased in the past fifteen minutes, Allah smiling on his mission.

The young man lowered his window. Fifteen feet away.

The gun was ready in his hand. Ten feet away. He had to do this; he had to keep his nerve so he could qualify himself for a much greater battle.

He raised his arm and asked Allah to guide his aim and fired the modified semiautomatic at the family, hoping the drizzling rain would not badly deflect his bullets.

The wife and the daughter, strolling in the front, fell screaming. He could see that the girl was dead in an instant, a bright cloud of blood settling on her skull; the wife shrieked, badly wounded. The professor—He Who Must Die—stumbled, trying to catch his family, a dawning horror on his face.

The gunman fired again, another spurt of bullets drumming through tender flesh and mortal bone. The three of them lay sprawled in the blood and the cleansing rain.

He had just killed an entire family and for a moment the realization cut to his heart. Then he thought: *Good. Well done.*

They had dropped in front of a wine bar and a man ran out, a woman stumbling behind him, trying to help the family.

Stupid or brave? the gunman thought. It did not matter. The gunman shot them both, biting his lip again, not caring now. He didn't want to be seen, didn't want his license plate noticed. He revved onto Sunset Boulevard, drove fast, blasted through two red lights, turned onto side streets. He had stolen it earlier that morning, changed the plates with a car at the airport. Now he drove the car to Orange County, parking in the shadow of a mosque, his breathing returning in even tides. He had committed a most brazen mass killing, in full daylight, and escaped. Now he could be part of Hellfire, his worth proven.

He made the phone call. He was told there had been a change in plans, that he would not go to Houston, that he must check an e-mail account that he had never seen before. He went to a computer at a public library and opened the account.

The message read: CHICAGO.

He had been chosen, not just by Allah, but by his brothers in arms, his fellow warriors, whoever they were. He lowered the window as he drove east, letting the damp air refresh his skin and nourish him for the battle and the glory that lay ahead.

31

Bridger lay bound and tied in the car trunk; Henry looked at him with a gaze free of pity. Snow's ex had been turned in by a Night Road member he knew, one that Bridger had run to in Alabama, begging for money and a place to hide. Per Henry's orders, the man drove Bridger in the trunk up to a rural field in northern Virginia.

Standing under the gleam of the stars, Henry wanted a cigarette for the first time in several years. The conversation with Luke had unnerved him badly. He had thought before that Luke would at least be willing to hear him out. If he could simply get a word in, he was sure he could make Luke understand. Barbara kept crowding into his thoughts, her final words to him much like Luke's: *I know what you are.* She had said them right before the crash, when he'd only grabbed the steering wheel to get her to pull over, so he could work his magic, convince her that she was wrong. If she'd only listened, the car wouldn't have plowed through the guardrail, somersaulted down the hill. He had kept his eyes open during the whole crash, screaming Barbara's name, watching her die.

If only Luke would listen, a certain tragedy would be avoided.

Barbara had only found a phone in his desk. A cell phone he kept for contacts in the Middle East. The balance sheet for the think tank had grown thin, and he would spend late nights rereading his 9/11 papers, wondering. *When I saw September eleventh coming, why did no one believe me?* He would ignore that he had failed to include so many vital details that actually happened in the attack. His anger at being overlooked would heat like a fever and he would think, like a bullied child, *I'll show them all.* He would sip his whiskey, grow morose. He knew many people in the Middle East, some of them with loose connections to the terrorists he'd interviewed and psychologically dissected. He had sent out feelers, calling them, asking for meetings, trying to find a solution to his problem: How could he predict terrorist attacks with greater accuracy. How could he win wider acclaim, grow his business, be seen as a power player?

He'd finally realized he'd needed someone that could help him make his vision work.

She'd found the phone and she'd listened to a voice mail he'd forgotten to erase, from an associate of the Arab billionaire. Stupid of him. But he had been listening to it when she interrupted him and he'd just switched off the phone. But she knew it wasn't the phone he normally used. What had possessed her to pry, to listen to the voice mail? Had she been afraid he was unfaithful, that the phone was used for contact with a mistress? He worshipped Barbara. He knew how lucky he was. And she had waited until they were in the car, a day later, to confront him. He should have denied it all while they were driving but he was too rattled.

He would not make such a mistake again. It had cost him Barbara; it would not cost him his son.

He had driven from his Alexandria home to the deserted field, careful that Drummond or someone else was not following him. There was no sign of a shadow; then he reminded himself that if Drummond was part of the government still, then they could simply train a satellite on him and follow him.

You're not that important, he told himself. *And that is your strength. If they'd realized you were important, maybe you'd still be with State. Maybe you'd be where you started, on the side of the angels.*

Then the little stinger of his conscience: *If you had been treated as important, then none of this would have happened.*

"I need to speak with him alone."

"I'll take a walk," said the young Alabama man who'd delivered Bridger. He strolled off into the darkness. Henry dragged Bridger out of the trunk, propped him against the car's bumper. He still wore the leather jacket with its emblazoned eagle.

"I've had a very bad day," Henry said. "You know, in my business, I have to e-mail out position papers on policy and theory to some of the most powerful people in the world."

Bridger stared.

"I've warned my clients about all sorts of impending attacks today: a follow-up on the chlorine bombing, an assault on our fuel supplies, a rise in neo-Nazi hatred. Everything I've predicted is coming true."

Bridger moaned behind the gag.

"I've had violence on my mind, Bridger. And you know, thinking about violence can make one more violent. That's unlucky for you."

Bridger's eyes widened with terror.

Henry unwrapped the gag, let the fabric fall from Bridger's mouth, and the man screamed for help.

"No one can hear you," Henry said. "God, it feels good to say that. You're the best part of my day, Bridger."

Bridger, to Henry's disgust, started to cry.

"Your mouth is what's gotten you in trouble."

"I didn't do nothing, honest."

"You didn't do anything because your Quicksilver contact got killed before you could sell us out."

"No. I don't know what you're talking about."

"You're on the Houston traffic intersection tape we accessed, son."

"It ain't me, it ain't me." He was not a brave man, in any sense of the word, and his stark fear shuddered off him in waves, as though it had its own energy his skin could not contain.

"It's you. Even if we hadn't pulled your face off the tape, your extremely badass leather jacket with the embroidered eagle on the back is too tasteful and refined to belong to anyone but you, Bridger."

Bridger hung his head.

"You've broken Snow's heart."

"She . . . you don't need to hurt her."

"I don't blame her for your betrayal. Plus, she's useful. She's already found a guy to fill your shoes and to warm her bed." Henry's smile shifted. "When you don't amount to much, it's easy to replace you." He smiled to himself. He knew this truth. Warren Dantry hadn't been much of a father or husband, in Henry's eyes, and he'd slipped into Warren's life with an astonishing ease.

"Now. We can be friends again, and the Night Road can forgive you." Henry squatted on the cool grass next to him. "If you tell me who Quicksilver is."

"I don't know that name."

"The man you were meeting worked for a company called Quicksilver. Who are they?"

"I don't know. They said . . ." and Bridger stopped as though searching for words.

Henry reached over to him, found a finger. And broke it, with a clean snap. Drummond had taught him the technique, years ago, for self-defense.

Bridger howled, kicked a muddy trench in the grass, knocked his shoulders and head hard against the bumper. When he could speak coherent words again he begged, "Don't, don't, no!"

"You have nine more. One minute to change your mind, and I crack another." He let the pain sink in, let the horror rise in Bridger.

Bridger clenched teeth.

"I mean, do you think Quicksilver's going to charge through the woods and rescue you? I think not. I'm your only hope for mercy and kindness, Bridger. We can forgive you. We can hide you. But not if you don't help us."

The minute passed, the only sound Bridger's clenched moans. He was nothing more than a loser, a guy who'd drifted from one racist extremist group to another across the South, usually doing no more than building their Web sites and waving a placard during poorly attended demonstrations. He'd met Snow five months ago and they'd moved in together; he had an interest in learning how to build bombs, but no skill, and he'd been demoted to solely being the guy in charge of fetching her supplies.

Gently, Henry reached for the next finger, caressed it from nail to joint, and before he could break it, a desperate spill of words came from Bridger's throat:

"I got a call on my cell phone. From this man."

"What was his name?"

"He didn't give it. He said, real blunt, that he knew I had acquired bomb gear for Snow. That if I didn't want to go to prison for the rest of my life, I needed to cooperate." Bridger swallowed.

But how had Allen Clifford known about Snow in the first place? Henry wondered. And the answer was clear: *We have a spy inside the Night Road.*

"The guy said they'd pay me, they'd hide me, make sure I didn't go to prison. If I just gave everything I knew to him, he'd come meet me in Houston."

"How did you know about what Snow was working on?"

"I heard Snow talking to you." He shook his head in shame.

"You were spying on her."

"I knew she made a few simple bombs, for people to pick up and use. A guy from Minnesota, a guy from Missouri, a bunch of hippies from Seattle. But then she was working on a huge number of bombs, for days and days." Bridger bit his lip. "So I thought, I'll go meet this dude, then I was gonna capture him and bring him back to you. So we could know who the enemy was, you know. I'm on your side."

"We? You're not part of us. You're not smart enough to be one of us." Henry broke another finger and Bridger vomited onto his own lap. "That's for lying and not even being good at it."

Bridger howled and cried and spat a green rope of spit onto the ground. "I thought I'd . . . prove I was useful to you." His voice sank into a quicksand of pathetic whining. "I ain't a traitor."

"Then prove it. Tell me everything and I'll let you call Snow and you can apologize to her."

"So I agreed. The guy said he'd meet me in downtown Houston. I wanted it on the streets in case it was a trap. So I could run." As though a trap couldn't be sprung on Bridger in the streets of Houston, as it clearly had been, and one of Jane's own design. "Told him he had to dress like a homeless man, throw me a hand signal that all was clear."

"And the point of this meeting?"

"I'd tell him everything I knew about Snow and the bombs. I knew about the Web site she goes on, to talk to folks around the world, you know, people like us. How to access the Web site, what Snow was planning. Give 'em any names. I only knew yours and Snow's."

"And Clifford—that's the man's name, by the way—would give you what?"

"Protection. A fresh start overseas. I thought I'd go to Sweden or Iceland or one of those countries that's nearly all white folks. That's just what I told him. Of course my plan was to capture him, bring him back to Snow so y'all could question him."

"Of course. Did he know about Hellfire? About the members of the Night Road?"

For a second it looked like Bridger was giving the matter serious thought, as much as his lax brain could summon. Then he shook his head. "He knew something big might be coming. He didn't know what specifically, I don't think."

"Thank you, Bridger. I'd like to know if Clifford mentioned my name."

"No."

"Did he mention Luke Dantry?"

"No."

"Did he ever suggest that he was part of a police or government agency?"

"No."

"Did he use the word *Quicksilver*?"

"No."

"How did Clifford assure you he could protect you?"

"He said they could hide me better than the feds or the police could because there would be no record, no paperwork, no trail for me to be found."

No paperwork? Then Quicksilver didn't play by government rules. Henry rubbed his temples, a throbbing headache blossomed in his brain. Bridger's claims only deepened the mystery.

But he had to act before either Jane or Quicksilver could derail Hellfire. Apparently Quicksilver didn't know in advance about the first wave of attacks; nothing had interfered with the execution of those operations. But they suspected the first wave was just a prelude to something bigger.

He patted Bridger's cheek. "Okay. Let me get your fingers fixed up and we'll get you on your way."

"Really? Really?"

Henry nodded at the pathetic desire to believe. "Really."

He went to his own car, pulled out a video recorder and a tripod, mounted a night-vision lens, and turned it on.

"What's that for?"

"Discouragement."

His back was to the camera, but he still lowered a black balaclava, drawn from his jacket, over his face to hide it. Bridger started to whimper. "But you promised . . . you promised."

Henry could edit the words out later. He broke the remaining eight fingers. By the fourth one Bridger was unconscious from the pain. He kicked Bridger in the testicles, to waken him. Bridger's eyes jerked wide with numbed fear. Henry cut his throat with a straight razor, one swift move.

He put his hand on Bridger's shoulder, felt the life and the pain seeping out of him, and said, "This is what happens when you attempt to betray the Night Road." The video clip would be put up on the group's Web site in short order, and that should take care of any loyalty issues.

Ten minutes later the boy from Alabama returned from his stroll. He stared down at Bridger's body and Henry heard the click of his swallow. "Well."

"Get rid of him for me, please. Make sure he's not found. Dig deep. Then go home. You'll receive extra money or extra training at our expense, your choice."

The Alabamian nodded, his face pale. "I want to learn how to make bombs."

"I'll see that you do."

Henry drove home to Alexandria. He sat down at his computer.

Quicksilver—he needed to know who they were. And they would have to be eliminated. If they were a new incarnation of the Book Club, a group working outside government constraints, then their activities could be mapped, followed, discovered.

Among the clients of the Shawcross Group think tank were leading telecommunications companies, concerned about infrastructure attacks; transportation companies, worried that they themselves could be terrorist targets; and financial services companies, always knowing that a wave of terrorism could slash their profits in the event of a massive financial collapse.

He would use his clients' resources to find Quicksilver.

He crafted his e-mail carefully, then sent it to his highest, most discreet contact in each client.

As one of my key clients, I urgently seek your help. I have been requested by a high government official to test how quickly both government and private databases can unearth covert operatives working on American soil, and to determine how consistent the information is. I suspect forthcoming lucrative contracts may be at the basis of his decision.

I have created two false identities: Allen Clifford and Kevin Drummond. Please use your databases in communications, financial, transportation, credit, security, and so on to find them. I have given them an association with a legitimate firm called Quicksilver Risk Management. Please forward any results, time-stamped, on these two identities or this firm. Thank you and please know that our confidentiality agreement applies.

Henry suspected he wouldn't have long to wait. And this would give him the best opportunity to find out about his enemy.

Afterward, he sent out another private e-mail to his clients. The first line of the e-mail read:

Forthcoming from Shawcross Group research, a new series of papers outlining the most likely attacks against the United States.

Hellfire was going to make him look like a very smart man.

32

Luke woke up from his doze, leaning against the airplane's back wall. Frankie Wu stood over him. Luke's head throbbed, thick with sleep. He blinked himself to full wakefulness. "What's wrong?"

"Nothing, Mr. Lindoe. I just wanted to be sure you were all right. You're not in your seat."

"Sorry. I sat to have a think and I thought too much." He stood awkwardly.

Frankie Wu watched him, arms crossed.

"Shouldn't you be flying the airplane?" Luke said. He went back to his seat. His knapsack lay tilted on its side and he wondered if that was the position it had been in when he dozed off. Had Wu searched it?

"Autopilot. Just wanted to see if either of you needed anything, Mr. Lindoe."

The use of the false name again, the barest emphasis. *He knows. But he's not calling you on it. Not yet. He doesn't want trouble in the air.* "When do we land in New York?"

"Forty minutes."

Luke glanced at Aubrey; she was asleep. He wasn't surprised, not even at his own heavy slumber. Sleep was escape. Hunger was a sudden, sharp fist of pain.

Wu turned without a word and went back to the cockpit. Closed the door.

Luke opened the knapsack. The gun was still there. He checked it. Unloaded. The clip was gone, and nowhere in the backpack. The gun was now useless. The cash he'd taken from Eric's stash was still there, though. The laptop from Eric's was there, too, cool to the touch. It hadn't been fired up.

Wu had searched the bag.

Luke went to the tiny galley. Quietly, he checked the drawers. In one he found a flight manifest for the food and drinks on the flight. The charges paid for by Quicksilver Risk, with a New York City address. Quicksilver.

His stomach sank to his toes. He picked up the phone in the galley. He called information for Braintree. He remembered the name of the property company of the cabin, from its sign near the gate. He got the number and called. If they rented cabins, there ought to be an emergency number in case the renters had a problem at night. He got an answering machine that fed him such a number; he redialed.

"Yes?"

"Hello. My father has gone missing and he may have rented a cabin from you. Cabin number three. At the edge of the property. Was it rented by a company called Quicksilver?"

"I sure am getting calls about this rental." The clerk sounded huffy.

"Please. Allen Clifford, he's missing. . . ."

"Well, he left the cabin a mess, destroyed the bedroom furniture, and we charged his card again for damages."

"How did he pay? I'll make sure you're compensated."

"Charge card. Company card. Quicksilver Risk Management."

"Thank you." Luke hung up. Jesus, they had paid for the cabin, Henry was right. That didn't mean he could trust Henry. But it sure didn't mean he could trust these people either. He took a calming breath.

He tore the page with the address from the manifest. Eric's escape route was a trap.

He found sandwiches in the galley and ate one. The city that never sleeps looked like a creamy miniature galaxy below. He guessed they would be landing in New Jersey, right across the river.

He shook Aubrey. She blinked at him, awake and ready. He handed her a sandwich and mouthed the words, *The pilot knows. We have to run.* Her eyes widened in fear and she mouthed back, *What's the plan?*

He wished they'd had this discussion back in her car, but they hadn't known they'd be able to con their way onto Eric's flight. They'd have to improvise. He whispered into her ear: "A company called Quicksilver paid for the cabin we were held in and for this flight."

Her eyes widened in fright.

Who are they? she mouthed.

He shook his head. *Follow my lead,* he mouthed, and she nodded.

He took her hand, and they waited to land.

The plane taxied toward the small terminal at the private airfield. Wu asked, through the intercom, for them to remain in their seats.

Luke disobeyed. He got up, went to the door, popped the lever. The door swung open and an alarm brayed into the cold night air. Aubrey was at his back and they jumped to the tarmac. Aubrey landed next to him and they ran.

Cutting through the roar of the engines, he heard Frankie Wu's once-friendly voice yelling in rage. The airport's runway was between them and a fence, and another commuter jet was preparing to take off, now that Wu's plane was clear.

Luke and Aubrey ran to the edge of the runway—then he heard voices bellowing his name. "Luke! Luke Dantry! Stop!"

He glanced back, causing Aubrey to collide into him, and saw two men, running past where Frankie Wu had screeched his jet to a stop. Wu was in the doorway, pointing at them. Closing fast. Quicksilver's welcoming party, he thought. If he and Aubrey stayed put they'd be dead. The other commuter jet approached.

We can make it, he thought, Aubrey's hand clenched in his.

They ran across the runway, the departing jet catching them in its lights, rising, knocking them in a battering wash of engine, both stumbling to their knees from the wake.

He looked back—one of the Quicksilver men held a collapsible rifle and was unslinging it from a knapsack on his back. "Aubrey, run!" he yelled.

They bolted back to their feet, running, nearly in a headlong drive, both intent on reaching the fence. Forty feet; beyond the mesh lay a parking lot, a scattering of cars. A stream of light beckoned beyond, the hazy glow of a highway.

The grass erupted in front of his feet, shots spewing green bits of lawn. They kept running.

They hit the fence. He slowed to help her but Aubrey was quicker, clambering up the chain link with an assured grace. She reached the concertina wire and paused, pulling her coat free. She balled it over her head in a tight dome and wiggled through the slicing spiral.

"I don't want to get caught again," she screamed. And he knew to his bones her fear, that helpless, this-is-not-happening-to-me terror. He'd felt it when Eric Lindoe stuck the gun into his rib cage, steered him out of normalcy into the rapids of nightmare. He knew she'd felt it when that burlap bag went over her head as she left her office.

She was through, on the ground, pants torn along the leg where the razor-wire scored.

He ripped off his own coat, following her lead, yelling at her to keep running, don't look back.

He covered his head with the cheap windbreaker just as he heard the voices closing in, one saying, "No way." Then thumps against the fence, the boom of the rifle.

The lined windbreaker made a fragile cocoon. The curling wire cut past his defenses—he felt a slash along his scalp, his back, his butt. Then gravity superseded fear, yanking him through the last curve, the concertina cutting at his suddenly bare stomach.

He hit the ground, panicked, rolling free of the tattered windbreaker, running for the lot.

Aubrey was gone. It wasn't that big of a parking lot and she wasn't moving through the moonlight. Where was she?

She's hiding, he thought, and then he saw a car racing away from the lot, far faster than normal traffic. And in a blur, her face, struggling at the window.

"Aubrey!" he yelled. He glanced back. The Quicksilver men who'd dogged him to the fence ran, yelling into cell phones. Not in such a hurry. Of course not. They had friends waiting to catch Aubrey and him, maybe a team for each. A car powered up, raced straight toward him as he ran off the curb.

33

Luke ran. Not deeper into the parking lot, where he knew the Mercedes sedan could corner him as their partners had caught Aubrey; nor back toward the razor-tipped fence where the two men had corralled him.

He ran toward the highway.

The grass funneled out into a short expanse—maybe sixty feet across—and then a service road and then the torrent of cars, traffic still brisk at a late hour, people returning from Manhattan.

Behind him, the Quicksilver Mercedes vroomed off the asphalt lot, onto the dry grass.

Blood coursed down his calves where the wire had bit. He did not dare glance behind him; he did not want to see. It was worse than being pursued by Mouser and Snow because this was *teams,* coordinated, an inexorable fist closing around him.

Luke hit the service road and a minivan laid on its horn, nearly veering off the road trying to avoid him. The van revved past him, leaving a wake of burnt stench and a scream of *You crazy asshole* as he ran. The pursuing Mercedes lurched across the grass, closing the distance fast, and now he glanced back, saw a rear window powering down.

He measured his options in one glance. He could go to the right, where the service road curved toward a distant intersection and the Mercedes could run him down or scoop him up. Or he could go left, where he'd be running headlong into one-way traffic. But to the left was an entrance ramp onto the highway, bordered by a crash wall, so the Mercedes would have to both go against the one-way traffic *and* make a 180-degree, sharp-as-nails turn to follow him onto the highway.

He headed for the ramp.

Two cars hurtled at him, both screaming with their horns, and he ran between them, feet snapping on the white line. He ran like a machine, the wind carrying him, trying to urge every bit of speed from his tired muscles.

A screech yowled behind him, metal sliding, skimming hard against other metal. He turned as he sprinted along the highway entrance ramp, another car zooming past him in a blur.

Luke stormed up the ramp, and he glanced back. The Mercedes began a sharp turn to navigate the entrance, smoke misting the wheels.

Five lanes of traffic, a median wall, and then five more lanes. They would catch him if he hugged the shoulder and ran in the direction of the traffic. Or smear him like jam along the concrete.

But a stream of traffic coursed by, and he couldn't get across the lanes in time; it would be a violent waltz where one wrong step or one veering driver would kill him.

No time to hesitate. He saw the approaching cars and their headlights, and he had to dodge them.

A belching semi rocketed past him and he ran the first lane in its wake, seeing a station wagon in the second lane. The wagon slammed brakes and he jumped and ran around it, clearing it and the third lane as the station wagon resumed speed.

The Mercedes powered fast onto the highway. He froze, no choice, five zooming sedans powering past him. He was trapped, the Mercedes approaching, trying to navigate to his lane.

The Mercedes aimed dead on for him as the fifth car blasted by and he ran, brakes screeching, a crunch as a car swerved over into another lane, its side crumpling against another sedan. The Mercedes cut around the cars, heading straight for Luke. He could see the triumph on the driver's face.

Then the Mercedes was rear-ended by a brake-slamming truck.

Luke turned and ran through the final lane and vaulted the concrete wall. The slowing of traffic had already started due to the human urge to rubberneck, and while the New York–bound traffic didn't slam to a standstill, he managed a short, brutal dash to the opposite side.

A truck barreled past him on the exit ramp, clearing him by inches, and he fell on the concrete and saw the tires just miss his outstretched fingertips. He looked up and the truck was past him, slowing at the end of the ramp, brake lights brightening. He cleared the ramp by hurtling himself over its edge, dropping fifteen feet to soft dirt. He went to one knee, weary with the cold, shaking, and the adrenaline turning on him, burning like poison in his veins. He staggered back to his feet and caught his breath, the quavering in his legs finally easing.

He ran down the service road, the weight of the knapsack heavy on him.

They'd gotten Aubrey. He had to get her back.

He ran to the intersection, where an all-night mart sat in a puddle of streetlight. He walked in and heard the soft sounds of Indian sitar music drifting above the shelves. A few minutes ago he was dodging cars, now he was shopping. He wondered if he looked shell-shocked. He bought a first-aid kit and a hot coffee and a bottled water. He went to the bathroom and inspected his cuts. A thin, shallow one marked his stomach—the concertina wire had nipped him where his shirt had been hiked and twisted. Another cut sliced through the back of his jeans, a scoring across his calf and lower back that stung even more when he saw them. He smeared on disinfectant gel, applied adhesive bandages to the worst of the cuts, and swallowed aspirin. He downed the cold water in four long gulps. He drank the still-warm coffee and the heat began to seep into his blood, under his skin.

Luke left the mini-mart and walked away from the highway. He had to keep moving. But it was late and they would not stop hunting him. He did not feel panic; but rather the calm of resolution.

He was going to take the war back to these people.

First things first. He was still entirely too close to the air park and the highway, and the Quicksilver team might have friends.

He found a taxi letting off passengers close to a bus station. He showed the cabbie the address for Quicksilver he'd stolen from the food manifest.

"That address, you know what part of the city that is?"

"That is near NYU in Greenwich Village," the cabbie said, after consulting a detailed map.

"Let's go."

The cabbie informed him of everything wrong about New York, a city Luke had always enjoyed visiting. Luke sat in the backseat and listened only enough to make agreeing grunts when required for politeness. When they reached Washington Square, Luke asked the cabbie to let him out at the entrance to the park. Luke walked along the darkened paths and sat down on a bench. He surveyed the immediate area for trouble and police and saw only a drunk reclining on a bench thirty feet away, staring at the grass as though it held the secrets of the universe.

What will they do with Aubrey?

He imagined the worst for a long while, and when the drunk approached and asked if he had five bucks, he got up and walked out of the park. He did not walk to the Quicksilver address. He found a small hotel that catered to New York University visitors and paid cash for a minuscule room. He registered under a fake name, Brian Blue, because a weird abstract blue painting hung in the lobby, and Brian was the name of the annoying neighbor who'd bad-mouthed him on the television news. He sprawled on the lumpy bed. He wanted to curl into the cocoon of sleep but he couldn't. They had Aubrey. She had been kidnapped, again, and the thought of what she must be enduring burned. Being kidnapped at gunpoint, he knew, was not a skill that improved with practice.

He had thought he was taking them to safety. He wished he had talked her into going to the police; by now she'd have been safe. And he would have been able to give up this fight, just vanish, run, find a nice big rock to hide under.

He stared out the window. Running was no life. Hiding was no life. He couldn't give up, not yet. He had never felt so alone, even chained in the cabin. There, escape had been the only option he could pursue. But now, he could try to save Aubrey, or go to the police and surrender, or try and fight the Night Road and Henry.

He unpacked the knapsack. The useless gun, the laptop that he'd already picked clean. He pulled Eric's key ring from his pocket. The Chicago Bulls toy basketball on the end of the ring caught on the pocket's inside lining. He yanked it free.

There was a slight catch on the edge of the toy ball, under the Bulls logo. He hadn't noticed it before. He worked his thumb on the catch.

The ball popped open.

Inside was a USB plug, the kind that slid into a computer port.

The other half of the basketball was solid. It was a hidden thumb drive; a portable way to carry computer files.

"Oh, my God," Luke said in the silence of the room. He powered up the laptop and logged in. Then he slid the secret thumb drive into the laptop.

The thumb drive appeared on the screen. Holding his breath, biting his lip, he clicked on it. Inside was a single file. He tried to click it open, but all he got was a dance of gobbledygook, glowing random numbers and letters, across his screen.

The file was encrypted.

Eric had started his career in bank operations; he would know about encryption. Luke knew then this must be the file that contained the whereabouts of the fifty million dollars. Nothing else could be so important. The thumb drive was Eric's insurance in the face of certain death from the Night Road, his bargaining chip for Quicksilver. He'd simply carried it in his pocket.

This held the information on where the fifty million was hidden, and the key, he knew, to stopping Henry and the Night Road.

But he had no idea how he could access the information. The encryption key needed to be on the computer, and it wasn't on this laptop.

He tucked the gun under his pillow; even empty, it reassured him. And he put the key ring under the pillow as well. Luke closed his eyes and the weight of what he knew he must do pressed him into fitful exhaustion.

As the night pressed against the windows, the eyes of the Night Road and Quicksilver kept watch, scanning every credit charge, every hotel database, looking for Luke's name, Eric's name, any sign, any mistake that would signal his location.

And while the thousand electronic eyes watched, he slept.

34

The day had nearly driven Mouser mad. Snow made a poor patient; she slept fitfully, waking often to worry if Hellfire would be canceled. Mouser kept waiting on the Night Road hacker to pierce the GPS database and hand him Aubrey and Luke. He'd paced tracks in the already questionable carpet of the South Chicago motel room. Snow alternated between uncomfortable sleep and watching him fret.

"You had him in the basement," she said finally. "Is that what's preying on your mind, baby? Because I had him in the woods and he got away from me."

"I'm not happy with how we've done. We can do better."

"Come here," she said. "Lie down next to me and see if you can't calm down."

He swallowed, thinking he shouldn't. "I hate this waiting."

"I need a little more warmth than the blanket," she said. He lay down next to her, certain she couldn't want him, not after being shot in the shoulder. But she did. He was conscious of her bandages and was very gentle with her. The whole time her small mouth was a hard little O and he wasn't sure if she was happy or angry until the savoring smile broke across her face at the end. Afterward he watched the ceiling and thought: *God sent her to me, to be my helper against the Beast. I've had bad luck with catching Luke but that all changes now. He's running out of rope. He can't go to the police. He can't go much anywhere where the Night Road can't find him.*

"You know why I hate the government. Why do you?" Her breath warmed his shoulder.

He didn't intend to answer but then her fingers began a slow meander across his stomach.

"I knew Tim McVeigh," he said.

"Oh."

"I'm not bragging. We weren't buddies, but we'd met at a couple of . . . meetings of folks who didn't like the government infringing on people's rights. I had some acquaintances, who decided they would emulate McVeigh by bombing a big shopping mall. I didn't know about the plot, but I got hit with a jail sentence because they'd called me and asked me about acquiring explosives, and I didn't turn them in. They blabbed about me, I hadn't done anything wrong, and yet I went to prison for five years."

Snow was silent.

"So. In there I met a guy. Henry. Interviewing so-called domestic terrorists, delving into our heads. Trying to figure out if I hated my dad, was dominated by my mother, psychobabble crap."

"He thinks terrorists hate their dads?"

"Some of them. He said it was a consistent pattern. I got a friend outside to send me one of his books."

"I would have died for my dad," Snow said softly. "I know what loyalty is."

"He and I kept talking. I liked talking with Henry. I got out and I sort of bummed around, did mechanic's work when I could find it. And kept thinking about how I could make the Beast pay for taking five years of my life."

He felt her fingers grope along his chest, skirt the tattoos reading GLORY and DEATH that spread across his muscles, move down across the flat of his belly.

"We lost a lot from the government," she said.

"You more than me. Your family. I remember the rage I felt, after Waco, after Ruby Ridge, after what happened to your compound in Wyoming. . . ."

"Show me," she whispered, closing her hand around him. "Show me that rage."

He made rougher love to her in answer, not caring about her injured shoulder. She gasped and writhed, gritting her teeth. When they were done she put his head on her stomach and rubbed his hair, gently. He felt he could have stayed there forever, safe against her skin. Wrong feeling. The mission was more important. The mission trumped all.

Just before ten o'clock at night, his cell phone rang. Mouser scooped it up. "Yes?"

The Night Road hacker said, "I found your target."

"Where?"

"I got a lead on them from a traffic camera last night. That gave me a starting point for searching the GPS database and getting a read on them. Aubrey Perrault's car is now at Lakefront Air Park. Private aviation field north of the city." He fed Mouser the address.

"Thank you."

"When you kill the cop for me . . . send me the news clipping." The hacker hung up.

Mouser got off the bed and climbed into his clothes. A private air park. First Eric's name forged on a passenger manifest, now a private jet to whisk them out of Chicago. He and Snow and Henry were clearly up against someone with serious resources. "Get up," he said, sharper than he intended.

Snow sat up, let the sheets pool at her waist. "I need my bandage changed."

"Get up. Now. They're at an airport. They're leaving the city. We got to go now." All gentleness in him was gone. Nothing else mattered.

Mouser parked. The small air park appeared closed. He spotted a security guard—older, African American, heavyset—walking along the sidewalk in front of the terminal building.

They surprised him with their guns, hurried him into the building, using his electronic passkey.

The guard was afraid for his life. He kept telling Mouser he had a wife, two daughters, three grandsons. He kept repeating their names, a thread-bare litany. Like invoking saints who would protect him.

Snow studied the computer's database; it had not been locked. "Two people logged as taking a flight to New Jersey's Ridgecliff Air Park. Pilot, Frankie Wu. Passengers, Eric Lindoe and Aubrey Perrault."

"That smart bastard." Mouser shook his head.

Snow raised an eyebrow. "I strongly suggest you lose that slight tone of admiration."

"Nita. Shawnelle. Latika. Joy. Trevor. David. Shawn," the guard said, eyes on the floor, as though he could see the faces of the loved ones in the texture of the carpet.

"Hold them in your thoughts," Mouser said. "May I ask you a question?"

The guard—in his sixties—looked up, his face crumpling with grief. *I guess you don't get any more ready to die even when you're old,* Mouser thought.

"Before you worked here, what did you do?"

"I'm retired. From the police department."

"Thank you," Mouser said, and paid his bill to the hacker with one quick shot.

Snow watched, then put her gaze back to the screen.

"On the computer, who paid for the flight?" Mouser asked.

"Quicksilver Risk Management."

"Get us tickets on a red-eye to New York." He smiled; he had not even smiled when they'd made love. "I'm glad to finally know who our enemy is."

35

Aubrey thought she was dead.

Darkness surrounded her. She blinked and awareness slowly warmed her. Her hand lay stretched above her head, tingling from lack of circulation, and she thought for one surprising second that she was lying back on the narrow hard bed in the East Texas cabin, waiting for Eric to come save her, the poor gallant fool. Of course she wasn't and she gave a half-laugh, half-cough.

She moved, stretched, let her fear subside, and let herself drink in her surroundings. Her hand lay bound above her head and her desert-dry mouth tasted of chemical gunk. Thirst crushed her throat.

She moaned. The flight to New York had gone so wrong. Why had she gotten involved in this madness? The plan hadn't worked. She remembered the men closing in on her, roughly manhandling her into the backseat of a car, her trying to fight. Screaming. A needle piercing her flesh, then an awful sodden blackness that smothered her. Vague notions of a buzzing noise, darkness, the hum of machinery. She felt as though she'd slept for days. Years.

Everything had gone wrong. Luke. Had they gotten Luke?

A faint light switched on and Aubrey could see she was lying in a narrow bedroom. She tried to blink past the medicinal haze that fogged her thoughts and focus on the man's face that appeared above hers.

A man's face. Familiar, maybe? But then she closed her eyes. She opened them again and the haze cleared and she didn't know this man.

"Aubrey."

Her lips formed an answer. "Where am I?"

"Where is a good start. Tell me where Luke Dantry will go."

"I don't know."

The voice—she kept her eyes closed because she did not want to look at him again—did not respond. Fingertips moved hair from her eyes. "Am I to believe that two kidnapping victims who have endured as much as you and Luke Dantry made no contingency plan if you were separated?"

"No. We slept on the plane."

A soft, low, patient laugh. "Yes, you like to sleep on planes." She risked opening her eyes again. "I almost believe you when you say you don't know where Luke will run. But I don't."

"I'm telling you the truth."

A long pause. "Let's talk about Eric. He was going to give us information."

"Information?"

"Tell me about this Night Road."

She wasn't sure what to say. "Eric just told me the name . . . extremists, a bunch of different causes. He kept it all secret from me. We broke up," she added. She felt woozy. The bed gave a slight lurch and she became aware that the heavy droning noise wasn't a rattling in her head, a leftover from a drug-addled daze. The white noise sounded like jet engines. She blinked again at the unadorned, curved metal ceiling and she thought: *I am on a plane again. Where are they taking me?*

"Wise of you." He stared at her. In the dim glow she could see the ice in his gaze. A person stripped of every decent feeling, she thought. She tried to remember if he had been one of the men in New York who had grabbed her. She thought not. He stood. He wore black slacks, a navy shirt, and she saw a bit of silver chain peeking out from under the shirt. "You're going to help me find Luke Dantry."

"I don't know where he is. Or where he'll go."

"Let's call him and let him know you're still alive."

"Oh, God, please don't kill me. Don't hurt me." She hated the begging in her voice but the fear surged and her heart swelled in her chest, as though the muscle would explode.

"We're going to call Luke. Tell him that you're alive." He unfolded a cell phone, dialed, and then listened. After what seemed like a century he closed the phone.

"Didn't he have Eric's phone?"

"He broke it."

Without another word the man turned and walked away from her cot.

She raised her head. It looked like she was in a cargo plane or transport of some sort. At the other end of the cabin she could see the man issuing orders to a younger man who sat at a desk, a set of computer screens before him. The young man answered with a French accent in words she could barely make out. The boss and the Frenchman, she named them in her head. The Frenchman glanced back at her and she saw an ugly half-circle scar on his cheek.

French. Paris? Were they taking her to Paris, as Frankie Wu had mentioned back in Chicago?

It didn't make sense. Why were they were taking her and leaving Luke behind?

"Why?" she said. "Why?" She wanted to know. She held her breath.

The boss glanced back at her, came back to the bed. "How much do you mean to him?"

"I don't know."

"Will he try and find you or keep running?"

"I don't know."

"Why did he run?"

"I don't know. He said he had to run." Aubrey didn't want to say that they knew Quicksilver had funded the cabin where they were held. She was afraid of what would happen.

The boss looked at her for the longest ten seconds of her life.

"Get some sleep," he said. "You're safe now."

Aubrey didn't believe him. She didn't believe him at all. But she closed her eyes, and she pretended to sleep, and she tried to listen to every sound, every word, anything that would help her figure out where she was and how she could escape.

36

The address for Quicksilver Risk was a twelve-story building a few blocks from Washington Square. The tower glittered glass and chrome, more modern than its surrounding fellows. It did not carry the purple flag of NYU, like other structures did in the area, and Luke did not see students gathered around its entrance. In the fifteen minutes he'd stood sentinel he did not see anyone leave or arrive.

He'd checked in the phone book—no listing for Quicksilver Risk. A company that didn't bother to be in the phone book, in a building that no one entered or left.

Luke stood on a corner down from the building. He slowly read a *Times* he'd salvaged from the trash, glancing now and then at his watch.

So now what? Saunter in and see what happened to him? He could be walking into a trap. If Frankie Wu noticed the charge manifest was missing from the galley, or if they'd made Aubrey talk, they'd know Luke had learned this address. They'd be waiting for him.

Maybe Aubrey was here. Inside. In trouble.

But he needed help. He needed a way to break into that encrypted file. If Quicksilver wanted this fifty million from the terrorists, he'd strike a deal with them. Trade them the file for Aubrey. Of course, there was nothing to prevent them from just taking the drive from him and killing him and Aubrey.

Luke made his decision. The lion's den had to be braved. Luke folded the paper and walked toward the building. At the front door, Luke could see a doorman through the heavy glass. He was an imposing sort, barrel-chested, thick hands peeking from the cuffs of the navy wool uniform. Everything about him was hard and he looked like he could deck Luke into a hospital bed with one punch. Was he one of the men at the airport? Luke didn't recognize him.

Luke tapped at the glass. Thicker than normal glass, he noticed.

"Good day, sir," the doorman said. He stood beyond the locked door, hands behind his back, but he didn't open it. "Who are you here to see?"

Not just a doorman. A guard.

"Mr. Drummond." He remembered the name from the e-mail to Eric about the flight from Chicago, and mentioned by Henry. "I'm Luke Dantry. He's expecting me."

The doorman stepped inside after holding the door for Luke. The entryway was cool, tiled, with a massive desk, with a large raised granite counter around it, the kind that concealed monitors. No building directory—no tenants. The lobby was small, with two doors behind the desk. Both were heavy steel. No décor.

The air felt very still. The soft hum in the walls seemed to be made by machinery, not people moving and talking in offices beyond. Luke had the oddest sense of entering a bunker, a hideaway, like an old comic book hero's lair. The doorman kept a polite gaze on Luke as he keyed in a message onto a keyboard. Apparently phones weren't good enough. Or he didn't want Luke to hear the message he was communicating.

Luke glanced up at the camera perched in the corner. Let it read his face.

"Mr. Drummond will see you." The doorman moved his hand to another part of the desk. The locks on the front door engaged with a soft click.

He was locked in.

"Follow me, please," the doorman said.

Apparently the front door was not to be left unattended. A fortress in Manhattan. An elevator door slid open and the doorman gestured Luke inside.

They rose in stately silence. It was the quietest elevator that Luke had ever ridden. The car stopped, suddenly, with a soft shrill whistle. The doorman pulled out a huge gun from under his jacket and pressed it against Luke's skull.

"You have weapons on you. Spare us both the indignity of a search."

"A gun in the back of my pants. But it's unloaded." He tried a provocation. "Your buddy Frankie Wu took my ammo clip."

The doorman stripped the gun from his back. "At least Frankie did something right before he flew back to Chicago."

Luke glanced up at the elevator ceiling. "Metal detector?"

"Nothing so primitive." The doorman entered in a key on a pad and the elevator resumed its ascent. He lowered the gun away from Luke's face and Luke remembered to breathe again.

"This building is, um, unusual. Prime real estate but unoccupied."

"Mr. Drummond can explain it to you. If he chooses."

A soft *ping* as they reached the top floor. The doors slid open onto a hallway. It had a spare wooden floor, and an elegant Persian rug running down its stretch. A doorway stood at the end.

They stepped into the hallway and the far door opened.

"He had a weapon, sir. The scans show him now as clear," the doorman said.

At the end of the hall stood a man in a dark turtleneck and jeans, salt-and-pepper hair, broad shoulders. Not tall but heavily muscled. He had a pugnacious face that looked like it had been battered over the years. His eyes were slightly pinched; it made Luke think of a reader who spent a great deal of time peering through books he found disagreeable. "A weapon. I blush with pride. Hello, Luke." He didn't smile.

"Hi, Mr. Drummond," Luke said. He wondered if Drummond knew Eric was dead. *He must know. This man looks like he knows everything.* "May we talk?"

"I have dreamed of the day." Drummond raised an eyebrow. He seemed to survey Luke's face, as though it were a map he'd seen once before but that had been redrawn over time.

The doorman turned and left.

Drummond watched him. A slight smile crept onto his face.

Luke decided to play his card. "Is Aubrey Perrault here?"

"No."

"Do you know where she is?"

"Yes, I do, and she's safe."

"I doubt that. Your people shot at us last night."

"Rubber bullets. They hurt but they don't kill unless you don't know what you're doing."

He remembered the bullets spraying up the grass at their feet. They could have shot him and Aubrey in the legs, but they didn't.

"You gave everyone a fright running into traffic. You could have gotten yourself killed, Luke."

"You look at me like you think you know me."

"I know who you were, Luke. I'm more interested," Drummond said, "in who you're going to be."

37

The apartment had the most disturbing walls Luke had ever seen. Giant photos covered them like wallpaper. One image per wall, each a massive enlargement. One picture was a young girl, huddling in the bombed ruins of a stone cabin. Her face looked like a surprised ghost. Another photo showed people in a Mideast bazaar, expressions contorted in naked fear as they looked over their shoulders at an unbidden and dawning threat. A gunman, a car bomb? Who knew? The terror and the resignation on their faces was a timeless stamp. Another photo of a man Luke recognized, a former senator, clearly staggered by loss, leaning against a porch railing.

"That senator. His son died. I remember it in the papers. Shot to death by a terrorist in Japan while studying abroad," Luke said. "You have odd décor."

"I am an odd man," Drummond said. "After all, I am welcoming you into my office and you had a hand in my friend's death."

"You kidnapped my friend last night."

"Your friend is perfectly safe. My friend is dead."

"I had nothing to do with Allen Clifford's death. I was kidnapped, forced to drive at gunpoint. Then chained up in a cabin your company paid for."

Drummond raised an eyebrow. "We financed a cabin. You being taken there was not our doing. But you killed Allen Clifford—"

"I didn't kill Allen Clifford. I know who did."

"Who?"

"Eric Lindoe. Operating under orders from a British woman named Jane, who kidnapped Eric's girlfriend. Kidnapping me and killing your friend was Jane's ransom demand for Aubrey's safety."

"Convenient to blame him, since he's not here to defend himself."

"He's dead. Back in Chicago. He kidnapped me in Austin to force information from my stepfather." He thought it would be better to hold off on mentioning the fifty million; it would take over the conversation and he wanted to know more first.

"Tell me everything," Drummond said. "I think to get to the truth, we must trust each other. We've been pitted against each other, Luke, and we should not be enemies. You must think the same, or you wouldn't have come here after running from us last night." Drummond gestured at a large glass table. "Sit."

Luke sat down and Drummond sat across from him.

Drummond's faint smile inched wider, went crooked. "Like Eric, you wish to make a deal. Tell me everything and I'll give you something in exchange."

"I ask, then you ask, we can hammer out a deal."

"All right. You first; you're the guest," Drummond said. "I'll judge whether or not to trust you further by the intelligence you show in what you ask."

If he failed—if he asked the wrong questions—he might never learn the truth. Or Drummond could be playing him. He wasn't ready to offer the encrypted file yet; he wanted to see what he could learn first. Drummond studied him, a cat easing on its haunches before the mouse hole.

"First question. Is Quicksilver behind my kidnapping?"

"No. The cabin had been rented in advance, to be used by Clifford for an interrogation of a suspect. The man he was meeting—a loser named Bridger, who ran when you and Eric approached—was selling information on a domestic terrorist network to Clifford. I suspect that he was killed, and the cabin used, to make your stepfather and the Night Road aware of Quicksilver's existence, since Clifford and the cabin point back to Quicksilver. Someone wanted the Night Road to know Quicksilver is chasing them. To put us in each other's sights."

"You know about the Night Road?"

"I didn't know the name until Eric mentioned it two days ago. We know it's a loose affiliation of extremist groups, turning toward violence, working together to share resources, tactics, and information. And I suspect the Road's hand in the Ripley attack, and the attacks over the past week."

"Attacks?"

"*E. coli* infecting a food plant in Tennessee. Pipeline bomb in Canada. Attempted bombing of a pipeline in Alaska. And last night, a bombing at a high school football game in Kansas City, eight dead, a hundred injured. And one of our leading thinkers in counterterrorism was slaughtered last night with his family while leaving a restaurant in Los Angeles."

"Oh, God, no. You should know I found these people."

"You found all these people for who? Henry?" When he said Henry's name his mouth made a curl of distaste.

"Under his false pretense of doing psychological profiling for his think tank. I gave him thousands of names. He whittled it down to the most committed and dangerous. I'm a pawn who got played."

"Henry used you. And you're a pawn who's pissed off about it," Drummond said.

"Yes. What is Quicksilver?"

It was as though Drummond did not hear the question. "I can offer you what I offered Eric. Get you out of the country, hide you under another name. You'll be safe. You give me all the information you have on the Night Road. That's the deal."

"No. I don't want to be stashed away. I want my life back. My good name. I want to be cleared of Clifford's death, and the officer's death in Chicago. And I want to help stop the Night Road."

"Noble of you, but unnecessary." Drummond said. "My offer is what it is. You're not part of this battle, Luke, and I think it best you hide until the danger's passed. Know that you're helping us by telling us everything about the Night Road. That's your contribution."

"It's not enough. Please. I helped build that network. I want to help destroy it. I can't just sit someplace safe while Henry runs a terror cell."

Drummond studied him. "Why did Henry use you?"

"I don't know; I was handy, I guess. What is Quicksilver? Are you CIA? FBI? A black ops group? What?" He took a breath. "Are you like the Book Club?"

"How did you know about the Book Club?"

"Henry. He was desperate that I not see you."

"Oh, I'll bet he was."

"Did you know my dad? Did you work with him in the government? What did he do?"

"I said no more on Quicksilver."

They stared at each other. Luke tried a different tack. Drummond wouldn't answer his questions but he oddly seemed to want to hear what Luke wanted to ask. "What are all these pictures?"

"My many failures."

Luke turned away from the portraits of suffering. "What, you screwed over all these people yourself?"

"Consider them salt in the wound. I failed in these instances, so these people suffered. I remember them. Every day. I have no choice."

"The Book Club tried to help people?"

"Mostly succeeding but not always. Good doesn't always win out."

"You could take the pictures down."

"I would still see their faces. It's easier to see them on the walls than in my dreams."

"I don't understand why you would help Eric get out of Chicago when he killed your friend."

"Because stopping the Night Road is more important than revenge. Eric made a bad choice, under tremendous pressure, and then when it all unraveled he was ready to betray the Night Road. I didn't like him but I do what's necessary to save lives."

"I will trade everything I know for Aubrey's release and information about Quicksilver. Otherwise, we have no deal."

"You assume that we would hurt Aubrey. We won't. We're the good guys," Drummond said.

"Then, please, tell me what I need to know."

"I can't. I need you to trust me, entirely. I need you to tell me everything, Luke, and to please, please ask me no questions. I need you, for the sake of your country, to cooperate fully and to let me hide you someplace where you'll be safe."

"Why should I trust you when you won't trust me?" Luke said.

Drummond sighed. He reached under his turtleneck and lifted up a piece of silver from under the sweater's black weight. A Saint Michael's medal, an exact duplicate of the one that Luke wore. The archangel stood tall, sword in one hand, shield in the other, wings of steel spread.

Luke's eyes widened. "Where did you get that?"

"An old friend gave it to me, a few weeks before he died."

"An old friend," Luke echoed.

"Your father. One of my closest friends. Now. Knowing that, will you trust me?"

Luke studied Drummond's face. "I will." Seeing the twin of his own medal around Drummond's neck filled his head with a hundred questions. "My dad—"

"Would order you to listen to me and to do as I say. Please. For your own safety, I cannot explain more. Now. Help me the only way you can. Tell me everything about the Night Road."

"I guess I should start with the most important part. The fifty million dollars."

Drummond raised an eyebrow. Luke could see he hated to be surprised. But he was.

"The fifty million what?" Drummond asked.

38

Henry Shawcross leaned forward across the table and said, "Quicksilver has my son. We are going to get him back."

Mouser and Snow glanced at each other. A thin haze of smoke from Mouser's cigarette hung above the hotel room table; they sat at a window, but Snow insisted the curtains be kept drawn. She said satellites could spy on them. Henry thought she might be right. He studied their faces; they looked haggard, tired. They could not be. He needed them sharp.

"There was a police incident report filed, shots fired near the air park where Luke's plane landed, a man running into traffic, causing a couple of accidents. Quicksilver grabbed him." He'd driven up from Washington late last night when the news came from Mouser that Luke was headed for New York.

"Who the hell are these Quicksilver clowns?" Mouser asked.

Henry waved the smoke away from his face. "I gave some of my think-tank clients a security exercise to perform last night, to find every record affecting Quicksilver Risk and my old friends Drummond and Clifford, who are not much more than hired guns. Quicksilver is a small risk-management consulting group, but I'm sure it's just a front. But they have also bought, sometimes through front companies, buildings around the United States, Europe, Asia, and the Middle East. They have accounts in banks around the world, again, under a set of holding company names."

"Are they CIA?"

"Drummond used to be State Department. I don't think it's State. But

I'm not sure why the CIA or FBI would go to this trouble to hide, unless they're simply breaking the law and avoiding congressional oversight."

"You want us to attack a building," Snow said.

"I live for this," Mouser said.

"It's not a typical building. There are no tenants. They will have a skeleton staff. All you have to do is get Luke back. Kill everyone else, I don't care."

"And this is to save Luke? You know we're just going to have to kill him, Henry. Face facts. He's not coming over to your side."

"I want to talk with him. Hustle him into a van and bring him to me."

"Face facts," Mouser repeated. "You're deluded."

"I am in command here, Mouser. Not you."

Mouser said, "For the moment."

Henry ignored him. "Quicksilver knows of us, thanks to Bridger. So we have to decapitate them before they can act."

"Just the two of us and you?" Snow said.

"I have some important Hellfire work to do. I've arranged for some Night Road help for the two of you." He looked at Snow. "And, Snow, we need to move your bombs. I need to know you didn't leave booby traps around your storage space in Houston."

"Why?"

"You're not there to handle the distribution. I've gotten a Night Road team to go to Houston to transport the bombs to a new location."

"Where are you taking the bombs?" Snow asked.

"That's need-to-know. You're about to go on a job where you could be captured."

"No traps," Snow said after a moment. "Take good care of my babies."

"You're running this show," Mouser said, "but it's your fault we're in the hole we're in."

"Your continued failure to capture Luke is our hole," Henry said, "but I've gotten you some more muscle."

Sweet Bird was not a man who enjoyed waiting for other people, but impatience got you killed these days. Mr. Shawcross had offered him enough arms to eliminate every rival gang in Queens and New Jersey. The Albanians, the leftover Italians, the mean Russians, and the Asian tongs. He couldn't say no to such a deal. Even if the risk was high. His grandmother, who never lived to see him become a leading kingpin and had hoped he would become a physician, had drilled that lesson into his head, by soft cajole and hard belt: Take your opportunities, don't waste them.

So when Shawcross called him early this morning, he'd listened to the delicious sound of a rare chance to make a powerful friend.

I may need you to assault a building.

A building? You're kidding me.

I don't like the sound of hesitation.

Ain't hesitating, I'm listening. You probably don't like the sound of some idiot leaping before he looks.

You do this, you'll be one of the most powerful men in New York by the end of the day. I have a lot of work for you. Mr. Shawcross's voice had carried a low gleam over the phone. And Mr. Shawcross always delivered. In the past two months he'd sent Sweet Bird real nice Belgian rifles to use, trained his men, helped them take down rival drug lords and a bothersome DA. Given him army-quality grenades to eliminate a couple of informants, right in their cars, no need to bother with unreliable handmade pipe bombs. And, from the Night Road Web site, handed him a couple of small insurance agencies that sold cheap policies, made it easy to shine and polish and legitimize the cocaine money.

He was waiting for Shawcross's two people at a back room at one of the agencies, a few blocks from Greenwich Village. He waited with five of his regular guys, one who was Sweet Bird's cousin, a violent gangster wannabe Luke had found two months ago on a board discussing urban warfare, the others hardened street fighters. He watched as they double-checked their weapons. He had one of the nice Belgian rifles and he ran his hands over the cool fine metal. He had modified a raincoat so he could carry the rifle in it unseen. In the background CNN played, talking about the spate of attacks across America, a rapid rising of violence that was undercutting Americans' confidence to simply go about their lives.

Two minutes later there was a knock on the door, and he opened it to find a lean, muscled guy with a crew cut and a pretty but scowling woman who had a scary mop of white hair. They gave the right password.

"Mouser. Snow. Pleased to make your acquaintance. I ain't never met anyone from Night Road face-to-face."

"You understand the plan as presented?" Mouser said. "And you understand I'm in charge."

"It's not rocket science," Sweet Bird said. "Let's go get it done."

They left, in two cars. Mouser drove. Snow said, "Did you tell that guy you want Luke Dantry dead if he's there?"

"No," Mouser said. "You and I will handle it. I don't trust anyone else."

"He's Night Road—he's okay."

"Nobody's okay. I thought Henry was. He's distracted by his affection for his stepson. It's become a problem. If Luke's at this building—he stops being a problem for us."

39

"You don't know about the fifty million dollars," Luke said. "You have to be kidding."

Drummond measured his expression, looking for a sign of bluff. "No, I didn't." His head tilted slightly, as though he were listening to the soft whir of the air conditioner. He flicked his glance at the kitchen corner, for the barest of moments. If Luke had not been watching him so closely for his reaction, he wouldn't have noticed. Luke glanced at the corner as well. He saw a pinpoint hole in the ceiling. A camera, maybe.

He had the sudden sense they were being watched. Maybe his imagination. But the past few days had taught him to trust his instincts.

"A man as desperate as Eric would have mentioned every asset to win his safety." Luke put his gaze back on Drummond's face. "He wouldn't forget to mention fifty million."

"Offering us information on the Night Road would have won him ample protection. He didn't have to mention money." For the first time Drummond looked shaken. "We were working on IDing him from the airport garage video and the speeding ticket video. He contacted me."

"Wait—how did Eric know how to find you?"

"That was a mystery. But he knew Quicksilver was more than a risk company. He wanted protection and he gave me enough info on Night Road for me to know it was legit. I hadn't even met him face-to-face yet."

Luke realized Drummond had no reason to lie. "Then Eric was going to keep the money for himself. You pick his brain, you hide him away where the Night Road can't kill him, and then he vanishes, with fifty million stashed away and waiting for him, and neither the Night Road nor Quicksilver gets the cash. You're too busy waging war against each other to care what he does." It was a simple but brilliant plan.

"Where is this money?" Drummond said.

"I thought you said it didn't matter."

"Money is lifeblood for terrorism. Where is it, Luke? We've got to secure that money before the Night Road uses it."

"Tell me who Quicksilver is and I'll give you the fifty million."

Drummond paused, as though holding in his anger, and then Luke saw it: a minuscule earpiece in Drummond's ear. "Okay," Drummond said. "You give me the location of the money and I'll answer your questions."

"I go first." Luke watched the corner of the kitchen where Drummond had seemed to pause. "Are we being watched? Or listened to?"

"Does it matter?" Which to Luke meant yes.

He took a deep breath and then asked again: "I want to know what the connection is between you and my stepfather and my dad. Why do you have a Saint Michael's medal like mine?"

Drummond tented fingers under his chin, put on a frown.

"That connection is the key to why I was targeted. You're on one side of this fight, Henry on another, and you're both part of my father's past."

Drummond was silent for ten long seconds. "Seeing you brings back a lot of memories. I carried you once on my shoulders. I remember when you were a small kid, I saw you a few times at your parents' house. There were three of us at the beginning. Me. Your stepfather. And your father."

The words unnerved Luke. His father had led an entirely secret life, and the foundation of what Luke had always believed about his dad seemed to shift under his feet. A wave of dizziness hit him and passed. "The beginning, you said. Beginning of this Book Club?"

"Book Club was a joke name, because it was mostly professors and writers, but it stuck. The State Department recruited your stepdad, then your dad. And your father found several others, including me. To work with a secret group, unofficial, to approach and solve the world's problems in new and fresh ways. What do you do if there's a foreign leader who becomes an enemy? You can't assassinate him; that's always a temporary solution. But maybe, the Book Club would say, we find an unsuspected way to erode the guy's power among his base. Perhaps involving subtle economic changes that hurt his biggest backers, or political pressure that he doesn't see as coming from the West. It's more effective than assassination. But it takes imagination, and then some muscle and well-applied arm-twisting to make the situation happen. That's just an example. The professors were the thinkers; me and Clifford, and sometimes the professors, carried out the missions. We had a few successes. Sometimes subtlety is greater than force." He gestured at the photos. "We had a few failures. Subtlety doesn't always work."

"I'm having trouble picturing this." Luke shook his head. "My dad was a history professor. Tweed jackets, and obscure books crammed in every space, and chalk dusting his fingers. Now you say he was some sort of counter-terrorist?"

"One of the best. You don't realize how good they were."

Luke sat back down. It felt like the air had vanished from the room. "That's why he had so many visiting professorships. Europe, Asia, Africa. It wasn't about being a teacher, or research. It was about . . . spying."

"Yes."

"Did my mother know?"

"I don't know."

"Don't lie. Did she know?"

"No," Drummond said after a moment. "Most of us weren't married. Only your dad was. He kept it from her. Orders."

Orders. His father had been an operative for a secret group. How many secrets had hidden behind Warren Dantry's smile? Tears came close to Luke's eyes and he blinked them back. "And my stepfather?"

"The same."

He glanced around the room, trying to see where the other cameras might be. It was strange how claustrophobic you could feel in a room full of windows.

"Yes. But of course, when your father and everyone on the plane died, the Book Club died. He'd wanted to start a new group in the weeks before; the Book Club had problems. Your father and your stepfather disagreed fairly often. Henry wanted to lobby for more money, more attention inside State; your dad wanted to keep a low profile, just get the work done."

"And Quicksilver is the heir apparent to the Book Club."

Drummond rubbed his face. "Yes, we started Quicksilver. Your father died before he could see it take shape. Quicksilver grew out of our earlier work, a new way to fight the bad guys, to stop terrorism before it starts, to bring new strategies to the problem."

A new way. He wondered where the money came from, for this building, for the security, for the private jet, for all the resources that Quicksilver had. "Are you still part of the State Department?"

He gave a jagged laugh, shook his head. "We started Quicksilver, and in a wonderful symmetry, you helped start the Night Road." Sweat was on Drummond's face, as though the silent listeners would be measuring him, watching him.

The phone began to ring, a soft, repetitive warble. Drummond didn't move.

"I'm not going to answer it," Drummond said. "Because I'm going to tell you why I want to keep you safe. Your father saved me once, and I'm repaying the karma the best way I can. I'm going to get you out of the way of a war."

"War."

"There is a war beginning. A secret war."

The phone stopped. The silence hung between them like a mist. "You can't fight a war in secret. People tend to notice armies and bullets and missiles." Luke shook his head.

"That sort of war is dying. This war started a long time ago. Skirmishes, and in both cases each side used governments as their proxies. Their pawns. Influence was their currency, and then there were only two sides, not a thousand like now, and each was able to say that their concerns matched those of their governments—that these interests were aligned—and the governments believed it." Drummond sounded for a moment like he couldn't continue. The phone's insistent buzzing began again. "But—the governments—they didn't stop September eleventh. Or the Bali or Madrid or London or Jordan bombings. Do you know how much they cost?"

"Thousands of lives."

"Yes. Of course, and that's incalculable, but think: How much they *cost*? The economic damage. Who suffers economic damage?"

"Well, everyone."

"Everyone?" Drummond's voice oozed contempt.

The phone stopped ringing.

"Okay. Then I guess governments and big companies lost the most. Then it trickles down."

"Then it trickles down, Luke. Yes. And after those attacks, we are simply supposed to trust that government will do its job. Protect us. That the various governments of the world, and their multitude of agencies, with their well-intentioned but million moving parts, handcuffed by rules and bureaucracy, will shift into efficiency and suddenly develop all the human capital and infrastructure to"—he paused—"fight and eliminate every shadow and nutcase, every asshole with a laptop and an agenda? You know what kind of people you found for the Night Road. How they can vanish like smoke, how badly they can hurt the world with a small investment and their own fanaticism. The playing field must be even." The glare in his eyes grew cold. "Now. I am here to protect you. But you give me this fifty million, Luke. You tell me everything you know about Hellfire."

"I don't even know what kind of attack Hellfire is." It frightened him that Drummond knew the name. The thought flooded him: What did the Saint Michael's medal prove? Nothing. Medals could be copied to win trust. Lies could be told. There was nothing to prove what Drummond had said was truth.

"Think. It's coming out of the Night Road, all those thousands of postings you made. You must know what they would target if they made a big hit. What would be their dream attack, one they could actually execute?"

"They're already executing attacks." Luke paused. "But I think these attacks, they're *not* Hellfire. Hellfire is bigger. On their Web site they are chattering about the attacks, but there's no word on Hellfire. Hellfire has got to be something distinct from this group of small attacks; it's much more tied to this money they want. It's not unusual in terrorist psychology to consider smaller jobs as dry runs, or as qualifiers for more dangerous work."

"You're right. As awful as they are, these attacks are too small. Too localized." Drummond frowned. "Maybe they need that fifty million to finance a huge new series of operations, and you not giving it to us is leaving open the chance that Night Road will get their hands on the money."

"If someone else is listening to or watching us," Luke shouted at the ceiling, "if they have Aubrey, I want to talk to them. Please."

Drummond made a choked laugh. "You're a smart kid. You figured it out we were under a camera. I'm pleased."

The phone began to ring again. Drummond answered it. He listened and then said, "For God's sake. He gives us what he knows first, then we decide."

Drummond turned away to go into the other room, as if to finish his discussion.

Luke stood and picked up the chair and the voice on the phone must have warned him because Drummond turned. Luke swung the chair with all his might and it crashed and splintered into Drummond's head. He didn't pause. He hit him again and Drummond went down.

Drummond groaned, the back of his head bloodied, his eyelids at half-mast. The phone lay on the floor.

Luke picked it up. "Hello? Did you see Drummond's taking a nap?"

Silence. The line was dead. He dropped the phone and looked up again where he thought the hidden cameras might be. "I'm not playing your game. All right?" he yelled to the air. "I want Aubrey back. I'll give you all the information on the Night Road, the accounts, everything I know, but you give me Aubrey and you tell me who you people are. Do you hear me?"

Drummond groaned. "I'm sorry," Luke said. He dragged Drummond into the walk-in pantry, slammed the door, and jammed the other kitchen chair under the knob. Leaving Drummond with the cake mixes and the bottles of beer, he turned back toward where the cameras might be hidden.

"Hey! Why you hiding behind an old man?" Luke taunted.

The phone rang. He answered it.

"Let Drummond out of the pantry." It was Aubrey. "They have me. You have to let him out."

"Aubrey. Are you okay?"

"I'm all right. They haven't hurt me, Luke—I think these are the good guys."

"Let me talk to whoever's in charge."

A few moments passed. For a moment the silence made Luke think they'd been disconnected. A man's voice came on the line, one he didn't recognize. "Release Mr. Drummond. You must get out of the building. Now."

The accent was French—slight but noticeable.

"What's happening?"

"Get out of the building now. It's under attack."

"By who?" He opened the closet door and dragged Drummond out. He was groggy, bleeding from the ear and the temple.

Luke put the phone back to his ear. "Who the hell are you people?"

"Get out, Luke. Get out of there now!"

He hung up the phone and started to search the apartment for a weapon.

He found a bedroom, a small office next to it. Inside the desk drawers, he found a manila file folder, crammed in crookedly as though it had been put away in haste.

In it were papers. The first was a news account of his father's death; the plane that had gone down with several noted professors aboard. A file on Ace Beere, the man who had confessed to sabotaging the plane before he blew his brains out. A large sticky note said, *Check airport surveillance photos from last Book Club flight, compare with Night Road suspect, ask photo archive for facial comparison and confirmation.*

Under the note was an old photo of Mouser. Then a new photo, that looked like it had been taken from a security camera, stamped LAKEFRONT AIR PARK, Mouser and Snow heading toward an entrance. Another image of Mouser, taken from what might have been a traffic camera on Armitage, during the chase from Eric's shooting. The photo was grainier but it still looked like Mouser.

Luke's stomach felt a dark pang. Mouser. Was he connected to his father's death? And how could Quicksilver access these surveillance cameras?

The final document was attached to a photo of the man who had died in Houston. The photo was grainy, slightly, hazed by sunlight. It looked like it had been taken in a desert setting; a long stretch of sand lay behind the man. In the photo, his father stood next to the man. Hands on shoulders. They were dressed in military garb, guns at their sides. Next to his father stood Drummond, smiling, an arm around his father's shoulders.

Attached to the photo was a readout, a service record from the State Department, of a man named Allen Clifford. He had retired from the State Department two weeks after Luke's dad died.

He hurried back to the kitchen. Drummond sat up from lying curled on the floor, holding his head. "Drummond!"

"What?" A harsh grunt, low and pained.

"I'm really sorry. Your friends say we have to get out of here now, we're under attack."

Drummond focused his gaze on a blinking red light on the kitchen wall. "Someone's trying to get past the security systems." He rose unsteadily to his feet. "We have unwanted company, Luke. The Night Road must have tracked you here. I hope you're ready for a fight."

40

Ten minutes earlier, Snow had knocked at the door of the Quicksilver building. The doorman stood up, peered at her both on the camera that monitored the street and through the bulletproof glass.

"Yes, I'm here to here to see Mr. Drummond at Quicksilver Risk Management," Snow said with a coy, slightly crooked smile.

The doorman did not seem at all impressed with her smile. He gave her a hard, measured stare.

"No sales calls," he said through the intercom.

"I'm not a salesperson. I represent a software company that has already registered the trademark of Quicksilver Risk Management in the state of New York and I've been trying every way I can to get in contact with Quicksilver at this address and nothing has worked." She tapped her foot on the pavement and ran a hand through her snow-white hair.

"We're not interested."

"Well, you might be interested that my client is planning to sue you for use of a registered trademark. And if you don't let me in to speak with someone in charge, then I shall have to simply summon the police and the press here and say that you are refusing to accept legal papers."

The doorman was not privy to the name of the building's owner. And he privately thought the police wouldn't care less. But the woman was making a fuss and one of the overriding descriptions of his job was to keep the building out of public and police notice.

She stepped inside as he deactivated the electronic locks on the door. She reached into her purse and pulled out a thick envelope. "Honestly, how do your clients get ahold of you?"

The doorman reached for the package and the end of it exploded. The bullet tore through his flesh like it was paper and he toppled toward the granite counter.

She thought of the uniformed men who had swarmed the burning compound, the only home she'd ever known, and she was glad the man was dead. She walked to the front door and admitted Mouser. She propped the door open with a metal wedge. They dragged the doorman's body out of sight.

They hurried toward the elevator. She swiped an electronic code scanner card, connected to a modified handheld computer, that Sweet Bird had given them to unlock the elevator; it tested thousands of combinations within thirty seconds, scored the right one, and the doors closed. She pressed the button for the top floor. They would start their search there.

The elevator began to rise. At floor five it jolted to a hard stop.

Sweet Bird listened to a call in his earpiece. "Understood," he said. He turned to his Birdies. "The show-offs got themselves trapped." He did not want to spend his day playing soldier; he did not like putting himself or his people in unwarranted danger. But he had no choice.

He and his five Birdies got out of the van, their guns hidden under their coats. The driver moved the van along into traffic, to start his ongoing orbit of the building until needed.

The front door was propped open, but Sweet Bird kicked the prop loose and the door shut itself again.

"Get on the computer system," he told one of the Birdies. "See if there's an override for the elevator, or if we got stairs to take." Suddenly two uniformed men barreled in from a door at the end of the small lobby, guns drawn.

The gunfire erupted just as Sweet Bird dove for the cover of the counter.

"Look for an override button," Snow spoke into her mike. The distant sound of gunfire, five floors below, stopped abruptly.

A long quiet filled the elevator while she waited for an answer, hoping that Sweet Bird and his flock were still on their feet.

"Got it," Sweet Bird said. Suddenly the elevator lurched into life, began its ascent toward the top floor.

"If Luke or these assholes have our money, we kill them as soon as we've got our hands on it."

"I get Schoolboy," Snow said. "He hurt me worse than he hurt you. A bullet beats a blade."

"Do you know who killed my dad? Was it Mouser?"

"Not now, Luke, for God's sake. Here, take this gun. We're getting the hell out of here."

"Tell your friends on the other side of the camera to call the police if we're in danger."

"They're far away. They can't help us."

"Where's far away?"

"Europe."

"Why are they taking Aubrey to Europe?" Then he remembered Frankie Wu's words back in Chicago, discussing their itinerary. New York. *Paris.*

"Can you shoot this?" Drummond pulled a Glock 9 from a kitchen cabinet, pressed it into Luke's hand.

"If I have lots of time to aim."

"Don't be a perfectionist." They turned the corner into the entryway. The elevator doors were already open and Mouser leveled his semiautomatic and opened fire. Rounds exploded into the walnut paneling near Luke's head. Drummond shoved him back around the corner, returning fire.

They retreated toward the kitchen. The finery of the living room—the cleanly upholstered sofas, the glass tabletops, the vivid photos of misspent suffering on the walls—all were splintered and dusted in the gunfire.

Drummond and Luke went over the kitchen counter. A few more bullets thrummed into the granite-topped island.

Then silence.

Drummond pointed at the doorway at the end of the kitchen, gestured that it meant the roof. It would be a run of a dozen feet, uncovered.

Luke shook his head.

"Schoolboy," Luke heard Snow call to him. "You left marks on my throat with those chains, and a hole in my shoulder"—and then she went silent.

Luke knew what would happen to him if she got those pale, tender hands on him. She would pay him back with agony.

He stared at Drummond and listened for the shuffle of feet on broken glass. But there was only silence. The quiet filled his chest with a crushing dread.

The silence stretched.

"No neighbors to call for help, Mr. Drummond," Mouser called. "This is one empty building. We got people going floor to floor and nobody's home. How can you afford that in New York?"

"Family money." Drummond reached into a drawer and yanked out a large knife.

"Luke, how you doing?" Mouser called.

"Better than Snow," Luke said. *Did you kill my dad?* He wanted to ask the question but the words wouldn't form in his mouth.

"You're a nothing punk to me," Mouser said. "You cooperate, you get to go home to Stepdaddy. You don't, I'm giving you to my girl, and it's not going to be sunshine and lollipops. Now, shut up and let the big boys talk. Mr. Drummond?"

"What, asshole?"

"Tell me who's trying to screw the Night Road."

Drummond said nothing.

"You help me, I help you." Mouser's voice grew closer.

"Fine. Here's the deal," Drummond said. "You leave and I won't kill you."

Snow was silent; Luke thought she might be drawing close, grinning at him under her bottle-white hair. He risked a glance around the counter's edge but didn't see her.

"I'll leave, but with Luke. You get to live."

Drummond said, "Eric stole your money. Not us. And I walk out with Luke."

"You're outgunned. I got street gangbangers in the lobby. We're over a dozen stories up. You got no place to fly."

"Except into my arms." Snow sounded like she was just on the other side of the counter.

Mouser continued his negotiation. "Eric hid the goods and you were gonna fly his ass out here. I think Eric gave Luke and Aubrey our money."

"You want to know what Eric did with your money?" Luke said. "I know exactly where he stashed it. You kill us, you'll never ever find it." They had nothing left but a bluff. Luke's fear rose in a tide inside his heart. But he would not let it control him.

Drummond gestured again at the stairs. No way, Luke thought, *no way*. But they had no choice.

"Luke. Aren't you tired of running?" Mouser said.

Luke held up a hand to Drummond, five fingers spread, and then pointed at the escape route to the rooftop garden. He opened his hands again to five. Then four fingers. A countdown.

Luke wanted to shoot Mouser. He could feel the hate, the rage, swelling in his chest.

Three. Two.

"Luke, don't you want to see your stepdad again? You two got lots to discuss," Mouser said.

"No," Luke said. "You talk to him. You're both traitors."

One finger, upraised, holding. Drummond mouthed: *You just run.* There was no arguing with him. Luke couldn't look back.

Go, Drummond mouthed. He had the knife in one hand, the gun in the other.

"You're the one who's a traitor," Mouser said in a snarl, and Luke bolted for the stairs. He expected the rip of bullets. He ducked low, hiking fast up the stairs, and he heard gunfire, a cry of fury from Mouser, and a scream from Snow.

The roof. He ran through the door and Drummond was seconds behind him, his shoulder bloodied. Luke slammed the door closed and engaged the bolt. Weird that there was a lock on the outside of the door—it meant this really was Drummond's escape route. "We have nowhere to go."

"Wrong. Down." Drummond gritted his teeth against the pain.

"It's suicide."

Bullets began to pan hard against the metal of the door around the lock.

Drummond grabbed Luke, shoved him away from the door. Over the pounding of blows against the reinforced door Luke could hear, hundreds of feet below, the hum of traffic, the whisper of endless shuffles of feet against the pavement.

"Never let yourself get cornered," Drummond said.

"We are cornered."

Drummond kicked the layer of gravel away near the slightly raised box of metal that looked like a maintenance access point. It was secured by a digital keypad lock. "We have only a window of fifteen seconds."

"What the hell are we doing?"

"If they have gunmen below, you are going to have to shoot. You can be scared, but don't think about it. It's time to be your father's son."

The hatchway opened and Drummond gestured to Luke to crawl inside. Behind them the roof door began to creak free from its hinges. "Be quiet. Not a sound."

Luke wriggled into the darkness. The narrow crawlway led into the elevator housing. Below him, eight feet or so, he could see the top of the elevator car. With a hatch.

Drummond must've intended to go through the elevator and attack Snow and Mouser from behind. They'd surprise them with bullets in the back. But as soon as Mouser and Snow broke through the door and saw the roof was empty—in a matter of seconds—then Mouser would figure they'd reentered the building. And then he would alert the other gunmen inside.

Drummond closed the access hatch behind him and raised a grimy finger to his lips. In the dim light given off by the controls and from the glow of the elevator cabin below, Luke thought Drummond looked like a tired old lion. Blood soaked his shoulder.

They'd shot him. Luke had to get him to a doctor.

Wincing with pain, Drummond punched in a key command on the elevator's roof and the soft click sounded of a lock released. He punched other buttons, presumably disabling the weapons scanner so it wouldn't refuse to lower the car. They slid open the hatch to the elevator, but only an inch. Luke started to shift the hatch open more and Drummond stopped him with a firm grip on his arm. Drummond pointed.

In the narrow gap, looking down into the elevator, Luke saw a handheld computer dangling from a card feeder at the bottom of the elevator keys. Luke guessed Snow and Mouser had used a digital lock pick to bypass the security in the elevator.

He heard the roof door at the top of the stairs smash open, Mouser warning Snow to stay back.

Luke slid the rest of the hatch open, eased himself down into the elevator. If they heard him . . .

Snow and Mouser were soon going to see the roof was empty and figure out they were back inside. Within seconds, they would charge back into the building and head for the elevator.

Luke pressed the ground floor button.

Nothing happened. The doors stayed open; the elevator did not move.

In the distance, he could hear Mouser calling an all-clear to Snow.

He jabbed at the button again. Nothing. He slid the electronic passkey from the card reader. Tested the button. Nothing. An elevator that wouldn't move.

They'd reset the code for the elevator. To keep Drummond and Luke trapped. There was no escape route.

Luke studied the card reader. He'd spent way too much time on computers cobbling together the Night Road research, couldn't he figure out this one? If the passcard had broken the original code—he slid the passkey back into the card reader. The PDA, tied to the card by a thin strip of plastic, blinked to life. A series of numbers raced across the screen.

He heard the sound of footsteps returning down the stairs. Fevered breathing.

Combinations of numbers flashed across the readout.

Luke put himself flat against the door, out of sight from the hallway. They couldn't see him, and he couldn't see them. He heard voices barely ten feet away.

"Not over the roof, goddamn it, no broken windows, nothing to lower themselves," Mouser said, as if speaking to someone not there. "So they're back in, Sweet Bird."

The elevator gave a soft, traitorous *ping* and the doors began to slide, slowly, closed.

He heard running footsteps and then the end of a gun jammed into the closing door. The door began, like an obliging devil, to open.

The only thought that seared into Luke's head was that hesitation meant death. He seized the gun's barrel before it could pivot the rest of the way toward him.

Snow stumbled into the elevator. She swung toward him, trying to wrench back control of the gun and aim it into his stomach. Over her bloodied shoulder, in the gunfire-sprayed hallways, Mouser ran for the elevator, full sprint, gun up.

Snow was crazy-strong and she sank her teeth into Luke's wrist, still trying to turn the gun into his flesh. She crouched between Luke and Mouser.

Mouser, running full-tilt down the hall, gun raised, screamed at Snow: *"Move out of the way!"*

Luke kicked the buttons as he fought with Snow, hitting the door-close button. The doors whooshed shut and the car began to descend.

Luke tangled with Snow, her mouth smeared with his blood. He saw her gun swing free of his grip. She pivoted the gun toward him. No place to retreat. He pushed her away, yanking the gun back from her, stumbling, falling into a corner of the elevator.

Then a sudden stop, a screech of metal against metal. Snow collapsed onto him, her hands clawing for the gun, and he barely felt the soft *phut* of the gun's discharge.

She doubled over, spat blood onto his foot. He couldn't tell if it was his or hers. Her eyes widened as she sank to her knees.

Drummond dropped through the opening and went to one knee.

Luke could see the fear in her eyes and her hand went to her shot chest, fist clenched, as though she could hold her life in with her fingers.

She spat in his face as he leaned close and she died.

"I—I . . ." Luke could hardly speak.

"She would have killed you and laughed about it later," Drummond said. "Let it go. Let's see what floor we're on."

Above, he heard Mouser screaming Snow's name.

41

It took Mouser only seconds to reason it out. The two bastards—the old man and the nine-lives punk—had entered the elevator shaft from the roof.

He forced the doors open with a mighty shove. It took all his strength but he peered down into the darkness of the elevator shaft.

He heard the crack of a shot, saw Drummond, sliding from the roof of the cabin into its interior. The hatch clanged shut.

"Snow!" he screamed down the shaft. It made an echo: *No. No.*

He could see the support rails inside the shaft. He leaped inside, landed on metal, and grabbed hold. He began a mad, spidery scramble downward.

Seventh floor. They ran for the stairwell. The floor was a huge, empty open space. Soft light made squares on the concrete floor. There was no place to take cover.

They moved quietly but quickly down the stairs. Several floors below them, they heard the clang of a door.

"Hell," Drummond whispered, leaning against Luke. The injuries to his head and his shoulder made his voice thick, his walk shaky. "Don't let your heart guide you. Stay cool. Remote. Always."

"Shut up with the advice," Luke said.

"By the way, my gun is empty."

"I have the one you gave me."

They reached the third floor. Storage space, empty of tenants. Crates and boxes everywhere. Plastic-wrapped office furniture—chairs, desks.

Drummond listened. "I hear them coming. I think they're in the stairwell."

"Then we go out the window." Luke hurried along the windows, peering down. One side of the building was scarce of foot traffic.

He stripped plastic from a heavy desk, he braided the fire hose through the drawer's opening, and he rammed the desk through the window. Glass exploded and the desk plummeted, unfurling the heavy hose. The desk stopped ten feet above the pavement, dangling like a broken pendulum against the building.

"Come on!" Luke yelled. "On my back." No time for them both to climb down the hose. Luke felt Drummond's solid weight go on his back and he threw himself out onto the makeshift rope.

42

The cameras in Drummond's kitchen had been destroyed in the hail of Snow and Mouser's gunfire, so the watchers—the boss, the scarred Frenchman, and Aubrey—had to settle for a satellite view of the Quicksilver building. They'd seen Luke and Drummond retreat to the roof, vanish into the hatch, then saw Mouser and Snow come onto the roof and disappear back into the building moments later.

Aubrey made a horrified noise in her throat.

The computer screens were set up in a corner of the hold, and Aubrey could hardly hear what was said over the drone of the engines. They'd given her drugs, first to make her sleep, then to make her talk, or so she suspected. She'd been lying on a cot, staring at the gray ceiling, when the boss had come and pulled her up and made her speak to Luke on the phone.

Luke was alive. But the boss told her what to say and she said it. Then she saw and heard the *tat-tat-tat* of the bullets in the kitchen, then nothing.

The boss pushed Aubrey away from the black screen.

"You have to help Luke," she said. "Please." She felt hazy from the drugs.

The boss ignored her. "Response from the security team?"

"None," the scarred Frenchman said. "We have to assume the ground-floor gunmen killed them."

"Drummond?"

"Not answering. I imagine he's busy."

"Access the building's computer systems. Wipe everything clean. What can you install in its place to soften the police inquiry?"

"We have a backup story: The building is a prototype, being built to test security technologies for sale. We will wipe and then reinstall data to that effect."

"Fine. Keep it simple." The Frenchman began his work.

"That's not helping them!" Aubrey yelled.

The boss looked at her. "I know. Go back and lie down. We'll be landing soon." The old cargo plane creaked and Aubrey looked past the man's shoulder. On the satellite feed that monitored the building, glass shimmered as a large desk burst through a third-story window.

"Luke?" Aubrey said.

43

The hose held, the desk dangling a good ten feet above the pavement.

Luke held hard to the fabric of the hose, slid down to the desk's surface. Drummond was wiry, all muscle, and he weighed a ton.

Luke looked up and saw a sparrow-thin man staring down at them from the broken window.

The thin man raised a sleek rifle, aimed it with confidence in his eyes. He let five seconds pass, saying, "You made it easy now."

Against his back, Drummond twisted. The weight of Luke's gun, jammed in the back of his pants, came free and a thundering boom went off near Luke's head.

The thin man ducked back or fell dead, Luke didn't know. He lost his grip on the hose and he and Drummond hit the canted desk, slid, hit air again. He felt Drummond's arms wrapping around him to cocoon him, to drink the impact of the concrete.

And it *hurt*. Luke felt all the air drive out of him. Drummond lay beneath him, breathing in short sharp pants. Luke's vision swam—he saw the desk, swinging above him.

Move.

Luke scrambled to his feet—muscles feeling like they'd been pulled from his body and hastily stuffed back inside his skin—and tried to lift Drummond from the sidewalk.

"Can't—leg broken—go." His voice was a hiss.

No way he was leaving Drummond behind. Luke hiked the older man up. Supported him on his shoulders. The hard shrill knife of a police siren sliced the afternoon, cutting through the Manhattan hum.

He pulled Drummond into his arms and carried him, heading for the cross street. He wanted to put buildings between him and the killers.

"My keys." Drummond patted at his pocket.

"You have a car?"

"My keys," he repeated and then the shot rang out, piercing him in the back, near where Luke's hand held him. The bullet tumbled through spine and organs and the impact nearly knocked him loose from Luke's grip.

The crowd that had been starting to close around them scattered, a woman shrieking, students bolting.

But Luke did not stop. A tea shop was a few yards away and he stumbled through its door as the proprietor opened it to see what fresh hell had erupted in the Village. At tables people with laptops looked up from their Web-induced isolation and gasped; the counterperson erupted with a series of short screams.

"Call 911," Luke said. "Please."

Drummond opened his eyes with visible effort. "My keys. Run. No police." His eyes focused on Luke's face. He clutched at Luke's Saint Michael's medal, which dangled above his face as Luke knelt by him. Then his hand went to his pocket and he died.

Oh, God, Luke thought. In the pocket he found a ring of car keys with a bottle opener. He grabbed the keys and Snow's gun, still nestled in Drummond's hand.

When he grabbed the gun everyone in the tea shop scrambled backward. He paused. Then he tore the Saint Michael's medal from Drummond's throat, cupped it in his hand. He hurried past a counter and ran into a small side alley of brick. It was closed to the main streets by an iron gate.

Keys. A car. Drummond must have a car. A rental garage's address was printed on the back of the bottle opener. Four blocks away.

Luke climbed over the iron gate, dropped to the next street, and ran.

44

The final bullet of Drummond's long career had caught Sweet Bird under the jaw and he'd fallen back with an astonished look on his thin face.

Mouser had picked up the rifle next to Sweet Bird's body. He'd gotten a single shot off, and if he was lucky one bullet had nailed both Drummond and Luke.

Chaos was about to descend on this building. He had to get out. There was no time to say good-bye to Snow. He'd left her behind in the elevator cab, one kiss good-bye. He blinked away the hot feeling behind his eyes as he bolted out the back of the building, avoiding the arrival of the police, blending in with the crowd. Sweet Bird's crew was either dead or had fled.

Luke and Drummond had killed her. The vengeance against Drummond had come quickly but Luke still walked and breathed. He felt the cold bloodthirstiness from Snow begin to fill him, as though her spirit was settling in his bones, seeping into this skin. A stirring in his chest took its final breath and shriveled. He had not even known her real name.

He turned into the tea shop's back door; he'd seen where Luke ran. Drummond's body still lay sprawled on the tiles. He frisked the body. Nothing. No cops yet; outside, a woman in a barista's apron spoke with the police in the street, pointing toward her store.

He retreated out the back door. The alleyway remained empty, the backs of other buildings fronting on to the space. Which way had Luke gone? And where would he go?

He remembered the manifest for Eric's charter—he'd seen it at the air park in Chicago—had said New York, then Paris.

He ran down the alley's iron gate, fury toward Luke filling him, and fury for Henry, who had sent him on this fool's errand.

The garage was four stories tall and Luke hurried along the row, testing the remote, until the lights on a plain Ford sedan beeped. He opened the trunk and found a briefcase and a packed bag. He took the briefcase and set it on the front passenger seat. The car still smelled new; the miles on the car were fewer than a hundred. Luke rifled through the glove compartment. The car had been sold to a James Morgan.

The charter pilot, Frankie Wu, had mentioned Paris. There had to be a reason that Eric would have stopped in New York—perhaps to meet Drummond and seal a deal on information—and then fly on to Paris.

For what? A final meeting? Drummond had said the people watching their interview were headed to Paris.

He steered into traffic, heading away from the chaos at Drummond's building, watching his rearview mirror for Mouser. His mind kept replaying the bullet he'd put into Snow. Intent didn't matter. He had killed her. He had ended another human life, but she had brought on her own fate with her choices.

At a stoplight he snapped open the briefcase. Two Canadian passports, one for Drummond, one for him. In the names of James Morgan and, for Luke, Tom Morgan. The passport photo was a modified version of his driver's license photo, cleverly expanded to fit the passport parameters. They were stamped with entry for the United States and the Bahamas. They looked real to him. He counted the cash, around two thousand dollars. He found credit cards in the name of Tom Morgan. The promise to hide him had been real and would have been immediate. And two tickets, the seats together, on the red-eye to Paris for tonight, under the same false names.

The car had a GPS system, and at the next light, he plugged in a request for directions to JFK Airport.

Aubrey lay on the cot and she heard the scarred Frenchman say to the boss: "We have a live signal from Drummond's car."

"He got out?" the boss asked. The satellite picture of the street had indicated Drummond might have been hit.

A pause. "I wonder where they'll go," the Frenchman said.

"Track the car. And find Henry Shawcross. I want to know if he's on a plane, a train, where he is."

"Do we still send a cleanup team?"

Aubrey closed her eyes and pretended to be asleep. They might be tempted to speak a little more freely, over the rumble of the plane, if they thought she had dozed off again.

"No. If anyone's still alive they're on their own," the boss said, and she could hear the awful bitterness under his words. "Sometimes you have to leave people behind."

"We could just call the car," the Frenchman said. "If it's Luke alone, he's probably scared to death."

"We clearly have to build trust with young Mr. Dantry," the boss said. "You play it out, you talk to him."

Aubrey felt a shadow over her. She opened her eyes. The boss, staring down, wore a frown on his hard face. "How is Luke doing it?"

"What?"

"Escaping these people. Finding us. Being so clever. Was he trained by Shawcross?"

"*Trained?* He's a grad student in psychology and you people have scared the crap out of him. A smart person who's scared can be dangerous."

"You better tell me the truth, Aubrey."

"I am. I am." She licked at her dry lips. "He and I, we just want out, we just want our old lives back. Please."

The man leaned close to her. "You get to go home when you help us. This fifty million Luke mentioned to Drummond. Where is it?"

"I don't know. I want nothing to do with that money. I want to go home."

"Home," the boss said. "I hope you can."

45

Henry wanted to be present for Luke's capture—or at least in the van that would be taking him away from the Quicksilver building. But an absolutely critical component to Hellfire required his attention. He especially wanted to be there to kill Drummond personally, if Drummond was at the address. But priorities were priorities. He could not delegate this task.

The storefront in a quiet street in Queens read READY-ABLE SERVICES. A recent change in ownership was not reflected in the storefront. The company, which was headquartered in New York and had branches in fourteen major metropolitan markets, contracted out cleaning and maintenance services to government and corporations. The workers were bonded and underwent background checks. The company was twenty years old, successful, and privately held. The inside man had been hired, inserted at Henry's suggestion four months ago. He'd cleared the background check because he had no record; he had never been caught. He took a salary cut for the job at Ready-Able, and his boss thought the company lucky to have landed such a smart, hard worker.

Henry went inside and gave a false name. The inside man, with the rank of supervisor, was expecting him. The two of them walked past the other supervisors and employees and headed for a storeroom at the back of the facility.

In the storeroom, the supervisor opened the box. "You can see," he began in Arabic.

"English," Henry said. "I don't wish to draw attention."

"Yes, well," the supervisor said in lightly accented English. "As you asked. Twenty surgical masks."

"It's not uncommon for the employees to wear these?"

"No. Cleaning can be a nasty job. They go with the uniforms. I have provided twenty, in the sizes you asked for."

Henry looked at the uniforms. "The pocket here is big enough to hold a gun."

"Yes, a variety of models. I tested it myself."

"And the access passes?"

"Activated. That took a bit of fiddling with the master database. You cannot have substitutions of personnel, though. I cannot issue new picture IDs at this late date."

"I understand." Henry carefully inspected all twenty passes. They looked entirely genuine because they were. Ready-Able had just added twenty employees who had not been hired or interviewed, hidden inside an access pass database that held information about two thousand employees around the country.

"The database audit was completed yesterday. I added the new records immediately afterward. We should be good for two or three days. I hope your operation takes place by then—"

"Not your concern."

"The company will be seen as a common element of the attack's targets when Hellfire is completed."

"You will be extracted and sent wherever you like. Go to the airport, go to the Travport cargo office. They will smuggle you out of the country."

"Understood."

The supervisor and Henry resealed the boxes and loaded them into Henry's van. Henry drove to a Travport satellite office and shipped the boxes to an address in Chicago.

This was the next-to-last stage before Hellfire could be launched. If only he had Luke under his thumb, then all would be well.

Henry's phone rang, and he opened it, sure that it would be good news.

The car's phone rang as Luke pulled into airport parking. He hit the talk button. "Hello?"

"Is this Luke?" A man's French-accented voice, the same one from Drummond's phone.

"Yes."

"Are you all right?"

"Yes, but Drummond is dead. I'm sorry I couldn't save him. He saved me."

"We mourn him more than you know. I can tell you he had a rewarding life."

Luke didn't know what to say, so he took refuge in the business at hand. "I have the fifty million the Night Road wants. I will trade it to you for information on my father's past, and for you to set up Aubrey someplace where she is safe."

"I do not understand. Your father's past?"

"Drummond was investigating one of our attackers, a man known as Mouser. I want to know if Mouser is suspected of killing my dad."

"And what about you?"

A surprising certainty filled him. "I want to keep fighting these people. I want to join you."

A pause, and then: "This is not your fight, Luke."

"It is entirely my fight. I don't want to hide under a name somewhere and hope you defeat Night Road. I am in this fight."

"Luke, you fought hard for someone who was cast as simply a pawn."

"Are you in Paris? Because I found tickets for today's flight. Drummond was supposed to bring me to Paris, wasn't he?"

"Yes. If we agreed it was best. But—"

"Then I'll see you soon." He switched off the phone.

46

The red-eye to Paris was close to full. Luke's tongue felt like a rock in his mouth when he had to present his false passport, but the airline's scans did not raise an alarm. Drummond had bought tickets in business class. The seats were plush, in a plastic-and-steel half-shell that let you recline without intruding on the space of the passenger behind you. He had the window seat and he kept his sunglasses in place, a cap pulled low on his head.

Drummond's seat next to him remained empty. He gave a sigh of relief. He pulled Drummond's medal from his pocket and studied it next to his own. Exact duplicates, in every detail.

This will keep you safe, his father had said. What exactly had that meant? Luke had taken it to mean a metaphysical safety, in terms of a moral compass; but now he thought his father might have meant a more concrete promise. He put Drummond's medal back in his pocket.

He ate the dinner of salad, lamb, couscous, and ice cream sundae. He pulled a blanket up to his chin and fell into a heavy sleep.

He awoke, hours later, as the breakfast service was being completed and first he saw out the window the spill of clouds over the French countryside. Then he sat up, rubbing his eyes under the dark glasses, and Mouser said, "You slept well. I didn't."

Luke blinked. It couldn't be. But Mouser was sitting right next to him.

And then he gave Luke a twitch of a smile, the kind the devil might flex. Somehow that quasi-grin was worse than the thrust of a blade.

"If you make a scene, you'll ruin the flight for everyone else. In the worst way."

Luke spoke past the rock in his throat. "How did you . . . ?"

"We both needed to get to Paris. There's not an infinite number of flights."

Luke let his gaze dart past Mouser's aisle seat. The middle row was occupied by an older couple who looked like vacationers. Behind him were two businessmen, one asleep, the other immersed in a laptop. Everyone in their own first-class cocoon.

"I'm not going to hurt you," Mouser said in a soft whisper.

"Liar." He thought of Drummond, bleeding his life out. His father's face boarding that plane.

Did you kill my father? Why are you a suspect, years later? The thoughts blazed through his mind as if blasted from a flamethrower. His hands clenched into fists.

In his pocket was the secret thumb drive, hidden in the little basketball. The key to the money.

"Why are you going to Paris, Luke?" Mouser sipped red wine from a glass that sat on his foldout tray. "I guess you need a vacation after all your adventures."

Luke gave no answer. He had to get away. The pilot announced that they'd be landing in twenty minutes.

"Do tell me. Because if I alert the attendants to the fact you happen to be traveling on a false passport—mine is legit, by the way—this was a giant risk for you. What would be worth such a risk, I wonder. I can only think that it's the money. Eric wanted to go to Paris too. You're following that dog's trail."

I have to incapacitate him, Luke thought. *Fight him here and get away without getting caught.*

"You give me the money," Mouser said, "and you walk. Our battle is over."

"I won't, on either count."

"I don't blame you for New York. I blame Snow. She rushed where she shouldn't have." His gaze was steady on Luke's face.

"But I do blame you for Drummond. And . . ." He stopped.

"And what?" Mouser hissed.

"Did you ever . . ." He waited as the flight attendant walked past. "Did you sabotage a private plane? Heading from D.C. to North Carolina? Ten years ago?"

The silence hung between him, Luke staring at him. The twitchy smile stayed on Mouser's face.

"No. I don't know anything about planes or their systems."

Luke watched him. He didn't believe him. Terrorist psychology showed extremists did not like to admit a shortcoming in knowledge. It was a consistent thread. They were know-it-alls. A simple no would have sufficed. Luke had said nothing about the systems of the plane being involved. His tongue felt locked to the top of his mouth.

If Mouser was curious about the North Carolina question, he didn't ask. "I've answered your question, you answer mine. Where is the money?"

He told his first lie: "Eric hid the money in a bunch of accounts."

"Give me the account numbers."

Luke tapped his temple.

"I don't believe you memorized a bunch of bank account numbers. They're long."

"I was highly motivated. If you kill me, you'll never get them."

Mouser looked at him. "You're giving the info to someone in Paris. To get Aubrey back."

"Yes." And to keep the money away from the Night Road. He had no intention of funding terrorism. But he wondered: Could he turn this meeting into a trap for Mouser? A way to give him to Quicksilver? The outline of a plan began to take shape in his mind.

"You barely know that woman." Now Mouser looked straight ahead. "I barely knew Snow. Sometimes barely is all you need." He paused. "A college kid like you, you don't want this kind of life. Give me the info on the accounts and you're free."

Tires hit pavement as the airliner coasted onto the runway.

What had Henry told him, a lifetime ago back in Austin, about his work? You're good at baiting the hook. "I'm meeting Quicksilver. They have the capability to do a lot more damage to you and the Night Road than I ever could," Luke said.

The captain was announcing to the passengers that the plane would first taxi to the bus that would take them to the terminal.

"You cut a deal with them."

"No," Luke lied. "They only want the money. So I have a suggestion."

"What?"

"Come with me to the meeting. You can grab one of their people, find out what Quicksilver really is. But me and Aubrey walk. You get the money, you get your enemies."

"Why would you help me?"

"Because I just want to be left alone. By you, by Quicksilver. The fight is between you two." Luke knew if he made a scene to get Mouser arrested in the airport, he'd be arrested too. And he wouldn't ever find out the truth.

Quicksilver would be watching their every move. *They have the resources; they'll see Mouser coming well ahead. And they'll kill him,* Luke thought.

"Me help you save your woman after you killed mine." Mouser's whisper was so soft that, as the plane parked and the passengers stood to gather their belongings, Luke could barely hear him. "I feel like I'm making a deal with the devil."

Me too, Luke thought.

47

PARIS

Luke had not been here since he was an undergraduate. He had accompanied his stepfather and his mother to Paris for a conference. At nineteen he had wandered the streets in blissful freedom—bookstores, bars, the expansive parks, the old student quarter near Notre Dame. He had loved the city, but he had not been back since.

But he hoped his brief familiarity with Paris would save him. Mouser had given no signs of even a basic comprehension of French beyond *oui* or *non,* and that might be his salvation. Neither had a suitcase other than his carry-on, and after a desultory check of their documents in customs he and Mouser walked out into the dull gray morning, toward the taxi line.

He checked his cell phone as they walked outside and retrieved a voice mail: *Meet at the Eiffel Tower for Aubrey one hour after your plane lands.* Mouser grabbed the phone, listened as Luke did.

"But they don't know I'm here," Mouser said.

"No." Considering Quicksilver's reach it would not surprise him if they did know. But let Mouser be surprised.

"The Eiffel Tower. How touristy," Mouser muttered in a low growl. "Give me your phone."

"Why?"

"I don't want you calling them and letting them know I'm with you."

He'd thought of trying to text just the word *Mouser* or *Help* to the number that had just called him. To warn Quicksilver. He hesitated.

"I will kill you the second you pull a fast one on me," Mouser said. "Give me the phone."

Luke gave it to him.

Mouser put a steel grip on his shoulder. "Come on. I have a ride for us."

The car sat in the parking garage in a back corner. Mouser found keys in a container locked under the bumper. It was a Mercedes sedan, gleaming, high-end.

He opened the trunk. Inside were bags and cases. Some were long and narrow, marked with the logo of a golf club manufacturer. Luke figured they were not golf clubs. Weapons. Someone had given this man an armory and driven it to the airport for him. So Mouser had allies in France.

The Night Road was bigger than just a group inside America. He had only researched American extremists, but if those domestic terrorists were linked to, cooperating with, other extremists around the world . . . the thought was frightening.

"Get in the car," Mouser said.

Luke obeyed. Mouser didn't slide behind the wheel; rather he seemed to be studying the phone. As though he'd gotten an e-mail. He turned his back to Luke. Thirty seconds later he slid into the car, an angry look on his face.

Mouser roared out of the garage.

48

Mouser had taken one of the long cases—marked with the logo of a British golf manufacturer—and slipped the earpiece into Luke's ear, saying, "I'll be able to hear your every word. Dump this and you're dead."

"Where will you be?"

"Watching. Don't screw this up or I'll shoot you, accounts or not. You play nice, you and Aubrey walk."

No, Luke thought, *you're the one who's going down.* But he turned and walked toward the tower. When he glanced back, Mouser was gone. He had not counted on Mouser being able to eavesdrop on his conversation. This made his plan much harder. And if he ditched the earpiece, he had no doubt: Mouser would shoot him—and Aubrey. He had to think of another way to warn Quicksilver.

The base of the Eiffel Tower was broader and the plaza wider than Luke remembered. He saw French soldiers with assault rifles wandering the sprawling grounds, scanning faces in the scattered crowd of hundreds of tourists and sightseers, watching for the unusual or the threatening. A kiss of sunshine came through the late spring clouds.

His phone rang. He answered it.

It was Aubrey's voice, scared. "Luke."

"Are you all right?"

"Yes. I'm going to give you your directions now." She steadied her voice. "Walk away from the river, away from the tower, go toward the half-circle where the tour buses stop. You'll see me."

He could see in the distance, past the walkways and the low shrubberies, a wide loop of street, a double-decker bus parked, tourists not bothering to get off the bus but snapping photos of the grand tower. "All right."

In his other ear, he heard the whisper of Mouser's voice: "If you warn them, I'll shoot first and learn to live without the money."

"Yes," he said, as if to both Aubrey and Mouser.

So much for his brilliant trap. He had brought this maniac to the meeting, and he could only hope that the Quicksilver people had spotted his uninvited guest. If they hadn't . . . then he was going to have talk through the meeting without handing over the encrypted thumb drive, get Aubrey, and figure out a way to get the Quicksilver people and Aubrey to safety.

He walked past a beggar woman, with outstretched hands, who said, "Speak English?" past a fellow wearing a belt of cheap Eiffel Tower replicas that jingled. Luke glanced around to see if he could see where Mouser had gone.

To his right was another pathway that led to a shuttered gazebo and a playground that was unoccupied. Beyond that was a large wide walking and jogging trail; and beyond that was a cluster of grand mansions, one of which, he remembered from strolling around here before, was the Czech Embassy. He didn't think Mouser could hide there, so he cast his gaze toward the half-circle, looking for the spot where Mouser would be and trying to spot Aubrey in the dozens of faces.

Mouser had walked down the broad jogging path in the shadow of the tower, Allée Léon Bourgeois, after sending Luke on his way to the rendezvous. The *allée* was not busy; a few joggers, iPods insulating them from the world. He scanned the area, looking for the best point to make his stand. To his right, shaded trees bordered the *allée*, with an empty playground and a shuttered gazebo that sold treats on warmer days. He walked with complete purpose, which was always the most convincing camouflage. He went to the back of the gazebo, stepped onto an electrical unit, and climbed onto its green roof. He would not be concealed for long; anyone on the *allée* who looked up would see him sprawled on the roof, but the joggers were absorbed in their solitary orbits. That was the problem with everyone today, Mouser thought. *They're all in their own world, oblivious to civilization around them descending into hell.*

He slid the rifle free from the golf bag. Just a matter of seconds and his work would be done. He put the crosshairs on Luke's head.

Luke tried not to panic. So where was she? A flock of tourists herded and moved between him and the bus, which pulled out, to be replaced by another bright red bus.

"Speak English?" another woman asked him. He ignored her and pushed past a small group of Japanese visitors. And saw Aubrey, several yards away, on the edge of the walkway. Aubrey wore a raincoat, a heavy hat on her head, her face pale and gaunt.

And standing next to her was a man who turned and met his gaze.

His dead father.

Luke froze. Blinked. No. The man was bald; his dad, frozen in memory, had a full head of graying hair. But the eyes. The mouth, set in a nervous frown. The nose, straight as iron.

He stared at Luke. Luke felt as though the crowded acreage of the tower were contracting, the mass of people around him fading to a misty blur, the hum and rumble of Paris devolving to a giant white-noise hiss. Mouser said something in his earpiece and Luke could not register a single word. The air left his chest; his knees buckled. He kept himself standing through sheer force of will.

This could not be. But it was. His father did not smile at him, but he closed his eyes, as though conscious of Luke's pain, as though it were a wave he could feel or hear or taste. Ten years. Ten years of grieving and missing his father, feeling his absence like a raggedy gap in his chest, and clutching a piece of silver as his father's last gift of presence in his life.

His father's words on their last parting: *I'll miss you every moment.* They rang and echoed in his head. It had all been a lie, the kind of monumental lie that did not just sting feelings but cut down to heart and bone. A lie that undid lives.

His father was alive. He was here. The shock suffocated him until his chest began to ache. Heat burned the back of his eyes. He took two steps to start running toward his father . . . but then he remembered where he was. Not just in the gray light of the Paris morning. He was in the crosshairs of a terrorist's gun.

Every plan and stratagem vanished from his mind. A tremble took his body. "Dad?" he said, more gasp than word. No. It was too much to ask. He couldn't do this anymore. But he had to.

"What?" Mouser asked in Luke's ear.

He couldn't let Mouser close his trap. He had to think past the maelstrom of emotion.

"I said damn. I don't see her." Luke blinked. He felt tears on his face before he realized he'd shed them. "They're not here. We should go. I'll just give you the money. Please, let's go." He turned to walk away.

"I see her. The woman you were with in Chicago. Straight ahead of you, standing with some bald guy. What the hell's the matter?" Mouser said in a low growl of menace.

"That's not her." He could think of nothing else to say.

"Luke. Don't you fuck with me."

Maybe he won't recognize Dad, he thought. *Maybe he doesn't remember everyone he kills.*

A man he didn't know stopped in passing, grabbed his arm. "Luke, it's okay." He recognized the voice as that of the Frenchman who'd spoken to him on the phone.

Luke tried to shake his head. "Get them out of here. Please get them out of here."

"What?"

"Sniper, run, scatter." Luke bolted toward his father and Aubrey. "Aubrey, Dad, run! Run!"

"Dad?" Mouser hissed into his earpiece. "What the hell game you"—and then he stopped, as words no longer mattered.

The crack of the bullet hummed through the air, the dirt kicking up at Luke's feet. He stopped, nearly fell. A second shot boomed in the air, and now panic rippled through the crowd approaching the tower.

"Sniper!" Luke screamed. Another shot and people scattered, screaming, knocking into one another as they fled. He looked back at the Frenchman—he was racing across the grass toward where the shots were coming from, a weapon drawn, and then he was cut down, a bullet slicing through his throat.

Luke got knocked off his feet by a line of tourists scrambling back toward their bus at the sound of the gunfire. His sunglasses fell from his face.

Feet trampled him and agony rushed up from his hand, boots landed on his scalp, his cheek. He fought to stand. He saw his father and Aubrey, surrounded by three men, guns jammed to the back of their heads, being shoved through the chaos of the crowd.

This was a trap. The Night Road had wanted to flush out their enemy, and now they had. Luke had handed Quicksilver to Mouser—who wasn't working alone.

"Dad!" Luke yelled. Luke saw the group headed rapidly toward the bus drop-off, borne along by the rest of the fleeing crowd. Luke struggled to catch up with them. He broke free of the main crowd and saw his father and Aubrey being shoved into the back of a van. The van was marked with a logo of a cake and read Trois Petits Gâteaux. Three Little Cakes.

The doors slammed and the van peeled out onto the road. Luke cut across the grassland and ran out onto the broad, tree-lined walking trail, trying to keep the van in sight on the street.

But suddenly the van wheeled hard and zoomed right. Along the *allée*, heading directly toward him. The driver was pointing at him. Coming back for him.

Luke turned and ran, back toward the tower. He shot a panicked glance over his shoulder and he could see the driver's face, frowning in concentration, teeth gritted, intent on running him down.

He had nowhere to hide. The van veered past him, a rifle butt from the window slamming him, knocking him over. The van skidded to a stop. He heard the shrill high cry of the police sirens booming across the air, through the trees, closer to the tower, the armed guards clearing out the people, hunting for the unseen source of the shots. No more shooting; Mouser was gone. Of course. His buddies could finish the work.

"Help me!" Luke yelled. *"Aidez-moi!"* But in the panic, no one heard him.

One of the black-suited men jumped out of the van, raced toward Luke, gun drawn, screaming at him—in English—to get in the van. He saw in a flash Aubrey and his father, facedown on the van floor.

Make the creep come to you, Luke realized. The thought came with shimmering clarity. The past few days had awakened a brutal, long-drowsing instinct in him, as though the bookish Web-surfer who had never thought about the reality of danger had been whittled away. Seeing his father, alive, had changed him, changed everything. He was not going to lose him again.

Luke went flat on the ground. The gunman ran up to him and Luke timed it to the second, spun, and scissor-kicked hard. It was awkward but forceful enough and the gunman stumbled. Luke delivered a pile-driver kick into the gunman's groin. The guy grunted in agony and folded and Luke kicked him in the head without hesitation and wrenched the gun from him. He ran toward the van, gun raised.

One of the gunmen inside the van leveled a pistol at him. Then he saw Aubrey launch herself from the floor, claw at the gunman's arm. The doors slammed and he heard the sound of a shot fired inside the van.

He fired at the van's tires, hitting too high, nailing the bumper. Then a swarm of people fleeing ran between him and the van, and he couldn't risk another shot. He rammed his way through the crowd, trying to get close enough to shred a tire.

But the van revved and accelerated, knocking through the thinning crowd. They'd run out of time to execute the grab on him, with French police swarming the grounds. The van blasted onto Avenue Charles Floquet and was gone.

Luke tucked the stolen gun under his jacket and ran. His mind raced. Mouser. Mouser would know where they would be taken.

The sniper fire had ended, as far as he could tell. Which meant it was too risky for Mouser to stay in place. Mouser would have to run and wouldn't he run to the Mercedes? If he couldn't rendezvous with the Night Road team in the van after using Luke as bait, he would have to make a fast escape in the chaos. But with the immediately snarling traffic as pedestrians and every bus in the area fled, and police shutting down roads, the sedan they'd driven to the tower would offer a difficult solution for escape. No sniper wanted to be caught in the mother of all traffic jams.

But the Paris subway, the Métro, was close by. He could be wrong. But Mouser would want safety more than retrieving an asset like a car; it was the terrorist way. He headed for the sign indicating the Métro.

49

Luke followed part of the fleeing mass of people and ran to the Champs de Mars Métro station across the street from the tower, hurried down into the tunnel. The lines to buy a ticket were long and he jumped the turnstile, apologizing to the man in front of him. No one seemed to care about his lack of a ticket in the rush to get away from the shooting. It was a big station, different-colored signs pointing to different lines, and then he caught an edge of what looked like Mouser's burr haircut making a turn. He followed, cutting through the crowd.

Mouser. For sure. He headed for a station with a yellow line, an RER station with the large trains that traveled the lines running parallel to the Seine. The crowd—dozens thick—pressed forward as a large double-decker train pulled into the station. Children cried, people talked in a hubbub. Panic steamed the air. No one looked at Luke, even glanced at him. He was the cause of it all and he felt as small and anonymous as an ant.

He lost sight of Mouser. He pressed the earpiece Mouser had put in his ear but heard nothing. Mouser had killed the connection. Luke threw it on the floor. He didn't want Mouser reactivating it and hearing him.

Luke went on tiptoe and surveyed the dozens of faces stretching away from him in a jostling human quilt. Damn it. Then he saw Mouser. Thirty feet away and to his left, scanning the crowd himself, his head slowly turning toward Luke's position.

The sunglasses that had helped camouflage Luke on the plane were gone, lost in the scuffles. Luke ducked, crowding a young woman, who spat a vol-

ley of outraged French that questioned Luke's basic intelligence. Her hair
was a spike of black dye; her boyfriend next to her had shaved off his hair.
A pair of sunglasses sat on his head.

The roar of an approaching train sounded. The crowd eased forward bare
centimeters.

"Are you trying to kiss asses?" Luke thought he heard the boyfriend say.
Luke ignored the comment and stayed kneeling on the floor.

The double-decker train stopped, and the doors slid open.

The human tide surged forward. Luke grabbed a fistful of Drummond's
dollars from his pocket, handed them to the boyfriend, and said in bad
French, "I would like to buy," then said in English, "your sunglasses," pan-
tomiming the shades.

"What is wrong with you?" the boyfriend said. "No. I don't want your
dollars."

But the girlfriend laughed and pulled the shades from his head, stuck
them on Luke's face. She grabbed the money. "There you go. I bought them
cheap for him on the street. Now I can buy a dozen more in ugly match-
ing colors." Her English was good. She gave Luke a thoughtful, measuring
stare, as though trying to guess his motives for the bizarre offer.

From behind the dark lenses, Luke watched Mouser moving toward a seat
on the ground car. Luke knew if he stayed on the ground car Mouser would
see him, sunglasses or not. So he went up the steps, following the girlfriend
and the boyfriend, his heart a piston in his throat. Mouser could get off at any
station and he would lose him; he couldn't easily monitor who got off and on
the ground car. He stood near the stairs; it was his only hope. If Mouser came
to the stairs and glanced up, he'd see Luke. Then Luke was dead.

If I lose him, how will I ever find Aubrey and my dad?

My dad. The two words were like two muffled explosions in his chest. The
entire past ten years of his life had been a charade. His father was alive.

Now that he had time to think, a hard bite of anger closed on his heart.
Why? Why would his father pretend to leave his wife and child—why
would he abandon them to a man like Henry Shawcross? Why would he let
his wife and child suffer through a devastating grief? Why would he hide
behind the deaths of his friends?

Luke had thought he didn't know the real Henry; he clearly didn't know
his father either. The realization felt like a punch in the stomach. He shook

his head, as though physically clearing the thoughts from his mind. No. If he pondered this now, emotion would drown him. Grief and bewilderment could wait.

The train jolted forward, people crowding on the stairs.

"Are you still enjoying my sunglasses, crazy man?" the boyfriend said, in serviceable English. He had apparently decided to indulge his girlfriend's whim. "You want to buy a shirt next? Nice pants?"

The girlfriend giggled.

"No. But I need help," Luke said. "You heard the shooting?"

The boyfriend rolled his eyes. "We walk out of the station, everyone running this way, we head back inside." He shrugged. "Crazy. The tower will be there tomorrow for us to see."

"How do you need help?" the girlfriend said. Luke saw she was the power in the relationship.

"My girlfriend, she is a student here. She's seeing a guy. Who's not me." The train jostled them slightly as it picked up speed.

"Ah," the girlfriend said. The boyfriend frowned.

"He was going to meet her at the tower today. She didn't show and now I'm following him."

"Ah, the shooting was you shooting at him," the boyfriend joked. "Revenge is sweet, yes."

"Ah, no."

"And this man knows your face," the girlfriend guessed.

"She had a picture of us on the bedside table. I'm sure he's seen me." The lying was easy, because a real sense of betrayal swelled in his chest. His father had been the greatest liar of them all. "But he's dangerous. A little crazy. I want to find out where he lives. But he's below, on the ground car, and I don't want him to see me."

The girlfriend raised an eyebrow in amusement. "And he will be convinced by a disguise of cheap sunglasses," she muttered in French, unzipped the boyfriend's backpack, pulled out a knit cap. "Cover your hair with this."

"That's not, what you say, hygienic," the boyfriend complained. He spoke in a flood of French.

"Your head is clean." She yanked the cap onto Luke's head, tucked his light hair under its rainbow folds. Then she pulled out a scarf to match. Both were pink and green. "I make these for him; he never wears them."

"He will not wear them either," the boyfriend said.

"I will," Luke said. He pushed some more cash into her hand. Her kindness overwhelmed him.

The girlfriend's finger lingered against his palm, but she made a point of putting the hand she'd touched Luke with firmly against her boyfriend's cheek. "And you, my sweet, you will get a new hat."

"A cowboy hat," the boyfriend said. The girlfriend laughed.

"Where is the next stop?" Luke asked, rubbing his arms. He couldn't keep still.

"Pont de l'Alma," the boyfriend said. "Les Invalides, the next one, is more of a center for more lines."

People around them were chattering, mostly in French and English, about the shootings. The girlfriend kept a look locked on Luke and he thought she saw the deception beneath the surface of his smile.

"You must love this girl a lot to forgive her," she said.

"Her I love," Luke said. "Him I don't." The boyfriend laughed.

The train slowed as it approached the station. People pushed past them, eager to get down the few steps to the exit.

"Are you getting off here?" he asked them.

They shook their heads after a shared glance.

Luke risked a few steps down to the ground car, inching for position. He had wanted to ask them to see if they could spot if Mouser got off the train, but too many people jammed the car. He couldn't take the risk that they would miss him. He peered down, scanned the crowd. He could see the back of Mouser's head. It looked like he was text-messaging on a phone, furiously. But not rising to leave.

The train stopped and the doors hissed open. A number of people left but many stayed. Few climbed on.

Mouser remained in his seat, his back to Luke. The gun hidden along Luke's side, covered by his jacket, pressed like an iron weight. The RER train pulled out of Pont de l'Alma. Mouser stood, began to move past the other seated passengers. He had a smile on his face.

Luke retreated up the stairs. "He's getting off at the next station. Thank you for your help."

"You're welcome. Thanks for the money." The boyfriend shook Luke's hand, and then Luke saw that the girlfriend had noticed his gun. Her mouth narrowed and her eyes widened. They knew there had been shots fired at the tower, and now here was a man asking for glasses and hat for an instant disguise, with a gun tucked in the side of his pants, under his jacket.

The fear in her eyes churned his heart. She could scream. She could go to the first policeman in the next station.

"Please," he said. "I'm not the bad guy. I'm not." He didn't know what else to say.

She seemed unsure of what step to take next, and the boyfriend looked at her, aware of a strained communication passing between her and Luke, and misreading it. Suddenly not happy about it. He eased the girlfriend away from Luke, down the steps, toward the door. She looked at Luke with stark terror; her mouth trembled.

I'm not the bad guy, he mouthed again.

Les Invalides. The train stopped. Much more of the crowd poured out for this station, but Luke tried to hang back until the last second to see if Mouser exited. And this time he did, passing within fifteen feet of Luke, hurrying. He stepped off last, Mouser a good twenty feet ahead of him, the boyfriend and girlfriend between him and Luke.

Luke considered ducking behind on the garish orange pillars but decided he had to risk staying close. He kept following the couple. The girlfriend pulled a phone from her purse and started talking into it.

At the top of the stairs, Mouser shot a glance across the crowd behind him. His gaze raked across where Luke walked but he did not notice Luke, wearing dark glasses and heavy cap and an ugly scarf across his chin and mouth.

Mouser turned back toward the front.

Luke hurried up the stairs, half expecting to see Mouser waiting for him, but he wasn't. Mouser stood on a long moving sidewalk, feeding past abstract art, and Mouser returned attention to the phone, texting, eyes close to the screen. An angry expression colored his face.

Luke realized that the girlfriend and the boyfriend were gone. Vanished. Maybe they'd tucked into another line.

Mouser reached the end of the moving sidewalk and stepped off without a backward glance. Then Luke looked back at the end of the conveyor belt, spotted the boyfriend and girlfriend from the train.

Talking to a policeman.

He had to hurry. If the cops stopped him before he stopped Mouser . . .

the panic tore through his chest. He'd put his father and Aubrey in this danger, he had to save them from it.

He hurried toward the station's exit and took an escalator up. Ahead of him, across a stretch of parkland, was Les Invalides, the golden-domed complex of museum and monuments of French military history. To his right was the Musée d'Orsay, a more recent jewel of Parisian museums. Around him was a stretch of grass, a playground, people walking in lazy surrender to the brightening day.

Fifty feet ahead of him a black BMW stopped, the back door opened, and Mouser slid into the backseat. Luke pivoted; he couldn't risk Mouser seeing him and now the car was headed toward him.

He heard the purr of the approaching motor and the air felt sealed in his lungs as he headed back toward the escalator that led down to the Invalides station.

The policeman came out of the station. Looking straight at him.

Trapped. Between the cop and Mouser in the BMW. He took the risk and stopped. The sedan shot past, not braking. Luke crossed the street in the wake of the BMW's passage.

In the backseat, he saw the burr of Mouser's head. Then the driver turned full to speak to Mouser.

Henry Shawcross. His stepfather.

Oh, you bastard, he thought. Finally, to see the betrayal with his own eyes, Mouser and Henry together. No way he could let them escape, no way. Luke's eyes darted everywhere; no taxi stand in sight. No means to follow them. He ran across the street now, in a full-blown sprint, toward the Musée d'Orsay.

He glanced back. The policeman was running now too. Chasing him. The girlfriend had sold him out.

He reached the taxi stand at the museum and one of the cabs cut hard to the front of the line, earning a squeal of honks from the other drivers. Luke got in the backseat.

"Thank you, go. *Vite.* Fast. Eiffel Tower."

The driver, a young man about his age, nodded and roared down the street. Past the winded policeman, who had stopped running.

"The tower, very hectic, too much traffic," the cabbie said. "A shooting . . ." His English was serviceable.

"Okay," Luke said. He didn't care where they went. The black BMW was gone. How was he going to find his dad or Aubrey, now? "Then—the police station."

The cabbie kept watching him in the mirror. "You run from a policeman and now you want to go to the police."

"He mistook me for someone else."

The cabbie did not seem to understand.

"Wait." Drummond said that he and Henry and his dad had all worked for the State Department. If Quicksilver was the replacement for the Book Club, then he should turn to State for help. "Take me to the American Embassy, please."

"I must call for address." He flipped open a phone, spoke a flurry of what sounded like Russian into it.

Luke fell against the back of the seat. The cabbie made turn after turn, speaking into the phone. He reached for a radio and turned it off.

"How far to the embassy?"

The cabbie clicked off the phone and took a hard turn into a quiet street. He slammed the brakes and twisted in the seat. He raised a small gun from the seat and aimed it at Luke. A pop sound, and Luke felt a thump hit the crocheted wool of the ugly scarf and a slight weight lodged in the fabric. He grabbed at the gun, his head scraping the ceiling. He turned the little gun back toward the cabbie and it fired again.

The dart pierced the cabbie's throat and he sagged against the steering wheel. The car lurched forward, crumpling into a parked van. Luke yanked a dart from the scarf; it had gotten stuck in the thick knitting. The girl-friend's impulsive gift had saved him.

Jesus, Luke thought. *He was waiting for me. Cut ahead of the line to make sure I was his fare. He knew I was at that subway station. How?*

The cabbie kept breathing in shallow panting gasps. Drugged.

Luke fumbled with the dart in the guy's throat; his fingertip touched a leather string. He pulled on the cord and a small medal of an armed angel crept out of the cabbie's shirt.

Saint Michael. Like his, like Drummond's.

Was the angel a sign of Quicksilver? Drummond had the medal and was clearly part of Quicksilver. But if the medal was the sign of a Quicksilver member, why would the cabbie attack him?

Luke picked up the dart gun and the cell phone the guy had used. He grabbed the cabbie's wallet. He got out of the cab and ran. Three streets over, he opened the cell phone and looked in the call log. The number was one he recognized, one seared in his memory.

Jane. The kidnapping mastermind.

Never mind Quicksilver, never mind the Night Road, never mind the fifty million. Jane was the woman who had orchestrated all the chaos. The woman responsible for the hellish chessboard his life had turned into; she had sent this cabbie after him.

If the cabbie was part of Quicksilver, then he must be a traitor, working with Jane.

That was going to be her mistake, Luke thought. Because she'd just given him a way to track her down.

Pawn takes queen, he thought, as he ran away from the cab.

Luke knew he needed to avoid anyplace with security cameras—maybe the surveillance in the Métro had helped the cabbie find him at Les Invalides, he thought—and so he ran until he found a library. But even the library had a camera near the door. He ducked his head, averted his gaze from its unblinking view.

He opened the cabbie's wallet. A wad of euros, a French driver's license, a gray blank card. Like an electronic passkey.

Now he just needed to find an address to match the passkey.

He sat at a computer terminal. He entered in the Web address he'd seen on Eric's laptop in the old house: the Night Road's online meeting room. He got to the television fan site, entered in Eric's password. It still worked; someone at the Night Road was being sloppy.

Or maybe they were just busy getting ready for Hellfire, whatever horror it was, and the thought chilled him.

He signed in as Eric and he started a new discussion with a request for help: *I have a cell phone that I need to track. Immediately. Help please.* And he typed in Jane's cell phone number.

He waited. He clicked on a posting about a video link and to his horror the video started with a close-up of a guy he recognized as the man in Houston who'd been standing at the intersection waiting for Allen Clifford. The cheap jacket, the scarred cheeks—Luke remembered him running away in the dim streetlight in Houston. His eyes were wide and a razor began a slow draw across his throat.

Luke turned off the video before anyone around him could see the execution. He felt sick. *That's what they'll do to you if they catch you. That's what they'll do to Aubrey and Dad.*

He jumped to an English-language news site, and the shooting at the tower was the top story. No suspects caught yet.

He went back to the Night Road site, hoping against hope. A reply waited for him. *I have your phone info. What do you have to trade?*

Inspiration struck and he wrote the kind of lie he thought would appeal: *I have a nice set of bank accounts, established, ready for cleaned money.*

He waited. It took an hour and he fought his impatience. *Fine,* the answer came in a private message to Eric's account. The phone was registered to a Jane Mornay, she had a Paris address near Saint-Germain, on a street called rue de l'Abbé-Grégoire. He signed off without posting the promised set of accounts. Betraying the guy who'd traced the phone probably meant his password would be invalidated and he couldn't use the site again, but it didn't matter. He would have the woman behind all his misery, the woman who had stolen his life.

And he would be closer to the truth about his father, his life, Hellfire. He thought Jane was at the nexus of all these events, an unseen hand, one he was about to drag into the sunlight.

He walked out the door, shielding his face again at the library's doors. He was afraid every camera was an eye watching him.

50

Mouser kicked Aubrey and Warren Dantry out of the back of the van, sending them sprawling at Henry Shawcross's feet. The packed dirt of the old, vast barn smelled of horse, of hay. Aubrey blinked. Shafts of light made yellow bars on the brown of the floor. She saw a BMW parked behind Henry. She tried to make herself tiny, curling into a ball. One of the men had hit her after she'd spoiled his shot at Luke, kept a gun on her head to force Warren Dantry to sit still. She looked up at Mouser, Henry, the two remaining thugs. She realized no one was looking at her. They were all looking at her fellow prisoner.

Warren Dantry rolled onto his back and Henry stared. Mouser said, "You recognize—" and Henry raised a hand to silence him.

"You were on the plane. You died," Henry said.

"Hello, asshole," Warren said.

Mouser saw Henry's hands start to tremble, clenching into fists.

"Luke is gone," Mouser said. "No way he's an amateur. I think he's been working for his dad this whole time. You've been played for the biggest effing fool on the planet, Henry."

"No," Henry said. "No, no. Not possible."

"No to what?" Warren said. "No that I'm here or no to Luke having handed you your ass on a plate?"

"Leave us," Henry said. "I want to talk to the walking dead alone."

"No," Mouser said. "You're blinded, Henry. You're blinded by your affection for your stepson. It ends now. You are incapable of calling the shots.

You've put our money, our whole network, and Hellfire at risk. I'm in command now."

Henry slid him a look of utter poison. "No, you're not."

"Jesus, Henry, you really can't run anything," Warren Dantry said. "Even when you're supposedly the smartest guy in the room."

"Shut up. Shut up, shut up, you're dead." Steel coated his tone, but underneath everyone could see a murderous rage.

"Academics must take the evidence before their eyes into account," Warren said.

Henry seized the bound Warren and half dragged him into an unused room off the main barn floor. He slammed the door closed. He shoved Warren to the floor.

"What is Quicksilver?" Henry said.

"It's your death," Warren said. "Unlike mine, yours will be for real."

Henry studied Warren's face. "Whoever they are, they must have paid you a fortune to abandon your wife and child. I would have enjoyed your funeral except I could see the agony Barbara and Luke suffered. I don't think you gave them a moment's thought." He knelt close to him. "You think I've lost? You lost, you heartless bastard. You lost the last ten years."

"You had to take over my life because you never could have built one for yourself."

"I loved being married to Barbara, loved being Luke's father. And I was better at it than you were."

"Please. You destroyed it all. Barbara knew what you were, what you were becoming."

Henry staggered on his feet.

"I'm guessing she confronted you about your illicit activities while you were on your drive that day. I knew her better than anyone else. She wouldn't have been able to contain her outrage. She called you out, didn't she?"

I know what you are, Henry. You can't lie it away. Her words, coated with venom. Him trying to explain, convince her she was wrong. Grabbing at the wheel, begging her to pull over. *I want you out of the house, Henry, out of our lives. Gone forever.* The car wheeling loose, the guardrail suddenly crunching and giving way, the car tumbling through air.

"And you killed her."

"It was an accident. Just a stupid accident."

"There are no accidents around you, Henry. You're the Black Death in a bad suit."

Henry kicked Warren in the stomach. Hard. "Shut up." Then he kicked him in the face. Blood burst from Warren's mouth, a chip of tooth pebbled across the packed dirt. Then Henry leaned down, grabbed Warren's head, and started pounding it against the ground.

"You're dead, you're dead, I'm going to make you dead again," Henry screamed.

"Let him go." Mouser stood in the doorway, holding Aubrey. He held a gun aimed at Henry's head.

"I told you to leave us alone," Henry said.

"We need him alive." Mouser guided Aubrey to a corner chair. "For information, or for ransom."

"No, he has to die, now."

"Go back to being dead?" Mouser pushed the gun against Henry's skin, between the nose and the upper lip. "Listen to yourself. We need him."

Henry slapped the gun away. "Why? I can tell you what Quicksilver is if this bastard's behind it. It's a group of eggheads, with a bit of muscle thrown in, to evaluate threats and fight them off the books. Just like Book Club. He took it over from me; he stole all the credit."

"Quicksilver is far more than Book Club ever was. Just like Luke is far more of a man than you'll ever be." Warren spat out another sliver of tooth and blood.

"You," Mouser said to Warren. "How much do you know about us? Specifics."

Warren hesitated and Mouser aimed his gun at Aubrey's head. "Talk or she dies."

"You're going to kill us anyway." Warren looked at Aubrey, sadness in his eyes. "I'm sorry, Aubrey, but it's true."

"I know." Aubrey closed her eyes. As if waiting for the bullet to end the nightmare.

"But I think if you want this money you're after so bad, you won't shoot her. Luke might still be willing to make an exchange."

Mouser weighed his words. "Oh, I want to shoot her. Badly. Just because Luke killed my woman." Mouser twisted Aubrey's breast until she gasped in pain. He gave her a rough, angry kiss on the cheek as she tried to wrench her face away. But then he turned the gun back toward Warren. "You work for the Beast, right?"

"The Beast?"

"The United States government."

"I don't work for the government. Not anymore." Warren raised an eyebrow. "I mean, Henry takes the government's money at his think tank. I don't." He said this like it was a sign of moral superiority.

"How did you survive?" Mouser said.

"Don't you have other things to worry about?" Warren said.

"Answer me. You should have died on the Book Club flight."

"I missed my plane."

Mouser licked his upper lip. "Those two guys outside. They used to commit gang rapes in Bosnia when they wouldn't get answers from pissant villagers. They'd love a few hours with Aubrey."

Warren said, "I didn't get on the plane at the last minute."

"Why?"

"I got a phone call before the flight took off. I got a job offer I had to give immediate and private consideration. I told my friends I'd fly down later and meet them. And when the plane crashed, I knew it wasn't an accident. My new employers thought it best to hide me. For me, and for my family. So they wouldn't be targets."

"You're a cold bastard," Aubrey said. "Luke worshipped you. You don't deserve his love."

"My enemies thinking I was dead protected Luke. Until now." Warren stared at Henry. "You tried to make him into you. You failed."

"Shush," Mouser said. "You say you're not part of the Beast. Only the Beast can mount a group that's so well funded."

"Night Road is an army but isn't part of any government either," Warren said. "We're opposite sides of the same coin."

Mouser frowned.

"You're nonstate, so are we," Warren said. "Welcome to the future of warfare."

"What, you're a bunch of well-heeled international vigilantes? Please."

"We don't have to follow the laws. Same as you. Scary for you, a level playing field."

"Shut up, Warren." Henry seemed calmer, collected. He turned to

Mouser. "He won't tell us specifics. Maybe if Luke were threatened. But he won't talk."

Mouser leaned down into Warren's face and shouted, "What do you know about Hellfire?"

"You're not going to be able to pull your big attack off," Warren said.

"You didn't answer my question."

Warren closed his mouth.

"You're a lot like your son," Mouser said.

"Thank you," Warren said.

"By that, I mean you are too stupid to know when you are in deep trouble. He's had luck. Yours has run out."

"If you kill him, you won't get the money."

"You see, that was wishful thinking on Henry's part. I think we get a man inside Eric's bank, we hack our way in, and we track where he hid the money. That's a hell of a lot simpler than trying to find Luke, who may or may not know where the money is."

"Luke doesn't know." Aubrey practically spat the words at Mouser. "You might as well not spend your time chasing him. Eric was too smart for you. You killed him in cold blood but he made sure you're not ever going to get that money. He hid it too well."

Mouser kicked her in the chest and she went down, gasping. He turned back to Warren. "Where will your son go?"

"His only option is the police."

"I don't think he'll run to the cops," Mouser said. "I think he'll look for Quicksilver to help him. We are interested in them, and in one other person. A British woman who calls herself Jane."

"I don't know a Jane," Warren said.

"I think you must," Mouser said. "She's pitted us against each other. She's responsible for the deaths of your man in Houston and she tried to steal our money. We have a common enemy in her."

Warren stared silently, his lips pressed into a tight line.

"You don't know her," Mouser said.

"No. No idea who she is."

"I think you don't know her by the name Jane, but maybe by another name. Maybe Jane's just her kidnapper name. I think maybe she screwed you over," Mouser said.

Warren remained silent, but Aubrey could see a flash of painful realization on his face.

"Is your son working for you? Was he a spy for Quicksilver?" Mouser asked.

Warren measured the tension in the air. He watched Aubrey staring at him. "Yes. Yes, Luke works for Quicksilver."

"Goddamn it, he's lying, to make me look bad," Henry said.

"You're doing that perfectly well yourself," Mouser said. "I'm not blind to the fact this man wants to see you stripped of your power."

"I want to see him stripped of his life," Warren said.

"But I'm not blind, either, to the one fact you both ignore. The catalyst to this entire situation is Luke. He is the one and only person with a personal link to both Quicksilver and to the Night Road. This Jane bitch knew it. She's not part of the Night Road. So I think she must know about Quicksilver." Mouser crossed his arms.

Henry and Warren glared at each other.

Mouser went to the desk, opened the laptop. "I left Eric's account alive on the Night Road Web site to see if they would come back. It was accessed once, after Eric was dead, and I figured it had to be Luke or Aubrey. Someone using Eric's account just posted a request to trace a phone."

"Luke's looking for someone," Henry said. "Where is he? Can you find where he logged in from?"

Mouser studied the screen. "He's gotten a promise to respond from a member. Call the member, Henry. Tell him to give us the information on who's registered to that phone but well before he passes it to Luke. I want to know where they are, and who owns that property. I think Luke will go there."

"You want to set a trap," Henry said. "Let me go, let me talk to him."

"No. Much more than a trap. This ends now, Henry. There are other ways to get our money back." Mouser glanced at Aubrey. "She was his woman. She can get us inside that bank. She knows Eric's friends there, his coworkers. We can get inside, we can track where he moved the money."

The answer from the hacker came quickly, Mouser read it off the screen: "Registered to a Jane Mornay, at this address. On rue de l'Abbé-Grégoire."

"Send me. If Luke is there, I can talk to him."

"Grow up. You cannot have it both ways. Didn't your mama ever teach you that?" Mouser clicked open his phone, began to dial. "I've got friends here beyond you, Henry, people I've traded information with before. It's time for a very big gun. Then we go back home and we launch Hellfire, Henry, now. The money is not more important than the mission. We can get more money to fund the Night Road."

"We can't. You don't know who our financiers are. They'll kill us for losing the fifty million."

"Not us. You."

Henry stared.

"I do know who's sending us the fifty million. Did you think I wouldn't check you out when you approached me about the Night Road, you idiot? I have my own contacts, Henry. When I explain your incompetence, your lack of focus, the prince will give us fresh cash. He has plenty and he'll pay plenty to fund us for years to come. And if you argue with me, I will shoot you to death. I'm taking command. Fight me and I'll kill you."

"What the hell are you planning?" Henry's voice rose.

"Two birds," Mouser said, "one stone."

51

Rue du l'Abbé-Grégoire was a quiet street and Luke used the cabbie's passkey to open the ground-level door of the building. He walked in.

The lion's den. The truth behind his kidnapping. The truth behind his past.

It was tomb quiet. He walked up a narrow stairway. He had the cabbie's passkey still in one hand and the gun he'd taken from the Night Road thug at the tower in his other hand. The cabbie could have regained consciousness, called in, and warned Jane.

Launcelot Consulting, read the sign on the doorway. He tested the knob. Locked. He tried the passkey on the electronic pad next to it. It didn't work. Tried again. Still didn't work.

An idea struck him. He took his Saint Michael's medal and pressed it against the pad.

The door opened.

He pushed open the door.

His breath felt frozen in his chest. Because here was a threat far scarier than kidnapping or bullets or the unmoored violence of a Snow or a Mouser. Because here might be the truth. About his father, his stepfather, the shadows that had lain quiet close to his life, waiting to waken, and now dominated him. He raised the gun ahead of him and stepped into the empty reception area. He closed the door behind him and heard the lock take hold.

Dead quiet.

He moved through the rest of the office suite. The passkey opened every door but one. He saw cots, a table with guns, a small kitchen. It smelled like a small camp cabin: a lingering air of food, of cigarettes, of sweat. In one of the rooms, the corner held a single cot. Long dark strands of hair threaded the pillow. Aubrey's rings, her watch, lay on a bedside table.

Aubrey. They had kept her here.

He went into the next room.

Paper covered the walls. Clippings, photos, writings. Of Mouser and Snow and the thin black guy who'd nearly killed Luke and Drummond in New York.

It reminded him of his father's study. His dad liked to post index cards and notes on a blank wall, scraps of history, economics, and politics, to find the common links that would help him delve into a past mystery or outline a scholarly article or book. The sight of the collage of paper struck him; his father's thoughts, put up on the wall.

He looked at the clippings and photos. The word *HELLFIRE?* was written on a piece of paper in the center, in his father's handwriting. The wall looked like a project interrupted, as Quicksilver—his dad—tried to piece together the evidence about the Night Road.

Luke recognized the first photo as the man who'd been at the Houston rendezvous with Allen Clifford, recently shown executed on the Night Road's site. He had small eyes, a weak mouth, nice hair. His driver's license was next to him; his name was Bridger. A list of former addresses were posted next to his picture. But the photo next to him was a face seared into Luke's brain, that of Allen Clifford. Alive, and then the press photos of him dead after Eric shot him. Luke read the handwritten notes beneath the pictures: *Subject that Clifford is meeting with wishes to sell information on an impending multicity terrorist attack,* a date four days ago scrawled in: *Subject meeting with Clifford, demands that they meet in open. Will not meet indoors, extreme paranoia. Insists on meeting at corner near Episcopal shelter on McCoy Street, near downtown, 9 P.M., Clifford to dress as homeless man, at subject's request.*

Mouser's real name was Dwayne York. A blow-up of his Texas driver's license hung on the wall. He was a freelance Web designer in Dallas. Ex-military. Dishonorable discharge. His friends called him Mouser because he got written up for shooting mice on the base. He had progressed to cats and dogs. A long history of loose ties to paramilitary groups; he had been implicated and spent time in prison for a loose connection to a radical group that tried to bomb a government building.

A picture, dated on the day his father's plane went down. It was a security photo, a man in a maintenance suit, walking past a camera, head ducked slightly. It could be Mouser.

The bastard did it, Luke thought. He sabotaged my dad's plane, he killed my dad's friends, the son of a bitch.

Snow. Her real name was Roanna Snowden. One of the few survivors of the Lamb of the Blood religious cult. He remembered the feds besieging their compound; they had been massing weapons. He had just been a kid then, and so had Snow. She'd gotten a chemistry degree and then dropped out of sight. To make bombs, apparently.

The thin guy from New York. David Byrd, nicknamed Sweet Bird. A long list of crimes, a web of names with his at the center, prisons and terms served. Many of the names on the list were tied back to another network, a mosque in Queens, one with links to Wahhabi radicalists in Saudi Arabia. Stories of unsolved crimes where he had fallen under suspicion, including the murder of an assistant DA, were chronicled below his picture. Financial accounts that showed one of his associates had signed for cargo shipments carried by Travport. Luke remembered the name; Travport was the company that had bank accounts with Eric. Then a long list of recent attacks, small ones, against the city's infrastructure: power stations, traffic lights. Small acts of sabotage, knife swipes at the soft tissue of everyday life.

There were photos, all overlaid on a map, of a shooting in Los Angeles, a bombing in Kansas City, a ruptured pipeline in Canada, the chlorine attack in Texas, as if whoever had built this collage—his father—was trying to piece together the people and the attacks, find the common links.

As he looked at the map, a thought rose to his mind. The scattered bank accounts Eric had set up. California, Minnesota, Missouri, Texas—the locales of, or very close to, the attacks. Even the one failed attack—in Alaska, where the extremists had been arrested—he remembered the news account said the men were from Seattle. Washington State had been on the bank account list as well.

He stepped over to an array of computer screens. One screen showed a feed from the Invalides station. In the screen's corner was a frozen photo of him, stepping onto the train at Champs de Mars. The cabbie must have gotten radioed reports, driven fast to each stop. Another photo of him, on the Invalides automated walkway.

He could not believe that the place was empty. But then he considered. His father was a captive of the Night Road. The Frenchman was dead at the tower and the cabbie was unconscious in the taxi. Maybe Quicksilver's numbers in Paris were few. But where was Jane Mornay?

And if she was part of Quicksilver—part of his father's organization—why had she done this? Why had she put Luke's life at risk?

He tried the one door that the passkey denied again. Locked.

He tore down a curtain and wrapped it around the gun. He fired into the lock.

It took twenty minutes of intense arguing and haggling, but Mouser struck the unholiest of deals. The Islamic terror cell knew and trusted Mouser; he had previously sold them stolen credit card data from hijacked PCs. The cell's leader listened to Mouser as he outlined his difficult request.

He needed a bomb, and he needed it right now.

The cell's next martyr had planned to execute its Paris operation three weeks from now, during a visit by the Israeli prime minister. Everything was prepared. The martyr wanted to do his work.

Mouser convinced the cell's leader that they needed to strike an office of the Israeli intelligence service, hidden in a quiet neighborhood. But they had to act immediately. An attack on the office would be a great blow before the Zionist's visit. And Mouser could guarantee a strike, in payment, on Zionist targets inside the United States. As well, Mouser told the handlers what corporate stocks would be most affected in a massive planned American attack he referred to as Hellfire, due to be launched in the next forty-eight hours: They could sell and buy accordingly, and realize a nice profit.

The cell's leader was convinced. Sacrificing a martyr now could build a useful alliance.

Ten minutes after Mouser's call, the martyr's prayers were completed, and he was on his way, driving with deliberate care through the busy streets of Paris.

*   *   *

Behind the locked door was a small room. Luke saw a scattering of paper files, printouts; a large shredder sat in the corner. File cabinets filled a wall. He tested one. It slid open easily. It was empty. Another also empty, but he could see flecks of paper left in the bottom, like forgotten snow standing its ground in shadow. The third cabinet was locked.

He shot out the lock. His hands trembled. Inside were paper files, but only a few.

A file on his stepfather. Thick, and some of the papers torn free. They were old memos written by Henry on State Department letterhead, with sticky notes attached. Most of the memos touched on the rising challenge of inexpensive terrorism—how radicalist groups could gut a nation on the cheap with attacks on its infrastructure. Apparently this was Henry's favorite topic during his earliest think-tank days. Scribbled, handwritten notes clipped to the various reports validated Henry's long-ago musings. *9/11 cost a half-million dollars, inflicted $80 billion. Bali bombings, $2 billion in damage for a $60,000 investment. The Madrid bombings, $50 billion in damage for around $12,000 in marijuana, Ecstasy, and money. The London bombings, $3 billion in damage inflicted for $18,000 in expenditures.*

As though these horrors had merely been the first act to what the Night Road might unleash on America and its allies. How high could they aim with fifty million dollars at their disposal? They could create a wave of 9/11s, an endless chain of attacks and horror, stretching over months, over years. And if the enemy was already inside the borders, working together across ideologies for their common goal—how much more dangerous could they be? Luke stuffed the file back into the cabinet. He was past feeling sickened; now he only felt a steady rage at how he had been used.

Files on Eric. Lots of notes about his bank, Marolt Gold, which seemed to specialize in nice wealthy Americans and a few people of dubious integrity. The notes suggested the bank had been under Quicksilver's eye for the past several months due to its connection to a certain Arab billionaire, who was suspected of funding terrorism. A photo of Eric and Aubrey, taken in happier times, thick sunglasses hiding most of Aubrey's face but not her happy smile. Photos of the two of them walking through Versailles—he remembered that Aubrey had particularly wanted to go there, and that a variant of *versailles* had been used as a password on Eric's laptop.

Good God, he thought. How long had Quicksilver been watching Eric?

A file on Luke. The words Do Not Contact were stamped in red on a photo of himself, a fairly recent one, him leaving Henry's house in Washington last Christmas.

Christmas back in his ordinary life, and *his father had been watching him.* How many holidays had he mourned his father's passing, felt it most acutely with the taste of eggnog and the smell of pine, and his father had been watching him? Watching him mourn, watching him live his life.

Unless it hadn't been his father watching him.

What if it had been Jane instead? Jane's phone was registered to this address. How did she connect to his father?

A file on his mother. The word *eliminated?* and the date of her death stamped on the file.

He sank to his knees. *Eliminated?* The question mark made it worse. Had Henry killed her, even though he himself had nearly died in the accident? He rifled through the file but nothing announced a brutal truth—photos of her and Henry, taken under surveillance, a history of her personal life. Photos of the wrecked car.

"Mom," he said, and then he couldn't speak. Couldn't think. His chest ached. What truth about her had been hidden from him? Had she known his father was alive? It was inconceivable she could have kept such a secret from him. And she had gone from being married to a man Luke considered a hero to a man Luke knew was a contemptible snake, the basest traitor.

He gathered the papers. Tucked them into his knapsack, sealed it shut. The other files were on people he did not know, dozens of people whose names meant nothing to him. Except one. A file on Aubrey Perrault, with the word *Lindoe* alongside in parentheses. He opened it. Empty. All the papers, whatever had been here, were gone. As though Aubrey had been erased.

He heard the whisper of the door opening and turned and a young woman stood there, gun in hand. Leveled at him.

"Don't raise your gun. Drop it." Her accent was British.

He obeyed. She didn't lower her gun.

"You're a bit too late for the reunion," she said. "Hello, Luke Dantry."

"Hello, Jane."

"Kick the weapon over to me." She sounded like a teacher gently issuing an order at a preschooler.

He did. She kicked the gun under a table.

If she was surprised by his use of her name she didn't show it. She looked as calm as if she'd just sauntered into a good restaurant to enjoy a glass of wine with friends. But she still didn't lower the gun. Her voice sounded like ice chipping, falling onto cold steel. She flexed a smile. She might have been pretty once but a hardness cast into her face made her unattractive. "Well, thank God you're safe."

"Yes. Thank God I'm safe," Luke said. "Because I'm the key to all this, aren't I?"

"Key?"

"To your plan. Your scheme."

"*Scheme* sounds so vicious."

"I couldn't figure it out at first. My stepfather thought Quicksilver was behind my kidnapping. It wasn't them. It was you. *You alone.* You're part of Quicksilver, but you were working on your own. You betrayed Quicksilver. You had Eric kill Allen Clifford to get Quicksilver's attention, to set them off after the Night Road. You were the Quicksilver agent assigned to watch Henry, to watch me, after my mom died. And you discovered the Night Road, and that Henry was getting all this money. You started a war between the two groups. Just so you could grab the Night Road's money and let Quicksilver take the blame for it."

"Very good. I watched your stepfather and a thoroughly nasty billionaire finalize a deal in a London park. That's why I knew I could steal the money." She flexed that awful superior smile again. "One can hardly be a traitor to a private company. I prefer the term *free agent.*"

"Drummond, and the rest of Quicksilver, didn't know about the fifty million. Only you did. You kept the information from my dad and the others."

"A waste, really," she said. "You might be smarter than both your fathers."

"And I was the perfect pawn for you to use. I had a father in Quicksilver, a stepfather in the Night Road. I get involved, and both sides heat up the war. This is the secret war that Drummond referred to. It's not going to be fought in the open. It's like the new CIA versus KGB."

Her smile flickered.

Luke said, "And that war gives you ample smoke and fire to make a getaway, drop out of sight. You could be presumed dead or captured by the Night Road. You brought Eric to Drummond's attention, promised him you could hide him from the wrath of the Night Road. He could trade information on the Night Road, Mouser, my stepfather, for his new life. But the fifty million was a secret between the two of you. You've let your own friends be murdered and captured. Just for dirty money."

"Money isn't bad. Money's joy, security, a life free from worry. Rather different than a job with Quicksilver. The benefits package, I found lacking." She raised the gun, ever so slightly. Better to hit him between the eyes. "You offered Quicksilver the accounts where the money's been hidden for Aubrey."

"Yes. I have the file with the account information."

"I have the encryption key."

"Two halves of the puzzle. Held by the queen and the pawn."

"I despise chess," she said, frowning. "Give me the account numbers, Luke. Now."

The martyr watched the target building. He was nervous; he had not expected to go to paradise for weeks, and now he had no time to comport his mind toward calm. People strolled past the building; no one came in or out. On the other side was a Christian bookstore, with apartments above it; on the opposite side was an art supply store. Selling the tools to make godless images, he told himself. He tried not to think about the two pretty young women standing outside in the dank air, finishing their Gitanes cigarettes, laughing. He smoked Gitanes too. He tried not to look at them but their lovely faces drew his gaze like a magnet. He was weak and temptation was strong. They laughed and the smoke wreathed their faces, and he reminded himself they were devils, nothing more. Paris was a city full of devils. The virgins given in heaven would be far more desirable, flashing eyes, water-pearled thighs, and smiles of rapture.

He drove past twice, looking the part of the man seeking that simplest of urban pleasures, a parking spot. When he completed his orbit back in front of the target building he was glad the two girls had either left the street or gone back inside the art shop. He didn't want to look at them again.

"You can put the gun down, Jane."

"Can I?"

"Let's discuss terms," Luke said.

The softening of her smile was an acknowledgment that they were moving toward the truth. "Terms. You give me the fifty million and you walk away, and you hope the Night Road never finds you. Mouser might flay you alive if he gets his hands on you, and he might not be the worst of it." She gestured at the photos of Mouser, Snow, and Sweet Bird. "They're insane but functional. I'm sure they could take a very memorable vengeance against you."

"Two of the three are dead," he said. "I'm not exactly scared of them the way I was."

"I'd kill Mouser if I were you. He won't give up."

"So I give you the money and I get nothing." No way she would let him live. She had nothing to gain from it.

"I'll offer the same deal I gave Eric. I promised I could buy a new life for him and Aubrey. You keep a quarter-million. You vanish. I'll help you set up in a nice backwater."

"You're just as bad as the Night Road. You completely screwed up my life, you bitch. For what? So you can have what you want, and everyone else be damned, and you don't give a shit about innocent people."

"You make me sound so bad, Luke. Honestly. It's a day's work. We're keeping cash away from terrorists, after all. I'm much less nasty than the Night Road. Now, the file, please. I have the encryption key on the computer in the other room."

He stepped into the corridor. He would only get this one chance. She stepped away from the window, the pistol focused on him.

Finally a parking spot directly in front of the building opened up. An elderly man eased his Peugeot out of a slot and, talking to himself, drove down rue de l'Abbé-Grégoire.

The martyr parked with care; one had to be a good parallel parker to survive in Paris, and he was. He did not weep but he thought of his father, dead two years from a cancer, his mother, who would not understand. The sky was milky with rain. He wondered if there would be cool rain in paradise; he could not remember if weather was mentioned. It felt like someone else was operating his muscles, as though they moved of a different accord than his own brain and heart. He wished for his mother's touch, he wished he had not seen the girls in the art shop, he wished he had finished school, but none of that would matter. He was being weak. The glory that awaited would surpass all. Wouldn't it?

The martyr lifted a device that had once been a game controller. Wires led to the gateway to paradise. He was afraid. A tiny voice inside him screamed, *Do not do this*.

He silenced the voice with a heaving breath and he pressed the button to the game controller.

52

Jane had followed him into the room with the computer. It sat on a desk, in front of the window. She went behind the desk, gestured the gun at him to make him stay put.

"Toss me the key ring."

He obeyed. She opened the toy, slid the thumb drive into the USB port.

With one hand, she ran her fingers along the keyboard, typing. She kept the gun aimed at him with the other hand.

She would have to glance down if the account information appeared. He could rush her then. She would shoot him, he was sure, but it might be the only time her attention was divided. If he waited, he was dead.

She kept flickering her glance between the computer screen—which he couldn't see, but which gave off a dim glow in the darkened room that lit her face with an otherworldly blue—and to him. She wouldn't kill him until she was sure she had what she wanted.

He tensed to jump at her.

"There it is." But Jane's voice—so confident and snarky—suddenly sounded shaken. "Hidden in plain sight, that little b—"

The window—and the world—where Jane stood vanished. A flash, like God opening an eye, blinded Luke. There and gone, only light and dust remaining. He tumbled up and down and sideways through the air and grit where the walls had been and landed against a fist of stone, rubble rained past him where Jane had stood with her rotten gun and her smug smile.

Junk hammered a hundred blows into him. Everything seemed pulverized to powder. His scream got lost in his throat and then it was done, the sound and fury gone and then an enormous, wrenching silence.

Luke grew aware that he was still breathing, since he was coughing and every hack pierced his rib cage with pain. He tried to move and every muscle cried against the bones and flesh. He could see bits of a milk-colored sky above him; the roof was gone, half of it in the street, the other half on top of him. The front of the building was a memory; a curtain of dust marked where the walls had stood. Smoke filled his nose. Parts of the rooftop had fallen atop him in a wide scattering. The wall had held, shielding him from the heaviest of the rubble. He blinked. Tried again. He could move his feet. His hands. The floor sagged and a fearsome crack in the floor inched toward him. Beyond that, the mist of dust.

He rose on hands and knees now, testing the bones to see what was broken. His face hurt. His eyes were swollen, blinking hard against the onslaught of grit and the bright sun-smashing flash of the blast. He crawled away from the crack, from the edge of the floor—he remembered that he was six stories up.

"What the hell, what the hell, what the hell," he mumbled to himself. He tried to get his bearings. The building could collapse. Would collapse. He had a horror of being trapped, entombed alive with tons of rubble sealing him away, succumbing to a slow, lonely death. The fear cut through the haze. He crawled along hands and knees. The stairs he had come up must be gone now, in the front of the building, but there had to be back stairs.

The floor groaned, sagged, and he nearly fell. Below him he heard a rumble, walls tumbling away. The floor canted hard; he could not see past the swirling dust. He heard the shrill cry of a police siren. Help was coming.

He tried to remember the layout of the building. Stairs. Reception. Hallway. Offices on both sides.

He realized he was crawling the wrong way through the gritty fog. He turned and hoped he didn't crawl off the edge. He splayed his fingers in front of him, feeling, reaching. He found a wall. A door. Blown inward by the blast, at a broken angle, wrenched clean of the hinges. He fumbled forward. Nothing but wall, more wall. A dead end. No back stairs. He crawled back out into the shattered hallway.

The building moaned. He thought it might well have been built before the days of steel beams and might be straining to stay erect, held together only by chance.

He found another door, also caved in by the force. He crawled under its twisted wreckage and the floor ended. He reached a few inches below and found only space. Stuck out a leg and his toes found the rest of the shattered stairway. He put his weight on a step and it held. Then both feet, and he lowered himself down. He sat down on his butt, shivering. Then he eased down on his belly, snaking along the stairs.

He slid down the top three stories. At the next one the walls didn't look so cracked from the force of the roof's collapse and he got to his feet. He tested the stairs with his feet. Behind him the stairway stood in a crazy, dust-choked warp.

When he reached the bottom, the stairway was slashed apart at the bottom floor. What looked like large chunks of a smoldering car were wedged where the steps would have once been.

He jumped down from the stairs into broken glass, burning rubber, twisted hot metal. Rubble made a moonscape of the street. The buildings on both sides were damaged as well, their façades ripped away, but their frames holding. Fire surged out the top of one of the buildings.

He stumbled through broken brick and scorched stone. Wreckage choked the street.

No sign of Jane. She'd been vaporized in the blast. But what the hell had happened?

Bomb.

The Night Road was attacking Quicksilver. They'd found his father's people—maybe his father had talked. Or Aubrey. And they'd gone after Quicksilver with a murderous rage. They'd used bombs in the attacks at the high school and the chlorine train. And now here.

He coughed and spat blood. Hands touched him. He looked up. A young woman spoke French to him in soothing tones. He could start to hear her words over the hum in his ears. She tried to help him walk. He saw walking wounded, stunned, a woman clutching her broken arm, an old man with a brutal gash across his bald pate. Luke touched his own face and probed a wet mask of blood. The pain in his body turned savage, like a beast awakening inside his bones.

The young woman kept talking, soothingly in the lovely French, supporting him, and through the dust he saw the cream-colored sky.

He pulled away from her. She wouldn't let him go and at the end of the road, he could see police arriving, ambulances with lights, fire trucks.

"Non," he said.

She spoke French he didn't understand and pulled at him. No doubt she thought he was in shock. No doubt she was right. But the police, no. They would want to know who he was. Why he was there. And they would find out he was wanted in the United States. No.

He abandoned his kind savior with a thank-you, shrugged free of her grasp. He stumbled past the crowds that were gathering at one end of the street and people stopped him, trying to help him, sure that he was shaken. He pulled away. He staggered past a crowd that had spilled out of a restaurant. He went inside, to the bathroom, and was sick. He stood and studied himself in the mirror. Both his eyes were swollen, blackening with bruising. A tooth on the left side of his mouth was gone. His lips were heavy, like he'd taken a punch. A score of cuts along his forehead, up into the hairline, a bad one across his nose. Another one on his chin. His whole body throbbed like a bruise. His hair stood in spikes, dusty. His shirt was in shreds and he could see the red, scraped skin underneath. He felt the silver medal of Saint Michael, covered in grit.

He washed the blood and gunk from his face. He realized he'd lost his gun. In the dining area he saw an array of cutlery at a service station, and selected a large knife. He didn't want to be unarmed. He put the knife in his waistband.

He went back out into the street and a man wearing an apron stopped him and in French said, "You should go to hospital, sir. Do you need help?"

The man's face was full of kindness. Of course it was, Luke thought. Most people in this world were decent. Good. They did not turn a blind eye to the suffering they saw. There is good in the world, Luke thought, and the Night Road wants to stamp it out. Destroy it.

"I am okay," Luke said. "Thank you."

He headed down the crowded street. The police cordoned off the avenues. How many innocent people? he thought. How many buried in the rubble, or killed outright? Nausea and anger shook him, vied for control. The ambulances were pulling away now, loading the first evacuees to the hospital. Surrounded by the onlookers, he felt marked, alone, as though he wandered among them like a ghost.

And then, a block away in the milling crowd, he saw him. Henry Shaw-cross. Standing close to the cordon, looking down rue de l'Abbé-Grégoire at the devastation. Standing on tiptoe. His face might have been carved of stone. He stood on tiptoes, peering down the street, firsthand witness to the carnage he'd helped create.

Henry turned away from the crowd, started to walk toward the ambulances that remained, where the injured were being loaded in.

He's looking for me. To see if I survived, Luke thought. He walked up to Henry, grabbed his shoulder, and said, "Are you here to leave flowers on my grave?"

Henry didn't move; he just sucked in a breath of surprise.

"I'm armed. Are you here alone?"

Henry nodded.

"If you lie to me, you'll die. I'll kill you and I won't even blink. Start walking toward your car."

"Luke."

"Tables are turned, asshole. This is me kidnapping you."

Henry obeyed. Luke kept a grip on his arm, and under his hand Henry's flesh trembled.

"Thank God you're alive—" Henry started.

"Don't give me your crappy lies. You sold me out. You left me to die."

"I did no such thing. Everything I've tried to do—"

Luke's hand glided down to Henry's and gave the little finger a savage twist. Henry gasped and nearly stopped. "I am, oddly enough, not in the mood for one of your lectures about me or my life. Heard that, done that." They walked in the middle of the closed street, away from the other pedestrians who might overhear Luke's harsh whispers.

"The Night Road did this. Yes or no?" Luke said.

Henry nodded. Misery on his face. "Mouser ordered this done. He's no longer following my orders. I tried to stop him."

"Yeah, I can really see you called the police."

"Luke, please. I was going to walk up and shoot the bomber before he could detonate. I didn't get here in time. I took an enormous risk in coming here—"

"Spare me the heroic self-portrait. They have Aubrey and my father?"

Henry nodded again.

"Alive?"

"Yes."

"So. All this to kill me?"

"And to wipe out Quicksilver."

"You've killed innocent people."

"This is a war."

"You're playing at war, but this isn't a war."

"Look around you. Look at what you've been through, Luke. War. War of a different sort. Fought in secret. But still a war."

"And you're on the side of the bad guys," Luke said.

"The good guys didn't want me anymore." He looked away from Luke.

"What?"

"This is my car." Henry stopped by a BMW sedan.

"In, drive."

Henry obeyed. When he got behind the wheel Luke put the knife along his ribs. "I drove for four hours with a weapon in my side. I hope you enjoy it more than I did."

"Luke, let me explain."

"You are going to take me to where my father and Aubrey are. Do you understand?"

"Yes. I do."

"Whether or not I kill you when we get there depends on how well you act. Do you understand?"

"Yes, Luke."

"Drive."

Henry inched out into traffic, headed toward the Pont Neuf, crossed the Seine. Luke couldn't take his gaze off Henry. It was like seeing something human, but knowing that a devil dwelt under the skin. Hurt, anger, loathing, all tore at him. No explanation could satisfy. But he still wanted to hear one, in Henry's words.

"Why?" Luke asked.

"There are so many whys." A bit of the cool confidence inched back into Henry's tone. "I hardly know where to start."

"I want to know why you're a traitor."

Silence for a long while. Luke stabbed him. Not deep; but he drove the knife into the cotton of the shirt and into the soft fat underneath.

"Ahhh." Henry didn't scream but it was close. A choking cry. "Do you want me to wreck?" Henry slapped a palm against the steering wheel in pain. "The police might ask why I'm bloodied and why you're holding a knife."

"Did I stutter? Answer me. Why? You owe me, Henry. For years you pretended to be what you weren't; you acted like you cared about me and my mom."

"I did."

"Why. Why. Why. Why."

Then the answer came, the words as flat as the blade of the knife. "No one listened to me."

It was such a petty confession; a small gripe by a small man. On such a little wheel could turn betrayals of country, of family, of honor.

The confession left Luke nearly speechless. All the rage he felt toward Henry turned into a confusion. "Henry, I always listened to you. I trusted you."

"You and your mother were better to me than anyone ever was, Luke. You just don't know."

"I'm listening now."

"The Book Club was my first think tank. It was formed of a group of professors with international postings, recruited by the State Department. We all worked secretly for the department, doing analysis, talking with other academics in the target countries and regions we studied. We were much closer to the action than most analysts. We would conceive of new ways to acquire intelligence, to affect situations in foreign governments, and our muscle—"

"Drummond and Clifford."

"Yes, they'd carry the plans out. I did some missions as well, so did your father. I did a lot of profiling of terrorists and extremists. We would write papers. But not for public release, they were policy papers. The deal was that we would never be named; we were working for State's own version of the CIA, the one they're not supposed to have."

"An illegal branch."

"A secret branch. None of us were formal spies, although we were trained in tradecraft; they were afraid we might get kidnapped, they wanted us to be capable of protecting ourselves. They called us thinkers and thugs. But we mostly focused on keeping our ears to the ground in a way that tapped into broad social changes that other researchers were not studying." He wiped at his lip. "We predicted the fall of the Soviet Union six years before it happened. We were ignored; just a bunch of State eggheads who were working in secret and didn't even acknowledge our own names. We predicted the jihadists would arise after the fall of the Soviets. Guys with guns in Afghanistan would start hating America as much as they hated Russia and decide to open terrorist training camps. No one believed us." His voice broke. "I predicted September eleventh, the use of jetliners as weapons, the same selection of targets, ten years before. No one believed me. No one took me seriously. Do you know what that felt like?"

Luke did not feel sympathy for him, but it was hard not to feel a sickening pity. "You don't get a pass because your feelings got bruised."

"No. It was more than feeling hurt. I started Book Club. But your father took it over. Every good idea I had he smothered. I brought in the other professors, gave them this one great opportunity, but it was your father they wanted to follow. They thought I was just a chalk jockey, a book reader, I wasn't a leader, I wasn't as smart. I'd had one good idea, the Book Club itself, and then I was useless."

"So, ignored and unloved, you had Mouser kill them and make it look like an accident."

Henry opened his mouth, shut it, opened it. Like a fish looking for the cooling water. But a knife in his side, he said, "Yes. No one was listening to us anyway. After September eleventh we were an embarrassment—can you imagine the damage if my predictions saw the light of day? The government wasn't willing to risk it. Ever. So there was no successor formed to the Book Club."

"And Mouser framed an innocent man for sabotaging the plane and killed him too. And you found Mouser where?"

Henry coughed. "It was my job to profile terrorists, see what we could learn from them. I met him in prison. I liked him. He wasn't quite so extreme then. He's gotten worse."

"You tried to kill my father and then you have the gall to claim you care about me? Just because you were jealous of him?"

"You're just like him. Just like him. I thought you were like your mother but I see you're just like Warren."

Luke let the silence build. He thought he might kill Henry right now, even if it wrecked the car and killed them both. "Did you kill my mom too?"

Henry's face broke with grief. "You know better."

"I don't know anything about you."

"It was an accident. She was driving. You know I nearly died. It was an accident."

"I feel you're leaving gaps."

"Then go ahead and kill me, Luke. I am telling you that I would never have hurt your mother, and you can believe me or not. Kill me if you have to."

"You think I won't kill you? Do you really doubt me now?"

"I know you are fundamentally a decent person who will not kill a man whom he loved as a father," Henry said. "We can help each other escape our problems."

"Ah. Having betrayed your friends, your family, and your country, now you're going to betray the Night Road."

"Would you prefer I stay loyal to them or help you?" Henry asked. The traffic thickened and he laid on the horn, fighting his way through a tangle of cars and buses at the Place de la Concorde.

"Help me. How do I stop the Night Road?"

"You can't, there are too many of them."

"What is Hellfire?"

"Hellfire is the second phase. The first wave was an audition."

"What?"

"Think it through, Luke." Like this was an intellectual exercise.

"An audition," Luke repeated. "Like a gang initiation, a smaller crime before you get responsibility for the bigger crime? Is that what these recent attacks are? The chlorine train in Texas, the *E. coli* in Tennessee, the pipeline bombing. The high school attack?"

Henry nodded.

"Proving grounds," Luke said. "Pull them off and you get to play on a bigger stage. Which is Hellfire."

"Yes."

"The money," Luke said. "The fifty million. You get a slice of that if you qualify, more if you contribute to executing the Hellfire attack."

"Yes."

"Where's it coming from? The funds had to be brought in and cleaned, Eric said. From where?"

Henry's tongue played along his lip. His breathing grew ragged. "I need to explain."

An audition. He thought of the various terrorist wannabes on the Night Road site, asking for and getting expertise, the words they'd used. "It's an investment. Someone overseas is investing in American-based terrorists."

Henry nodded.

"Your researches into terrorism. You interviewed people overseas too." Now he put the knife close to Henry's tender throat. He didn't care if anyone else in a passing car saw.

"Who?"

"An elderly Saudi prince. He's backing the fifty million. More to come if we succeed. He is funding networks all over Europe, in east Africa, in the Philippines, in Australia."

Luke lowered the knife. He'd thought he knew how deep this betrayal went, but this staggered him. "Why?"

"I told you, I've been warning people about this for years, even with the new think tank, I write the papers, not enough people listen, but now . . . they have to. I've predicted everything that's going to happen. All my papers over the past six months. All the papers I've got coming out this week."

"You predict the future and then you make it happen. And now— everyone will listen to you. And pay you handsomely for your insights. And think you're incredibly smart."

Henry moved his mouth to say yes but no word issued from his breath, his lips.

"Do you realize how utterly pathetic you are? Truly?"

Henry wiped at his mouth.

"Why?"

"I told you."

"Why me? Why involve me?"

"I thought I could just write the papers—with you—and then when our 'predictions' came true, we'd be a success together. I didn't know I'd have to run the show. Handle the money, recruit the Night Road proper. But it was all my idea, so the prince wanted me involved. I couldn't say no. I thought it would just be us together in the think tank—not us together in the Night Road."

Henry drove onto a highway that snaked through the northern suburbs of Paris.

Luke couldn't look at him. It was as though he'd glanced into a well and seen bodies piled and rotting in the water, a sickening sight that would haunt him forever. "Hellfire. It's bombs, isn't it, with Snow involved."

"Snow made a lot of bombs. They've been planted in six cities."

"Planted where?"

The car's phone rang. "Mouser," Henry whispered.

"Tell him you saw me dead."

Henry glanced at him.

"I want him to think I'm dead."

Henry answered the phone. He kept it on speakerphone.

Mouser sounded impatient. "Well? What happened?"

"You won, Mouser. You won."

"Luke?"

"Dead. I saw it myself. Lying in the street."

"His father's people?"

"Same."

"Excellent. Anything else?"

"No."

Mouser hung up. No good-byes.

"Where are these bombs, Henry?"

"I'll tell you if we can make a deal." Henry gave him a sidelong glance. "And if you kill me, you won't get your dad or Aubrey back."

"What's the deal?"

"Mouser resents my efforts to protect you. He's going to kill me, I feel sure, and take control of the Night Road entirely. I want immunity. I want protection."

"I can't really give that to you."

"Quicksilver is more than that office in Paris or Drummond in New York. They can protect you. I want protection."

"All right."

"It will be a wave of bombings. A hundred and forty."

A hundred and forty bombs. My God.

"Where? What cities?" He thought of the map of the previous attacks. Would they strike the same areas? Or entirely different ones?

"When I'm safe, I'll tell you. Not before." Henry glanced at his watch. "You better hurry. Mouser's moving your father and Aubrey in the next hour."

"Describe where they're being held."

Henry remained silent and it was only when Luke shifted position to slice at him again that he said, "Don't be an idiot. If you want them out, you need me. I can't go in there bloodied. They'll know something is wrong. Start using your brain, Luke." He reached out, grabbed Luke's wrist. Squeezed. Released it. "You hate me. Fine. We're still stuck together in this mess. You should tell me what you plan to do. Marching in with a knife on me buys you nothing."

"True. I need a gun."

"Glove compartment."

Luke opened it, fished out a small Beretta. He checked; it was loaded. He didn't say thank you.

"Tell me what the plan is," Henry said. "I just gave you a gun."

"We're going to go in and I'm killing Mouser."

"He has hired men with him. You have no chance. I want you alive, Luke. Look at me. I raised you, for God's sake."

"I don't see tears in your eyes."

"I don't cry. You know that."

"Thanks, but I'll handle it myself. Where are they?"

"The prince has a compound just outside Paris. I drove like the devil to get there in time to try to stop the bomber."

"Or to make sure his work was done."

"You know that's not true. If you believe I want you dead, stab me right now. Do it. Kill me."

"I need you breathing, Henry." He thought of the words of Chicago-Chris; now Luke was the one trying to earn admittance to the club. "You're my golden ticket."

53

A stone fence surrounded the compound. The home beyond looked like a château, grand but slightly soiled. The landscaping had been ripped up around the house but not replaced, giving the house the air of neglect. Three miles away was a former French air force station, used as a hub by Travport for its legitimate courier service.

"The prince, he owns Travport, through a series of limited partnerships."

"And he put you in touch with Eric." Luke remembered the photos in Eric's room at his parents' house, him posing with a businessman type in the shimmer of the desert.

"Yes." Henry paused. "Eric did banking for him when he worked on overseas projects. Mouser will fly us back on a Travport jet, with the prince's permission. Easier with prisoners. You're an idiot to try this."

"Not asking your opinion," Luke said from the backseat. Henry had given him a basic layout of the compound. In the center was the old small château that the prince's money had renewed from ruin. Behind it was a large barn, a guesthouse. Beyond that was another house, and that was where Warren Dantry and Aubrey Perrault were now being held.

Or so Henry said. But Henry was the king of lies.

"Guards?"

"Two remaining. Now that Quicksilver's Paris base is gone, and presumably the remains of Quicksilver scattered with it, I suspect that the guards will not have further reinforcements."

"I'm going to shoot the guards," Luke said. "If you give me away, I'll shoot you too."

"Is it liberating to order me about?" Henry sounded almost amused.

"The spine, Henry, is where I'll put the bullet. If you survive, a nurse will wipe your chin and change your diaper." He knew Henry well enough to know the merest thought of a lack of control would frighten him.

Henry steered the car to an entrance. "The camera's on me," he said.

"Don't talk. I don't want them wondering who you're talking to."

Henry shut up. He entered an access code; the tasteless baroque iron gates hinged back and swung open with a false grandeur. He drove in.

"What will be expected of you?" Luke asked.

"For me to drive to the back house."

The odds were bad. Four to one, really, because Henry wasn't on his side. Henry was only on his own side. Luke leaned closer to the floor of the sedan, keeping a tight grip on the knife. Fear prickled every bone in his body, and then the fear shrank, became smaller than himself.

The sedan stopped. "We're at the house. The doors will be locked."

Luke peered over the edge of the backseat. The back house was crafted of stone, studded with a few windows. "Do you have a key?"

"Yes, Luke, I do."

"Out."

Henry got out of the car. Luke stood and slid the knife into the back of his pants. He walked close behind him and kept the Beretta close to his ribs.

Henry unlocked the door. Luke pushed him, used him as a shield, and Henry didn't complain. They moved from the front door, across a living room, into a back kitchen. The house was as silent as a grave. Or maybe, Luke thought crazily, a grave was louder. For a hub of terrorist activity, it was far too silent. Luke's skin tingled as though warmed by fire.

"They're gone," Henry said.

Luke listened to the pressing silence of the house. He heard a creak on the stairs.

Henry was a liar.

Luke kept his grip on Henry's shoulder but he moved the gun away from Henry's ribs, kept it aimed over Henry's shoulder. He listened for the next creak. Heard nothing. He kicked open a back door, yanked Henry away from the wash of cool air, pulled him back into a corner.

Five seconds later he saw the gun come into sight from around the open door. The edge of the barrel, then hand gripping the guard, then arm.

Luke aimed and fired twice in rapid succession. The gun kicked more than he thought it would. The first bullet scored; the second missed. The sleeve, halfway up, pulled and smoked and produced a bright flush of blood. The thug fell against the door and raised the gun up but Luke threw Henry into the thug. Henry tackled the thug, closing arms around him. They staggered together into the wall, then slid to the floor.

The thug screamed a babble of rage in his own language. He punched Henry hard; Henry went down, but clawed at the thug's hair. They grappled, and Luke looked for the shot.

Just shoot them both, he thought, but he couldn't.

The thug shoved Henry clear, sending him crashing into and over a kitchen table. The thug slid to the floor, his arm bright with blood. His hands empty.

Where the hell was the guy's gun? Gone.

Henry. That conniving bastard had grabbed it. He glanced over at the corner of the kitchen where Henry had landed. Gone.

Luke pulled the trigger. The gun jammed. Or the clip was now empty. Or he didn't know how to use it. The gun was useless.

The thug launched himself at Luke; his fingers dug into Luke's throat, squeezed into the flesh. Luke gripped his hands, tried to pry them free, kicked his feet along the floor. He was bigger and taller than his attacker but the guy had the advantage of strength and experience.

The guy slammed Luke's head against the tile. Luke released his futile grip on the guy's hands. Luke pushed off the floor, came close to the guy's chest. He threw an arm around him in an embrace and rummaged along his own back. His fingers closed around the knife he'd taken from the restaurant after the bombing.

Luke slid the blade hard into the guy's side. Felt it touch bone, and the guy howled. No second chance. Luke stabbed and pulled out again and the wash of blood was warm, awful; and he drove the blade upward, into the guy's throat.

The guy toppled. Dying. Luke kicked out from under him, hand slick with blood, the breath frozen in his half-strangled throat.

He looked up from the dying man and Henry stood above him, gun in hand.

"No one else is here. The house is empty. I had to be sure," Henry said calmly.

Luke stared at him, kicked away from the dying terrorist. The thug lay on the floor, gasping out air and blood, a froth on his lips. His eyes stretched wide in fear, in horror, in pain. Luke couldn't look away. It was all the ugliness of slow death, laid bare. He had killed Snow, but she had died within seconds. It did not matter that the man deserved it. Luke felt something shift in his chest, his brain, watching death unfold.

The dying thug coughed and writhed and his eyes pleaded for a question he couldn't ask. Unlike the near-instant deaths he had seen—Snow, Chris, the poor officer in the Chicago alleyway—this dying took time. They watched his pain.

"For God's sake, put him out of his misery," Luke said.

Henry glanced at the gun he held and stayed still.

The thug coughed and gurgled blood, clutching his wound, and then he lay still.

"My God, that was messy. You for sure killed him," Henry said. "Let's get you washed."

Luke tore his gaze away from the dead man and looked up at Henry. *Get me washed, like I was a child caught playing in the mud.* Henry held the gun but it wasn't aimed at him.

"You could have shot him," Luke said. "You could have ended the fight so I didn't have to . . ."

"So you didn't have to do what was necessary? You handled it." Henry's voice was flat. "I had to make sure no one else was here, attacking our flank. Everyone else is gone."

Our flank. Like they were a team. The shock of killing eroded in the anger he felt toward Henry. But Henry had the gun.

Luke wondered if Henry would shoot him. He didn't really know Henry. He only knew the lie Henry was.

"You hung back to see if I'd win. What are you trying to make me into? You?" Luke stood and the rage he'd felt while stabbing the thug tingled hard in his hands. "You used me to build your terrorist network. You made it so I can't go to the police. That I can only turn to you."

"We're family," he said quietly.

"You involved me only to bind me to you. You destroyed my options in life and left me with yours. So I would join you?" It was the horrifying truth that lay between them. "You think that because you had me build the Night Road, and hide from the police, and now made me kill, I'm somehow more like you?" He spat at Henry's shoe. "We could not be more different."

"You're all the family I have, Luke. The only family I've ever had." He mouthed the words with difficulty. He tried an expression that was distantly related to a smile. "I wanted us together."

"What, in jail cells? If you wanted to be my family, you could have had your normal life and let me have mine. You don't know what family is."

"I know we don't turn on each other in a time of need." Henry wet a hand towel, tossed it to Luke, as though cleaning the blood off his hands was as everyday an act for him as a gardener wiping off dirt. "Clearly, since Mouser and everyone else is gone, and this man was waiting here to kill me, I'm on the outs with Mouser and the Night Road," Henry said. "You and I have to come to an agreement, Luke. An opportunity confronts us."

"This isn't like we've had a fight about a family issue," Luke said. "There is no agreement. No opportunity. You tell me where Mouser took them."

"I assume Chicago, on a Travport plane. He thinks he can find the fifty million by tracing Eric's activities at the private bank that Eric worked for. The money, Luke. Where is that money?"

"Your so-clever bomb destroyed the encrypted file that contained the account info. Jane decrypted it. But I didn't see it and all the evidence was destroyed."

"She said nothing about where it was?"

"No." Only her final words of anger. *Hidden in plain sight, that little b—*

"If you and I take the fifty million before they do, well, the Night Road is done. It will fall apart without the promised money, and the billionaire won't try and invest in terror again. You and I can hide. All is well."

"Not for my father and Aubrey."

Henry's lips thinned. Laughing, but not wanting to show he was laughing. Because Henry had the gun. "Trying to save them is suicide. They'll kill you."

He punched his stepfather, hard, fist to jaw. Henry sagged to the floor, agony on his face. He swung the gun back toward Luke. But he didn't fire.

Henry said thickly, "I'm trying to save you—"

"Quit lying. Just quit." Luke kicked his stepfather. Hard. In the stomach. He did it before he even realized it. All the air went out of Henry's lungs. Luke hit him again in the face and a great sorrow rose in him, for this man who'd cared for him, been his friend, tried to be his father. It was all a most vicious, damnable lie. He could kill him. But there were things worse than death.

"Tell me where these bombs will be placed. Or I'll kill you."

"They'll change their targets, beeause Mouser's shut me out. They'll be afraid I'll cut a deal with the authorities."

"Humor me. What are the original targets?"

"Shopping centers. Striking at ordinary people. Easy to deploy." Henry turned his face to the floor. "But I'm telling you, they'll abandon that plan because they're under such pressure and so much has gone wrong. Mouser will . . . think bigger. He'll make Hellfire a memorial to Snow."

He dragged Henry into the kitchen. He went into the bedroom off the hall; a pair of abandoned handcuffs lay on the bed, probably used for his father or Aubrey. He went back into the kitchen; Henry lay curled on the floor, in a fetal position, coughing. Luke dragged Henry to the dead guard. Snapped the cuffs on Henry's right wrist, reached for the dead man's wrist.

"Please, Luke, don't!"

The cuff clicked home. "I'll leave you with your friend. You belong together more than you and I do."

"Don't! I can help you!"

"Tell me where in Chicago Mouser will take them."

"You'll really let me go?"

"Yes, Henry. Tell me where they will be."

Henry took a hard breath. "He's got the Night Road members who are carrying out the attack meeting at Aubrey's office."

"For Hellfire."

"Yes. The final meeting before they launch the attack. Take me with you. I can talk to them for you."

"Give me something valuable," Luke said.

"You'll need a password. They'll kill you at first sight without a password," Henry called. "Let me go and I'll tell it to you."

"Tell me."

"It's *determination*."

Luke turned and started to walk away.

"You said you'd let me go." Henry's whisper became a wail. He raised his arm; the dead man's arm went up as well, as if in a final plea for mercy.

"I lied." He stared at his stepfather. "If I ever see you again, I will kill you."

Luke went upstairs and he washed his face, his hair, scrubbing the blood away.

"Luke?"

In a closet, he found a clean shirt and clean pants that nearly fit. He dumped his bloody clothes on the floor.

"Luke? Please. Don't leave me."

He searched through a briefcase he recognized as Henry's bag. There was an electronic passkey on it, labeled PERRAULT IMPORTS. Aubrey's company. He held it up to Henry.

"Eric sent it, so we would have access when the time came."

Luke didn't speak a word; he walked past Henry, shackled to the dead man, and he never looked back at his stepfather.

"Luke! Luke! Please don't leave me like this."

Luke shut the door behind him.

Luke got into Henry's car and drove to the Charles de Gaulle Airport. When he got there, he rebooked his flight on the return ticket he had in the system and changed it to Chicago. He had a while to wait. He found a pay phone, and he called the police. In broken French he told them where they could find one of the people responsible for the afternoon's bombing in Paris, chained to a dead man. Then he hung up.

Henry, he thought, would not do prison well.

54

On the long flight to Chicago, Luke Dantry sat with his battered, bruised face behind dark glasses and made his plans, filling a little notebook he'd bought at the airport with scribblings, and put it in his pocket. Things he wanted to tell his father, ask his father, if they made it alive through this horror. But he also thought about how the Night Road might use its hundred-plus bombs.

The plane, to his horror, was grounded in New York due to inclement weather in Chicago. They sat on the runway for an extra six hours. Luke felt sick with waiting. Finally the jet took off again; it lost another hour orbiting Chicago as the last of a violent storm cell cleared out from the city.

When he got off the plane into the dark Chicago midnight, he knew the Night Road could be waiting for him.

He could not shake Henry from his thoughts. Let him know abandonment, let him feel what it was like to have your life taken from you and wadded up like trash.

He walked toward the rental car station. He kept glancing over his shoulder, because whether it was Quicksilver or the Night Road, they had known how to find him when he traveled. To trap him. Not again. He signed off the rental car paperwork, using the false ID and credit card Drummond had left him. He walked out into the parking garage and found his car on the top level. The attendant had him inspect the car for preexisting damage and sign the form. He barely looked at the rental, a Lincoln Navigator SUV, and scrawled his false passport name on the paper.

The attendant said, "One second, I'll get you the keys." He vanished into the office and when the door opened again it wasn't the attendant, it was Frankie Wu, the pilot who had flown him and Aubrey to Chicago for Quicksilver.

Luke froze. Glanced around. All the attendants seemed to be gone.

"Are you all right?" Frankie Wu asked.

"Yes." *He's part of Quicksilver, he'll help me,* Luke thought. Luke wouldn't have to do this alone.

"Let's get in the car," Frankie said gently. "We can talk about your dad."

Wu got behind the driver's wheel. The passenger seat was full of gear, and Wu didn't move it, so Luke sat in the back.

They got in the Navigator, drove out of the garage—Luke noticed that the guard at the exit simply waved Frankie Wu through, no checking of the rental car papers—and into the night.

"My dad. I have to go help my dad," Luke said. "You have to help me."

"No, Luke," Wu said, "I have my orders. We don't engage with the Night Road. I'm sorry."

55

"How did you find me?" Luke asked. His voice sounded small in the quiet of the car.

"You traveled under the ID Drummond got for you. We get a ping every time you use it. Especially after Paris was charged with recovering you and the office got blown the hell up." Anger stormed Wu's voice.

"Then be mad at the Night Road. They attacked your offices, in New York and Paris."

"We've lost a lot of good people because of you."

"Because of a traitor inside Quicksilver. A British woman who called herself Jane. I don't know what her real name was. But she's the one who's put the Night Road and Quicksilver at each other's throats, she was behind my kidnapping, killing Allen Clifford in Houston, trying to steal the Night Road's money."

"What matters is us surviving another day to fight them. They've taken out two of our centers trying to kill you. You matter to them. So it's my job, and my only job, to get you somewhere safe. Another team will arrive soon to help me."

Frustration was a claw in Luke's chest. "That will be too late. You have to help me *now*. They're here. They're planning a massive bombing attack, maybe on shopping centers, maybe on some other target. They have dozens of bombs ready. We can't wait, we have to act now."

Wu looked at him in the rearview with a gaze as cold as chrome. "I have my orders. Get you to a safe place where you can be protected and debriefed about the Night Road."

"You don't understand. They have my father. They have my friend. They've brought them here."

"I have my orders. I'm sorry. I'm just one guy."

Wu said nothing, steering onto a highway.

"For God's sake. Please. Aren't you part of the CIA or something? You can't be just one guy left."

Wu didn't answer.

"Listen to me." He told Wu how Paris had gone wrong. "They're here, within our grasp. They've kept my dad alive to pick his brain about Quicksilver, and don't doubt for a second they will torture him within an inch of his life. And they're keeping Aubrey alive to access Eric's accounts at the bank; they think she can help them get inside the bank, since she's a client. If they find this fifty million, they can subsidize terrorists all over America, they can wreak a hell of a lot more havoc. Terrorism is cheap, they can fund an endless chaos, far more than we've ever seen before. They've got an Arab billionaire investing in domestic terrorism. Don't you realize how dangerous they are?"

"The last thing I can do, with Quicksilver in tatters, is to attack alone."

"You have me."

"You. No. You're not trained."

"I've held my own."

"It would be suicide."

"Then let me call the police," Luke said. "Tell them."

"Tell them what?"

"I have information on a gigantic attack that the Night Road is planning. They're massing here in Chicago, to distribute dozens of bombs to their members, but I don't know which cities they'll hit."

"No evidence. No certainty. And you tell them about this, you have to tell them about Quicksilver. I'm not authorized."

"There could be thousands of lives at stake. Tens of thousands. I don't care if you get exposed."

"I'm not authorized. I'm just one guy."

Just one guy. "Quicksilver. What exactly is it?"

Frankie Wu said, "Quicksilver? Just an element. Just another name for the fleet-footed god Mercury."

"Yeah, you all are real fleet right now." Luke lifted his Saint Michael's medal from his shirt. "You wear one?"

"Yeah," Wu said, but he didn't take his hands off the wheel.

"Why Saint Michael?"

"When people in the Roman Empire stopped worshipping Mercury, a number of his temples were rededicated to Saint Michael—a symbol of good overcoming evil."

His father must have been thinking about starting Quicksilver before the Book Club was wiped out. "The successor to the Book Club. Thinking in new ways about how to fight threats. Except Quicksilver is much more about the fight, not the theory."

"Whatever you say."

"My father belonged to a secret State Department think tank called the Book Club. So did my stepfather and Drummond and the guy who died in Houston."

He waited for Frankie Wu to speak, but Wu just arched an eyebrow.

"So. The Book Club kept predicting with accuracy how the world was changing but kept getting ignored and pushed aside due to political concerns; no one wanted to give credence to a bunch of eggheads who weren't part of the power structure. But someone knew about Book Club, and knew my dad was right. Maybe someone in State who'd moved to CIA. Dad got a better job offer and decided to play dead. Maybe to do what he was already doing, concepting and identifying forthcoming threats. The government finally decided to give him a real job. One that no one could know about. The CIA isn't supposed to operate on American soil—"

"You're wrong. We're not CIA." Frankie Wu shook his head.

He thought of the papers he'd seen in the Paris apartment before the bomb blast incinerated everything. The memos, the reports, all were old State Department, not new, annotated to reflect new thoughts, new threats, the notes in the memo. The relatively minor costs of attacks, compared to their huge inflicted economic damage. He remembered the account of the pipeline bombing a few days ago in Canada: a few thousand for the explosives, but millions in unrecoverable economic damage.

It was very cheap to wage highly effective war on the infrastructure of civilization.

What had Drummond said: *Quicksilver grew out of our earlier work, a new way to fight the bad guys, to stop terrorism before it starts, to bring new thinking to the problem.*

A new way.

And after those attacks, we are simply supposed to trust that government will do its job. Protect us. That the various governments of the world, and their multitude of agencies, with their well-intentioned but million moving parts, handcuffed by law and order, will shift into a hitherto unseen efficiency and suddenly develop all the human capital and infrastructure to fight and eliminate every shadow and nutcase, every asshole with a laptop and an agenda?

Uneasiness settled into Luke's chest. "I get it. Quicksilver is funded by private industry. Not any government."

Frankie Wu met his gaze in the rearview. "Should the world's most powerful companies just sit and wait to get bloodied again? Trust law enforcement and the military and the government to win every battle in a shadowy war? The good guys need help beyond political donations. Help not constrained by legal bureaucracy or political expediency that tries to fight global terrorism like it's the West versus the Soviets or the Nazis again. It's not two armies battling each other. It's not even nations battling each other.

"It's networks of people battling each other." Wu leaned back. "Which is basically the same as corporate warfare, except this time with guns. Your father was a genius."

Was. Like he was dead again.

"He was the real brain behind the Book Club. Your stepfather was just a wannabe, an opportunistic coat-tailer. And while your father took his philosophy to help those who want peace and stability and trade, your stepfather signed on with the opposite team."

"Henry thinks he predicted September eleventh," Luke said. "And that no one listened to him."

Wu snorted. "Jesus and Mary, man. Do you think if anyone had written a detailed forecast of September eleventh, it would have been ignored? I saw his paper; Drummond sent it to us all when this hell started breaking loose, as part of a psych profile of Henry Shawcross. It was vague in the extreme;

he only suggested the possibility that jetliners could be weapons, and he never identified specific targets or groups that could carry it out. Henry Shawcross convinced himself—and only himself—that he was the ignored prophet who could save the world and then got pissed when no one paid attention to him. He's crazy." Wu shook his head. "With the bad guys is the only place a man like Shawcross could be a star."

Quicksilver. A private CIA for the world's most powerful corporations. Luke could see it, money funneled carefully into security initiatives or perhaps hidden inside fat corporate contracts. Or research. It would be comparatively cheap insurance; fund and field a group of operatives who worked beyond the law to fight terrorists. The operations' cost might well be less than the economic damage they would suffer in another cataclysmic attack. You could hide just enough financing, spread out among enough of the companies most sensitive to terrorism. And even if such a group couldn't be entirely invisible to governments—would they turn a blind eye? Perhaps governments would even offer subtle or implicit support. Another army to fight the rising darkness, one with its hands not tied so closely by bureaucracy, could be a help. Or a disaster.

"You all aren't legal."

"No. But, until now, we got the job done."

"Until now," Luke said. "Now you're all too scared to fight back."

"What exactly were you planning to trade for your dad?" Wu said. "They weren't just going to give him to you."

"Trade? Get real. I was just going to kill them and get my dad and my friend back." Luke spoke with a matter-of-factness that would have appalled him a week ago. But he meant what he said.

"Are you suicidal?"

"No," Luke said quietly. "But I helped build the Night Road. My stepfather tricked me, but the Night Road exists as a network because of me. I have to stop them."

"We have to think big picture," Wu said.

"Big picture?" He remembered the words often in his father's mouth. "How's this for a big picture. They are launching a huge attack." He checked his watch. "The planning meeting for the attack is taking place right now. You can decapitate their organization, but only if you act," Luke said, his voice rising.

"As you said, you helped build the Night Road. You can help us reconstruct who's involved, where they might be. We can't risk losing you in an ill-planned attack on a terrorist cell. We'll hide you. Find a way to put you to use. You know them better than anyone—you're a valuable resource."

Which meant walking away from his life. Leaving it all behind.

He believed Wu. Quicksilver was not bound by law. He had no idea if they were bound by decency, although he wanted to believe that any group run by his father would be guided by good.

"Please. Please. I need to help my dad. You may never get another opportunity to take down Mouser. And thousands of lives are at stake."

"Orders say no."

"Screw your orders. I thought you were supposed to be nimble and fast and responsive. Well, I'm handing you these assholes on a plate and you're too afraid."

The stubbornness—bureaucratic idiocy—frustrated him. He gave Wu the details of the rendezvous at Aubrey's office; it made no difference.

"I won't tell you a thing I know about the Night Road unless you help my dad."

Wu acted like he hadn't spoken.

"What is wrong with you? You're no better than the bureaucrats you claim to replace," Luke said. "At the least, call the police or the FBI, tell them that Mouser and these bad guys will be there."

Wu said, "That would expose us, potentially, but I'll consider it."

Luke heaved back in the seat in complete frustration.

He glanced at his watch. *I'm only one guy,* Wu had said. Well, so was Luke. And he had made it this far. Sometimes one person had to be enough to make a difference.

He lapsed into silence and conjured up a half-baked plan. Drummond had told him not to get cornered. Wu was a trained Quicksilver operative, and who knew what that meant? Ex-CIA or ex-FBI or maybe just a guy who wasn't afraid of trouble if he was paid enough. He was trained to fight. So Luke would have to be smarter.

Scare him in a way he wasn't expecting.

"I have a confession," he said.

Wu glanced at him. "What?"

"I'm not going with you." Luke threw open the Navigator's door. At sixty miles an hour.

"What the hell?" Wu yelled. "Get the hell back in here."

Luke stood in the open doorway, firming a grip on the Navigator's roof.

Wu wasn't slowing down.

Luke hoisted himself onto the car's roof just as Wu veered across the lanes of traffic, horn blaring as he made for the highway exit. "Are you crazy?" Wu screamed.

He was forcing his hand, at huge risk. He could not fight Wu without crashing the car; and he needed the Navigator. He just needed Wu lured out of it, and he didn't have time to wait for Wu to get him to a safe house. He had to move now.

The car veered without slowing, and Wu swerved to avoid another car and the swerve nearly threw Luke from the speeding Navigator.

The Navigator careened toward the shoulder, which was all railing rushing by as the driver sped toward an exit.

They kissed the railing, sparks showering from metal biting against metal, erupting past Luke. The roaring of a honking semi tore within ten feet of them. Wu veered hard, taking the next exit, which was in downtown Chicago.

The car peeled through a red light.

He's not slowing? Why? Because, dummy, he needs the speed. To toss you off. You've pissed him off. And he needs you unable to fight.

Wu aimed the careening Navigator toward the parking lot of a convenience store, and as he crossed into the lot he slammed hard on the brakes. But Luke timed Wu's approach toward the building and slid back into the car through the open window as Wu jammed the brakes.

The brake slam threw Luke into the front seats, landing him on Wu's head and sending him crashing into the front windshield, which buckled and cracked. But the force of his body hammered Wu into the steering wheel.

The car skidded to a stop.

Luke, dazed, bleeding from the back of his head, slid onto Wu, fumbled for the gun under the jacket. His fingers found it and he yanked it free as Wu struggled to grasp the weapon.

Luke put the gun at Wu's temple. Wu went very still.

"Stop! Out! Leave the keys in the ignition," Luke ordered.

"You won't shoot me," Wu said.

Luke moved the gun to the side an inch and fired. The bullet shattered the driver's window. "Yes, I will."

Wu stepped out of the Navigator. "You're a suicidal idiot."

"Yeah," Luke said. "I'm just one guy." Luke kept the gun aimed at him, slid behind the wheel, and roared off, the wind hard in his face from the shattered window.

56

Luke knew he'd be a cop magnet, driving with a shattered wind-shield.

But he had to risk it. If a cop pulled him over he would tell everything he knew. He'd given Wu information that could stop the attack, if he himself couldn't. Calling the police now would take too much time, involve too much explanation—they might not believe him. He was wanted in connection with the death of a Chicago cop. And the Night Road could meet and vanish, carrying their deadly cargoes to the target cities.

He had to act. Now.

I'm just one guy. Wu's words. But one guy could make a difference in fighting the worst impulses of humanity.

Which was exactly what Mouser and the rest of the Night Road represented. Take away choices, take away security, and replace it with a twisted, bitter view of the world they thought best. It was the common thread linking the ideologies of the various fringes in the Night Road. They wanted the strength they would get—that they could only get—from creating a grave and constant terror that undermined everyday life.

He pulled back into the road and headed for Aubrey's import business. The meeting place for Hellfire was a small, sad, decrepit strip mall south of downtown. The night was cool and foggy and traffic was light the farther Luke drove from the freeway. He drove past the strip mall and saw a sign: PERRAULT IMPORTS. Aubrey's company.

Eric—or Henry—had set up her office space as the departure point for the bombs. It made sense. An import company would not raise eyebrows by having a number of vans arriving and departing at odd times of the day or night. Frequent deliveries would be seen as a part of that kind of business by any curious neighbors.

It made him feel sick, Aubrey pulled into Eric's world and used this way. Even if Eric had developed real regard for her, he had hijacked her life into the darkness—just as Henry had hijacked his.

He parked the Navigator behind a closed strip mall down the street. Few streetlights dotted the road. He opened his door, checked the clip in Wu's gun. There was a silencer mounted on the end and he'd never fired a gun with one before. He tucked the gun in the back of his pants.

He had the vaguest shape of a plan in his mind, but it depended on whether his father and Aubrey were being held at the office. He thought they would be. If they weren't, then he didn't have to worry about getting them out. If they were—he would face a choice. A hard one. Hellfire had to be stopped, no matter what.

No matter the cost.

He crossed the road. Aubrey's import emporium was the anchor at one end of the mall; the other stores belonged to an accountant and tax preparer; a women's clothing store; a nail and hair salon; a liquor store. Everyday America.

He could see six small moving vans parked in front of Perrault Imports. All from the same rental company.

He walked toward the vans and twenty feet away from the first one a shadow stepped out from between them.

A guard. He was skinny and looked scared and wasn't much older than Luke. "Hi," Luke said. "I'm here to see Mouser. I'm late, sorry."

The guard said, "Password?"

He prayed the password Henry gave him hadn't been changed. "Determination."

The guard nodded.

"I got orders to come here and get a van," Luke said.

"You walked?"

"I wanted to be sure cops weren't here. I look less suspicious walking than driving." He stopped now, five feet from the guard.

"Come here, put your hands on the side of the van. Everybody's got to be frisked."

He stepped close to Luke and Luke thought, *That's the kind of mistake I would have made.* Luke hit him hard, one in the face, and then pistol-whipped him with the gun. The guard collapsed, unconscious. He didn't need to use a bullet.

Luke searched the guard's clothing. He found keys with the van rental agency tag on it. He tried the door of the nearest van. Locked. He tried the one next to it. The door opened.

The van was empty. Which meant that some of the bombs, at least, were still inside. He pulled the guard into the van, left him there. Luke figured he would have won or would be dead by the time the guard was awake.

He tried the passkey he'd taken from Henry. The door clicked open.

The first floor was the wholesale showroom and delivery area. It was stuffed with décor, a mélange that showed just how small the world was getting. He made his way through a maze of cheap reproductions of African masks and wooden fertility symbols, Chinese lanterns and Asian-inspired furniture, stacks of china from Eastern Europe. A stairway with a bright orange arrow said MORE BARGAINS UPSTAIRS. He came to the bottom of the stairs and could hear voices.

He thought. The bombs would have been delivered here, since Snow could not distribute them from Houston. Chicago was central. But where would they be kept? Presumably the store had not been open with Aubrey gone, or Eric might have told her to tell her employees she was closing down. Aubrey had not mentioned a staff. The bombs would have to be kept where they would not elicit surprise or alarm if found.

He headed toward the back storage area. Boxes were stacked high in the dim light.

He saw unopened boxes of Chinese figurines, knockoffs of Swedish furniture, a desk, a scattering of papers. On the bulletin board were photos of Eric and Aubrey: at dinner, on a boat, walking along Lake Michigan.

Where would they hide the bombs? *Mouser's here, he would have checked them, and plus he has to show them how to work the mechanisms. Whatever packaging the bombs were in, they've been opened.*

He pulled an open box to him. Inside were gray uniforms and surgical-style masks, folded neatly. There was a stack of photo IDs, for a company called Ready-Able. At least twenty. They were photo IDs, with bar codes for electronic access. The first ones read NYC in small print. He thumbed through the others. Washington, Atlanta, Dallas, Chicago, Boston.

Each was keyed with the name of the mass transit system in the city. DART for Dallas, MARTA for Atlanta, CTA for Chicago, MBTA for Boston, Metro for Washington, MTA for New York. Henry had lied. It wasn't shopping centers. It was the transit systems. A hundred-plus bombs for the rail and bus systems in six major cities, separated by only a time zone, so a simultaneous attack would be devastating. Thousands would die; the sheer number of bombs would ensure a mind-numbing tally.

On a table across from the desk he saw a half-dozen boxes that had been opened. In Spanish they said on the side BOTIQUÍN DE PRIMEROS AUXILIOS. His Spanish wasn't good and he looked inside the box.

First-aid kits. Plain, white, with the red cross on them. But larger ones than you'd find at a store, ones that you might see mounted in a public place, like a shopping center, or an airport. Or a school.

Or a commuter rail train, or a subway.

He opened one of the cases. Inside were nails and screws, packed into thin plastic bags so they wouldn't rattle. And in the middle was an orange brick, like a clay, a simple lacing of wires webbing to a cell phone.

A bomb, armed with what he guessed was plastic explosive. He set it down carefully and began to count the first-aid kits. A dozen to a box. And how many opened boxes? A dozen. He checked kits in each box. Each contained a bomb.

A hundred and forty-four bombs. Henry had told him the truth. The first-aid kits could be placed on the transit system walls by the uniformed "cleaning crews," who need only show up, plant the bombs, and leave. The surgical masks—used by real cleaning crews—would hide their faces, since they weren't suicide bombers. One hundred and forty-four bombs, divided among six cities. Multiple cars on multiple tracks. Targeting people simply going to work for the day—just like 9/11 or the Madrid or London bombings. A dirt-cheap attack that would inflict millions—even billions—in damage to the economy and, worse, end thousands of innocent lives.

The thought made his blood chill.

The scale staggered him. The cell phone, it had to be the trigger. But would the bomb be detonated by calling the cell's number? No. There were far too many of them, and he suspected the bombs were supposed to go off simultaneously, or as near to it as possible. So. How?

Then he saw the simple answer. His throat went dry.

He had a choice. He could detonate one of the bombs now—killing himself but also the best of the Night Road, and his father and Aubrey if they were here. They'd be dead. The plan would be over. Or—there was another possibility.

And he heard the front door open and shut. Decision made. He didn't have much time.

What the hell, he thought. He'd be dead in a few minutes anyway.

A minute later, "Hello, Luke."

Henry Shawcross stepped into the storage room, gun leveled at his stepson, who knelt by an open file cabinet, rifling through its papers.

Luke stood.

"They don't know you're here, do they?" Henry said. Very quietly.

"No."

"You killed the guard outside."

"No, he's just beaten up and dumped in a van."

"You're nicer than I am."

"You got out. And got here." He didn't need to answer Henry's question.

"The keys to the handcuffs were in the pocket of the man you killed. Your grand gesture backfired."

Luke closed his eyes. A stupid mistake that was going to cost him dearly.

"I left quickly, right after you. I commandeered a Travport plane directly here." Henry flicked a smile. "I knew you'd be here. Playing the well-intentioned idiot. What possessed you? What were you looking for?"

"Evidence of where Eric hid the money."

"The money. Why do you care?"

"I need it. To hide." Luke put his gaze directly on Henry's. Let Henry think—if only for a moment—that Luke was as mercenary as he was, since he'd hoped Luke would become more like him. "What now?"

Henry shrugged. "Hard choices. The good things in my life are all gone, Luke. You've betrayed me too."

"You destroyed your life. Not me."

"No. Warren destroyed my life. It was hard enough to compete with a dead man. It's much harder when he turns up alive."

Luke said nothing. Henry cast a gaze around the room, as though checking that all was well, then put his stare back on Luke. "You're armed."

"Yes."

"Turn around. Hands on the cabinet."

Luke obeyed. Henry frisked him, took his guns.

"They're upstairs," Luke said. He had an idea. If only he could fool Henry. "My dad is up there, I think."

"Then let's go give you a proper reunion," Henry said, the hate thick in his voice.

They went up the stairs, Luke first, Henry's gun in the small of his back. Luke felt like he was walking up to a rickety gallows.

The second floor held import furnishings, and Mouser and six men sat around a patio table in an assortment of cheap chairs. Mouser saw Luke and Henry step inside. And he stood.

"What. The. Hell," he said.

A set of clocks stood above his head and Luke glanced at them. But they were set for a crazy quilt of times. He glanced past the table. His father and Aubrey were bound to chairs. Aubrey had a black eye; his father had been beaten, dried blood caking beneath his nose and mouth. They both met his gaze.

"What the hell are you doing here?" Mouser said.

"I'm here to lead the meeting," Henry said quietly.

The light above the table was dim, and Luke thought of the disaffected minds he'd studied in his psychology classes, trying to decipher their passions: the fire bloods of the French Revolution plotting the incineration of a social order and the collateral deaths of thousands of innocents; John Wilkes Booth, plotting the murder of the singular man who changed the course of history by keeping the Union together through a horrible trial by fire; the Bolsheviks, planning their paradise, who ended up with a discounted ruin built on the bones of millions.

"You said he was dead." Mouser stared at Luke.

"I lied," Henry said. "You're not in command here. I am."

"Not anymore." Mouser raised a gun and aimed it squarely at Henry's head.

"Gentlemen," Henry said. "You were promised a further, and much greater, investment in your causes if you accomplished your initial attacks. Mouser doesn't have your money. I do." He jerked his head at Luke. "And he does. Kill us and all investment in the Night Road stops, immediately."

"No," one of the men said. He had a pinched face that reminded Luke of a ferret's, a tattoo decorating the side of his neck. "You will give us our money now."

"Wrong." Henry smiled at Mouser. "You're such a punk idiot. You can't run this group."

"No one runs us," one of the other men said. "We do what we want. We succeed, we get funded. That was the deal."

An investment scheme, Luke thought. Terrorism Incorporated. The dark opposite of an idea like Quicksilver, which was Counterterrorism Incorporated.

"You won't get the money without *us*," Luke said, glancing at Henry. As if saying, *Okay, I'll play.* He had no doubt that Henry, now rejected and bitter, would shoot him the moment his usefulness was done.

His father stared at him, but Luke couldn't look at him. Every second ticking by was a heartbeat closer to death. But that was true of any ordinary day. The thought calmed him. He had to do this.

"Don't listen to this kid," Mouser said. "He and his friend killed our best bomb maker."

"Only because she tried to kill me. Funny how you can put your sorrow about Snow aside when it suits you, like in Paris."

Mouser's face purpled, his mouth worked.

"We're here about the money. For a trade," Luke lied.

"You didn't have the money," Mouser said.

"Eric did. Jane knew where it was. She told me." At this both Warren and Aubrey lifted their heads. "She used the Quicksilver computers to break the encryption that showed where Eric hid the fifty million. Right before genius boy here blew up their offices." Jane's final words echoed in his brain: *Hidden in plain sight. That little b——.* Eric, the bastard, who had betrayed her. He wished he knew what she'd meant. The answer had to be close. Eric was under enormous pressure. Where could he have stashed the money? *Hidden in plain sight.*

Mouser's gun swiveled toward Warren and Aubrey. "The money. Now. Or they die."

Luke glanced at Henry. "I'll give up the money. But only to Henry. That way, he's in control. My deal is with him. He lets my father and Aubrey go and I give him the cash. We worked it out." The lie was thick in his mouth. He looked at the men at the table. "I found you all. I pointed you to Henry. I made the Night Road happen. You owe me at least this deal."

"You're owed nothing," the neck-tattooed man said.

"You have nothing," Luke said. "What happens when the rest of the Night Road finds out that you've cut them off from potential millions to carry out their attacks?" He pointed at Mouser. "You're responsible, and your life will be worthless."

Mouser's face purpling in rage. "None of us are in this for money." He nearly spat out the last word.

"No, but the money makes pretending that you're badasses easier. To buy your bomb materials, to buy your guns, to do your dirty work. Without it you're nothing but assholes posting bullshit on the Internet, pretending you're important."

Mouser pointed at Henry. "He wanted you caught. Dead. Now you're on his side?"

"I never wanted him dead. That was your own mistake," Henry said. "Go. Do what you have to do for Hellfire. Mouser, you stay here. We'll work out the deal for the money."

"They saw our faces," Mouser said. "No witnesses."

"This is the only deal I'm offering," Luke said. Then he said the words that he knew would matter most: "Why don't you put it to a vote?"

"Did you really think I was going to negotiate with you?" Mouser said, nearly laughing.

Luke saw sharp glances pass between the Night Roaders. Mouser had ignored the call for a vote, and he knew that these men—leaders of their own movements or cells—did not relish taking orders. They were used to giving them as captains of their own causes.

"There is no vote. I have the access to the funds. You do as I say. Get going. You have your instructions, yes?" Henry said.

The men nodded. Luke noticed they each had sheets of paper outlining the bomb's operations, schematics of what looked like train tracks, photos and bios of train personnel at their target stations. Get in, stash their bombs, and get out.

"Go. You know the plan. Six-thirty A.M. Central, seven-thirty A.M. Eastern, day after tomorrow." Henry jerked with his head. "Go."

They had a day to return to the targets, to set the bombs.

"No," Mouser said. "I'm running the show."

"Do you have fifty million to reward and fund our friends here? Have you succeeded in anything I've asked you to do? Shut the hell up, Mouser." Henry cleared his throat. "Get going now. One of you will find the downstairs guard sleeping off a punch in your van."

The men filed past Luke; he could hear the shuffle of their feet on the steps. Then, from downstairs, the sounds of them loading the boxes, rushing them through the store, out of the front door.

"So," Mouser said. "It comes to this."

"You left a man to kill me back in Paris," Henry said.

"I didn't. He was supposed to keep you under wraps until Hellfire was done."

"You're a sorry liar, Mouser."

"Funny, isn't it?" Warren Dantry said. No one had been expecting him to speak and they all glanced at him. Underneath his bruises a smile flickered, the grin that Luke remembered from fishing trips, from sitting with his father on the back porch of their house. His voice sounded the same as it had before, a gentle baritone, older, wiser.

"Dad," Luke started. A thousand things to say, to know, rushed through his mind, then went blank.

"Funny," Warren Dantry repeated. "You really can't work with anyone, can you, Henry? First the good guys, now the bad. You always screw it up." He glanced up at Mouser. "You know, he thinks, he honestly believes, he predicted September eleventh."

Mouser glanced at Henry. "But you did."

"Hardly. He didn't." Warren snorted. "He would have risen to the highest posts in State or CIA if he had. Instead he's hanging out with these nothings."

Look at me, Dad, Luke thought, but Warren didn't.

"Shut up," Henry said. He swiveled the gun back toward Warren. "Shut up. Luke is my son now. Not yours. You gave him up. Shut the hell up."

"Luke. You know he's a nothing. A nothing." Warren now met his son's eyes. "He tried to kill me. Then your mother dies, under questionable circumstances."

"That was an accident!" Henry screamed, spittle flying from his mouth.

"Was it? Was it? Was it?" Warren said in a low, hypnotic mumble.

"It was an accident," and Henry brayed the last word as though a critical string had broken in his voice.

"Let's make peace, Henry," Mouser said. "Jesus, we've come this far. Let me talk to this bastard. Pry every secret from Quicksilver out of him."

"He won't talk. He just needs to die," Henry said. "Luke, look away."

"No!" Luke screamed. He lunged toward Henry.

And the world exploded.

57

Five of the trucks never made it out of the empty lot. Luke had reset the cell-phone timer of one bomb in each box to detonate in fifteen minutes. It had taken just enough time to load the trucks, light cigarettes, and gossip for a minute (the suggestion of going back in and killing Mouser and Henry both had been floated and shot down).

The trucks—save one—all went up at once in blossoms of fire as they started their convoy away from the store, within three seconds of one another, scattering debris and flaming tires and peppering shrapnel. The packed screws and twists of metal shredded the terrorists into raggedy men, tatters of flesh and bone.

The truck closest to the store stayed whole. Rushed to reset the timers, Luke had unknowingly pulled the wires loose on the last two cell phones, panicked to finish before he was caught, and did not realize his mistake. The cell phone's alarm did not detonate the blasting cap. The driver—the hardest and oldest of the men, the tattooed man responsible for the Kansas City high school bombing—stared at the wheeling masses of what had been his colleagues' trucks. He rose from the truck seat. His windows were blown out; as were the storefronts of the mall. One of the trucks crashed in the deserted street, burning. He could see what was left of one of his fellows, halved and crisped, twenty feet in front of him.

The bombs, he thought, *somebody screwed with the bombs.* For the next ten seconds he waited, knowing if his timers had been tampered with he'd be dead and there was no point in running.

But the tampered bombs had all gone off at once. None of his boxes had. He realized, with a certainty, that he was safe. He wheeled hard out of the lot, pressing his foot against the accelerator, thinking he would get the job done.

The edge of the blasts blew in the curtained windows of the second-floor showroom, lifted Luke off his feet, and tossed him into Henry. Luke tumbled over his stepfather and he didn't hear the gun's discharge. Bright balls of aftershock fire blinded his eyes; he blinked past the pain.

Resetting the phones' timers had worked. Luke scrambled to his feet. He saw Aubrey lying on her back, still tied in her chair, blood on her face. His father lay next to her, also knocked down by the explosions. Henry lay dazed. The gun that had been in his hands was gone.

Where was it? And Mouser?

Luke felt heat in a wave. Flame flickered along the curtains, blown in by fiery debris. The displays of imports—the African masks, the wooden tables, the bolts of Asian cloth—burst into flames, throughout the room. The building was ablaze.

He didn't see Mouser.

Suddenly an arm from behind closed around Luke's throat. He felt a gun barrel jam up against his forehead. Luke hammered his head back and caught Mouser in the face. Luke twisted and seized the gun in his hands and the fired bullet smashed into the concrete flooring. Luke nailed Mouser's jaw with a punch, the hardest he'd ever thrown. He felt the bone crack under his fist, felt his own fingers ache from the force of the blow.

Mouser staggered back, nearly tripping over Henry, who was struggling to his feet. The flames showed wild hate in Mouser's eyes and with a howl of pure hatred and rage he launched himself again at Luke. Tackling Luke, they skidded and rolled across the concrete, toward the now-flaming wall of windows.

They fought, arms grappling. Mouser's face twisted in a naked and bitter hatred. Mouser seized Luke's throat. They bounced off the windows, the burning curtains, and then fell back onto the floor. Luke felt his hair, his shirt, ignite. Luke dropped and rolled to quench the fire, clutching Mouser close to him.

Mouser screamed as the flames jumped to his own shirt. He yanked away; both men rolled to the floor, Luke smothering the blazing patch on his shirt. Mouser did the same and as he looked up, Luke kicked him savagely in the face, felt the man's nose and teeth break. He seized Mouser by the throat and belt and threw him toward the wall, the pain scouring up his back. Mouser fell through the burning curtains and the shattered window, arms wheeling, flames catching him from head to toe, slamming headfirst into the asphalt.

He lay still, and through the flames Luke could see his neck, bent at an utterly impossible angle.

Through the lick of fire and the smear of smoke Luke could see five wrecked trucks in a broken line across the lot, burning, ruptured.

Five. Not six.

"One got away!" he screamed. And he turned and saw Henry fleeing down the stairs.

No time to chase him. Luke pulled Aubrey to her feet, tore the ropes loose from her. She helped him free his father.

"Dad! Dad!" Luke screamed. His father opened his eyes, stared at Luke in shock as Luke untied him.

"Come on!" Aubrey screamed.

They ran toward the back, the flames jumping and dancing into the showroom.

"One of them got away," Luke said. No sign of Henry in the parking lot. They ran, Warren clutching him close, Aubrey holding his other hand. "We have to catch him."

"We don't know which way he would go," Aubrey started.

"He's going to head for a highway," Warren said.

"Then head west," Aubrey said. "Closest one."

They could hear the police and fire sirens wailing. Cars in the street—a few—had stopped, people staring at the devastation. At the car Warren embraced Luke. "Luke, Luke." He cupped Luke's face in his hands, tears on his face, shivering, shaking.

"Dad. Okay, we're okay, but we got to find this guy." A thousand words he wanted to hear and say burst in his head—his father's explanations, his father's love, his own anger to lash out at his dad for abandoning him—but it had to wait. The last bomber was running.

Luke remembered his father's false good-bye, his words: *I'll miss you every moment.* There had been years of missed moments as he stared at Warren Dantry. His father stepped back. "I'm sorry. I'm so sorry for what happened to you. Let that be a start."

Luke got behind the wheel, his father next to him, Aubrey in the backseat.

"My God," his dad said. "My God. Luke. Oh, Christ."

"Dad. Are you all right? Aubrey, you okay?"

"Yes. Fine. We're fine." His voice was hoarse, blood caked on his lips. "My God. I can't believe you did that. The timers, yes?" Surprise and pride colored his voice and he let out nearly a choking laugh.

"Luke?" Aubrey, touching his shoulder, squeezing it in reassurance. He looked back at her and she was wide-eyed, shaking, rubbing her hands together as if for warmth. "I'm glad you came for us," she said softly.

Luke roared hard onto the street. Emergency vehicles were making their way down the road, a fire truck, police cars. He shot past them. The Navigator was faster than the van. The driver would have to be rattled. Maybe he'd dumped the bombs in the lot, afraid they'd been set for early explosion as well.

Or maybe the guy had figured he'd caught a lucky break, and if he didn't blow up when everyone else did, he wasn't going to. Or he didn't care; terrorists loved their blazes of supposed glory.

He shot past the first group of responders and ran four red lights, heading up to a hundred miles an hour. It was one in the morning and the streets were empty. He saw taillights ahead, the only set.

A small moving van.

He'd caught up with the last bomber. He steered with one hand, fished out the gun with his other hand.

"Dad—here, you're the better shot."

"My hands." Warren raised them and for the first time Luke saw them, misshapen. Several fingers had been broken.

What those bastards had done to his father. He shoved down the accelerator, caught up with the moving van. "Dad, get in the back."

His father obeyed, sliding over the seat, Aubrey helping him.

Luke raised his gun, came even with the van.

The bomber leveled a gun, fired. Luke felt the heat of the bullet pass in front of his face, like a bolt, and he steadied his arm and fired. Missed. He fired again at the same time that the bomber did; the bomber's bullet hammered into the Navigator's roof, two inches from Luke's head. A black dot of blood appeared above the bomber's ear, his head jerked, the van careened onto the sidewalk. It crashed into the front of a closed Laundromat, sheets of windows shattering. Luke stopped, ran to the van. The bomber lolled, eyes open, dead.

"Luke. Get back here! We'll call the bomb squad. They'll know what to do," Warren called.

Luke ran back to the Navigator. His father moved into the front seat, staring at Luke as though he'd never seen him before, as though looking for traces of the lost boy in the man.

"Dad. Oh, God. You're okay. You're alive." All the things Luke wanted to say began to bubble up in his chest. "Really alive."

"I know you have a million questions."

"No. Just one. Why?"

"Okay, I know. But let's go, before the police arrive. Now."

Luke obeyed, pulling out onto the road. He set the gun down between him and his father. He didn't want to touch one, ever again. He turned onto the highway that led back toward downtown Chicago.

Silence filled the space between the three of them. A horrible, uncomfortable quiet. The adrenaline made Luke eager to talk but he didn't know what to say. Aubrey started to speak—Luke could hear the catch of her breath—and then she stopped.

Luke kept his gaze on the black ribbon of the street. He found his voice and it was calm. "So. Dad. Why? Why?"

Warren started to answer "I know that there is no—" Then he stopped.

"I want to forgive you," Luke started. "I just need to understand why—" He couldn't go on, his chest heavy with grief and shock.

His dad said nothing.

Luke glanced at his father and he saw the cool barrel of the gun against the back of his father's head.

58

"Where's the money, Luke?" Aubrey's mouth was close to his ear; the tickle of her breath froze him.

"What the hell are you doing?"

Warren Dantry didn't move. He glanced over at Luke, eyes wide in surprise.

"The money. I'd like to know where it is, please." Aubrey sounded steady, calm, as she had been during the crisis in Lincoln Park, on the jet to New York, in urging them toward the car back at the store. "You and Henry said you had it."

"Why do you"—and he saw it. The missing piece.

If Jane had arranged for Eric to grab him to ransom Aubrey, then she would have used a kidnapper to grab Aubrey. Just a man, Aubrey had said.

But what if there had been no kidnapper? The realization fell into his mind all at once. The burlap hood she said she'd been covered with, even after the kidnapper left. It hadn't been on the floor or under the bed. His wrists, after being tied to the bed one night, were raw. He remembered the smoothness of Aubrey's skin when he unlocked her shackles.

No one could prove Aubrey had ever actually been kidnapped. Except Aubrey.

She'd faked the kidnapping. Which meant . . . she was in with Jane.

It was you. You alone, he'd said to Jane. But she hadn't been alone. She'd had a partner, to keep an eye on the progress of the Night Road. Not a member, but sleeping with a member.

How had Jane ever found out about Eric's role in the Night Road in the first place?

"Dad. Did Quicksilver suspect Eric Lindoe of criminal ties?" He remembered seeing reports about Eric's bank in Eric's file in the Paris office.

"There have been a number of questionable accounts at that bank," he said quietly. "Yes, we've been watching the bank for a while. We sent the same agent to watch this Arab prince who seemed interested in financing terrorists." He swallowed. "I think you know her as—"

"Jane." Luke glanced back. He had to get her to see reason. If he told her where he thought the money was, she'd just kill them both. His tongue felt like concrete.

She said, her voice torn with panic: "I want to know where the money is."

Hidden in plain sight. That little b—, Jane had said. "Henry lied. He was bluffing."

"You know where it is," Aubrey insisted. "You have to. Tell me." Her voice cracked. "What I've been through, goddamn it, I get the money."

"I won't tell you unless you put the gun down."

"Tell me, Luke. Now. Don't pull over. Keep driving."

They raced down the highway, Luke dodging in and out among the scattering of cars.

"You won't believe me," Luke said. His father raised his mauled hands, his eyes wide in pain as Aubrey dug the barrel into the back of his head.

"You just got your dad back," Aubrey said. "I'll take him away. Tell me."

"I thought Eric was using you, but you were using him," Luke said. "An export-import business, lots of overseas money coming in, payments going out. A perfect way for Eric to stream in money, using your accounts. He thought he was using you, to a degree, at first. But you *wanted* him to use you. You thought he might be involved in money for the Night Road. Did he pillow-talk you, tell you what he was up to?"

"No. Jane and I figured it out on our own. From her spying on the prince for Quicksilver."

"Jane worked for us, but Aubrey doesn't," Warren said. The Navigator hit a bump and the gun jiggled against his father's head.

"We aimed me straight at Eric," she said, her voice calmer. "I got into his bed. I got into his head. After I was kidnapped I told him that these Quicksilver people might be willing to help us hide. He bought it."

Luke watched her in the rearview. "You were never kidnapped. It was just a lure to make him act and to keep *you* clean. And blameless and above suspicion."

She made a noise in her throat.

"Aubrey, you don't have to hurt anyone."

"Yes, I do. The money. Jane and I worked on it for months. Where is it?"

Luke saw a sedan speeding up behind them. Fast.

"I don't have it. I don't know where he moved it."

"You're lying! Tell me or your father dies."

Luke looked up at his father. His father shook his head. "Don't tell her. Don't let these people win."

That little b—. Jane hadn't meant Eric. She'd meant Aubrey. Jane thought Aubrey had betrayed her.

The speeding car passed, on the driver's side, edging Luke's Navigator.

Henry. Driving fast, a gun in his hand.

"Oh, Jesus," Luke said, slamming the Navigator against Henry's sedan. The Navigator rocked hard and Warren spun in his seat, grabbing at Aubrey's gun.

"Tell me where you put the money now!" she screamed.

"Don't shoot him!" Luke screamed back. "Eric hid it in plain sight! In your accounts at his bank!"

Aubrey fired. The bullet caught his father in the chest with a horrifying blast and he collapsed against the passenger door. Luke slammed on the brakes and the car slid into a long skid. Henry's car rode alongside them, Henry standing up through the sunroof as the cars spun on sheer momentum, not bothering to steer, aiming.

Luke felt the warmth of Aubrey's barrel against his neck and then the blast was loud in the car.

The Navigator skidded to a stop as the sedan hit its side. He could see his father slumped in his seat, eyelids fluttering, his chest a wet wreckage of blood. He wrenched around. Aubrey lay on the seat, bleeding from the side of her throat, eyes open, mouth slack.

Luke looked to his left and saw Henry, his car stopped parallel against Luke's, positioned just behind the driver's door. Henry still stood in the sunroof, a gun in his hand. Now aimed at Luke.

Luke had no gun.

"My last favor to you," Henry said. "Do you know where the money is?"

Luke shook his head. "No," he lied. "No."

They were the ten longest seconds of Luke's life. They stared into each other's eyes, the gun between them like a long-hidden truth.

Henry lowered the gun. "Don't come after me." Luke could see, for the first time, in the scant light of the highway lights, tears brimming in Henry's eyes. "I will not treat you like family again." Henry slid down into the driver's seat, roared his battered sedan off into the night. And out of sight, taking the first exit ramp.

Luke felt for his father's pulse. Weak. Erratic. He saw a call button on the Navigator and jabbed it.

Instead of an emergency service he heard Frankie Wu say, "Where the hell are you?"

"Dad needs a doctor—he's shot. Tell me where a hospital is."

"We got a doctor."

"He's been shot. He needs surgery."

"You can't take him to a hospital," Wu said. "Too many questions. I want you to do exactly as I say, Luke. Follow my directions."

And Luke Dantry, no longer the most dangerous man in the world, listened and drove off in the dark night, holding his father's hand, begging him to not leave him again.

59

A Week Later

Northern Michigan, Luke decided, was one of the nicest places you could go quietly insane. He sat on the porch watching the light dapple the waters of the lake, and he folded the newspaper and tucked it where his father would not see it.

The story had dominated headlines, but not in the way he had expected. A group of suspected extremists had been found dead after a series of explosions. Two had been identified: a dentist from Milwaukee known for sending threatening letters to oil companies, and a pharmacist from a small city in Tennessee, the same town where the *E. coli* scare had grabbed headlines the previous week. Another man, a known neo-Nazi from Kansas City, had been found several blocks away, with two dozen bombs hidden in first aid kits, and a uniform and passes that would have given him access to the Atlanta rail system. A man who had been dishonorably discharged from the military lay dead on the pavement, and recent information via anonymous phone calls tied him to an attack on an office building in New York. FBI officials suggested the group had planned a bombing in Atlanta, and most likely in other cities as well, but it had gone wrong. Theories as to why were as plentiful as the clouds in the sky. Editorials painted a grim picture of domestic groups of disaffection arming themselves with foreign-bought weaponry. No mention of networks called the Night Road or Quicksilver.

Aubrey Perrault found her rest in the quiet of an unmarked grave in this northern Michigan enclave, a quiet Luke guessed she hadn't known in her life. Every move she had made: urging Eric to flee with them, sticking close to Luke as he trailed the money, even, as his father told them, buying time for Jane to find Luke by insisting to Mouser that Luke didn't have the money . . . all of it an attempt for her or Jane to gain control of the funds. Investigators, as part of the bombing probe, found fifty million wired into her accounts; the FBI seized the money. Aubrey was connected, the investigators concluded, with the terrorist attack. Now the forensic accountants were trying to trace the money back to its source. Anonymous tips kept pointing back to a prominent Arab prince.

Luke watched the dappled light play on the water. How many names did Aubrey have? How many lies did she live? Luke wondered. He had been smart enough to fight the Night Road and win, but too blind to see she was no victim. She had been one of the architects of this carnage. It was strange to know she had stuck with him simply so he might help her find the money. If he'd discovered the hidden thumb drive in her presence, back in Chicago, she would have killed him and taken the file to Jane. Or if she'd checked her account balances, she would have seen the money and she could have taken it and run to Jane. They would have won.

Luke watched Frankie Wu on the fishing pier, reeling in an empty line. The past few days had been spent fretting over his father, recovering from surgery in a private clinic north of Chicago, one under Quicksilver control. That alone had made him realize the extent of this so-called loose network. They had money, they had resources.

But so did Henry.

"Have you decided?" His father wheeled his chair close to the door. Pale, gaunt, but he would recover, the doctors said.

"On dinner? I say steak. We deserve a steak. Now that you're up and chewing."

"Sounds good, but I meant more about what your future holds."

"I'm still a missing person."

"You don't have to be."

"Don't I? I hardly imagine Henry or the Night Road is going to let me walk back into my old life."

"We can do a great deal for you."

Now Luke watched his father, who was not looking at him, instead studying his hands folded in his lap. He felt a weird whirlpool of love and hate rise in his chest. He'd spent the past days watching his father sleep, recover, slowly regain his strength. And had not heard an answer to his one question yet.

"In gratitude for all you've done, Luke, Quicksilver can help you back into your old life."

"Is that how you make amends to me? Make all the trouble go away? You brought a lot of the trouble on me, Dad. This . . . war has been building my whole life, and I had no idea that I might be pulled into it. Other than you giving me a Saint Michael's medal and warning me I might one day have to fight. Were you assuming I'd simply follow in your footsteps? Thanks a lot."

Warren studied his splinted fingers, as though he hadn't heard the sharpness of Luke's words. "Eric's already been identified as a money launderer since his murder. He screwed around with the audit records, trying to cover his transfers. We can fake computer records, make it look like you had previous but innocent contact with him. That he thought you knew about his crimes and that he was pursuing you. We can clear your name in every way that it's been muddied, given time."

"Make up a lie so I can live a truth? My old life wasn't truth. It was all in the service of Henry. Because you left me behind. You abandoned us."

Now his father met his steady gaze. "I never would have picked this life for you, Luke. It was why I left."

"Why you lied. Let's call it what it is." Anger that he couldn't control steamed up in him. Before he was shot, they hadn't had enough time to talk. Only for his father to say he was sorry.

"Fine. Why I lied. But I thought I was doing the best for you and your mom. I didn't want anyone coming after me to come after you. They killed everyone I worked with. Do you think they would have hesitated to kill my family?"

"They? It was just Henry, Dad. He chased you off, you let him, and he slid into your life. For God's sake . . ."

"I didn't know it was Henry behind the attempt on me. I swear."

For the past week Luke had danced around this truth, unwilling to discuss it until his father was stronger. "What you said about Mom. That he killed her . . ."

"I will always believe he had a hand in her death. Your mother was a smart woman. She could have found out what he was doing. Confronted him. Knowing what we know now, he must have killed her."

"But she would have never been in danger if you'd had the guts to stick around. If you'd put us ahead of your work."

Warren reached for his son's hand, but Luke stepped back. A horrible silence settled between them for a long minute, broken only by the hiss of the wind in the oaks.

"Do you want me to be dead, Luke?" Warren asked. "I can be. It's what you know. You never have to see me again."

"You don't get off that easy, Dad. You did this so you could go fight this secret war, save people, prove all your theories. I have to matter as much as your work does. I fought that war when you couldn't, without any warning. But the war has to be worth fighting, for a personal reason. I have to matter to you. Why didn't you stay in New York, meet me there instead of relying on Drummond to take care of me? If I'd been willing to hide under a false name, like Drummond offered, would you even have stepped forward to let me know you were alive?"

"It wouldn't have been necessary."

Luke shook his head. "Even when I was in danger, you put Quicksilver's interests first."

"No, not true." Warren paused, as though he didn't know what words to use.

"Just say what you want to say, Dad."

"I was afraid of your hate. I could bear being away from you, but I couldn't bear knowing you hated me."

The silence between them was thick for a long moment. "I don't hate you. I don't know that I understand you yet. I may never. I will try. But I'm not sure what my next step is."

Warren cleared his throat. "You can go back, try to have a normal life again, or . . ."

"I can't. I can either hide or I can help. I don't want to hide, but I don't like the idea of being drafted into Quicksilver. And I'm not sure I'm ready to forgive you, much less work with you."

"I deserve every bit of anger you want to shove down my throat. I'll take it, Luke, and never argue that I could have made a better choice. But I want you to know, what you accomplished—the lives you saved . . . you make me so proud."

Luke watched the water. He had wanted to delve into minds defined by destructive purpose. He had, but now he understood less about them than he had before. No amount of study or theorizing had prepared him for Henry, or Mouser, or Snow. Yet he had survived.

Had he known, at some level, this wind of change was blowing? Had he sensed, even as a boy, that his father carried many secrets? His search for his father, his delving into the terrorist mind, his surprising determination to carry the battle forward, where had that come from inside him? All of this horror had burned away the old Luke, and left a different man standing.

If he tried to go back to a normal life, he would spend his life looking over his shoulder. Wars did not last forever. What if Quicksilver was the best hope of bringing this battle to a rapid conclusion? Be drafted. Do a tour of duty. Help his father. Stop Henry and make him pay for what he'd done. *Knowing what we know now he must have killed her.* He must have. Luke thought of the time he'd spent comforting Henry, reassuring him. A cold anger ignited in his chest.

"What would you have me do?"

"I think you could handle field assignments, given time." Warren cleared his throat, risked a smile. "But you would be brilliant as a terrorism profiler. You sifted through thousands of people to find the Night Road. You could find them again. You could help us find the next wave of terrorists long before they strike. Identify them, perhaps find ways to keep them from embracing violence, or alienate them from groups like the Night Road."

Henry had tried to make him believe, in his old innocence, that the world was not dangerous. That the world's most fearsome people were on the other side of the glass, in their own distant Wonderland, and he knew now they were everywhere. Waiting. Hoping to strike. And the world needed ordinary people like himself to stand and fight and to win that war. To not be afraid; to live for a while, in the secret wilds of the world. He didn't have to forgive his father right now. That would come in time. But he could take the anger he felt, channel it into kicking down the right doors. He could make a difference.

"We'll find Henry and the rest of the Night Road," Luke said, "you and me. I'll stay for a while."

And he sat with his father and he watched the sunset slide over the lake, creating a pool of a thousand colors, the first of the new memories.

60

Welcome to the new site for the Night Road. We have had a number of setbacks, but our strength as a network is our ability to recover quickly and with great nimbleness.

Despite the recent and unfortunate delays, I have relocated overseas and I have acquired new funding to share, based on appropriate projections of economic and mortal damage that you can inflict. As well, I have secured powerful friends around the world sympathetic to our cause. I expect further funding from them, so we can all pursue our plans.

Know that we face a real danger. The corporate titans—the globalizers, the power-mongers, the moneylenders of our enemies—have formed their own version of the CIA. They are called Quicksilver, and they will be hunting us. This is not the time to hide. Not the time to lose nerve. This is a time to rise and fight like we have never fought before. To join together in common cause. To know our enemy—the one who will engage us first, even if in secret—and to destroy him, utterly.

I made a mistake that I must confess. I placed my hopes in the wrong person. This caused our network no permanent or troubling harm, but it has reinforced to me that we must be careful in choosing our allies. In recognizing one another, in allowing no one to infiltrate us.

Instructions on proposals to be sent to me will follow shortly. Those who accomplish their initial missions will qualify for further investment. So think big, people.

Think very big.

Acknowledgments

Many thanks to everyone who helped me in the process of writing this book, and makes being a suspense writer such a joy for me.

I am fortunate to work with two of the best minds in the business: David Shelley of LittleBrown UK and Ben Sevier of Dutton. Their enthusiasm, support, and terrific insights are a constant inspiration.

Thanks also to:

Ursula Mackenzie, Hilary Hale, Alison Lindsay, Thalia Proctor, Sean Garrehy, Kirsteen Astor, Nathalie Morse, and everyone at LittleBrown UK, who have made me feel very welcome indeed in Great Britain;

Brian Tart, Christine Ball, Lisa Johnson, Erika Imranyi, Melissa Miller, Jamie McDonald, and everyone at Dutton, and Kristen Weber and Kara Walsh and everyone at NAL, for their advocacy and dedication.

As always, my deepest gratitude to Peter Ginsberg, Shirley Stewart, Dave Barbor, Holly Frederick, and Nathan Bransford, for extraordinary representation and ongoing brilliance.

Special thanks to those who shared their time to answer questions or guide me along the way: Simon Baril; Travis Wilhite; Marcus Sakey (also a terrific crime novelist); Rick Wall; Matt Willson. Any errors, or enhancements for the sake of drama, are my responsibility, not theirs. Thanks also to Steve Bennett and Nancy MacDonald.

There is an evil stepfather in this book; I am blessed with a kind one. Thanks to my mom, Elizabeth; my stepfather, Dub; and my in-laws, Becky and Malcolm.

For a variety of compelling thoughts about nonstate networks (such as the Night Road and Quicksilver) and terrorist psychology, I recommend the following: *Brave New War* by John Robb; *Thinking Like a Terrorist* by

Mike German; *The Mind of the Terrorist* by Jerrold M. Post; *Leaderless Jihad* by Marc Sageman; and *Terror and Consent: The Wars for the Twenty-first Century* by Philip Bobbitt.

Finally, my deepest thanks go to my muses: Leslie, Charles, and William, who are there every day with their love and support, which is more important than ink to a writer.

About the Author

Nominated for three Edgar and two Anthony Awards, Jeff Abbott is the internationally bestselling author of ten novels, including *Collision, Fear, Panic, Cut and Run, Black Jack Point,* and *A Kiss Gone Bad.* He lives in Austin, Texas, with his wife and family.